KENNETH BROWN

HASKELL
ORPHAN TO KING

The Mountain King Series - Prequel

Adgitize Press

COPYRIGHT PAGE

Haskell – Orphan to King

Published by Adgitize Press

Copyright 2021 by Kenneth Brown

All rights reserved, including the right to reproduce this book, or portions thereof, in any form.

An Adgitize Press Book

First Edition: January 2021

ISBN – 979-8-9890372-5-4

Library of Congress Control Number 2024915340

This eBook is licensed for your personal enjoyment only. This eBook may not be re-sold or given away to other people. If you would like to share this book with another person, please purchase an additional copy for each recipient. If you're reading this book and did not purchase it, or it was not purchased for your enjoyment only, then please purchase your own copy. Thank you for respecting the hard work of this author.

This is a work of fiction. All of the characters and events portrayed in this novel are either fictitious or used fictitiously. Names, characters, businesses, places, events, locales, and incidents are either the products of the author's imagination or used in a fictitious manner. Any resemblance to actual persons, living or dead, or actual events is purely coincidental.

Adgitize Press

https://kenbrownauthor.com

Cover Image Copyright 2021 – All rights reserved.

THANK YOU

Thank you for downloading this Adgitize Press eBook.

To find out more about the author, Kenneth Brown, and get advance notification about future books, check out the website, kenbrownauthor.com, https://kenbrownauthor.com.

Join the Readers Group to receive these great benefits.

- Get the latest information on New Releases
- Insider Looks at Outlines, Plots, Characters, Deleted Scenes and Exclusive behind the Scenes looks at Kenneth Brown's Writing
- Sneak Peeks at Chapters of Upcoming Books
- Ask the Author Questions
- Exclusive Offers
- And MORE

Go to https://kenbrownauthor.com for more information.

DEDICATION

Dedicated to Young Adult Fantasy Readers around the World

CHAPTER 1

Fourteen-year-old Haskell sprinted through the village of Whiterock Grove. This time, the big boys chased him. He was faster than kids his age, but could he outrun the larger, older teens? Haskell needed ninety-seconds to outrun his attackers. That's how long it took him to reach his home on Pine Street from this part of town.

The older boys chased, which proved involvement from Gadiel. That white-bearded old man had killed his friend, Russell.

He veered onto Blackthorn Road on the village's east side, where crowded shops and tents in the marketplace allowed him to sneak into small places without being caught. Haskell needed to reach the blacksmith's forge at road's end. It contained a tunnel that small Haskell could shimmy through, but the smell of the tight space always stopped the larger boys.

Benny's forge stood twenty seconds away, but the large market crowd today made the passage difficult. It was a perfect day to pick-pocket the village's wealthy ladies and rich lords, but not while being hunted. The teenager searched for paths through the throng to escape the five thugs chasing him. They were fast and gaining on Haskell. He stepped left to bypass a fruit stand.

A hand reached out from behind, and touched Haskell's shoulder and grabbed his tunic. A quick duck under a horse-drawn carriage and the attacker released.

"Stop, you little mongrel," the carriage driver cried out.

Haskell didn't stop. If they caught him, then Gadiel would kill Haskell.

He closed the distance to the blacksmith's shop. He was only ten seconds from the first escape tunnel. Haskell had used this escape route numerous times this year since moving from Velidred Castle after his father and mother died. Living on the streets of Whiterock Grove required learning methods to escape from the people he robbed.

How did Gadiel locate him? Haskell tried to stay invisible to that evil man. Rumors told of Gadiel's ability at deep dark magic. They said when he killed you; the unbearable pain of magic caused you to scream for centuries after your death. Why did he seek Haskell?

The chasing thugs gained on the boy. He doubted his ability to outrun his pursuers. Haskell changed his mind about going straight to the blacksmith's shop and veered left into the street. Horses reared up on the dirt road as the short, thin street urchin scooted under the horses' raised hoofs. The confusion and change of direction surprised his assailants. As Haskell glanced back, the boys had stopped behind carriages and horses.

The city constables, guarding the businesses, shouted at the thugs chasing Haskell. "Stop punks." The constables chased after the boys.

Perfect, the extra time I need. He ran through a linen shop, knocking over the handmaids, who held lengths of fabric for viewing by their ladies. Women screamed at the racing boy as he upended a table loaded with bolts of cloth.

Haskell dashed under the tent into the next shop, and scooted behind a constable, watching the commotion on the street. Haskell hurried back across the street; thirty yards closer to the blacksmith's stable. A quick glance backwards showed his attackers had resumed hunting him. Three constables chased in hot pursuit.

He broke through the clasped hands of a young, romantic couple walking by the shops.

"Hey stop that," said the man.

It's only five steps to the blacksmith's stable and then the tunnel. Next to the blacksmith's forge, a tinker fashioned body armor for the lords, knights and men who fought in the king's army. Many times, the tinker had closed the path between the tinker's shop and the blacksmith's shop, which blocked the easy path to the tunnel Haskell used.

Another member of Gadiel's gang darted out of the tin worker's shop. *They must have discovered my path and waited for me to flee in this direction.* The tall boy, sporting a small goatee, gained speed and reached his hand out to Haskell's shoulder. He grabbed Haskell's tunic.

Haskell wore an old, filthy and ragged tunic. The cloth needed washing. He had learned to hand sew the rips and tears in the fabric, but it still had more holes than sewed areas.

Goatee Boy grabbed the cloth tight, and the fabric ripped from the neck hole to the hole over Haskell's right shoulder. As the cloth tore, Goatee Boy lost his balance and smacked head first into the blacksmith's horse railing. He released his grip.

Haskell dived under the railing, between horses, into the blacksmith's shop. He scooted around the heated furnace and dropped to his knees, crawling through a small tunnel used to shove horse dung into the back alley for shipment to the king's garden. He hated the smell of horse dung and the filth made him gag, but Haskell's path grew easier once he reached the alley.

The teenager gasped for breath as he crawled six feet through the tunnel of dung. Though the stench disgusted Haskell, the scent of horse dung represented freedom and the thrill of escape. Once Haskell reached the alley, it'd force the chasing boys to detour to the end of the street, and divert around a building to reach this alley. That would allow Haskell time to travel one street farther from his pursuers. He had never been captured after the blacksmith's dung tunnel.

Haskell slipped through the muck and found open air in the alley. He wiped the filth from his face and took deep, calming breaths. He smiled, a joyous expression of freedom.

Then he sprinted fifteen feet through the alley, vaulted over a junk wagon and hurried between two buildings onto Causle Street. Many lords and ladies frequented Causle Street, which might slow him. But he only needed ten fast seconds to attain his next exit.

"There he is, get him," shouted another member of Gadiel's gang.

Haskell sprinted down the middle of the street as three thugs bolted after him. The boys wore shoes, but poor Haskell ran in bare feet. He hadn't worn shoes since he outgrew the pair he wore when his father died. It didn't matter, because with or without shoes Haskell hustled, knowing his life depended on escaping.

He breathed hard, the sprinting thugs gaining ground on the smaller teenager. The gang had never chased him this far. Even with only thirty seconds to the hidey-hole, he pushed the limits of his endurance. He hadn't paced his speed this trip, and he bit hard on his bottom lip as he realized he might not make it to the hidey-hole this time.

His chest tightened, and breathing became difficult. He must escape from the man with the white beard if he expected to live another day. He pumped his arms faster, shoulders curling forward causing his chest to tighten more. The oxygen exchange between lungs and legs didn't transition fast enough, and his legs stiffened from the effort.

He reached the end of Causle Street and turned right, heading toward Gambit Gristmill, a small flour mill next to the King's River. The gristmill used river water to rotate the waterwheel that powered the meal grinder for the large village. Haskell bounded up concrete steps, darted through the open door, avoided the rotating grinding stone and leaped through the window.

A chasing thug yelled, "Stop that boy."

Nobody in the mill stopped Haskell.

He glanced over his left shoulder as he stepped onto the turning waterwheel. No thugs were close enough to stop him, and this next part promised a challenge for the older teens. Haskell hadn't watched his step, and he slipped on the wet, mossy waterwheel landing hard on his back on the turning wheel.

Haskell sucked in a scream as his body rotated toward the river. He felt dizzy after the fall, as the spinning wheel carried him to certain death. The original plan required jumping from the wooden paddle wheel to the metal bracket holding the wheel in place. Then a short leap to the bridge's lower support beams. Once he reached the bridge beams, he could scurry across the river like a tightrope walker.

That plan had failed, and the wheel groaned in anticipation of grinding him between the wheel and the sluice. He regained his control and placed his foot on a water wheel bucket, but the old mossy wood didn't allow a solid foothold. This escape route allowed no easy fall into the water. Friends had shared stories of street urchins grounded into pieces between water wheel and sluice after tripping on the water wheel. He talked to himself, "Come on. Find a foothold."

Three buckets of water remained before Haskell's life ended. He scrunched up his face, his eyes squinting. "Come on, take a chance, and jump." He leapt off the bucket, his foot slipped, and he dropped face first into the water sluice, sliding ten feet in the chilly water.

He closed his eyes as exhaustion overpowered his body. Is this how it ends? I drown in water, or will the boys capture me and drag me to Gadiel as an unwilling sacrifice with goats, magic and fire?

The cold water felt refreshing, allowing him to raise his head and catch his breath. Where were his pursuers? Did he lose them because they expected him to reach the east side of the river?

Sliding to the end of the sluice, Haskell tumbled fifteen feet and splashed into the river. He submerged and swam with the current. Twenty-five yards later, he surfaced with a whisper of noise and floated into the reeds near shore.

He stayed in the weeds until sunset. He clambered out of the bone chilling water, and continued his journey home watching for the white-bearded man's gang. He sauntered home in satisfaction at beating the old man, but needed a plan for tomorrow. He should leave the city and find a safer village. He must escape Gadiel's influence.

Haskell grabbed an apple from a tree and ambled home. He lived in a small space beneath a row house. He could enter the space through a hole and short tunnel that ran beneath the house. The space under the house's wooden floor gave him plenty of free-living space.

He crunched on the apple, and noticed the white-bearded man walk off the porch and block Haskell's entrance.

CHAPTER 2

Haskell turned to run, but found all paths blocked by the larger boys. His freedom had expired and now he found himself captured by the old man and his gang. No chance to grow up and live a long life. He knew with no doubt the man planned to kill him.

He didn't run. What would be the point?

Two boys grabbed his arms as a taller boy punched him hard in the stomach. Haskell hunched over in pain. The boys dragged him down the street.

Haskell spent the night in a cramped box, a wooden cell with limited space. It was difficult for the small boy to even stretch his legs. How would they kill him? Maybe not feed him? Would Gadiel release a flash of magic and poof, gone? Would the older boys pummel the life from his little body, or burn him in a sacrificial offering to the god of Velidred? What evil lurked in Gadiel's mind?

####

The next day the door opened and an arm reached into the box for Haskell.

He felt the hand and pushed himself back into a corner of the box.

"Come here you rotten little runt." The jailer put his head into the box while Haskell backed up farther.

"Leave me alone."

"Gadiel wants to see you."

"I don't want to see him. Let me go."

"You ain't being released, now come here." The boy reached into the container and grabbed Haskell's arm.

Haskell kicked the kid in the head.

"Ouch. That's gonna cost ya."

"I don't wanna die."

"I'm gonna kill you myself if you don't stop struggling. Do you need more softening? Lenny and Sims get over here and help me with this varmint."

"Ha, Dakarai, you can't bring him out yourself?"

Haskell struggled but to no avail. The two boys grabbed his wrists, twisted his arm to the point he couldn't take it anymore, and Haskell relented. They hauled him out of the box and held him. Dakarai punched the boy's face.

Haskell's heart raced in his chest as pain flashed across his eyes. His mouth fell open and blood and spittle flew across the room. He flailed his arms to free himself from the other boys' grasp, but only floundered uselessly.

"Listen up you little runt," Dakarai said.

Blood trickled down Haskell's forehead into his left eyebrow. "What do you guys want with me? I'm not hurting you or your trade."

"Gadiel wants to talk with you, and we want to make the introductions."

Lenny and Sims laughed.

Dakarai slammed a fist into Haskell's gut.

Haskell contorted in pain as he spit blood.

He remembered a couple of friends that lived in the streets like him, making do by thieving and doing odd jobs. One boy, Russell, nick-named, Rusty, because of his red hair, taught Haskell special tricks to relieve royals of their purses. Rusty was caught by Gadiel's web of thugs and the next day found floating face-down in the river.

Dakarai grabbed Haskell's jaw and squeezed, drawing Haskell to stare into the boy's brown eyes. "Do you want me to hit you more or are you ready to meet the boss?"

Haskell closed his eyes. Another strike to the gut like the last one and Haskell suspected he could die, but he didn't want to be in Gadiel's presence.

Toby, another street thief captured by Gadiel's thugs, had escaped and ran, but rumors told of a boy, with Toby's face, swinging from a tree in a nearby village.

Lenny and Sims dragged Haskell through a hallway while Dakarai led the way.

How long could Haskell last in Gadiel's presence? If he could escape from the boys' grasp, then he could high-tail it out of the city and make his way back to his home town of Velidred. He'd be safe there, out of the reach of Gadiel and his thugs.

Dakarai stopped and knocked on a door.

Haskell wriggled and flailed, but the boys held tight. He believed the rumors on the street that Gadiel's eyes flashed red flames, and those who looked in the man's eyes died.

A voice sounded from within, "Enter."

Dakarai opened the door.

Haskell hadn't stayed alive as an orphan by being weak. He stepped on Sims' foot.

Sims let go and screamed in pain.

Lenny looked confused at why Sims was screaming, but he held tight to Haskell.

With a hard right, Haskell hit Lenny in the jaw.

Lenny held tight.

Dakarai grabbed the front of what was left of Haskell's tunic and punched Haskell in the stomach with his other hand.

Haskell bunched over and dropped to his knees.

With a quick twist of his hand, Dakarai had a handful of Haskell's hair and produced a knife which he held to the prisoner's neck. "One more stupid move like that and your life's over. You mean nothing to us and nothing to Gadiel. Do you understand?"

Too afraid to shake his head, Haskell mumbled, "Yeah."

The knife pushed into Haskell's neck. "What did you say?"

He couldn't move his head back because of Dakarai's tight grip on his hair. Haskell said, "Yes."

"Yes, what?"

He coughed up blood. "Yes, I won't struggle."

"That's better. I knew we could agree on this." Dakarai raised his prisoner to his feet.

Numbness overcame Haskell as he shuffled into Gadiel's office.

CHAPTER 3

Dakarai said, "We have a runner and a fighter, sir."

Gadiel sat in a chair behind a mahogany desk. A bookcase behind the desk displayed over a hundred books. The books interested Haskell; he had never seen so many at once, but alas he had never learned to read.

Gadiel said, "What's your name, son?"

"Haskell," he mumbled as he searched the room for means of escape.

"Welcome to my office." Gadiel moved his arm like a salesman displaying his wares.

A large map tacked to a wall showed the Goodwin castle and the surrounding countryside. Beside that map was one that showed Velidred, Kalluri and Goodwin castles.

Haskell studied the map looking for places to hide if he found a way to escape.

"Do you know why you're here, young fellow?"

"Because you want to kill me."

Gadiel cackled a dry, wheezing laugh. "Quite the opposite. I have a proposition for you. I'm told you're quite capable at relieving the lords and ladies of their purses."

Haskell smirked and stood straighter, which caused him to cough. Blood sprayed across the desk.

The old man produced a black handkerchief from the top pocket of his black jacket and wiped the desk. "I see Dakarai educated you on proper behavior in my presence. Most unfortunate." Gadiel pointed at the two boys holding Haskell and said, "Lenny and Sims, guard the door in case our friend thinks he can escape."

The thugs released their grip on Haskell, lumbered from the room and shut the door.

A glance around the room showed a window, but it was too high above the floor for Haskell to use it as an escape route.

"Let's get down to business." Gadiel rose from his chair and walked to the front of the desk, within inches of Haskell.

Haskell thought about kicking the old man in the shins and making a run for the door, but Dakarai stood with the knife right next to Haskell. "I don't want to do business with you. I'm doing fine by myself."

"Are you? The only reason you don't stink of horse dung is because you fell into the river. A blessing for Dakarai and me."

Dakarai laughed.

"The reason I fell into the river was because you and your thugs were chasing me. Otherwise, I didn't need to use that route."

"I want you to have an opportunity for the finer things in life, maybe your own cabin instead of a hole underneath one, sleeping with rats, raccoons and whatever else wants to bunk with you at night."

"How will I get that?" Haskell stared into the man's eyes, black as midnight, except for a red spot in the corner of the left eye.

Gadiel moved closer to Haskell and the eye's red spot moved toward the middle of the old man's eye, changing into the shape of a scorpion. Haskell noticed the man's right eyelid appeared to droop. The sunlight from the window diminished as Gadiel came closer. *Was that because he blocked the sunlight, a trick of the light, or Gadiel's magical power?*

"I will train you to steal more than pies and apples, and apply your skills to earn more than the meager gold and silver found in a lord's leather purse."

"And if I choose not to work with you?"

"Not a wise decision. Tell me how you came to the streets?"

"Why do you care?"

"Should Dakarai show you how much I care?"

Haskell scowled at Dakarai and returned his gaze to Gadiel. The scorpion in his eye grew larger. Haskell couldn't look away from the expanding red spot. *How did he do that?*

Gadiel touched Haskell's arm making him jump. "Relax, Young Man. You're among friends. Tell me how you became an orphan."

Haskell didn't want to tell the man in black his story, but he couldn't help himself. "My mother was a seamstress and my father a blacksmith in Velidred.

He was a good blacksmith, well liked in the village and respected enough to shoe the king's horses."

Memories flooded into his mind of the day that everything changed for Haskell. "I handled the horses, kept them quiet while Dad shod them."

Dakarai said, "A blacksmith's son. Hah."

Gadiel glared at Dakarai.

Haskell knew the reason he became an orphan was his own fault. His Mom and Dad didn't do anything wrong. It was a childish mistake by Haskell. A mistake any twelve-year-old could make.

"Continue."

Haskell's mouth was parched, as dried blood clung to his lower lip. He felt a thickness in his throat. His cheeks burned. "The caravan was in town."

"For the Ice Castle?" Gadiel asked.

He nodded. "I enjoyed watching the mastodons and hoped to become a tug puller."

"A shrimp like you a mastodon handler?" Dakarai asked.

"Dakarai, it's time for you to leave."

"Sir, is it safe? He's a feisty one and quick."

"He isn't going anywhere, are you Haskell?"

The red scorpion in Gadiel's eye mesmerized Haskell. "No, sir."

"See? Now, leave the room."

Dakarai glowered at Haskell as he exited.

Gadiel said, "Bring my chair from behind the desk."

Haskell didn't understand what forced him to want to serve Gadiel. He pulled the chair from behind the desk and set it in front of Gadiel. Gadiel sat. "Continue your story."

He watched the scorpion pulse in Gadiel's eye. "That day, my friend Vali came to me in the morning." Haskell was transported to that day two years earlier.

Vali said, "I'm heading to watch the mastodons, are you coming?"

Haskell scanned the horses in the stable, two farmer's horses and one for the king. Dad stood by the forge heating metal shoes for the king's horses. "I have five minutes."

He didn't tell Dad he was leaving. He raced out of the blacksmith's shop with Vali close behind. When they reached the caravan, the handlers were arranging their wagons and had backed up the mastodons for hookup. Haskell loved the sound of the animals bellowing, and the noise and excitement of the caravan as it prepared to travel.

"Let's get closer." Vali dashed toward the animals.

The smells of the animals bombarded the senses, but the rush of excitement, being this close to the animals, thrilled Haskell. He wanted one day to touch the animals, brush their fur and guide them to the Ice Castle. That would be exciting, but he knew Dad planned for him to become a blacksmith.

The massive mastodons were many different sizes. The larger animals pulled three wagons, others pulled two and Haskell saw ten of the animals pulling only one wagon each. The caravan hauled goods to the Ice Castle and supplies for the caravan itself.

Time passed on the field and Haskell and Vali watched till the sun reached midway in the sky. The last mastodon and wagon fell into line and trudged behind the long line of wagons on their way to the Ice Castle. *What was it like at the Ice Castle?*

Vali said, "Hey we should get back, I bet your dad's angry with you."

"Oh man, we spent hours here. I'll be strapped." Haskell dashed back to the forge.

When he reached the blacksmith's shop Dad yelled, "Where have you been? The one day we have the king's horse in the shop and you disappear. Look at what you've done."

The king's horse stood on three legs in the stable. The fourth leg curled up in an irregular angle. "What happened, Dad?"

"Something spooked the horse and he kicked when I brought down the hammer to pound in the shoe nail. I hit the horse's leg instead of the nail." Dad sat on a barrel, his elbows on his thighs, and leaned his head on his hands.

"Will the horse be okay?"

"Listen." Dad jumped off the barrel and charged over to Haskell. He grabbed the front of Haskell's tunic and pulled him close. "You're going to be the man of the house. Take care of Mom."

"What are you talking about Dad?"

"Get your mother and head to—"

Three king's men came into the smithy at that moment. Dad showed them the injured horse. He didn't struggle when they seized his arms and escorted him to the castle. A king's guard stayed back, and killed the horse with a spear. "Boy, dispose of this horse."

He had to listen to the king's guard, so he cut up the horse the best he could and distributed it to neighbors. He cleaned up in the lake and went home.

Mom wasn't home. When he enquired about her, he had found they'd taken her to the castle dungeon.

Haskell took deep breaths, his neck stiff and muscles strained. Tears pooled in his eyes.

"Did they release your mother?" Gadiel asked.

"Not soon enough. That night they hanged my father for crimes against the king. I watched him drop and swing."

The room was silent.

Gadiel readjusted his position on the chair.

Haskell said, "They kept my mother one month in the dungeon. She lived for three days after returning home. They had no need to hold onto her at all. It wasn't her fault the horse went lame. The only reason they released her was because she caught a fever and they knew she wouldn't make it."

Haskell shook his head. "It's my fault. I wanted to watch the mastodons. I was a foolish little boy."

"I see." Gadiel said.

"I thieved a little in Velidred, living with friends of my parents. They fed me and let me bunk at their homes for a few days. But they weren't my parents, so I moved on. I knew the guards kept an eye on me, and Vali told me they planned to pick me up and make an example of me. Execute me like my father."

"So how did you get to Goodwin Castle?"

"Hitched a ride. The driver never knew I was on the wagon." Haskell said.

"Did you know you have magic in your blood?"

"What?"

"Magic. I can sense it. No one ever told you? I recognized it in you before I recruited you. That's why you're talented in thieving."

"I don't know what you're talking about, because if I had magic, I'd blast those guards, lords and kings. Give them a taste of what it's like to lose loved ones."

"Blasting people doesn't always get us what we want. I'd like to teach you to be a more civilized thief. I'll train you to use your talent."

Haskell's skin tingled and he raised his eyebrows in surprise. "You don't plan to kill me?"

"No. I see you as a strong resource to my team."

"How can I trust you? You've killed friends of mine, Rusty and Toby."

"Trust me, those were unfortunate accidents. I'm sure you won't have their problems."

Haskell looked at Gadiel. The scorpion retreated to the corner of his eye.

"Before I make promises to spare your life, I need you to complete a task for me."

CHAPTER 4

Haskell took a bite of stew as he thought about Gadiel's request. This had to be the best meal he'd had in months. Did Gadiel's gang eat like this all the time?

Lenny and Sims sat on the bench next to him eating stew. They didn't manhandle him after he left Gadiel's office. He thought about running, but Gadiel said he would feed Haskell and let him go to fulfill his request. If Haskell succeeded then he'd be allowed to stay in Gadiel's gang, but if he failed then the thugs would take their due.

Haskell didn't want to fulfill Gadiel's request. In fact, it wasn't a request, but the worst demand possible. Who in their right mind could trust Gadiel, and agree to his demand?

The boys spooned another bowl of stew, and Haskell followed suit. *Eat well today, and see if I live through the week.* Even when Haskell could return to the street, he wasn't sure he had the ability to fulfill Gadiel's command.

He looked at Dakarai sitting across the table. Was Haskell smarter than these boys? Could he outwit them and their master, and make a new life for himself somewhere else?

Dakarai said, "Eat up boy, you've got a big day ahead of you."

"I may not be able to complete the task."

"Gadiel won't be happy."

Haskell put another spoonful of stew in his mouth. He chewed the food and swallowed. He said, "You don't understand. Even I have trouble finding him."

"He's your friend, right?"

"Yeah, but … it's not like we meet up every day and eat like this. We live on the street, and I might not see him again for a week."

"You promised the boss."

He nodded. *Yes, but in hopes I can escape Gadiel's grasp.*

"The boss gave you twenty-four hours."

Haskell shook his head. Twenty-four hours wasn't going to be enough time for the task.

"We'll be watching you." Dakarai pointed his spoon at Haskell. "So don't try any funny tricks."

Gadiel's request surprised Haskell. He thought the old man might ask him to rob a lord or threaten a shopkeeper. But Gadiel had said, "I want you to bring Max to us."

Max! Gadiel wanted Haskell to fetch the most elusive thief in Whiterock Grove. Max taught Haskell the ropes of the village, and they enjoyed each other's company savoring a pie or a stolen rabbit on occasions. Haskell didn't know if he could locate Max in a day or in a week.

# # # #

They released Haskell into Whiterock Grove and Dakarai placed a knife to Haskell's neck. "I expect to see you with Max this time tomorrow. Don't try to run, we'll find you and . . ." He ran the knife in the air near Haskell's neck. "Understand boy?"

With a slight nod of his head, Haskell ran into the village. Free from Gadiel's grasp. Could he go back to Gadiel with or without Max?

Did Max confine his thieving to Whiterock Grove or did he work in the nearby villages? Haskell realized he'd never tried to find Max before today. They'd just meetup in the streets, sometimes by the castle walls, sawmill, gristmill or blacksmith's shop. Nothing was planned. He didn't search for Max, one minute Haskell stood alone, and then a friendly tap on the shoulder and Max stood beside him. *How do I find Max on purpose?*

Haskell wandered the streets of Whiterock Grove, keeping his eyes on the people strolling through the village for a sign of Max. How do you find someone that doesn't want to be found? Haskell went to the gristmill by the river and surveyed the crowd. He figured he'd stand in the normal places until he grew bored, and then try another neighborhood to see if Max showed his face.

He couldn't just stand and watch the villagers saunter by. Haskell scrutinized each passing villager with an eye for what he could steal from them. The lord and lady of Fairbury passed and Haskell had an itch for a purse, but he waived the opportunity. Widow McIntyre passed carrying her needlepoint to a prospective buyer. She'd fed Haskell in the early days. No need to rob her as she had no qualms about giving Haskell whatever he wanted. She was too generous.

The sun continued its path across the sky, making him hot. Haskell decided to move to the castle walls for better shade. Early afternoon could turn a number of treasures into a productive thief's possessions near the castle gates. Max taught Haskell how to work as a team, one boy catching the victim's attention while the other released a day's purchase or a half-full purse without their knowledge.

He saw opportunities, but ignored them for now. He needed to spot Max before dark to give them the best chance of escape. Haskell decided the best plan after finding Max was to ditch Whiterock Grove and return to Velidred. He wasn't sure if he could manage to escape the village by himself, but with Max's smarts they'd be halfway to Velidred before Dakarai and the others even knew they'd left the village.

A dumb thief might travel through the village's East gate, but Haskell was sure Dakarai and the others would mass their attention on that village exit. In fact, Gadiel would station his thugs at all the gates, but did they know about the hole in the wall?

Haskell stood near the castle walls for two hours, and still saw no sign of his friend. Despite building hunger, he moved to the lumber mill. This part of the village had a distinctive odor, a sweet, earthy scent, as cut logs floated from the villages in the mountains to this section of town. Sometimes he liked the smell, but today it added to the tension and tightness in his gut. The sun dipped lower in the sky, yet still no sign of Max.

He crossed his arms and uncrossed them, and shifted from foot to foot. Then he felt it. Someone watched him. Haskell scrutinized the nearby buildings for the watcher. Why did he feel it so strong? Were they Gadiel's people or another person? Was Max watching? Did standing in one place spook Max? Should Haskell act more natural, pick a pocket or two while he waited? His nerves felt jangled as he ran a hand through his hair. He rocked his head side to side to loosen his tight neck muscles.

Haskell couldn't stand in one place any longer, so he plodded along the river to a favorite tree of his. This tree had a huge canopy and he had learned how to climb its branches and find a spot in the tree from which to watch the world go by. The river reached a stony section by the tree and rushed a little faster and Haskell enjoyed the sounds of gurgling water as it fell over rocks and splashed in the sun.

He ran at the tree and used his feet to push off the trunk, allowing him to jump another five feet to grasp the lowest branch. His momentum carried him to higher branches and soon he had reached his destination branch.

"What took you so long?"

With a gasp, Haskell reset his hands. "How long have you been here?"

"Since I spotted you standing by the castle walls like a lonely, orphan boy."

"We're in danger Max."

"You shouldn't have gotten caught."

"It wasn't my fault. We gotta be careful, Gadiel's thugs might be tracking me."

"That's why you're only spending two minutes here."

"Gadiel wants me to bring you back to his base."

"That's not happening." Max said.

"We have to leave the village, but they'll watch the exits."

Max laughed, "Relax my little friend."

"I can't relax. I don't want them to find you. I don't want to stay in this village, and I don't want to go back to Gadiel. What are we gonna do?"

Max rubbed his long nose with the back of his hand. "You're in a pickle, aren't you?"

"Not just me, you too. Even if they kill me, they'll keep looking for you. It's not safe for us to stay in the village; we gotta bug out."

His friend looked pensive for a moment. "I have contacts in Velidred, though it isn't as lucrative as Whiterock Grove."

"The old man told me something." Haskell wasn't sure he should tell Max this. He wasn't sure it was true or just something the Gadiel told him.

Max smiled. "Yeah, what's that?"

"Wizard blood runs through my veins."

"Wow. Then blast the old man."

Haskell shook his head and smirked. "I don't know how to use magic. Gadiel said he could train me."

"Will you stay with Gadiel then to learn how to become a mighty wizard?"

"He says you have magic in your blood, too."

Max snorted. "I'm old enough to know if I have wizard blood and an inkling of magic. The man is talking nonsense."

"Maybe, but he says that's why we're so successful at thieving. Says we should team with him, and go after the big money."

"Happy with what I get now. Don't need the big money."

Haskell thought the same thing, but today he had wondered as he watched the lords wander in and out of the castle. *Could I grow up and become a lord? What's it like to have a lady on your arm and people come to you for help, money and decisions? Could I have that kind of life or will I always be a common village thief, in and out of the dungeon and always on the run?*

"We could make a good team with Gadiel. Imagine us running Gadiel's operation, we'd make a fortune," Haskell said.

Max said, "Are you gonna sell out on me? No, we'll run over to Velidred, find a wizard trainer and become grand wizards to impress the girls."

"I'm not selling out. But if we fail to escape the village, then they might kill us both."

"I'm not afraid of Gadiel and his thugs. I have tricks and ways to pass through small places unnoticed. Look, you've been up here too long. Head on down, and meet me at ten-bells behind the Sliced Pig Inn. I'll scout out a couple of escape routes and we'll be in Velidred tomorrow night enjoying the good life."

CHAPTER 5

Haskell hid in the dark behind the Sliced Pig Inn waiting for Max. He listened to two stablemen while he hid in the shadows.

"Then Lord William says, 'If you want to live, you'll saddle my horse now.'"

"What did you do?"

"I wanted to take his curly blonde head and smear it in the muck stall."

"He wouldn't like that."

A hand touched Haskell's shoulder and he jumped.

"Quiet," Max said.

Max led Haskell through the streets of Whiterock Grove. They headed toward the Northeast wall. Haskell wondered why Max led him in this direction. This was a dangerous area to sneak out of the village. If an exit existed in that quadrant without using a gate, they still needed to swim the moat and race across a hundred yards of meadow with no cover from the castle's archers. That plan had death by arrow written all over it.

Haskell checked the moons. The red Velidred moon showed full and bright, while white Pantaleon grew thinner. It still illuminated the village. Too bad they couldn't have chosen another night to escape.

The castle guards would see perfectly across the meadow and the two boys would become easy targets.

As they stood behind a log cabin on the edge of the village. Max pointed across the open area. "See that dark spot in the wall?"

"Yeah."

"There's a missing stone there. Dogs and little guys like you and I can get through it. I gave the guard money to ignore anybody he sees leaving through there tonight."

"We'll never make it across the meadow."

"I've timed the castle guards on the wall for an instance just like this. At the next bell the guards will change positions. When they do that, they chat among themselves and we have exactly two minutes to sprint across the meadow."

"And the moat?"

"Swim. You can swim, can't you?"

"Not well, but it's not the swimming that worries me. They have creatures in the moat. I've seen them."

"Ha, don't worry. What people don't know is they sleep during the night. Though I suggest you swim fast so you don't waken them."

Haskell's senses were on high alert. His toes and fingers tingled, and he bounced on the balls of his feet. He scanned the area near their location and the wall. Haskell didn't see Dakarai or any of Gadiel's thugs. Could they do a runner? He estimated they had five minutes before the next bells rang.

Max touched Haskell's arm. "Did you see that?"

"What did you see? Gadiel's thugs or guards?"

A dog wailed in the distance followed by a chorus of dogs barking. Yappy little dogs and the deep bass from the big dogs.

"I don't know if it was a person or an animal, I can't tell."

Haskell strained in the moonlight to see something or anything. "No, I don't see anything. Where did it go?"

He shook his head. "I don't know, one moment it was there and then gone."

"Gadiel's magic?"

Max didn't answer.

"Can we outrun them?" Haskell asked.

"Too risky. They can chase us for miles through the forest. We can't take a chance."

"I have an idea. I'll walk toward the wall. If anyone sees me and comes after me, then I'll tell them I'm looking for you. They'll think you aren't with me, and they'll stay here waiting for you and we can try somewhere else."

"Good plan. If they capture you, blast them with a fireball, that'll help."

Haskell wished he could blast someone with a fireball. He felt helpless not being able to get away from these thugs.

Max rubbed his chin. "We have three minutes at best. Go ahead, don't hurry, you need to draw them out of their hiding spots."

Haskell's heart palpitated in his chest as he took a breath to calm. He closed his eyes. "Here goes." He opened his eyes and dawdled into the clearing, only forty-yards from the wall. If Dakarai, Lenny or Sims were around he figured they'd try to jump him before he reached the wall. He didn't like the thought of being punched by Dakarai again. What would they do if they thought he was escaping by himself?

    With each step, Haskell checked the wall in front of him, the walls of the houses behind, and the empty space between the houses. He didn't see anyone. Ten yards closer to the wall and the space between wall and houses remained clear. Haskell crept nearer to the wall as he watched for the enemy. There wasn't anyone in this area, and he'd be right at the hole in the wall when the bell rang. Did Max really see something? If the boys found Max, Haskell planned to continue the escape plan. Gadiel wanted Haskell as an introduction to Max. Once he had Max then Haskell was free to run.

    Twenty yards to the wall and still no one appeared. There were no shouts to stop, and no castle guards patrolling the area. He'd be home free. He pictured heading home to Velidred, hooking up with some of his parent's friends, and see if he could join a wizard school. Wizarding meant money and prestige. Haskell didn't need Gadiel's help in becoming a wizard.

    Ten yards to the wall and Haskell was free and clear. A quick skinny through the hole, swim fast across the moat, and hope for the castle guards to not be paying attention for thirty seconds while he raced across the meadow.

    Haskell turned to look back at Max. He didn't see anyone in the shadows of the cabin. None of Gadiel's thugs showed. Had Max abandoned Haskell? That was smart of Max. Get Haskell out tonight and then Max could hide and sneak out at a more suitable time.

The first sound of the bell rang across the wall. He smiled. Haskell was leaving Gadiel and his gangsters and heading home. He checked one more time for Max, hoping to see him running toward him, but no one moved in the shadows.

Haskell pivoted back to the wall and the short distance to cover and Dakarai stood right in front of him.

Dakarai punched him in the jaw and Haskell's head rang in unison with the bells.

Dakarai said, "Where you going runt?"

Haskell felt pain in his jaw, the back of his throat and his chest constricted, preventing his breathing. Max's whole plan — blown up by Dakarai. How did Dakarai know where to set up to wait for them? There were multiple exit points they could have chosen. Plus, how did he hide himself from being seen this whole time? Haskell had to think fast. What excuse had they planned? "I'm waiting for Max, he agreed to meet me here. I thought I saw him over here, but it must have been you."

"You were leaving the village."

"No, I wanted to talk Max into going to see Gadiel." Haskell glanced at the shadows near the cabin and watched as three boys wrestled Max to the ground.

CHAPTER 6

The fifth day in the box and Haskell was roasting. All he'd received was a single mug of water each morning. The sun beat hard on the wooden box and he wondered how much longer he'd be able to last with only the meager water they gave him and without food. He didn't know what happened to Max. Was his friend still alive?

Was Haskell now a part of Gadiel's team of thugs, or were they planning to kill him? Why not throw him off the tower instead of forcing him to suffer through this torture?

Nothing about his time with Gadiel had made him want to stay with the group. Haskell needed to come up with an escape plan as soon as possible. This time a foolproof plan that gave him enough time to go somewhere they'd never find him. He realized Gadiel expected him to run to Velidred, the village he grew up in. So, Haskell would find another village where Gadiel didn't have influence.

Someone shuffled across the yard, which was unusual for this time of day. They finally decided to kill me, he thought. Fine. He was ready, but he decided to make a fight of it. Haskell tried to arrange his legs in the tiny box so he could strike with massive force when the lid opened, but the small box constricted movement.

Two boys laughed as they walked toward the box. They fumbled with the lock.

Haskell prepared his hand to strike the closest boy. He hoped Dakarai opened the lid, because Haskell owed him a few punches to the jaw. He worked his own jaw, still sore from the escape attempt.

The lid opened and sunlight blinded Haskell as he flailed his arms. The boys who opened the box laughed.

Max said, "Easy Haskell, it's me."

After being in the dark box so long, Haskell blinked his eyes to see in the blinding light. Was that really Max? "You're still alive?"

"Yeah, I'm okay." Max touched him on the shoulder.

Haskell flinched.

"Rough in there?"

"Were you locked up, too?"

Max shook his head. "Nope. Come on, you gotta be hungry after five days in the box."

####

A week later, Dakarai stood before Max and Haskell teaching them magic. "Use the spell for air to open a pocket and then it's easier to steal what you want. Go ahead, try it."

Max stood ten-feet from Haskell while Dakarai walked back and forth in front of them. Haskell thought the spell for air, and forced it into Dakarai's pocket. It didn't work.

Max cheered, "Got it." He lifted a purse of cheap coins into the air.

Haskell's friend had talent in magic. Dakarai would teach a technique twice and Max had it mastered in minutes.

"Haskell! I felt the air blast my tunic. Focus your magic and direct it into the pocket."

"Okay, give me another chance at it."

"Do that to a lord and you'll have a chance for the guillotine. Now focus."

Haskell rubbed the back of his neck. "I am focusing, your technique doesn't work."

"The technique works. Concentrate and try again."

Gadiel said Haskell had talent in magic, but it wasn't coming easy. Why was it so easy for Max, yet it required twenty more tries for Haskell to master the technique? He took a deep, calming breath.

Dakarai walked by Haskell and a breath of air opened Dakarai's pocket a little, but not enough to remove an item.

"Close, but I still felt my tunic push against my skin. Try again."

An hour later, with more coaching and practice Haskell resolved the problem where he forced the tunic against Dakarai's skin, but still the pocket didn't poof open.

Dakarai said, "Take a break."

Max patted Haskell on the shoulder, "You're almost there."

Haskell said through gritted teeth, "Leave me alone."

Max laughed. "I'm two years older than you. A person's magic ability improves in their late teens. The same way you couldn't expect to win a sword fight with a castle guard. Imagine that same fight after ten years of training. You'll get there, give it time."

Haskell shook his head and got a drink of water.

# # # #

A month passed and Haskell and Max waited by the castle gate. This was their first opportunity to try thieving using the magic skills taught by Dakarai. Max was going to try first. They searched for the perfect target to practice their newfound skills.

Dakarai stood twenty feet away under a crabapple tree to signal the boys.

Two guards came through the gate with their swords sheathed. Guards were never good candidates, as they didn't take kindly to losing their coins to thieves.

Three ladies walked together chatting about an acquaintance. Dakarai didn't want them robbing the ladies today. Focus on the lords.

The scent of baked apple pies wafted through the air and Haskell thought back to the days when an apple pie was enough thievery for a couple of days. He didn't like being forced to work at someone else's command, but as long as Gadiel controlled him,

Haskell followed Dakarai's directions. Learn magic and behave until he had power to escape.

A lord strutted under the tower and walked toward Haskell and Max. Dakarai touched his nose with his index finger which signaled them this was their mark. Haskell nodded at Dakarai and moved into position. The plan called for Haskell on one side of the lord and Max on the other. They would saunter in the same direction as the lord. Then poof, open the pockets, check for purse or coin, grab the treasure and disappear into the crowd.

Haskell had thieved for two years using a similar technique without the magic, but this new methodology scared him. Would he push too much air at the guy and get caught? He felt clumsy and ill prepared to do the task. He tried to swallow, but his mouth was dry, and his legs felt restless.

Because of months of practice by himself, Haskell knew the pocket on his side held no coin. He didn't have to do the poof of air thing because there was nothing to grab. The coin purse weighted the pocket on Max's side. Despite that knowledge, Dakarai wanted Haskell to practice the air poof anyway. He hoped the technique worked and he didn't get caught. The guards stood eight feet in front of them walking in the same direction as the lord.

They reached the lord's side and Haskell poofed the pocket. He reached in with his fingers, found nothing, as expected, and withdrew his hand. It worked perfectly. Haskell increased his foot speed to pass the lord when the lord cried out, "I've been robbed."

Did Max make a mistake? All the practice tries, Max never made a mistake. Years of thieving and Max didn't make mistakes. What happened?

Haskell's instinct made him calm his legs and suppress his desire to run. If you run, then the guards knew it was you, and they'd even hunt for you if they didn't catch you right away. Max still walked calm as a summer day with no worry, next to the lord.

The guards turned and grabbed Haskell.

"What are you doing?" Haskell asked.

"We're taking you in for hanging, you stinking pick-pocket."

"Look at me, I don't have anything." Haskell stopped and showed his hands and pockets. "I don't know what you're talking about, I've got nothing."

Max walked by the guards, a smile on his face.

The lord said, "I had a full coin purse in my pocket. This street urchin stole it."

"No, I didn't. If I took it then where is it?" He crossed his arms over his chest.

Dakarai and Max strolled past the guards once more on their way back to Gadiel's.

Those two are leaving me to the guards? He didn't believe it.

CHAPTER 7

Six months passed, and Haskell improved his magic and thievery skills. As he practiced more, he became adept at the techniques Dakarai taught. Max, Haskell and Dakarai worked as a team using magic and scoring treasures. Haskell didn't like that Gadiel took most of the loot and left little to Max and him. However, they did eat better with Gadiel than they had on their own.

Dakarai leaned against the brick wall of their magic-practicing room, wearing a white and yellow tunic. The bricks were red and black, a combination of the volcanic rock in the area and mud from the river.

Haskell asked, "How did you keep us from seeing you the night you captured Max?"

Max leaned in closer.

Dakarai smiled.

Haskell was thinking about the gaudy contrast of colors—Dakarai's tunic against the wall—when suddenly their teacher was gone.

"Did he disappear?" Max asked.

"I guess so, I don't see him." Haskell rushed toward the wall but bounced off an object two feet from the wall. An object he couldn't see.

Dakarai re-appeared in front of Haskell.

"Whoa, that is awesome." Max said. "Are you going to teach us that?"

"Not today. One of the requirements to learn that skill is participating in the Fire and Ice challenge."

Haskell inched back from Dakarai and asked, "The fire and what?"

"Fire and Ice challenge. It's a three-step challenge for young wizards. You have to be at least sixteen-years-old to take the challenge, and once completed, you're invited into a secret society of wizards. It's a tough test, which a handful of wizards don't survive, but if you want to become a great wizard you have to take the challenge."

"Where do I sign?" Max asked.

Haskell pouted, because he thought it'd be cool to take the challenge and learn to blend in with the background. He had another year before becoming eligible.

Dakarai said, "I'll talk with Gadiel and see if he thinks you're ready. If so, we can try to schedule it before the weather turns bad. The challenge requires a trip to the mountains. This late in the year it might not happen till spring."

####

A week later, Haskell caught Dakarai, Sims, Lenny and Max whispering among themselves as they waited for a lord to exit a tent.

"What're you guys whispering about?"

"Nothing that concerns you, punk," Sims said. "Get back to your watch position, and you better not miss signaling us.

Lenny laughed.

Haskell walked back to his station, where he watched the blacksmith's shop for two knights to finish their conversation with the blacksmith. Gadiel's team of thieves planned to rob the lord who was shopping in the tent, but wanted to wait until the knights finished their transaction and departed for the castle. The worst thing the thieving crew could do would be to get caught by the king's knights relieving coins from a lord. That never ended well. Lenny had a scar across his ear from a knight's sword proving how dangerous the transaction could be.

Dakarai taught Haskell techniques to listen in on conversations using magic, so he set up in position to watch the knights. He dispatched a magic stream to catch the conversation. He'd never tried this technique from this distance and deliberated about making the stream of magic wider. He thought Dakarai might be able to sense the magic, so he prepared a tiny, discreet stream, the size of a thread.

Max said, "And when the eclipse happens, any wizards at the volcano will—"

Two women, carrying clucking chickens to the castle, crossed the path of magic, and Haskell lost the thread of conversation.

When he picked up the conversation, Dakarai said, "Sixteen is the age a wizard has to be to attend this event."

"Are we taking Haskell?" Max asked.

"Too young. He's not sixteen."

Dakarai glanced in Haskell's direction and Haskell dropped the magic line and watched for the knights. What were they talking about and why couldn't they tell Haskell about it? If the age to attend was sixteen then he'd stay in the village. Whatever it was, it didn't have anything to do with him. He wondered if it had to do with Max's Fire and Ice experience, since that required a wizard to be sixteen-years-old.

The knights exited the blacksmith's shop, and Haskell whistled at the others to get their attention. Dakarai waved at Haskell and Haskell followed the knights toward the castle. If they didn't go straight to the castle, but stayed in the village near Gadiel's crew, then Haskell's responsibility required him to delay the knights or signal Dakarai to change plans.

Everything was going according to plan until the knights stopped three buildings past Gadiel's crew, and started a conversation with three women in castle finery. Haskell didn't know who the women were, but the knights stopping meant trouble for the team.

Haskell glanced back just as the lord exited the building. Were the knights far enough from the team for Dakarai to rob the lord? If Haskell didn't notify Dakarai, then they might put him back in the box. Then again, if they didn't get their money from the lord, they might take it out on Haskell, too. What should he do?

The lord ambled toward Haskell and the knights on his way back to the castle. The knights continued chatting up the women. Could the boys get their coins from the lord without the lord noticing? Max was supposed to do this job on his own, as a kind of graduation ceremony, but Haskell couldn't let his friend get caught.

No doubt Dakarai would throw Haskell in the box if he made the wrong decision. Was there a disturbance he could cause to disrupt the knights and the women? Throwing fireballs in the marketplace was frowned upon by Gadiel and his thieves, so Haskell needed something more subtle. But not something that might get him in trouble.

One of the ladies wore a veil and cap combination, and Haskell noticed she wore it loose around her hair. A puff of wind to blow the cap and veil off the woman's head would distract the knights as they helped a woman in distress.

A brief glance back at Max showed the lord one building closer and Max trailing the lord three-feet behind.

Time for Haskell to create the distraction. He sent a magical puff of air at the brim of the woman's cap, the veil puffed up, but it didn't fall off. She squeaked a little, "Oh!" and placed her hand on top of the cap holding it tight to her hair.

That represented a total failure on Haskell's part. Now what should he do? Max ambled next to the lord. They were only one and a half buildings distant from Haskell and the knights. Did Max see the knights, or was his friend too focused on his task?

Haskell had seconds to get the knights' attention to save his friend. It was too late to notify Max to stop the robbery. The knights wore their swords at their sides, nice weapons to slice Max's arm off or slash through his chest.

Two boys and a dog walked behind the knights at that moment and Haskell sent wind to buckle the knight's knees as if one of the boys hit the knight as they walked past.

The knight's legs bent, and he went to the ground to his knees. He yelled, "Stop."

The boys, barely ten-years-old stopped, then saw the knight on the ground and they did the only thing a ten-year-old can do when faced with a massive decision that might end in their death. They bolted from the marketplace.

The knight on the ground shouted, "Sir Timothy, chase after those scoundrels."

Sir Timothy, the other knight, didn't chase after the boys, but instead laughed, a big booming sound from the depths of his belly.

The ladies watched the boys run, and then joined in laughing at the knight on his knees. Sir Timothy helped his friend to his feet.

Max touched Haskell's shoulder as he walked past. The lord passed Haskell seconds later, but stopped and talked with the ladies and the knights and soon was also laughing at the spectacle of a ten-year-old taking down one of the king's knights.

When Haskell entered the main room back at the house Sims pushed him against the wall and held his forearm against Haskell's neck. "You were supposed to signal us if the knights stopped."

"They stopped too close to the time the lord exited the building. I didn't have time."

"That means you failed. Into the box you little creep."

Max said, "Leave him be, Sims, we got the coins." He rattled a purse of coins.

"We got lucky this time, next time he might fail and one of us will find a sword through our belly. Dakarai, what say you?"

Dakarai said in a monotone voice, "Put him in the box for two days. We have to follow discipline protocols."

# # # #

Two weeks later, Dakarai stepped into Max and Haskell's room. "Max, grab your jacket and boots, we're heading to the mountains."

Haskell cried out, "The Fire and Ice challenge?"

"Yeah."

"Can I tag along? I want to see what's involved."

"Sure." Dakarai said.

They walked for six hours straight up hill into the mountains. Winter hadn't reached the meadows of Whiterock Grove, yet, but in the mountains, snow drifts piled a foot deep. Flurries of snow fell on them as they climbed. Gadiel called a stop to the hike and said, "Set up camp here."

Dakarai and Max worked to set up tent, piling furs in the tent for sleeping. Lenny and Sims went into the forest hunting for food, while Haskell retrieved firewood before it turned dark.

They feasted on rabbit and squirrel while re-living thieving victories.

Haskell enjoyed the smell of the fire, the brisk mountain air with the scent of pine and the camaraderie around the fire. He hadn't been this happy since his parents died, and being out of the village helped raise his spirits. Maybe life as a thief would be okay. He'll take the Fire and Ice experience in a couple of years, learn new magic skills, and become a leader within the group like Dakarai.

Lenny was telling a story of a thieving victory and said, "Then Lord Braxton looked at the lamb standing where his horse once stood and said, 'Are you planning on pulling the wagon with a lamb?'"

The boys all laughed.

Gadiel said, "That horse turned a nice gold piece for us." He stood. "It's time for some work boys. Dakarai check on the coals, while Lenny and Sims make space on the lake and prepare the hole."

Haskell wondered what they would do with a hole on the lake. A hundred yards up the hill a twenty-foot-long bed of coals glowed red.

Dakarai returned from the hill of coals and said they were ready.

Gadiel asked, "Max, are you ready?"

Max's eyes sparkled red and yellow reflecting the fire. "Yes."

They trudged through the snow and reached the length of coals.

Gadiel said, "Take off your boots and socks."

Max removed his footwear and handed them to Haskell. "Keep them warm my friend." Max smiled.

"Drink this tea," Gadiel offered.

"Unusual flavor."

"Yes, it's designed to open your mind to sins you've committed against others. Maybe in the past, you've hurt a loved one. The fire experience once completed will rid you of those sins." Gadiel said.

Max drank the tea and a goofy smile crossed his face.

"Now inhale this incense to visualize your past mistakes." Gadiel placed an open jar of incense beneath Max's nose.

Max closed his eyes and inhaled.

They stood in the snow. Clouds that hid the sky during the day disappeared, showing a million stars in the night sky. The fresh, cold mountain air was unlike the smog-filled sky of the village.

Gadiel said, "Haskell, run over to the other side of the coals so Max can focus on you."

He clomped through the deep snow and made his way to the other end of the burning coals. What will happen? Haskell waved to let them know he was ready.

Max stepped on the coals and walked briskly toward Haskell.

Haskell didn't know what to expect. He imagined great magic like this would produce an exciting display of images in the sky.

Max didn't stop. No exciting images showed in the sky. Max's face changed as he walked across the coals. His smile changed to anger, and then Max quit looking at Haskell and averted his gaze. Max grimaced and flailed his arms like a man attacked by bees.

Haskell didn't see anything and couldn't tell what caused Max's problems.

Max stopped in the coals.

Gadiel yelled, "Keep going."

Max turned around on the coals, stopped and looked toward Gadiel, then rotated back toward Haskell.

Gadiel yelled, "Dakarai get him. Take him all the way across." Gadiel pushed Dakarai toward Max, and walked in the snow in Haskell's direction.

Dakarai ran to Max and grabbed one of his flailing arms.

Max pounded on Dakarai's arm.

Dakarai forced Max across the remaining coals.

Max collapsed to the snow when he reached Haskell.

Gadiel poured oil over Max's head and said, "Your past sins are forgiven, go into the future in peace of past mistakes."

# # # #

Haskell said, "His feet are burned."

Gadiel commanded, "Wrap his feet in snow. The burns will heal."

Max muttered meaningless words. Haskell wondered if it was a foreign language.

Haskell looked at Gadiel.

Gadiel shook his head. "The burns will heal, but the trauma is fatal."

"What do you mean the trauma is fatal? Aren't you doing the ice thing?"

"There's no need to do the smoke or ice experience. He's damaged."

Haskell asked, "What happened, did we do it wrong?" Max was supposed to walk across the coals, and then go on to the next experience. Sure, his feet got burned, but couldn't he go on?

"We didn't do it wrong," Dakarai said. "Max saw something that spooked him, a memory he wasn't ready to relive."

"Do we take him to a healer?"

"No."

They placed Max in an animal skin brought from the tent, and using the fur like a hammock the boys took turns carrying Max down the mountain.

Max mumbled unintelligible words all the way back to the village.

They placed Max in bed when they reached their home.

In the middle of the night, Max screamed and flailed his arms and feet.

Haskell grabbed his friend's legs and tried to calm him. "Wake up Max. You're home, everything's okay."

After twenty minutes, Max ran out of energy and returned to mumbling.

Haskell didn't get any sleep the first night.

As far as Haskell could determine, Max didn't sleep for eight days. His friend lay in bed sweating or freezing, mumbling or screaming, calm or flailing, and nothing helped.

On the ninth night, Haskell returned to the room after supper and Max had disappeared. Haskell ran through the village searching for Max and checking his favorite hiding places.

Haskell searched local inns, talked with Max's friends, searched in empty buildings and even went to his favorite tree, but he didn't locate Max.

He plodded along the river searching the grasses and prepared to cross over to the other side at the King's Bridge. This bridge spanned one-hundred-fifty yards across the river and the bridge was so wide wagons could travel three abreast.

Haskell trudged across the bridge. Where was Max and what happened to him during the fire experience? *I'm never taking the Fire and Ice challenge. It's too dangerous.*

He stopped in the middle of the bridge and watched the moons reflect off the river. The water slowed at this point in the river, making it difficult to tell if it was a lake or a river. Should he make another attempt to escape Gadiel's influence and thugs? He knew more than he did before, and could succeed as a thief in another village.

A wooden shuffling sound came from the top of the bridge. Haskell scanned above, and noticed Max balanced on the railing at the very peak, fifty feet high. How did his crazy friend get up there? "Come down Max. It's dangerous up there."

Max mumbled unintelligible words, but didn't move.

Haskell studied the bridge to find a way to scurry up to his friend to help him down. There was a method, though it included a five-foot leap from one bridge beam to another.

Haskell scurried up fifteen feet to the transition point, and gawked at Max who teetered on one leg while he screamed. Haskell shouted, "Max, it's Haskell. Are you okay?"

The screaming continued.

He searched for another method to reach the next beam. No choice but to jump the five-foot distance.

Then the screaming changed position and Max plummeted from the bridge past Haskell into the frigid water with a loud thud and small splash.

Haskell shouted, "No!"

He dove deep into the water after Max. The cold constricted his chest. He drove his arms and legs to swim hard back to the surface. Breaking the surface, Haskell sucked in lungsful of air. Gasping and coughing he searched for Max.

The current wasn't swift here, but was noticeable. The blue Anticletus full moon provided light on the water. Haskell spun in the water seeking movement, hoping to see Max swimming toward shore, but saw nothing.

Three times he rotated in the water, treading with arms and legs, and then he saw the body. Max floated facedown fifteen feet from Haskell, the drift from the current glided them both to the other side of the bridge. He needed to get Max's face out of the water if he hoped to save his friend.

Haskell struggled with the heavy, wet jacket he wore, but swam hard toward Max. How long did his friend have in the water? He wondered if the fall itself from that high might have killed him.

Within five feet of Max he yelled, "Max turn over."

Max didn't respond.

He reached Max and grappled with the body in an attempt to flip him to his back. The cold water soaked through his jacket and Haskell's body lost heat. His arms didn't have the strength to flip Max over and keep Haskell afloat in the water. He dove underneath the body and shot up to the surface propelling Max's body to his back.

Max lay limp, cold, blue and still.

# # # #

Haskell returned to his room. The cold sucked his will to live. He removed his wet clothing and dried off near the fireplace. Max was gone, just like Rusty and Toby, killed by Gadiel. The old man would pay for his crimes against Haskell's friends. Haskell grabbed a wooden chair and slammed it against the bed, over and over, until the chair splintered into twenty pieces. He threw the broken wood into the fireplace.

Why did Max take the Fire and Ice challenge? Dakarai told him it was dangerous, and he might die. Why didn't Max refuse to take the challenge?

For the second time, Haskell vowed to never take the challenge. He didn't need the benefits Gadiel promised. His life was more important than any magical promises.

He held a chair leg in his hands and pitched it into the fire. Haskell needed to come up with a plan to exact revenge on Gadiel and his thugs.

If Haskell threatened to kill Gadiel, that might end up being his own death sentence or at the least land him back in the box for a week or longer. That wouldn't help.

Did the boys and Gadiel trust Haskell enough to allow him space to do a runner? If he timed it right, and found the perfect location, Haskell could leave the village long before the thugs knew he'd left.

A third option he entertained was to break the legs of Gadiel's gang of thugs. That would deliver a blow to their ability to produce goods and revenue for Gadiel's schemes. What might happen if he failed or half had broken legs and half didn't? It'd be writing his own death sentence. Gadiel wouldn't care. The thugs could handle Haskell without Gadiel's involvement.

Haskell considered a long-range plan where he stayed with the team, learned the system, and pretended to be part of the gang. Then after sufficient training in magic and increased knowledge of the group; he'd plan his revenge or escape.

He considered refusing to help Gadiel with his thievery. Why not sit on the bed or go to the village and not pick pocket or provide an income for Gadiel? What could the man do to him? Haskell knew the answer. He'd be rewarded with an early trip to the grave.

    He lay in bed considering his options.

CHAPTER 8

Three nights in a row, Haskell dreamed of Max, and in each dream, he watched Max launch himself from the bridge. He dreamed finding Max alive when he returned to the room, but the next morning Max wasn't alive.

The fifth night, the dream started the same way, but then Max climbed down from the bridge and ran into the mountains. Haskell followed in the dream. Did this mean Max was still alive, and maybe in another dimension or plane, Haskell wondered.

Max led Haskell to the Velidred volcano. Velidred was an active volcano with a continuous explosion like a fountain erupting into a fiery display of lava. It had thrown lava into the sky for years. Max stopped and watched it blasting into the night sky.

"Are you trying to show me something?" Haskell asked.

Max pointed to the top of the volcano.

Haskell shrugged his shoulders. Why would Max bring him to this volcano? Didn't he know how dangerous volcanoes are? He wondered if a stray lava explosion could hurt Haskell in the dream.

Even though Haskell grew up in Velidred village, he'd never gotten this close to the volcano and he stood mesmerized watching the bubbling lava and listening to the roar as it splashed back into the boiling pit.

Max stared into Haskell's eyes for five minutes as if he was trying to perform a mind meld with Haskell, but nothing happened.

What did Max mean by bringing him here?

Then Max disappeared, and Haskell woke in his bed, sweating.

His friend never appeared in a dream after that night.

Six-weeks later, Haskell stood with Sims, getting the day's orders.

Gadiel said, "This job is easy. You go to the Widow McIntyre's seamstress shop. You ask for a pickup for Gadiel."

"What happens if she refuses? Do you want us to rough her up?" Sims asked.

"No, you don't have to do anything. She'll hand you the money. I'm giving you two this job because she's the easiest extortion client I have. You need to learn this part of the business. Do it right. No mistakes."

"Okay. Okay. I'm just making sure everything will go the way you want it to go." Sims paced back and forth.

Haskell watched Sims, who looked nervous. The Widow McIntyre was Haskell's friend and had provided comfort, food and money when he first came to Whiterock Grove. He never realized Gadiel had his claws in the nice old lady. The woman didn't make much more than she needed to live, and Gadiel extorted money from her? He wondered about her reaction when she found out he'd turned to a life of crime.

Haskell turned to leave Gadiel's office.

Gadiel grabbed Haskell's arm. "No mistakes. Don't get clever, don't take more from her than requested, and don't rough her up."

"We'll do it right." Haskell ripped his arm from Gadiel's grasp and stomped out the door. He planned to do it right, but he suspected Sims to do something stupid.

As they headed to the widow's home, Haskell fumed over Gadiel's insistence he do it right. Of course, he wasn't planning on taking any shortcuts and definitely had no plans to mistreat the nice woman. He considered her a friend, and his chest tightened at the possibility of confronting her and taking cash from her. There was no way he could damage her shop if she didn't pay.

"How we gonna play this?" Sims asked.

"The way Gadiel told us."

"We're gonna rough her up right?"

"No, we're not gonna rough her up. We follow the plan, ask her for Gadiel's pick up and leave. You got that?"

"You don't think Gadiel was telling us that for deniability reasons? Don't rough her up, wink, wink."

Haskell pinched his lips and poked his index finger in Sim's shoulder. "Listen, Widow McIntyre is a nice lady. If Gadiel said she'd give us the money then we don't have to rough her up, because she'll give us the money."

Sims said, "I came into this group first, why do you think you're my boss?"

"Simple, I have common sense and you don't. Plus, I know magic, and you're just fast on your feet. Get your head in the game. No funny business. Get in, get the money and get out." Haskell shook his head. He had a feeling that Sims planned to do something stupid. He didn't want to go in and see the widow. He had told her that he planned to follow his father's footsteps and become a blacksmith.

They stood at the door to the widow's home and business. She had the door open and was the only one in the building.

"Are we going in or just standing on the doorstep?" Sims asked.

"I'm thinking."

"Think about this, if you don't get the money, Gadiel will throw you in the box."

Haskell felt heaviness in his gut, and his arms and shoulders tensed. Could he trust Sims to do the job alone? Surely, Sims couldn't ruin something this simple. It's just an easy in and out.

"Can you do this job by yourself?"

"Why, because you don't want to see the widow? Do you have a thing for her?"

"No. Get in there and get the money. Don't take too long, there's a guard heading this way. Can you do it?"

Sims sneered and walked through the widow's door.

Haskell kept his eye on the guard. It'd only take a minute for Sims to get the coins, and they'd be on their way before the guard reached their location. The guard talked with other businessmen sometimes, and that might allow Sims more time to get the money.

The guard stopped at the tailor's and walked into the shop. Perfect thought Haskell.

Something fell in the widow's shop with a loud crash.

What was that? Haskell rushed into the widow's workshop.

A display of ribbons and thread lay scattered across the floor and Sims had straddled the widow and threatened her with a knife. "Where's Gadiel's money, lady?"

"What are you doing, Sims?"

"Getting the money the way Gadiel told us."

Haskell pulled Sims off the old lady. "He said don't rough her up." He pushed Sims against a bench, and Sims fell to the floor screaming about hurting his knee.

"Are you okay, Widow McIntyre?" Haskell helped her to her feet.

She touched the back of her head and blood showed on her hand.

Haskell wasn't sure if she recognized him or not.

The guard walked in and said, "What's going on here?"

"These boys are trying to rob me." She screamed.

The guard blew his whistle, and lowered his lance at Haskell.

Sims made a dash for the door but the guard, a burly man, turned his lance and blocked Sims' escape and knocked him to the floor.

Three more guards entered the room and secured Haskell and Sims.

# # # #

Sims and Haskell sat on the castle dungeon floor secured to the wall with chains.

Haskell said, "What did you do?"

"I asked for the money, and she refused."

Haskell rolled his eyes, "Gadiel said she never refuses to make the payment. Tell the truth. What did you do?"

"I don't have to tell you anything. You're not my boss."

"Listen, Gadiel's gonna ask, and he won't be happy."

"Not my problem."

"It is your problem, because you beat up the nice old lady."

"I'm following the boss's orders."

Haskell's muscles ached from being chained to the wall. He shook his head at Sims. "Gadiel specifically told us not to rough her up."

"Not Gadiel, I'm following your orders. You're my boss."

Haskell snorted. "You better not tell Gadiel I ordered you to beat her up. I have no qualms about killing you."

"If Gadiel asks, that's what I'm telling him."

"You're a piece of work, Sims. Gadiel won't believe you, because he knows I listen to him and you don't listen to anyone."

"I'm getting out of here whole, but you're leaving without a hand."

Haskell wondered if that could be true. Is there some way that Sims could pin this horrendous mistake on him? He needed to talk to Gadiel before Sims, so Gadiel had the right information about Sims' attack, rather than the lies Sims wanted to tell.

CHAPTER 9

The bells pealed ten times in the castle tower. Haskell wanted to sleep, but he couldn't find a comfortable position on the dungeon floor that didn't involve an awkward twist of his arms. The sound of someone snoring came from the guard station outside the metal gates of their cell.

Haskell wondered what the rest of the castle looked like. He'd never been in the Goodwin castle, but he had heard tales of rich tapestries and golden vases. He wondered if he could take a little stroll through the castle.

Sims slept.

With a little magic spell, Dakarai had taught him, Haskell released the chains that held him to the dungeon walls. They dropped to the stone floor and clanged. Sims snorted in his sleep, moved to a new position and in a few moments returned to sleeping.

Haskell stood and rubbed his tender wrists and ankles. He wondered if the spell could work on the dungeon door, and if he made it through the door, what reaction would he get from the guard?

Who was the stupid one now thought Haskell? Sims lay asleep, and Haskell planned a walk through the castle even though he was supposed to be a prisoner. He stood on his tiptoes and noticed the guard sleeping with his head on the table.

Dakarai had taught Haskell how to encase a person in air, and he thought his skill level could handle the guard. Since the bells had just rung ten, when was the next guard change? In a few moments or did Haskell have an hour or two to roam? Was there another guard that he couldn't see from his position? That'd be horrible to walk out the door into the guard's hands.

A tingle of excitement ran down his back, and he shook the feeling out of his body. Using a slight amount of magic, Haskell encased the sleeping guard in air. That would hold the man. Then he manipulated the lock with a thread of magic, and the lock disengaged.

He took a deep breath and opened the door a crack; just enough to peek into the guard area. Something moved across the floor, and Haskell shut the door. Then he realized he had scared a rat from its nightly rounds. He chuckled under his breath, and opened the door.

No other men guarded the room. Haskell grabbed a mug of ale left by the sleeping guard and drained it. He wiped his lips with the sleeves of his dirty tunic.

This had to be the most stupid thing he'd done in his life, but excitement and adrenaline pulsed through his body. Haskell crept down the long corridor, staying close to the wall. He had no idea what he'd do if he encountered anyone, and now that he'd escaped from the dungeon, what did he plan to do?

Haskell admired a tapestry hung on the wall, portraying four women in a forest while two lords rode horses. The tapestry didn't impress him, nor did the second tapestry he encountered. That one showed a man and woman kissing outdoors while eight others ate and drank around an outdoor table.

His stomach reminded him that he hadn't eaten in a while, so he decided to search for the kitchen. Maybe he'd find cheese or nuts to munch on while he took a tour of the Goodwin castle. He reached a landing, and realized he didn't know how to find the kitchen.

Haskell had no idea what he'd do if he encountered a castle guard. *What do you say? I'm a prisoner, and I thought I'd roam the hallways.* He needed to learn how to do the surface trick that allows you disappear next to a wall the way Dakarai did the night they captured Max.

He snuck along the corridor watching all around him. The first room he reached was unoccupied and had a large fireplace. No fire blazed at this time of night. Books lined two shelves in the room, and a couch and two chairs had been placed on a large rug in the center of the room.

Haskell ran his hands across the leather-bound books, chose one and sat in a chair. He opened the book, and pretended to read and act like he was a king, enjoying the fine things in life. He imagined a servant bringing him food and drink, while he entertained other lords and ladies in fine clothing from the surrounding countryside.

He sat back in the chair, closed his eyes and pictured people coming into the room, bowing to him and asking him to make decisions on their lives. King Haskell, living a life of luxury while he solved the many problems plaguing the surrounding villages.

Footsteps sounded in the hall and Haskell dropped the book on a table next to the chair, and scurried behind the couch. A man entered the room, a servant not a guard. The servant picked up the book lying on the table and re-shelved it.

Haskell's senses went to high alert. *What if this servant catches me in the room?* He held his breath; afraid the man might hear him breathe.

The servant glanced around the room, must have been happy with what he saw and walked into the corridor.

Twenty seconds elapsed before Haskell thought it safe to breathe. That was close. He considered going back to the dungeon, but his stomach rumbled. He decided to continue his search for food.

A quick peek into the hallway showed it was empty, and Haskell scooted to the next room. This room was also empty. It had a full row of windows against one wall, and was larger with a table in the middle. He examined the candlesticks on the table, fine silver, worth a lot of money. If only he could find a way to take them out of the castle with him. Footsteps approached in the corridor.

A man said, "Someone snuck into the dining room."

Haskell ducked under the table.

"The princesses like to eat late night snacks. Was it one of them?"

"No, we would have seen them when they passed us."

"Are there other guests in the castle tonight?"

They stopped at the open door and Haskell made out the castle guard's uniform on both men.

"The commander didn't make mention of any guests."

"Have a look around. I will watch the hallway for other ghosts you might have seen."

"It wasn't a ghost."

"Then it's a princess. Did the person have blonde hair or dark?"

"I didn't get that close of a look." The guard searched the room, examining the corners and near the silver cabinets.

Haskell lay flat on the floor, under the table between the chair legs, watching the guard's search. His arm started to itch, but he was afraid to move.

The guard stopped his search five feet from Haskell, and though Haskell couldn't see the man's face, his feet faced toward Haskell.

He wanted to run. If the guards found him, he was sure to get the guillotine and not just to chop off a hand. His heart raced, and it beat loud enough he thought it'd wake the whole castle. He wondered if he could outrace the guards. Where would he go? He'd have to charge back to the dungeon and let himself back in before they caught him. Oh yeah, and remember to release the other guard. That's a laugh. He'd get caught before leaving the dining room.

The guard by the door said, "Which princess do you like best, Carol or Noreen?"

"Noreen's green eyes spook me. I'll take the blonde any day."

"Yeah, the blonde's a little older, closer to marrying age. I wonder which lucky prince will get her."

"Not you." The guard by the table moved away and ambled to the doorway.

"Yeah, we're not in her league."

The guards stood by the door for two minutes discussing the blonde princess.

Move away, and talk about girls somewhere else. Haskell was getting nervous.

They finally left their station by the door and continued their journey through the castle.

Haskell scurried from underneath the table. Should he return to the dungeon? He'd have to wait since the guards left in the direction he needed to travel. He would someday return and plunder the king's silver.

Where's the food? Haskell left through a servant door, and followed steps to the floor below where two girls were talking. He slowed his pace and snuck down the remaining steps until he could see the room. In the kitchen, an older blonde-hair girl, he figured she was older than he was, sat with a younger girl with black hair. The blonde was stunning, and the younger girl had green eyes, that seemed to glow.

"Daddy wants me to marry Gerard." The blonde said.

"Oh, that awful boorish old man who's always sniffing our hair?"

"Yeah, I think he's really creepy."

The dark-haired girl sliced off a bit of cheese and put it in her mouth.

Haskell had found the kitchen and the food. How long would the girls be there? His mouth watered, watching them eat. The blonde had an apple in her hand and kept gesturing with it as she talked. Haskell wanted to shout at her, "Just eat the apple and leave."

"Can you talk Daddy into letting you marry the very handsome knight, Preston?"

Both girls chuckled.

The blonde said, "He blushes every time I smile at him."

They giggled.

Haskell watched and listened to their banter. How long could he stay in this corridor until a servant or guard walked down the steps? He thought about the guard at the dungeon. If the guard was found tied up with air and the dungeon door opened, what trouble would that cause? Come on girls, stop giggling and finish eating.

CHAPTER 10

The castle bell pealed once, signaling the half hour. The blonde said, "Time for bed, Sweet Pea."

"Ah, I was having fun. I like hanging out with you instead of Mrs. Frey. She makes my head hurt, always trying to teach me to be a lady."

"Learn your lessons, and maybe Daddy will let you marry Preston."

They giggled. The eldest girl took the other's hand and moved around the table.

Haskell realized he was in a traffic zone into the kitchen. Would the princesses leave through this stairway? He'd been sitting on the stairs and stood, readying his legs to run.

Then footsteps sounded on the steps above him and one of the guards he'd seen before said, "Do you think the princesses are in the kitchen?"

"We won't know if we don't examine the kitchen for thieves and murderers."

The blonde said, "The guards are coming down the steps. Quick, Noreen, up the stairs."

They giggled, and changed direction.

Haskell counted to five, listening to the footsteps getting closer. Then he bolted into the kitchen. The girls left the food on the slicing table, but Haskell didn't have time to grab a block of cheese, an apple or a handful of nuts. He saw the stairs the girls took, but suspected that led to guarded living quarters. He searched for a place in the kitchen to hide.

"You think they left us any food, tonight?"

"I hope so, I'm starving."

The kitchen was a large room with arched ceilings over a fireplace. Grooves lined a stone and concrete floor where foot traffic trudged each day. The table the girls ate at fit under one of the arches, and pots and pans hung from the arch above the table. It looked like a surface the kitchen staff used to prepare food. Another table sat on the other side of the room.

Barrels of food and sacks of corn and peas lay in one of the corners. Haskell jumped on a bag of corn and moved it to burrow for a place to hide. Mice scurried away as he wriggled into the space. He hoped the guards didn't see him or hear him.

The guards reached the kitchen just as Haskell settled into his hiding spot.

"Did you hear something?"

"Not again. Did you see the same ghost as last time?"

"No. Heard something."

"The castle mice probably."

"No, it had to be someone."

"Nah, listen." The guard walked to within a couple of feet of Haskell's spot and kicked a barrel of pickles.

Mice scampered from their location and back into the area Haskell had settled. Two mice scampered up his leg and he squirmed. He wanted to scream, but bit his tongue instead.

"Mice. No ghosts. Now eat some cheese and nuts, and stop telling me about these ghosts you're imagining."

The other guard said something with cheese in his mouth, and Haskell couldn't understand the comment.

Haskell stayed hidden, his legs cramping, but he didn't twitch, despite the mice using his body as a plank to get to the castle provisions.

The guards didn't stay long, and he figured they had a certain time each hour to make specific checks to keep the castle safe. Haskell waited another minute after the guards left the kitchen.

He rushed to the table, grabbed a handful of walnuts, an apple which he stuck in his pocket and a small block of cheese he placed in his other pocket. With a salute of thanks to the castle cooks, Haskell hurried up the servants' stairs he had used to come into the kitchen. He hoped if he hustled, he could avoid another round of guards in the hallway, and get safely back to the dungeon.

The dining room was clear, and he sneaked to the corridor. It looked like a run of twenty yards to his turn to the dungeon, or did he have time for another search for treasure? He decided to forego any more adventure. It would be easy to explain food or give it to the dungeon rats, but if they found a silver knife or spoon in his pockets, he'd have no answer.

Haskell checked the corridor, first right, then left. No guards in either direction. The castle bells pealed eleven times as he sprinted through the hallway. He kept repeating, "no guards, no guards, no guards," in hopes that would save him.

He reached the intersection and rounded to the left. He scrambled down the steps to the dungeon door. Did the dungeon guards change at the eleventh hour? What might he find when he reached the guard he tied with air? He tiptoed the last few feet.

It took Haskell a second to gain the confidence to peek through the open door. Would the guard still be sleeping, or had Haskell taken too long? The guard lay in the same position Haskell had left him.

It required a little work to re-lock the door, undo the magic holding the guard and then prep the shackles for his limbs. He was going to enjoy dinner before he re-engaged the locks. Haskell took a bite of cheese. Delicious.

Sims said, "Where you been?"

"Getting supper."

"Give me some."

"Your hands are tied behind your back. How can you eat this delicious castle cheese? This cheese was cut by the lovely Princess Noreen, just for me."

"Free one of my hands, and give me a chunk of cheese."

"There's not enough for the both of us. If I'd known you were awake, you could have joined me in the kitchen."

"Give me some or I'll wake the guard."

"Sims, you're always ruining a good thing. The only reason we're down here tonight and not enjoying a delicious meal at home is because you have fewer brains than a cockroach."

Sims shouted, "Guard—."

Haskell used a burst of air and muffled Sims.

The guard woke and shouted, "Shut up in there, or I'll have to strap you."

Sims' nostrils flared, his face turned beet red and his neck muscles corded tight.

Haskell ate his supper in silence.

CHAPTER 11

The next morning, the guard opened the door, and Gadiel stepped into the dungeon. He said, "What happened?"

Sims spoke first, "Haskell told me to take the lady down."

Haskell shook his head and said, "That's a lie."

"He also took a stroll through the castle last night and visited the princesses."

Gadiel stared at Haskell.

"I was hungry, and they were in the kitchen," He smiled.

Gadiel rattled the dungeon door and when the guard returned, Gadiel pointed at Sims. "Release that one. You can leave the other one for another day."

"What are you doing?" Haskell asked. "I didn't do anything; we shouldn't even be in here. It's Sims' fault. I told him not to attack the lady."

The guard released Sims who jutted his chin, crossed his arms and sneered. Sims stood and stepped hard on Haskell's leg.

Haskell's first instinct was to use magic to inflict pain on Sims, but with Gadiel in the room, Haskell held back his anger. "I'll get you for this, Sims."

Sims smirked.

Gadiel and Sims left the dungeon, and the guard re-locked the door.

He sat on the cold hard floor, and wondered why Gadiel punished him. The man had to know Sims caused the problem and not Haskell. Was Gadiel angry at Haskell for sneaking out of the dungeon and wandering through the castle?

When will Gadiel return to spring me out of the dungeon? Is it possible Gadiel planned to test my ability to escape the dungeon and castle? If I stayed in the dungeon for a couple of days, can I expect Gadiel to return for me?

If Haskell escaped on his own, then the castle guards would have a reason to pick him up any time he planned to thieve for Gadiel. *What's the punishment for escaping the dungeon? Death? If I escape the castle then I'm a marked man.*

Staying in the dungeon might send a message that it would be okay for the guards to cut off Haskell's finger or a hand, which wasn't the ending Haskell wanted to see. How long could he last in the dungeon? He found food once, and figured if careful, he'd find it again.

Haskell thought of ways to hurt Sims when he returned to Gadiel's team. He'd stick it out in the dungeon for a couple of days and see what happened. Maybe he'd get another look at the pretty green-eyed princess.

CHAPTER 12

Three days later, Haskell relaxed in the dungeon. Whenever the guards came to the door he pretended to be locked up, but as soon as they left, he released his chains and walked about the small space.

He wondered why Gadiel didn't want him released. Gadiel had to know that Haskell hadn't done anything to the Widow McIntyre. Why didn't he return to release him?

The next day the guards brought in twelve young men and chained them in the dungeon next to Haskell.

"What's all this?" Haskell asked.

"Crazies from the eclipse. Anytime an eclipse is coming some kids get like this."

"What eclipse?"

The guard said, "The solar eclipse by the Velidred moon in two days."

After they got settled, Haskell asked, "Are you guys in here because of an eclipse?"

A young man, older than Haskell said, "During the solar eclipse, magic flows more readily near the Velidred volcano. Wizards with an affinity for Velidred magic can boost their magic if they're at the volcano during the eclipse."

Is this what Dakarai and Max were whispering about weeks ago? Haskell scanned the room of boys and men. Many looked younger than him. "Don't you have to be sixteen to attend the eclipse?" *That's what Dakarai had said, wasn't it?*

A boy shouted, "That's a lie. Those old people are afraid us younger wizards will steal all the magic."

A man responded, "Oakley, you don't know what you're talking about."

"Yes, I do. My dad told me it's true." Oakley glared at the other guy.

"Are you all wizards?"

"Oakley and another boy, much younger than Haskell, raised their hand."

"Then why are the rest of you in the dungeon?"

A towheaded boy said, "There are parties at the eclipse."

Haskell shook his head, "But why here?"

"There was a group of about forty of us planning to leave the village tonight to go to the Velidred Volcano, and a couple of the guys were getting soused. Most of us were outside of the tavern, just waiting to leave, and the guys inside got rowdy and tore up the place. The guards showed up, and now we're here."

Was that the problem with Gadiel and why he wanted me in the dungeon? He didn't want me to attend the eclipse. Maybe the whole issue with the widow was to put me in the dungeon until the eclipse was over. Can I receive magical power stronger than

Gadiel and his team? I need to get out of this dungeon.

Haskell said, "Hey guys, we need a plan to escape, so we can get to the volcano in time for the eclipse event."

The prisoners cheered.

Haskell would need to be able to leave the village without Gadiel knowing. He wondered if Gadiel and Dakarai planned to attend the eclipse event. Had they already left the village for the volcano?

He looked at the boys who had been dropped into the dungeon with him. Haskell could plan a mass jail breakout, which might allow him enough confusion to leave the castle. He didn't think these boys were very smart. With everyone running wild in the castle he'd have an advantage if the guards tried to herd them back to the dungeon. Maybe these other guys would get captured, but not Haskell.

A trip to the volcano required a minimum of a day, so Haskell needed to escape tonight.

# # # #

The bells knelled twelve times, and Haskell woke the boys in the dungeon. The numbers had grown to twenty-three and the room was crowded. Many of the boys were shackled to more than one other person.

Haskell released his restraints. "Do any of you want to get out of the dungeon tonight and head to Velidred?"

A chorus of, "Yes," filled the room.

Haskell evaluated the boys. He needed some crazies to run every which way, providing a distraction to the king's guards. Then he'd arrange the smarter boys to travel with him, helping him pick the best path through the castle. He picked his smart crew of seven.

"Here's what we'll do. I'll release you all. We'll all leave at once. As we travel through the castle you'll peel off and find multiple directions out of the castle."

One of the boys said, "I'm not a distraction, I'm going with you."

"Okay." *That one will stay in the dungeon.* "Do any of you know the best way to escape from the castle without being caught?"

Oakley, already a member of the seven, raised his hand. "My dad used to work in the castle, and he showed me a passage that's used by royalty when they want to leave without being seen by the commoners."

"Stick by me and we'll use that passage."

"Are you going to let the rest of us just get caught again?"

"No, it's important you work as hard as possible to escape. We don't know if the guards will expect a jailbreak. If they do, then they may close the passage my friend just mentioned. We might be the decoy, and you'll be the ones to escape."

The boys scrutinized each other as if wondering who might escape or get caught.

Haskell had mapped out a number of corridors during night runs for food, but he didn't know all of them. He feared his new friend might be leading him to the gallows.

####

They waited till the bells tolled twice, and then Haskell checked on the guard who normally slept every night. Haskell bound him in air, hoping the spell didn't injure the man, since he'd have no way to undo the spell after he left the castle.

Then Haskell released all the boys except the one who sounded like a troublemaker.

"I'm opening this door, and then we run like crazy through the castle. We can all meet up at the volcano."

"Yeah." They cheered.

Haskell opened the door and checked the guard station like he did every night, to make sure there wasn't another guard. Good so far. "Let's go, but stay quiet."

They bolted from the room. Haskell let them all go, then closed and locked the door. "See if the guards can discover how we escaped," he thought. Haskell ran hard and caught up with Oakley near the dining room.

Oakley turned into the dining room and raced down the stairs to the kitchen. Haskell assumed the passage led this way, but instead of leading them towards the stable, he sprinted up the stairs to the living quarters. It was a dangerous path as guards marched through the corridors, keeping the king's family safe from attack.

Their crew consisted of ten boys, six of Haskell's chosen ones and three of another group. Oakley reached the top of the stone stairs and stopped. He said, "We need someone to go left to distract the king's guards.

Haskell snagged the tunic of the smallest boy in the group. "You just volunteered."

The boy wanted to say something, but an older boy put his finger to his lips and shushed him.

Oakley said, "On the count of three, you go left, the rest of us will hold for ten counts and hustle right to a storeroom three doors away. "

Haskell realized at that moment that an arrow could stop him halfway to the doorway, and hoped the little boy chosen as a decoy fulfilled his role to distract the guards. He hoped the tyke didn't die along the way.

"Three." Oakley pushed the boy down the corridor.

Footsteps pounded through the hallway as Oakley counted to ten. On the count of seven, guards yelled, "Stop," and the footsteps continued.

"Let's go."

Haskell stayed right behind Oakley and made sure two boys ran behind him to take an arrow if needed. They reached the storeroom door and Oakley pulled on the door handle. It didn't budge.

"It's locked."

"I got it." Haskell used magic, and the door unlocked. He hoped it was a secret passage and not the guard's sleeping quarters.

Oakley pulled the handle, and nine boys squeezed into the tight quarters. The room contained buckets, mops, linens and brushes and smelled of lye. "Can you lock the door?"

Haskell locked the door as Oakley pushed shelving off to the side uncovering a hidden door in the floor. Two boys grabbed the ring and yanked. The wooden door rose and exposed a ladder. Oakley jumped to the ladder and climbed down.

All nine reached a room twenty feet below the storage room. The room was dark no light entered from outside.

"Where are we?" A boy asked.

Oakley said, "I'm not quite sure."

"Is this the way your dad showed you?"

"Yes, but it was daylight when he showed me, and I can't see in the dark."

"I got this." The boy, who raised his hand in the dungeon saying he was a wizard, produced a small globe of blue light.

"Whoa, you gotta teach me that," Haskell said.

The globe, the size of a tin mug, didn't provide much light, but they were able to search the room. The room contained swords, shields, bows and arrows, and lances.

Haskell said, "Is this the knight's weapons' storage room?"

"Yeah."

He rolled his eyes. Out of the frying pan into the fire.

Footsteps sounded on the floorboards above them.

"Get us out of here." Haskell commanded Oakley.

"Here's the door over here." One of the nine shouted.

Oakley said, "No not that door. That door opens to a corridor which houses the guards. Over here is a secret door." He moved a wooden shield and exposed a small door.

Oakley went first on hands and knees and Haskell followed behind. He'd let the others wrestle with the guards if they became a nuisance. The tiny passage required them to stay on hands and knees for ten feet then opened to a full-size corridor.

Why would royalty use this exit when they could walk out the front door? Haskell thought. Royalty can be so stupid at times.

Oakley asked, "Should we wait for the others?"

"No, go." Haskell's stomach fluttered and his senses prickled in high alert.

His guide led him past three doors on the right, one on the left and then stopped at the last door on his left. The corridor ended.

"Where do the other doors lead to?"

"I don't know. This is the one my dad showed me."

"Where does it lead?"

"Don't know really, he never opened this door."

"Did he say it leads outside the castle walls or inside the courtyard?" Haskell bounced on his toes. "Come on man, give me something positive. Will we encounter a bunch of guards?" *I can't believe I put my trust in this kid.* "Okay, open the door and let's see what's on the other side."

Haskell prepared for an onslaught of arrows or guards with lances. Could he encapsulate them all with air? If they exited outside the castle battlements, he'd have to worry about an arrow attack from the castle walls. Inside the courtyard, the guards could capture them, and they'd have no chance to escape. Maybe this wasn't a good plan.

The door opened to a small ledge which appeared to run along the side of the castle walls. The Anticletus moon showed bright in the sky lighting up a meadow. The moat stood between them and the meadow.

"They wouldn't cross a moat." Haskell pointed to the water.

"What?"

"The lords and ladies, they wouldn't swim across the moat. There must be a bridge."

"Yes, along the ledge. The bridge is within fifteen feet." Oakley pointed at the bridge.

Haskell heard screams in the corridor. The guards had found his group.

"Go." He pushed Oakley.

It was slow going, as Haskell didn't trust his footing on the narrow ledge, but they inched toward the bridge.

He examined the meadow. A forest stood two hundred yards from the moat; the same area his friend Max had wanted to use the night they were captured by Dakarai. If they had a head start in the meadow, he was convinced he could escape. If the guards on the tower weren't actively looking for escapees, then he'd be halfway across the meadow before an alarm was sounded.

They reached the bridge, a narrow wooden structure and Oakley bounded across it.

The attack bells rang from the bell tower, alerting every guard in the castle to get to their defense positions.

CHAPTER 13

How fast could Haskell race across the meadow? The guards on the tower expected to see attackers coming toward the castle walls, could running away from the castle prove a benefit? He dashed off the bridge to the meadow, and sprinted to the trees.

He was twenty yards away from the moat, and arrows rained around him. Dakarai had never taught him a magic shielding technique, so he shaped air to rush past his back hoping to push arrows off him before they struck.

Haskell ran faster than Oakley.

Then he heard boys yelling behind him, "Go, go, go." as they bolted across the meadow. More targets would give him a better chance at escape. He wondered how fast the many sleeping guards could reach the arrow slots to shoot at the escapees.

Three arrows slid off his back in the direction the magic air flowed and Haskell knew his shield strategy worked.

Cries of anguish grew in the meadow as the other boys fell to arrows.

At a hundred yards, Haskell's lungs cried for air. His legs churned, but lactic acid build up in his legs made each step painful. He didn't know if he'd make it to the forest.

Oakley passed him fifteen yards later. Arrows still pounded around their feet, missing their targets by inches. These boys weren't a risk to the king and his daughters. Why would the guards continue their arrow barrage?

With fifty yards to go, the number of arrows that came close to them lessened. Haskell wondered if the archer's arrows couldn't reach the forest, and maybe they didn't have to achieve the forest to escape.

Thirty yards from the forest, Oakley went down. Haskell stopped to check on him. An arrow had pierced the young guide's thigh. Should he leave him here? He increased his makeshift shield to include Oakley. He picked him up, threw an arm around his shoulder and forced his new friend onward.

Their paced slowed as Oakley yelped every time his bad leg touched the ground, but they hurried. Ten yards to go and Haskell couldn't see any more arrows striking the ground. Had they reached the archer's limits, or were the guards now in the meadow?

Haskell glanced back at the castle, but saw nothing.

They ran through the forest for at least a hundred yards. Haskell lost his sense of direction, as the vegetation changed to small bushes and briers, slowing their progress. They reached a shallow, dry ditch where Haskell and Oakley fell into a pile of leaves.

Haskell listened for people that might be following them. Would the guards continue their pursuit into the forest? He wanted to suck in huge breaths of air, but feared the noise would alert pursuers of their location. *Did any of the others from the dungeon reach the forest alive?*

Oakley moaned.

"Are you okay?" Haskell whispered. Dumb question, he could see the arrow in Oakley's thigh. They needed a healer.

"No," he gasped. Blood soaked Oakley's trousers.

"We should get the arrow out of your leg."

"How'll you do that?"

"Not sure." Haskell examined the arrow head, three inches above Oakley's knee and extending two inches past the front of the thigh. How do you remove an arrow? Can't pull it out with the arrowhead on it. He could break the arrow below the arrowhead, and drag the arrow through the thigh. What should he do if the arrow broke a bone as it pushed through Oakley's thigh?

There wasn't enough arrow on the arrowhead side to break with his hands, so Haskell rotated Oakley to position the feather side up. With a sharp snap, he broke the arrow with his hands and Oakley groaned.

"Almost done. Stay quiet and roll over."

He positioned Oakley on the leaves and placed his foot on Oakley's upper thigh causing Oakley to grunt.

"This'll be worse." Haskell grabbed the arrowhead with both hands and yanked. Oakley sobbed, but didn't yell. Tough boy, Haskell thought.

Haskell ripped off a bottom strip of Oakley's tunic and wrapped his leg at the arrow hole. He didn't know if Oakley would live.

CHAPTER 14

Haskell helped Oakley to Velidred, and found a healer to care for him. The boy was weak, had lost a lot of blood, and Haskell didn't think the boy would make it. Then he made his way to Velidred Volcano to see what the eclipse, his dreams and the volcano magic were all about.

A crowd of five hundred or more people swarmed the meadow area near the volcanic peak. Haskell felt the heat from the pulsing, lava as it bubbled like a fountain. He didn't know where to stand or what to expect.

Should he search for Gadiel and Dakarai? Had they come, and would Gadiel be angry with him for showing up at the volcano? He decided to wait to find them.

The range of people surprised Haskell. Lords and ladies with their servants ambled around the volcano. He noticed many wizards with staffs and wands. Groups of women and men formed circles as they chanted and sang. The noise from the bubbling volcano made it difficult to understand the words.

A petite woman stood on a large, flat rock, raising her above the group of people circled around her. The woman had to be in her late teens or early twenties, not much older than Haskell, and yet she transmitted poise and power.

Haskell edged into the circle to see what the woman was saying that captivated her audience. She wore ten or more gold and silver bracelets on her left arm and a large green jewel ringed a finger on her right hand. Her black hair cascaded to the middle of her back.

She said, "The god of Velidred calls for war, suffering, hate, and power. I say ignore Velidred, and seek a world of peace and love. Leave the volcano, now, and go back to your homes to seek peace with your troubles and neighbors."

Even a teenager like Haskell knew that the world was filled with hate and suffering. As a blacksmith's son, he'd seen the good and bad in people, especially from the ruling class. They looked down on people like him, orphans and blacksmiths. This woman must be from the ruling class to not see the pain and suffering of a commoner's life.

"There is no satisfaction on the volcano today. Even after the eclipse, you'll howl for more. Embrace Aloheno's nature, and feel her call for you to be as happy as the trees, never moving, always growing where they stand."

Two snickering men sauntered away from the woman.

A wizard in the group called out, "We seek Velidred's magic. If you can't embrace the magic of Velidred's goddess then return to your home in the mountains."

"Silence her with magic and show her Velidred's power."

"Nah, let her ramble on. How soon before the eclipse begins?"

The crowd dispersed leaving the young woman standing alone on the rock.

Haskell approached her. "Why are you here? Do you know magic?"

She spit at his feet, "No, I don't know magic, and I don't to. I live with nature, listening to the trees in the forest, and running with animals. Are you here to make fun of me?"

Haskell raised his hands. "No. I'm curious. I thought your speech was terrific."

She blushed.

He said, "I'm Haskell. Would you like help stepping down off the rock?"

She lifted her hand, and he clasped it. "I'm Forest River Blossom, spiritual adviser to kings and queens." She slid off the rock as Haskell helped.

"Impressive title for someone so young. Which kings have you advised?"

She stared at her feet. "None so far."

Haskell said, "Someday when I'm king, I'll hire you to advise me."

She reached out with her hand. "It's a deal."

He shook her hand and laughed. "Today, I'd be happy to find food."

"Are you a wizard?"

"Wizard-in-training over in Whiterock Grove."

"I didn't think wizard trainees were invited to the eclipse."

"Nobody stopped me." *Though many people tried.*

"There aren't many wizard kings," she said.

"Then I'll have to be the first."

Forest River Blossom smiled a beautiful smile. "Can I do a reading for you?"

"Don't have any money."

"You're a nice guy, I'll waive my fee." She dug into a bag slung over her shoulder and removed five objects. "Over here." They stepped to the flat rock she had stood on to give her speech and said, "With these five objects on this stone table, I'll read your past, present and future. Shake these objects in your hands, and I'll place them on the table."

Haskell had heard tales of fortune tellers, and he wondered if they were real and had the power to predict people's fortunes. He shook the objects in his hands and opened his hands like a bowl so she could remove them.

The five objects she gave him were a small pyramid with images on each side, a pink figurine in the shape of a pig, a blue marble, a bird's claw and a black obsidian rock. The rock was all black on one side with a red streak of a different mineral running through the other side.

She closed her eyes and chose one of the objects in Haskell's hands. It was the obsidian rock, and she took it and placed it on of the table with the red streak facing up. Forest River Blossom said, "The center position represents your present condition."

Appropriate. I'm standing on a meadow with a blackened volcanic peak spewing lava a few hundred yards above me.

Forest River Blossom didn't say anything else, but chose the next object from Haskell's hands. The blue marble she placed to the left of the obsidian rock. Her body posture perked up and she moaned. "West of the center is your past."

Haskell wondered what she saw in the objects. Were these runes or something else? He wanted to ask questions, but she seemed intense and focused on her task of reading his life.

She plucked the bird's claw and placed it above the obsidian rock. "Oh, unfortunate. North of center is the help you'll receive from others."

Should he be concerned that the bird's claw represents something bad?

The next object she placed below the obsidian rock and said, "The pig is placed south of center, representing acceptance of problems and outcomes."

That left the four-sided object, leaving Haskell wondering what the different images on the object meant, and how Forest River Blossom might read the object's placement.

She extracted the last piece and placed it right of center and said, "East is your future." Then she paused a moment. "Oh," her eyes widened and sparkled in the morning sunlight. She smiled.

Forest River Blossom chanted a long litany of words, a foreign language to Haskell. Meaningful or meaningless, he couldn't discern.

When she finished her chant, Haskell prepared to ask a question, she placed her finger on his lips. "Say nothing till I'm finished."

He raised his eyebrows and smirked. *The lady puts on a good show.*

"The blue marble represents your past. It was pleasant enough, but turned to sorrow and emptiness when your parents died."

He didn't remember telling her he was an orphan.

"Red in the obsidian rock tells us that the god of Velidred will play a major role in your life, and that you are destined to be on this volcano to receive the mantle of greatness."

That made him smile. *There's hope for this day to turn out okay.*

Forest River Blossom moved her hand to the four-sided object, but then stopped and picked up the bird's claw instead. "North of center tells us your path won't be accepted by others, and you'll struggle to reach your goals without the help you expect."

She studied him from head to foot as if assessing his abilities.

"South of center, the pig tells us that despite problems of acceptance by others, you'll push onward and receive your fat rewards."

Before handling the last object, the pyramid, she smiled sheepishly at him and batted her eyelids.

Why did she do that? He scratched his head.

Forest River Blossom inhaled and exhaled three slow breaths. She gazed at him as if seeing him for the first time. Snatching the last piece from the table she showed Haskell the bottom of the object.

CHAPTER 15

Haskell staggered away from the spiritualist and her predictions. He left Forest River Blossom at the flat volcanic rock after she read his fortune. He had only been kidding about getting his fortune read. How she could choose that piece remained astonishing. Were her predictions true, or just a game to entertain people?

She kissed him on the lips before he left, the first woman to ever kiss him. "Remember I expect you to hire me." She brushed volcanic ash off his shoulders.

He didn't know what she meant by that phrase, but she'd told him the unthinkable. A comment and future so preposterous, he didn't dare tell his friends or anyone. If his parents were still alive, he wouldn't even tell them. He thought of Princess Noreen.

A cheer rose from the crowd, "The eclipse is starting."

Haskell looked at the sun, and a hand pushed his shoulder, and the person said, "Don't look at the sun you idiot, you'll go blind."

"What?" Haskell pivoted.

Dakarai grinned at him. "Didn't your mom ever tell you not to look at the sun?"

"Yeah, but I want to see the eclipse."

"Still gotta be smart. The sky will darken and you'll know it when it's pitch black. I didn't think you'd make it."

The hair on the nape of Haskell's neck stiffened as he avoided eye contact. "Gadiel didn't want me to come. Left me in the dungeon."

Dakarai showed his hands and hunched his shoulders. "Didn't know. Gadiel is on the mountain today. Do you want to go see him? We could talk, there's probably a logical explanation. Sims will back you up."

"Is Sims here?" Haskell wanted payback for Sims landing him in the dungeon.

"Yeah, the little rat tags along wherever Gadiel goes these days, like a lost puppy."

Haskell chuckled. "How long does this eclipse thing take?"

"An hour or two for total eclipse."

"What are we supposed to do when the eclipse occurs?"

"I'm not sure, magic flows from the volcano, and we take some of it."

Haskell surveyed the crowd of wizards. "Will there be enough magic for all of us?"

"I guess so. Do you want to ask Gadiel?"

"Not yet. I want to check out an idea. Don't tell Sims or Gadiel I'm here, okay."

"Sure."

Haskell ambled toward the top of the volcano. They were near the peak, but he thought he saw another ledge by the lava pit. He wanted to see if he could reach the lava pit or at least get closer. Nobody else had walked up there, so he'd have the whole area to himself.

The closer he got to the peak the rougher the ground became. He went up old lava flows and then the same distance to a valley only to trudge up the next mound of black rock. The side of the mountain became steep, forcing him to all fours to climb higher.

Was this a mistake to want to be closer to the volcano pit? Lava danced thirty-feet high and splashed back into the molten pool. The colors changed from red, to orange, to yellow and then returned to the pit changing to black. The roar from the explosions was ear-splitting and his tunic got soaked with sweat and caked with ash. The stench of sulphur hung heavy in the air.

The mountain had darkened by the time he reached the peak. A level plateau stretched out to the lava pit. He attained the summit and glanced back at the eclipse partiers, small specks in the distance. *Am I that high above everybody else? Will Gadiel recognize me?*

The eclipse had to be more than halfway complete by now. With the rising and falling of the lava, Haskell noticed waves of blue, red, green and yellow flowing off the volcano. He relaxed and settled into the frame of mind to receive magic that Dakarai had taught him.

Peace and calm saturated his body as a dull, monotonous sound pulsed all around him. Somehow his body absorbed the magic as he leaned toward the powerful attraction of the volcano's power. The black art of Velidred magic swelled, crested and foamed over him like a rushing stream of water.

Haskell clutched his chest as the magic streamed into his mind and body. His limbs tingled in anticipation of more as it gushed and rippled back and forth.

Time passed, and the mountain grew darker. The eclipse wasn't full yet, but Haskell noticed a second wave of sorcery emanating from the Velidred moon. It came down like a blood red ribbon floating from the sky. The people below him tried to draw it toward them, but the ribbon of energy picked Haskell and joined with the volcano's waves of power.

He didn't know how he did it, but at times when wizards below the plateau reached out and plucked strands of energy, Haskell cut the ribbons. He consumed the magic cascading all around him.

At the time of total eclipse, a dark cloud rose from the volcano, and bolts of lightning struck the ground near Haskell, but he didn't move. Where did his body find space to store the magic streaming into it?

Haskell stayed in a catatonic trance for the next two hours while the magical forces from Velidred and the volcano saturated his body. When the Velidred moon moved off the sun, Haskell collapsed to the plateau floor in exhaustion.

CHAPTER 16

Haskell awoke as the sun neared the western horizon. He was dazed and confused as to his whereabouts and then realized the gravity of his location. He realized his position was perilous this close to the volcano cauldron, and feared a stay on the plateau overnight. If the wind changed direction the drops of hot lava might splatter on him. His body felt dehydrated, and he didn't want to climb down the steep, sharp cliff during the night.

A crowd of people mingled beneath him in the meadow below the volcano. He needed to reach that crowd before nightfall or he might fall to his death. Haskell wished for water.

He started his descent, but wasn't able to traverse the dangerous slopes before darkness settled over the mountain. Haskell stayed in one spot until the volcano spurted up an explosion of lava which allowed him to see the next two ridges before the light dissipated. He tripped twice coming down the hill but luckily didn't hit his face on the volcanic rock.

The time had to be eleven bells when he arrived at the meadow site where the rest of the wizards stood. It appeared were waiting for him to climb down from the volcano peak. Torches dotted the meadow and balls of blue light followed wizards about the field.

An elder wizard, with a grey beard to the middle of his chest, prepared a fireball to throw at Haskell, but the boy wizard sensed the fireball forming, and squashed it. The elder wizard sucked in a quick breath, and he covered his mouth.

Haskell's chest tingled and he felt lightheaded. He studied his palms wondering how he identified the wizard's intent and acted so fast, but he didn't have time to question his abilities as two other wizards attempted similar acts.

He pinpointed the two wizards and their intent, and Haskell suppressed their magic.

One wizard said, "I don't believe it. He's just a boy and can't know these techniques."

A wizard wearing a peaked gray hat with a wide brim said, "He absorbed all the magic from Velidred and the moon. We've never seen this before; we should study him."

"Good idea. I'll take him to my castle and examine the boy," A short, round man with a black, Van Dyke beard said.

Three wizards grabbed Haskell's arms and shoulder each pulling and saying, "Come with me."

Haskell emitted an electrical charge and they released him. Haskell pulled his shoulders back and asked, "Does anyone have water?"

Gadiel entered the group and said, "Haskell what have you done?"

"I didn't do anything. I climbed to the volcano rim and then the eclipse occurred."

Gray Hat Wizard said, "He consumed all of the eclipse magic at the rim, I've never seen this before today. There will be consequences."

The other wizards murmured in agreement.

"How old are you boy?"

Haskell's chest tightened as if a vise gripped it. Was he in trouble? He stared at the ground, filled his cheeks with air and exhaled. "Fifteen."

"Fifteen? Gadiel is this one yours? You know the mountain rules, sixteen and over."

"I arranged for him to stay back in Whiterock Grove, I don't know how he . . . escaped." The old man's lips pressed into a white slash as he sneered at Haskell.

Sims pushed Haskell in the shoulder and snarled, "We'll have to give you a few more days in the box."

Haskell visualized being locked back up in the box and shuddered. His head hurt and he wanted water, just thinking about the box, made him want water more. His throat ached, "Water, please?"

Gray Hat Wizard said, "Get the boy water. Now tell me boy, what did you experience?"

"What?"

"On the mountain top, during the eclipse, tell us what you saw and did."

Haskell blinked his eyes and shrugged to loosen the knot forming in his shoulders. Had he done something wrong? How much trouble had he caused with this community by his actions? "I didn't do anything." *Will they not train me in wizarding skills anymore?*

"Don't lie to us boy, you must have done something. Who taught you how to attract that much magical energy without burning out? Gadiel is this your doing?"

Gadiel's nostrils flared as his eyes turned cold and hard. "No, the boy managed it unaided by me."

Gray Hat Wizard stared at Haskell.

A wizard shoved a wineskin in Haskell's hands. "Drink this boy."

Haskell expected wine, but the skin contained tepid, stale water. He drank deeply.

He regarded Gray Hat Wizard and said, "The magic flowed toward me and I consumed it. I didn't consciously attract it. I observed the waves of magic emitted from the volcano and the moon and . . .," what was the right word to describe the experience, "engaged with the flows. I controlled them to do my bidding." What did all this mean that even elderly wizards didn't know how he did it?

"What training have you had?"

Haskell searched for Dakarai. All his magical training came from Dakarai.

Gadiel answered, "A wizard in my employ trained him, but that boy doesn't know enough to make this happen."

Gray Hat Wizard appeared as angry at Gadiel as at Haskell. "Gadiel you can't train wizards without a proper teacher. We've criticized you before on this behavior, and now we learn you're still engaging in improper techniques.

"Bah," Gadiel said. "The magic we teach is beginner's magic, nothing that compares with what we saw on the mountain today. You're the masters, why did you allow him access to the volcano top?"

"Don't turn this on us Gadiel, we've warned you before about irregularities in your training, and we're pulling your teaching license."

Gadiel's long bony arms grabbed Gray Hat's robe and pulled him close. "An untrained boy ascends the volcano, and steals your harvest, and you have the nerve to censure me? You claim to be the greatest wizards of the century. You assert that you wield the power of the ancients, and a boy diverts your glory. Now, you want to punish me?" He pushed the wizard to the ground.

Haskell saw it form, three weaves of magic from three wizards. The weaves of blue, violet, and gold intertwined to form a cage of magic around his body.

Gray Hat struggled with his robes as he stood, then swished the dirt off his robe with a swipe of his hand and said, "The boy will be imprisoned until the council meets. At that time, we'll determine the proper action, and then we can place him on trial."

Haskell's body heat soared as his stomach tightened and hardened. Could they do this to him? He hadn't committed a crime; and he only wanted to see the view from the top of the volcano. Would Gadiel allow these wizards to entrap him and place him on trial? "Gadiel, you can't let them do this to me."

Sims laughed, "You'll get what's coming to you now."

Gray Hat Wizard sneered, "My young wizard, you've committed a serious crime and will be punished. That's the wizarding way, you'd know that if you were properly trained." He waved his hand in dismissal. "Take him away."

Haskell's mouth fell open as he raised his hand toward Gadiel and Sims. "Help me." Did Gadiel have enough acumen to stop this?

Gadiel stepped back from the cage.

Sims said, "You should've stayed in the castle dungeon, boy." He smirked.

"What will you do to me?" Haskell asked.

"We have rules in the wizarding community and we don't tolerate people who violate those rules."

"Where will you take me?" He touched a railing within the cage and drew his hand back when the rail shocked him.

"The council meets twice a month. You'll stay in the council's prison until they meet next to determine your fate."

CHAPTER 17

The cage entrapping Haskell lifted from the ground and floated behind two wizards who controlled it with magic. Streams of magic connected the cage to the wizards.

Haskell gawked at Gadiel who didn't do anything to help him. He'd have to find a way to escape without Gadiel's assistance. He studied the cage to detect weak points or ways to beat the cage. Where might they take Haskell, and was there a way he could use it to his advantage? He wished he still held the wineskin, because the volcano's heat had sucked so much moisture from his body.

The streams of magic forming the cage intertwined to form a rope-like structure which Haskell couldn't touch. The bottom of the cage became an invisible floor that he stood on with no ill effects. The cage top resembled the walls with magic ropes that formed the impenetrable jail.

Haskell sat on the floor of the cage and reviewed all that happened this day. Based on snippets of conversations he picked up from Dakari and Max, he wasn't supposed to come to the eclipse. The other wizards had stayed on the volcano meadow whereas Haskell went to the volcano plateau to see the lava. He saw the flows of magic like a creek surging toward him from the volcano, and then during the eclipse the magic had flooded his body.

The magic filled a vessel within his body that he could draw on when needed, and he could feel this magic percolating ready for handling. When the wizards had attempted to throw fireballs at him, the magic reacted without any input or thinking on his part, at least not consciously. Would the magic work if he told it what to do? How could he exploit the power from Velidred?

Haskell folded his hands in his lap, his breathing slowed, and he decided to practice using the power given him today. He had manipulated wind readily in Whiterock Grove, and he wondered if he could control it within the cage. One of his captors wore a blue wool beret on his black hair, which Haskell thought made a wonderful target for his skills.

He wanted to start slowly, testing the cage and the magic, before forcing the beret off the wizard's head. He extended his hand toward the wizard and breathed over it with the expectation it would send a gentle puff of air and ruffle the beret a little. The air left his hand, but as it reached the space between the cage's crossbars, it didn't flow through the cage, but bounced off, and picked up speed within the cage. It bumped a second cage wall, and picked up speed again. Then it caromed off the ceiling and flew past his body, ruffling his own tunic.

The soft brush of air boomeranged off another wall, ricocheted off the next, and Haskell heard the wind gaining strength and power. After rebounding off three more walls, it smacked him in the side and knocked him over.

The air whistled in the cage as it increased speed. How could he stop this storm now? He needed to prevent it hitting the walls, because each bounce off a wall made it faster and stronger. He created walls inside the cage walls that caught the air and dampened its speed and power. After three more caroms off his springy walls, the next time the air struck him, it slowed, and finished its travels within the cage.

He felt relieved he hadn't tried to send a fireball at his captors.

Beret wizard looked back and smirked at Haskell.

####

Haskell wondered if they planned to kill him or keep him in prison the rest of his life. What else could they do to him?

The next morning his captives reached the Velidred Castle. The black volcanic rock walls were highlighted by the snow-covered mountains behind it. Haskell loved this village where he grew up and had lived until his parents died. It was a bustling village with a strong king and hard-working villagers.

He searched for his father's forge as his captors walked him to the castle. Someone had claimed it as their own, and the familiar clanging of hammer to melted iron rang through the village. The smell of burning coals, melting iron and fire triggered memories of home and family. He'd come back to Velidred to die where he would be with his parents once more in the belly of Velidred.

Haskell recognized villagers as they passed and realized he wasn't coming back as a hero, but a criminal. Not even a well-loved orphan, but just a simple thief. Or maybe he returned as a wizard criminal. Children his age or younger pointed at him as the wizards ferried him to the castle in their magical jail. Heat shot to his face and nerve endings throughout his body tingled. Why did he decide to attend the eclipse at the volcano? He didn't need to be there but had thought it would be fun to see the event.

The wizards transported him into the castle halls, the magic cage shrinking in size as it approached the doorways, and then refilling its space after passing through the door. Where were they taking him? After his escape from the Goodwin Castle and journey to Velidred Volcano, would he find himself back inside a dungeon?

His jailers hauled him to a room on the second floor of the castle. Haskell hoped they would release their prisoner into the room, and open the jail, a civilized action for a mighty wizard like him. Instead, the jail shrunk through the door, and then they dumped the jail and prisoner in the room.

"What are you going to do with me?" Haskell asked.

"The Council of Nine will evaluate your crime and decide on a course of action."

"What's the Council of Nine?"

"The ruling class for wizards, and you're lucky their headquarters is in Velidred Castle. Someone will come and interrogate you after we tell them your crime."

"What is my crime?"

"Blatant disregard to wizarding laws, theft of magic designed for all wizards, and poor etiquette during a Velidred Moon eclipse."

"I didn't know what I was doing. I wanted to see the lava."

"Tell that to the council."

They shut the door and left the room.

He wrinkled his eyebrow and pinched the skin at his throat. Haskell figured he'd die someday as a criminal, but never figured it would be because of theft of magic. Should he laugh or cry? At the moment he wanted food and water, his jailers had given him neither on the whole trip to the castle.

An hour later, three wizards entered the room. The first was a red-headed woman wearing a blue cape with an inch wide metal necklace clasped around her neck. The second was an old gentleman, graying, but with a touch of black on his sideburns and large eyebrows. The last man could barely stand by himself. He held a staff, for balance.

The wizard with the black and gray sideburns said, "My name is Master Wizard Titan and we're here to get your version of the occurrence at the volcano, so we can deliver your case to the Council of Nine." He stood with folded arms and narrowed his eyes. "Did you escape from the Goodwin Castle dungeon?"

"Yes, but I was in there for a crime I didn't commit."

"Okay."

"A guy named Sims beat up the old lady, I didn't touch her."

"Sims was released not guilty." Master Wizard Titan brushed lint off his red robe.

Haskell's stomach tightened as he shook his head. "I never touched her," He shouted.

"Getting angry with us won't help your case."

"Please help me get out of here. I didn't do anything."

"That's why we're getting information; we'll decide if you're guilty or not. How did you reach the volcano?"

"I walked."

"Do you have proof? We've heard stories that you mounted a dragon and flew to the volcano plateau."

"Where would I get a dragon? That's preposterous, I'm fifteen-years-old. I've never seen a dragon."

"What proof do you have about the dragon?"

"I walked. What proof can I present when I walked to the volcano?"

"Did you speak to anyone at the volcano?"

Haskell rolled his eyes. He didn't remember speaking to anyone there until after the event. These questions were lame and didn't prove anything.

The old wizard leaned his back against the wall, withdrew a pipe from a pouch and poked tobacco into the pipe.

"Wait, I did speak with someone."

"Yeah, who?"

"I don't know her name, a young spiritualist with long black hair and a large green ring on her right hand."

"That describes every spiritualist I've ever met."

"No, wait, she told me her name." He thought back to what she told him. Amazing information, that excited him so much, he couldn't think of anything else. He had just wandered off after she told him, but her name?

"We don't have all day young man," the red-headed wizard said.

"The woman's name had to do with trees and a creek."

"These lies aren't helping your case."

"Wait! I remember, her name is Forest River Blossom."

"Rhea, note the boy is associating with political agitator, Forest River Blossom."

Haskell rubbed his hands through his hair.

"When you reached the volcano plateau did you decide at that point to strip the magic from the moon and volcano, or had you made that decision while on the meadow?"

"I never made any decision. As I stood at the peak, I engaged with the magical flows. It seemed the right thing to do."

"Flagrant and shameless violations of the etiquettes of wizardry. Rhea, write it down."

"Yes, Master Wizard Titan."

"Very good then. We have everything we need. Is there anything you need?"

Haskell looked at the floor and said, "I haven't eaten for a day, can I get food?"

Wizard Rhea said, "I'll have some brought to you."

Haskell said, "What will happen to me?"

"Based on the answers to our questions, you'll be given the full sentence possible."

"How many years?" Haskell sighed.

"What do you mean, young man?"

"How many years in prison?"

"Oh, we aren't backwards peasants. We give you a choice."

That encouraged Haskell. Then he could choose the appropriate sentence for his life.

Master Wizard Titan said, "If found guilty, you decide on being beheaded or accept stripping of all your magic."

CHAPTER 18

Haskell rubbed his eyes. He'd been in prison all day, and he still hadn't received any food. He thought back to his time in the Goodwin Castle dungeon where he could fully roam the castle after ten bells and could find his own food. He was hungry and wondered if there was a way out of this magical jail?

Air didn't work and only magnified its power after he released it. A full-blown fireball cast into the cage would be fatal. There must be a spell or technique to escape this prison. How about all the magical power he received at the volcano? He needed to learn its potential and the proper way to use it, and fast.

Haskell sat on the floor and calmed his breath. He had seen its capability on the mountain, but needed to know if it contained a way out of this trap. How could he access its power? If he knew specific spells then maybe it'd help, but he didn't know any more than Dakarai had offered to teach him. Those were simple spells designed to remove coins from the rich.

His present skills were limited to air, puff pocket, a weak fireball designed to startle not kill, throw his voice to distract someone, and one Max had taught him before he died, called diminish plants. Yeah, just what he needed, make plants smaller. He smacked his hand on the floor of the jail, which made a hollow sound and hurt his hand, but it didn't make him feel better.

How do you escape a jail with walls so tight that even magic air can't break out? At the Goodwin dungeon he had manipulated a lock. Haskell examined his environment, careful not to touch the walls since he got shocked each time. He identified no door and no lock.

His throat was parched and his stomach rumbled. How much time did he have before they returned to chop off his head or relieve him of his magic? Magic so powerful, they were willing to kill him or take it from him, instead of training him to use it.

Haskell paced around his small room thinking of ways to beat the jail and the wizards. He lacked knowledge but had great power. He needed knowledge to beat this structure.

Could he visualize a pair of magic scissors and cut the magic threads creating the jail? Conjure a giant hammer to bust a hole in the wall or cast a spell to break the walls? If he knew Dakarai's trick to become invisible then he could wait until they came back and turn invisible. They'd think he'd escaped, and then disassemble the jail. He remembered Dakarai saying he'd have to take the Fire and Ice experience to learn that skill. No thanks, he'd never take it.

He thought about water, because he was so thirsty. Thirsty, hot, and hungry and he wanted out. Thinking about water, he remembered an experience when he was ten-years-old. He had left a ceramic jug filled with water outside during an extreme cold winter spell. The jug had a cork stopper on it to help carry the heavy load without spilling water. The next morning, he found the jug cracked into five large pieces and the water frozen into the shape of the Jug. His mom chastised him about leaving the jug outside, but Haskell didn't know that would happen.

Frozen water expands, and then if the object can't hold the shape then the container would break. Is that the answer for his jail? Just fill the cell with water, and then freeze the water. How could it work? No. He'd freeze to death before the jail broke. There must be a better solution. Plus, he had access to water he wouldn't be so thirsty.

As a blacksmith's son, he'd seen unbendable metals made soft and turned into knives and swords. Would he fare better heating his jail instead of freezing it? Can magic heat or freeze objects?

It was nighttime, and the castle bell chimed twice and Haskell still theorized ways to break through his prison. He must have thought of a thousand ways that might work, but most would kill him before he escaped., assuming his plans worked the way he thought they would.

His dad had taught Haskell logic as he learned the act of being a smithy. How much metal do you need to make a kitchen knife as opposed to a sword? If you heated a metal past a certain point, it'd melt and liquefy and become useless in the fire.

Haskell studied his prison walls once more. How difficult would it be to replicate the walls around his own body? Then he's the jail owner, and everything and everybody outside the wall couldn't enter his space. He studied the flows of magic that produced the walls, and he noticed a thin magic flow that he hadn't observed earlier. The jail rails were bold, bright magic, but this other stream of magic was thin as a human hair. This must be the key to making the magic grow exponentially within the space.

Could that thin stream make it possible for the wizards to lock the flows in place? Is the stream exploitable from inside the jail cell?

He wanted to smash it or throw a fireball at it. This tiny stream of magic probably prevented his escape. He wondered once more about already knowing how to stop a wizard's fireball as it formed at the volcano. Could he replicate that ability here and how?

He lay on his belly and reached his forefinger and thumb toward the thread of magic. The task was difficult, because he didn't want to be shocked once more. He came close to the thread, touched the imaginary wall, and pulled his fingers back in pain as the wall shocked him. Haskell removed his tunic and covered his fingers with the fabric, and then attempted to touch the thread.

CHAPTER 19

The tower bells pealed four-bells in the early morning hours and Haskell had managed to untie a sizable portion of the thin magic thread. He had decided that was what held back his ability to use magic within the cell without repercussions of ricocheting and increased magnification of his magic.

The process was slow going at first as Haskell feared manipulating the thread of magic could alert wizard guards to his plan, but as he untied the thread from the intertwined magic streams, he became more confident. He opened a space about the size of his body between him and the room door. His body couldn't get through the other magic bars, but he thought he could send a spell at anyone who entered the room.

He'd know for sure in a moment. He prepared to unleash a tiny stream of air to test his hypothesis. Haskell prepared a wall behind him to consume any bounce back. He stood and took a deep breath releasing it slowly. Here goes.

A slight curve of his hand and he sent a gentle breeze at the wall and prepared to duck under it if it boomeranged on him. The breeze flowed through the wall with no deflection.

"Woohoo. I did it." He whispered in exultation. Now what should he do? An attempt to cut through the jail bars sounded logical, as he preferred to escape the room before his captors returned with their decision.

Five-bells rang out in the bell tower. He was running out of time. He visualized a tree saw stored in his father's forge and imagined it slicing the magic rails. With a smooth motion of magic, he shaved particles off the bars. It took time to cut through a single bar, but he made the first cut without anyone entering the room to see what he was doing. Haskell worked the second cut higher on the bar and removed the bar, but still not enough space for him to escape. He'd have to remove a second.

Voices sounded in the hallway.

If wizards entered the room, they'd notice the missing rail, but what about commoners, could they see the jail?

Two men talked outside his room door. "On my way into the castle this morning, I noticed they had assembled the castle guillotine."

"The wizards always choose the guillotine to losing their ability at magic."

"My momma told me within a year after losing their magic they die a horrible painful death. Go crazy without their sauce."

"When do we bring this one to the Council of Nine?"

"The trial starts at seven-bells."

That's what Haskell needed to know, with that much time he could finish getting free of the jail. He re-started his tree saw, but had to use magic to cover up the sound. He didn't want to alert the guards to his escape. It took a half-hour to remove the second section and he was surprised that wizards hadn't noticed he'd altered their flows. Or had they, and they planned to jump him when he escaped the room?

Haskell stepped out of the prison and while still inside the room, stood by the door. Two guards were outside his room talking about girls and plans for the coming village celebration of the queen's birthday.

All this time, Haskell had figured getting out of the magic jail would be the hardest task, yet he now realized he had to escape the castle during daylight hours. His stomach rumbled reminding him he hadn't eaten.

He didn't know the inside of Velidred castle, but he'd visited the stable areas with his dad a few times. Could he reach the stables and hide there, or leave the castle gates that way? First, he needed a way past the guards beyond the door.

Six-bells chimed and he needed to hurry, but if he rushed too much, a mistake might cost him his life. Haskell decided he'd try to throw his voice on the other side of the door, in hopes the guards would move from the door. The technique didn't require much magic, so he figured it was safe from detection by any wizards also lingering in the corridor.

He closed his eyes and lowered his voice, sending it under the door and turning it right in the hallway. He forced it out twenty-five feet. He said, "Guards, I need you over here."

"Who said that?" A guard asked.

Haskell smiled, "Your commander. Hurry up and get over here."

"Did that sound like the commander?"

"No. Check it out. I'll stay here."

Haskell needed them both to leave not just one. "I want both of you, now hurry." He imagined the guards looking at each other in confusion.

Giving the guards ten seconds, Haskell unlocked the door with magic and opened it. The guards weren't there. He checked the hallway and guessed the direction to the stables.

His clothing still had traces of ash on it from the volcano, and his attire didn't fit in with any of the castle servants. It'd be difficult making it to the stables without being noticed.

Since he had the sent the guards to the right, Haskell hurried left, keeping alert for servants, guards and wizards. He was prepared to bolt at a moment's notice. He knew the stables were in the back of the castle, near the kitchens. Traffic in the kitchen at this hour could be problematic.

Like the Goodwin Castle, there had to be a special stairway the servants used, so they could do the castle work un-seen by royalty. He would start his escape by searching for the servant corridors. Voices sounded in the hallway behind him and he hurried. The wall ended ahead of him, which exposed a narrow, circular staircase going up and down. He stepped down, stopped and peered back in the hallway to see if anyone followed. Two men walked in the hallway talking. They didn't seem to notice Haskell or didn't care about him.

Haskell rushed down the spiral stone steps, watching for servants climbing to service the upper castle floors. He reached a landing, and peeked down the hallway of what he hoped led into the kitchen.

Instead, he saw it led into the grand castle foyer. His path had led him to the front of the building, instead of the rear.

Heading through the foyer would be certain and immediate death. Haskell retreated up the stairs to the previous level. He stopped at the landing and thought about his predicament. If he headed back in the original direction, he'd end up passing the guards.

The other wall, opposite the stairs, led to a cramped hallway for the servants. Should he go up a level or take the servant hallway? He chose the servant hallway and padded down the corridor. He reached another section running perpendicular, but worried that'd place him in harm's way.

He continued through the servant's hallway and noticed light coming through windows. He stopped and viewed the common area where the gardeners cultivated flowers and grew vegetables for the castle. A few men and women mingled, as they weeded or harvested for that day's meals. The gallows stood in the center of the court, with a guillotine arranged on one corner. Haskell closed his eyes and took a deep breath.

Before Haskell reached the next intersection a serving woman worked her way toward him. She narrowed her eyes and frowned when they met. She carried a chamber pot and the hallway was too narrow to pass without hugging tight to the walls.

Haskell leaned back and wrinkled his nose at the pot.

She stopped and stared into his eyes. "You're not supposed to be here."

"Yeah, I agree. I was supposed to go to the stables and got lost. Can you direct me?"

She didn't say anything for a moment, then said, "I will call the castle guards to help."

Haskell smiled. "No that won't be necessary, I'll find it myself."

The servant pinched her lips. Obviously, not the answer she wanted to hear.

He didn't wait to hear more or stick around for her to alert the castle guards. Haskell dashed down the hallway.

Would she tell someone? He didn't slow to examine the next hallway, but continued through the tight corridor. How much time did he have? If she told the guards, they'd make a general alert to all guards, either with bells or a horn. He had to hurry.

The castle was larger than he expected, and he passed two more hallways before reaching another circular staircase. Where did this one go, and should he take it? He headed down the stairs.

CHAPTER 20

When he reached the kitchens, he encountered a madhouse of kitchen workers, stemming green beans, cutting up a side of beef, mixing flour and eggs, and a man stacking wood into an oven.

A woman said, "Get out of here, boy."

Haskell hurried through the room, saying, "Excuse me. Pardon me." He dodged men and women working and carrying items through the kitchen. Haskell wanted to grab an apple as he zigzagged through the room, but they were near the man with the knife who was splitting the beef.

A man carried three freshly killed winter ducks into the kitchen. Haskell juked and swerved to miss toppling the man as they crossed paths. The man kicked Haskell after he passed, "Stay out of here, boy."

Haskell dashed into the stable area. He'd spent hours in stables with his dad, holding and feeding the horses, and slopping stalls. A pitchfork stood next to a doorway to the stalls and Haskell grabbed it as he passed. He swept up a pile of straw, and hurried into the stall. Three horses raised their heads as he entered and whinnied. The smell of horse sweat and manure made him smile. He missed these common chores, talking with his dad about things happening in the village and around the castle.

Just as he prepared to throw the straw into a stall, an old gentleman, wearing a leather apron over his tunic and a coif cap, poked his head into the stable and said, "What ya playing at boy? The stalls get mucked before you be laying down bedding. Who are you?"

He dropped the straw to the dirt floor, shrugged and dropped his head. "No one, sir. A villager wanting to see the king's horses."

"Well get out of here, before I call the king's guards. They can hang you along with that wizard they plan to kill today."

"Sorry sir, it won't happen again." Haskell looked at the man's eyes as he passed. Where should he go now? He had to get out of the castle and then leave the village. How much time did he have left, and how could he sneak out of the castle grounds?

At that moment, the king's shepherd led sheep out from their pens to pasture in the surrounding fields. Haskell scampered to get close enough to the sheep to make it appear like he belonged. The shepherd gave Haskell a dirty look, but he and the dogs continued to prod the sheep toward the pasture gate.

Could it be this easy? The gate to the pasture stood forty feet away and opened. Once they reached the pasture he would wander toward the forest and race back to Whiterock Grove. Two sheep strayed in his direction and he waved his hands to force them back into the group. No need to worry, fit in and help. All was good.

Then the bells rang and horns blared from the castle walls. A warning cry that a prisoner had escaped. The signal to close all castle gates to keep the escaped prisoner within the castle walls.

The shepherd didn't stop herding his sheep to the gate. Would the gatekeeper let the shepherd and his sheep pass? Haskell gazed at the guards, lackadaisical in their implementation of the clanging alarms.

Three sheep, frightened by the bells and horns, scattered into the yard, and two dogs fetched and guided them back toward the gate. The shepherd waved nonchalantly at the guards and they nodded at him.

Haskell raised his hand in greeting, and then guided another wayward sheep in the proper direction out through the gates. His plan to escape the castle grounds and certain death was working. With just another few feet, he'd be home free. His legs felt light and he wanted to dance.

The guard lowered his head and studied Haskell.

Haskell smiled and waved his hand like he was doing his daily chores. He thought with all the ash over his body and dirty clothing, he'd fit in with the boys that worked the stables and pens. At his age the guards wouldn't seriously think him a threat or a prisoner.

He glanced at the other guard who signaled the guard closest to Haskell with a head nod, which the other guard responded to with a slight nod of his own.

Should Haskell run? He might make it past the guards, but sheep might get in the way and cause him to stumble. Then a simple lance in his back and it'd be over for him. No way could he allow himself to get captured.

The guard on Haskell's side of the gate dropped his lance to block Haskell's progress. "Halt there, boy."

Haskell's pulse quickened and his chest tightened. This close to escape and a simple guard held his life in his hand. He clenched his jaw tight, "Are you talking to me?"

"Yes, halt."

"I gotta get these sheep to pasture, out of the way, guard. These are the king's sheep, are you stopping the good king's work-men?"

The guard looked confused for a moment. "Jeremiah, is that true? Is the boy with you?"

The shepherd glanced at Haskell and said, "Never seen the boy in my life, but he's a good shepherd."

Haskell grimaced. He wasn't done here, there had to be a way to save his skin.

CHAPTER 21

When Haskell came even with the guard's lance, the guard reached out to grab Haskell's tunic. Then Haskell shot a hard gust of air at the guard and another shot of air at the sheep which pinned the guard against the wall.

The second guard made an effort to get to Haskell, but the action on Haskell's side frightened the sheep, and they bunched up to the guard, climbing over each other in fear.

Haskell sprinted into the meadow. This close to the castle walls with the escaped prisoner horns blowing, a running villager meant trouble. The archers on the walls were trained to fire arrows at anyone who ran. Even Haskell's dad had trained him to stay still when the horns blew. He couldn't stay still today. Haskell created his shield of air that blew hard across his back, and hoped it would prevent arrows from reaching his body. Dakarai knew how to create a real shield, but even with the extra magic, Haskell hadn't figured it out. Haskell ran.

Arrows cascaded off his improvised air shield, falling to his left and not making contact. Good enough, thought Haskell. With fifty yards to run to reach the meadow he knew he'd make it. The arrows couldn't strike him, and he'd soon be in the forest just like when he escaped the Goodwin Castle. His lungs burned, and his legs felt like jelly, but he continued his breakout.

A purple rope of magic fell from the sky a few yards in front of Haskell. Followed by another ten dropping and locking to the ground blocking his way. "No way," he muttered to himself. The wizards were involved. *Why won't these guys leave me alone?* He gritted his teeth and bombarded the magic ropes with a spell sending out a thousand knives to hack against the ropes. Haskell didn't quite know how he did this.

The knives cut, chopped, clipped and lacerated the ropes, leaving them in snippets of purple littering the ground. Haskell powered through the wizard's attempted capture. How far did the wizard's power range? He couldn't run like this all day, maybe not even another two minutes. His breath came in short wheezes, as he struggled to reach the trees.

Five feet from the trees, another set of ropes dangled from the sky. This time the ropes were intertwined purple, red, yellow and green. Did that mean multiple wizards were joining forces to stop him? He sent out his knife attack again to slash and whack the magical ropes, but the ropes held. Haskell crashed into them and fell onto his back.

He jumped to his feet thinking of another way to break through the wizard's cage. They wouldn't capture him a second time. He didn't have time to look back. He knew wizards, guards, and knights would be chasing. The Council of Nine couldn't allow him to escape.

While captured in the castle, he thought of breaking the jail cell with ice, and that was all he could think of at the moment. He imagined the space around him cooling.

The wizards were using their magic to collapse the roped-in space smaller and smaller. He saw it closing in on him.

Haskell drew water from the air, forcing the water to react so fast that clouds formed. As the water flowed around him, he locked tiny particles of water to the intertwined rope flows. Then he froze the water droplets. He saw his breath in front of him, and frost formed on his exposed arms. Haskell made it even colder as the ropes pressed closer.

Snow fell within his enclosure, but he lowered the temperature even more, causing his teeth to chatter as he shivered to stay warm. Even if this worked, he wouldn't be able to move to save himself.

He imagined a large hammer that his father had built as a gift for a blacksmith friend. Four pounds, the hammer weighed. Haskell's dad told him the average blacksmith could use it for at best an hour before the weight of it sapped the blacksmith's strength.

Haskell's magic hammer walloped the frozen magical ropes and it caused a ringing sound painful to his ears. He closed his eyes and held his hands over his ears, and still he heard the ringing. Then he felt moisture and cold explode outward, and the magic cell disintegrated. He ran into the forest, stepping over fallen limbs and dodging trees.

He made so much noise, foraging deer dashed off ahead of him. Were knights chasing him on horses? He knew he couldn't outrun a horse, but he could hide and maybe prevent capture by using magic or threatening to use magic. He darted through the forest looking for a hiding place.

He wasn't able to see the sun in the thick foliage as he zigged and zagged through the forest. He assumed he was headed toward the mountains since the landscape changed from flat land to rocky outcrops. If he climbed an outcrop, he'd be able to hide from men on horses. He worried about wizards following on foot.

The land sloped up and he found a section he figured a horse couldn't traverse. He scrambled upward. Trees and small bushes became hand holds as he slipped on last fall's dead leaves. Twenty-feet higher he found an outcrop that met his needs.

It wasn't easy climbing to it. He had to grab rocks and place his feet carefully to keep from falling. With a final jump and a wish for success, he landed on the flat ledge. He found a small cave against the rock face. That would have to hide him until nightfall.

Haskell caught his breath and listened, too afraid to glance over the edge in case they might see him. Twenty minutes later, he heard voices below. Knights chased through the forest, making a lot of noise as their horses clomped over rocks, brush and logs. The knights complained of shrubs and tree limbs slapping their faces and arms. The search party moved on past Haskell's hideout.

Late in the afternoon, Haskell saw a thread of magic snaking over rocks in the distance. *A wizard is doing a more thorough search than the knights.* Haskell didn't think it wise to use magic to ward off the search thread, so he loosened rocks in the cave, and built a wall between him and the rest of the ledge.

He saw the thread bounce off the rocks, but not enter into his cave. Within a few minutes the wizard moved on. Haskell couldn't believe his attraction of the magic from the volcano had caused this much attention from the wizards. He needed to learn how to use the magic he had garnered and maybe he could become the strongest of wizards.

Where could he go to gain that knowledge? Unfortunately, he didn't know who to trust from the wizarding world. If they recognized him or heard about him, they might capture and punish him still. Who could he trust?

He shook his head. The last person he ever wanted to see again was Gadiel, but now he realized that Gadiel had a personal stake in helping Haskell hide. Gadiel always looked for an advantage and Haskell knew if they aligned, then he could provide an advantage with his newly superior magic skills. Dakarai could train Haskell and help him grow in knowledge and power.

Haskell wouldn't have to stay with them forever. Once he felt his skill level become strong enough to engage with the wizards searching for him, then he'd set out on his own to interact in a larger world.

Fatigue caught up with him before mid-afternoon, and he lay in the cave for a nap. He thought of Forest River Blossom's prediction and wondered if it was possible. With his newfound power, a little more knowledge on how to use the power, and Haskell could make it happen.

CHAPTER 22

It took Haskell two days to reach Whiterock Grove, as he only traveled at night and tried to travel quietly. He stayed off the roads and stopped any time he saw or heard people passing. He worried that once he reached Gadiel's place, that someone from the Council of Nine had already contacted Gadiel about Haskell's escape. Haskell suspected Gadiel would sell him back to the Council of Nine. The old man liked his money.

When he reached Whiterock Grove, he expected the Goodwin Castle guards would be searching for him. He suspected the wizards of Velidred had placed a price on his head, and Gadiel probably was searching for him, too. He didn't care. He needed training and experience, and he thought Gadiel enough of a businessman to strike a profitable deal for the both of them.

Haskell snuck into Gadiel's home after four-bells in the morning hours before the sun peeked over the horizon. He found his room, fell into bed and slept.

Sims poked him in the gut long before Haskell wanted to wake. "Get up you lard of slime. Gadiel heard you come in and wants to talk with you."

"Good because I want to talk with him."

"You aren't going to like steaming in the box."

"I might like the box." He waved his hand to dismiss Sims and then rubbed his eyes.

"The boss wants to see you now." Sims grabbed Haskell's leg and pulled.

Haskell just thought it, and Sims flew across the room and hit the wall hard.

Sims rolled to the floor, blood reddening his forehead. He wiped the blood with a sleeve and said, "That'll cost you five days in the box."

Haskell snorted, "I'm tired of being bullied by you, Sims. It's time for you to take instructions from me." Warmth radiated through his body, and he stood and crossed his arms over his chest.

"Make it six days in the box, Boy."

"Are you planning on being in the box for six days?" Haskell asked and moved toward his adversary.

Sims backed to the wall. "Remember Gadiel's rules of using magic against the team."

"The team. You think a stinking little eel like you is part of our team? Maybe it's time for me to banish you altogether."

"Stay away from me."

"Run as fast as you can because I'm not afraid of you and your games, Sims."

Sims glared at Haskell and ran from the room.

Dakarai walked through the door, "That won't make Sims or Gadiel happy, but it made me smile."

"Is there any food in the house? I'm starving."

"Yeah, let's see what we can find. You need to know that two wizards visited yesterday from the Council of Nine. You'll have to hide for a few weeks until they lose interest or think you died from magic burnout."

Haskell chomped on a roll as he headed to Gadiel's room. Would Gadiel be on board with his plan or hand him over to the Council of Nine? He knocked.

"Come in."

Sims opened the door and smirked.

"Causing trouble again, Sims?" Haskell raised his hands at Sims, and he ran out.

"You're more resourceful than I thought." Gadiel said.

Haskell stood straighter.

"I can't have you hurting Sims, though."

"He's a pain, sir."

"Member of the team. We can't have you injuring the team."

Haskell frowned.

"Council of Nine is looking for you."

"Yes, and I have an idea that I think you'll like."

"Okay?"

"I snatched all this extra magic, but I don't know how to use it. I thought Dakarai could teach me techniques and make me a stronger wizard. I'll stay on the team and use my magic to help the business."

"I see. Like you're my business partner instead of my servant." He sneered.

Haskell didn't like the direction this conversation was heading. "No sir. I work for you. I need training, and I don't know where to go to learn more magic."

"What do I get from it?"

"You still get the generous cut from our forays as you've always gotten. I don't want to change that. I need to learn how to use this magic, before I do something stupid, and burn out or kill a friend."

"My knowledge and Dakarai's knowledge will come at a price."

Haskell sighed. *Everything always comes at a price with Gadiel.* "I'm willing to pay you. You know how much I make, it's not a lot, but I don't need it. I'd rather have the skills and knowledge."

"I see." He paused, stood, and walked to the window. Gadiel stared out the window before speaking. "I want you to take the Fire and Ice challenge."

A picture entered his head of his friend Max yelling and screaming, flailing his arms acting crazy and confused. "I can't, I'm not sixteen."

"Sixteen is not an age set in stone. Many strong wizards took the challenge before sixteen and survived."

"I saw Max take the challenge and die. And what happened to Rusty and Toby? Did they take the challenge and die, too?"

"Without the Fire and Ice challenge, then I won't train you. I expect the wizards from the Council of Nine to visit me again to check if you've returned."

"Sir, either way, you're sending me to my death. I won't take the Fire and Ice challenge."

"Sims!" Gadiel shouted.

Sims entered the room.

"Put Haskell in the box for ten days. Hide him from the Council of Nine and the castle guards."

A sudden coldness smacked Haskell's core, and his legs locked. He stumbled backwards. He couldn't believe he'd be punished by Gadiel. Didn't the man acknowledge Haskell's newfound skills and how much more he could be worth to the old man?

"Punishment for escaping the Goodwin Castle prison without my approval, and for attending the Velidred eclipse without my permission. Ten days in the box. Any day you use magic, I'll add another two days to the sentence. Take him away, Sims. Use magic for three days, and I hand you over to the Council of Nine."

Haskell wanted to blast everyone in the room. He didn't need any of them to help him. His magic was stronger than either Gadiel's or Dakarai's magic. He didn't need to put up with this humiliation. Gadiel wanted to prove he still held power in the room. Should Haskell acquiesce or strike back with the magic he knew. The rumors implied Gadiel did know magic. Haskell suspected he'd be tied up in a moment and thrown in the box anyway. "Okay, put me in the box. I can take it." He scowled at Gadiel and snarled at Sims when Sims placed his hand on his arm.

Haskell spent fourteen days in the box.

CHAPTER 23

Six months later, Haskell and Sims stood in the tailor's shop waiting for the merchant to finish a transaction with his customer.

The tailor looked at his customer and then glanced at Haskell and Sims. The man bit his lip and fidgeted, rubbing his chest and then dry washing his hands.

Haskell wanted to yell at the man, relax, we're not going to hurt you. The customer, a lord from a neighboring village, responding to the tailor's nervousness, inspected Haskell and Sims out of the corner of his eye.

Sims was as jumpy as the merchant and couldn't keep his hands off the merchandise, fingering bolts of cloth, picking up thread and measuring sticks.

Was Haskell the only one in the room relaxed and in control? He wanted to come back later in the afternoon, but Gadiel wanted the money this morning. He had told them he had a business transaction later in the day and needed the coins from the tailor.

What else was Gadiel involved in that Haskell wasn't aware of? He knew the old man had a number of business enterprises going, and the thieving the boys did only brought in a few coins each week. They were doing business in the tailor's shop a week early, which concerned Haskell.

The lord's transaction finished and the well-dressed man took one more look at Sims and Haskell.

He pulled a handkerchief from his sleeve and took a deep whiff of the fragrant perfume sprayed on the cloth.

Haskell knew the sniffing of the cloth was a signal to the boys that they were beneath the dignity of a rich and powerful lord and landowner. He wished he could show the lord who had the real power in the room.

They waited until the lord exited the shop, and then approached the merchant.

Sims said, "Gadiel wants his money now."

"You're a week early."

"We'll break your arm if you don't give us our money now," Sims said.

Haskell stepped next to Sims. "What are you talking about? We'll do no such thing. How's he going to make money and do his tailoring work, if he has a broken arm?"

"Gadiel's money."

"Sir, can you pay us today?" Haskell asked.

The tailor looked at the floor.

Haskell had seen that look before from Gadiel's customers and it wasn't a good sign. "Can you give us anything?"

"Yeah, I can give you something, but I have a shipment coming in tomorrow and I need the money to buy supplies, otherwise I can't make any money."

Sims stepped behind the counter next to the tailor. "We don't care about what you have or don't have, we want our coins."

"You're a week early. Give me a week, and I'll have it for you."

Sims grabbed the tailor's arm.

"Leave him be, Sims."

"Says who?"

Someone walked into the shop and the boys turned and examined the new arrival.

Sims dropped the tailor's arm.

Haskell gawked at the woman who entered. Well, she wasn't quite a woman, maybe a year younger than Haskell, but next year she'd be a woman, and a beautiful woman at that. She wore a tight-fitting bodice of checkered emerald and gold, with a flowing navy-blue skirt that reached to her feet. The sleeves of her dress were tight at her biceps, but wide and long on her wrists, hiding her hands in cloth. He'd seen her before, the long black hair and green eyes were memorable. She was Princess Noreen, daughter of King Bryce Goodwin, and he remembered watching her and her sister that night he had snuck out of the Goodwin castle dungeon, and now she stood right next to him.

Sims came out from behind the counter.

Haskell kept his gaze on the princess. She met his eyes for a moment, pushed back a strand of hair that had fallen from her tall cone-shaped hennin. Princess Noreen licked her lips and when her lady-in-waiting entered the shop she broke eye contact with Haskell.

Haskell continued to stare at the princess until Sims poked him in the ribs and whispered, "Let's go for a few minutes."

He didn't want to leave. His heartbeat quickened, and heat rose to his face.

Sims grabbed Haskell's arm, "Let's go," and he walked Haskell out of the shop. They walked a few yards away and stood by the blacksmith's forge.

Haskell said, "Did you see that woman?"

"That woman is the king's daughter, and you can't have her."

"I could if I were a lord or king. Yeah, I should become king."

"Are you deaf? She's a princess and you'll never be worthy of a princess."

Haskell thought back to the words Forest River Blossom told him at the Velidred Volcano. A prediction that he thought of many times each day. She had revealed, based on the objects she placed on the flat stone table, that one day he'd be king. A king could marry a princess. They might have to marry for political reasons, but he didn't care. She was the most beautiful woman he'd seen in his life, and she'd matured in the last few months since he'd seen her at the castle. He said, "Someday I'll be king, and she'll be my wife."

Sims started laughing right there in the street. "You can't be serious. An orphan boy, born of a blacksmith, and you're going to be a king. That's the stupidest thing I've ever heard from you. It'll never happen."

Haskell didn't argue the point. He'd learned it wasn't worth his time to argue with Sims. His team member never backed down from an opinion he had, and if he didn't like your response, he always resorted to violence to win his point of view.

They stood and watched the blacksmith pound out a sword. Haskell got lost in the sound of a hard metal hammer walloping red-hot metal. He thought of Noreen as his heart pounded as hard as the hammer. Her eyes mesmerized him. She had given him a look as if she knew him. Had she noticed him sitting on the stairs watching her and her sister in the castle that night? She must know he wasn't at her social level. He smiled, not even close to her social level. Was Sims right and Haskell couldn't ever have Noreen no matter if he became king or not?

Sims poked his ribs. "The princess is coming out, do you want to go over there and smooch with her."

"Shut up." But, yeah, actually he did want to go over and smooch with her. He imagined his lips brushing against hers and then holding her close to his body.

"Let's go back to the tailor. I should let you know, the princess will be on her way to another kingdom in a couple of days." He laughed.

Haskell wasn't paying attention to Sims as he watched the princess and her entourage of three servants head back to the castle. Twice she peeked behind her and Haskell wanted to wave but knew Sims would make fun of him. How could he have her?

Sims volunteered, "Gadiel has already sold her to the highest bidder."

"What?"

"She'll bring a lot of money on the black market. She's pretty don't you think?" Sims poked Haskell in the ribs again.

"Gadiel is planning on kidnapping the princess?"

"Yeah, you saw her wandering around without a guard. Those three women with her can't stop us from grabbing her and selling her on the market."

I can't let Gadiel have her. Sure, she'll bring a high price, but . . . but what? There isn't anything I can do to save her. If Gadiel wants her, then he'll get her. If not today, then tomorrow. If I was king, I'd protect her.

"When's the pickup?" Haskell asked.

"In two days. She likes to wander around the market on Thursdays, and Dakarai, Lenny and I will grab her and make her disappear."

Make her disappear meant Dakarai planned to hold onto her, throw up his magic disappearing trick, and then walk her out of the marketplace without people seeing her.

Haskell had to stop this plan. What should he do? He'd go to Gadiel and plead with him not to kidnap her. No that couldn't work, because Gadiel thought more of money than moral activities. He'd think nothing of grabbing Noreen or her sister, Carol, the blonde.

They approached the shop and Haskell stared off toward the castle watching the Princess and her entourage disappear through the castle doors.

Sims pushed him in the back and said, "Let's go, we have work to do."

CHAPTER 24

Thursday morning broke sunny and bright, but Haskell's stomach knotted and burbled. He still hadn't come up with a way to save Princess Noreen from being kidnapped, and sold as a slave. He couldn't get any information about the kidnapping from the other members of the team other than the fact Sims disclosed that they'd handle it at two-bells.

It irritated Haskell that Sims might touch Noreen before he did, and he wanted to shoot a fireball at Sims that morning at breakfast. The other boys exhibited signs of nervousness. Sims' leg bounced up and down on the bench, which caused the whole bench to wobble. Lenny talked fast, babbling about nothing, and laughing longer and louder than normal. Even Dakarai rubbed his chest over and over with his knuckles.

Haskell planned to follow the boys at a distance and either yell at the guards before the boys grabbed her or stop them from grabbing her himself.

Haskell asked, "What are you guys doing today?"

Dakarai answered, "Special project Gadiel's assigned us."

"Yeah? Do you need help?"

"Nope, Gadiel has another task for you."

"What's that?"

Dakarai said, "He needs you to make a delivery and a pickup in Oak Ridge."

Haskell's heart dropped as a sudden coldness hit him in the core. Oak Ridge was miles away, and no way could he make a delivery and get back in time to rescue Princess Noreen.

"Maybe I can make that delivery tomorrow and help you guys today."

Dakarai had a chunk of bread in his hand and pointed it at Haskell. "No, you make the delivery today."

Sims laughed and smirked. "The boy king has to make a delivery to Oak Ridge. Maybe the locals will bow down to you when you walk through town."

That meant Sims had told Dakarai and probably Gadiel about Haskell's desire to be a king. Did Gadiel think Haskell might be a problem today if he helped the team, or was this a legitimate task?

"Shut up, Sims," Haskell said.

Sims said, "Are you still upset you didn't get a chance to smooch the princess?"

Dakarai kicked Sims' leg underneath the table. "Shut up."

Sims smirked at Haskell.

Before twelve bells Gadiel called Haskell into his office. "I've a job for you."

Haskell scowled. Should he refuse the task and see what Gadiel did? Haskell thought he had learned enough to beat the old man in a magic fight, though he'd never seen the old man wield magic. What if Gadiel didn't have any magic at all, and he grabbed these young kids and led them to believe he was more powerful than they were with magic, yet his magic was all a sham? A trick.

"Yes, sir?"

"Dakarai's busy today and the others are too stupid to deliver this for me." He handed Haskell a travel pouch. "Take this to Lord Jorgensen in Oak Ridge. Hand it to him directly and ask him to review immediately. Then he will give you a message to return to me. Can you handle that?"

Haskell stared at Gadiel. "Yes." He threw the pouch straps over his shoulder and left the room. What was in the pouch that was so important Haskell had to carry it instead of one of the messengers Gadiel normally employed for these tasks? He wondered if Gadiel was trying to get him away from the princess.

Oak Ridge was a tiny village seven miles from Whiterock Grove. Haskell calculated travel times in his head. The pouch wasn't heavy and he figured he could run the distance and arrive before one bell. Then get Lord Jorgensen to respond to the request and run back. It'd be two bells at the latest, meaning Haskell could return in time to rescue Princess Noreen. He was faster than most of the kids on Gadiel's team, but a round-trip represented fourteen miles. That'd be a hard run at top speed.

He walked out of the village with the pouch and exited the village gates. He waited until he'd lost sight of the castle and village before jogging. Half-a-mile later he felt comfortable and ran faster, passing people ambling on the dirt road.

He reached Oak Ridge village just as the bells rang one. He made inquiries in a small shop and found the location of Lord Jorgensen's manor. The merchant was quick to not call it a castle.

Good thought Haskell, that'd make the task faster if he didn't have to deal with any guards. Haskell's legs tightened when he had stopped, and he had trouble returning to his previous speed. The lord's place turned out to be a little over a mile from the village and in ten minutes Haskell reached the lord's large, brick house.

A gardener stopped him just inside the gate and asked, "Where are you heading?"

Haskell had to catch his breath then said, "I have information for Lord Jorgensen."

The gardener had a folksy style about him and said, "Well, give it to me and I'll make sure it gets to Lord Jorgensen."

"Can't do that. I'm under strict orders to personally deliver it to Lord Jorgensen."

"Okay, follow me. The lord and lady eat at this time, which means you might have to wait until after dinner, before he responds."

Haskell wrinkled his brow. "Oh, that'll never do, Gadiel needs an immediate response."

"Gadiel, you say?"

"Yes, sir. An immediate response."

The gardener smiled as if he knew an inside joke and led Haskell to the house. They entered the foyer, and the gardener said, "I'll get Lord Jorgensen, why don't you take a moment and wash up in there." He pointed to a kitchen.

Haskell wanted to tag along with the gardener but walked into the kitchen area and found a bucket with water in it. He splashed water over his face and drank. If the lord was eating, would it take long to get the man to come see him? Haskell didn't have much time. He had to run eight miles back to the castle and he didn't think he could run as fast going back as he ran to get to Oak Ridge. His legs burned with fatigue.

The gardener didn't return right away, and Haskell sat down on a stool in the kitchen. How long would this take?

A female servant rushed into the kitchen and shooed Haskell off the stool. "You can't sit here. Go away."

Haskell wandered back into the foyer, peeking into rooms that contained tapestries, paintings and even a piano in one of the rooms. He held back from strolling in and plinking the piano keys, something he'd always wanted to do. Lord Jorgensen needed to hurry for Haskell to have time to save Princess Noreen.

Time stretched and Haskell watched a shadow move across the porch. He couldn't take it any longer. He'd find Lord Jorgensen himself. Haskell strolled through the hallway looking into rooms for signs of the lord or the gardener. Three doorways later, he found two people sitting at an elaborate table, fifteen feet long. A man sat on one end and a woman on the other. There was no sign of the gardener.

"Excuse me sir," Haskell said.

"Oh, are you still here?"

"Yes, sir, I have a pouch for you that requires your attention and an answer."

"What is it dear?"

"I'm sure something from Gadiel. I'm guessing he wants more money for the wayward orphans in Whiterock Grove."

Wayward orphans? Gadiel sent me here to ask for money for wayward orphans?

The lady said, "Are you a wayward orphan, young man?"

Haskell smirked. "Yes, I guess I am."

"Rolf, my dear, you should give him one of your jackets. Look at those old dirty clothes the boy's wearing."

Haskell peered at his clothing and glanced back at the lord at the table. Lord Jorgensen wore a brown doublet with a white lace collar around the neck and hands. If Haskell wore a doublet like that what would Princess Noreen think of him? The princess. He had to finish this transaction before it was too late. "Thank you for your kindness, my Lady," Haskell bowed, "but I must return with an answer for Gadiel, or I might lose my job." He thought the comment about losing his job might help motivate these people to move.

The lady rang a bell on the table and a servant walked through a doorway. "My Lady?"

"Carl, can you go to Lord Jorgensen's cabinet and bring back the blue doublet with the silver scrollwork."

"That one, dear? Are you sure?" Lord Jorgensen asked.

"Oh yes, it's quite out of style now, and it'll look wonderful on our wayward orphan."

What was Haskell going to do with a doublet? Lenny and Sims would laugh him out of the building, and what would Gadiel think? "No, my lady, it's inappropriate for me to wear clothing so fine."

"I insist, young man. Even though you're an orphan, you're entitled to nice clothing."

"Hurry Carl, before the boy runs off."

"Yes ma'am."

The servant was an old man and he didn't move fast. Haskell hoped the lord's room wasn't too far away. He was sure he could run back to Whiterock Grove before the servant returned with the doublet.

"Okay, young man, let's examine what Gadiel has sent me."

"He asked me to stay for a response." Haskell handed the lord the pouch.

Lord Jorgensen removed a leather document pouch and un-twirled the strings holding it closed. Then he opened the document pouch, and retrieved an envelope with a red seal, representing Gadiel's family coat of arms, on the back cover.

"It's sealed tight. I'll have to wait for Carl to return to open it."

Haskell snorted. *The man can push his lily-white fingers under the envelope cover and rip across it.* He'd seen others do that same thing.

They waited.

Waiting for Carl to return made Haskell's hair hurt, as he felt a numbness creep over his skin. Haven't these people ever hurried in their lives?

They waited.

"Are you hungry?" The lady of the house asked Haskell.

"No ma'am, I had a big meal before I started my journey." Haskell was starving and his mouth watered gazing at the plate of ham and sweet potatoes on the table. He wanted some of the food, and any other day, he'd have taken them up on their generosity. But today he had to leave and save Princess Noreen. He tilted his head back and focused on the ceiling.

Haskell decided he could help this process, "If you tell me where to find your letter opener, I'd be happy to get it for you."

"Oh, we can't have you doing that. Carl is perfectly capable of doing his job."

No, Haskell thought, he isn't. We're all going to die of boredom before he returns.

Ten minutes later, Carl returned with the doublet. It was a beautiful jacket, dark blue, maybe navy, with exquisite scroll work above the waist done in silver thread. Haskell wondered how much he could sell it for in Whiterock Grove. Then he thought of Princess Noreen. Could he impress her if he wore the doublet?

Carl handed the doublet to Haskell.

"Put it on, Boy, let's see how it fits." Lady Jorgensen said.

Haskell placed it on over his sweat stained tunic. It fit pretty well, but was a little large.

"Carl, give the boy two gold coins. That'll allow him to have it altered to fit better. A good tailor can alter the jacket for you in a week."

"Thank you, ma'am." Haskell bowed to the lady. "Now about the document, sir."

"Oh yes. Carl, fetch the letter opener, I'm anxious to see what news Gadiel has for me."

Haskell's body temperature increased with impatience. How long would this task take?

Carl stepped over to a side table two feet out of Lord Jorgensen's reach and grasped the silver letter opener.

Haskell rolled his eyes. Really? The man couldn't get out of his chair and take two steps to pick up a letter opener?

"Very good, Carl. Now, let's see." Lord Jorgensen slit the envelope and pulled a letter from it. He read the letter and nodded. "Honey, Gadiel has found us an orphan girl to work with you in your boudoir to replace that horrible girl from the village."

"Oh, that's brilliant dear."

"I'll respond with a yes. Carl, fetch paper, an envelope and my seal."

"I could give Gadiel your answer verbally."

"We're civilized folks. Even though we aren't in the big village next to the castle, we still follow etiquette protocols, don't we Rolf."

Lord Jorgensen nodded. "My father always used to say, 'It only takes a moment to be civilized.'"

Carl returned with paper, pen, envelope and a jar of wax.

Lord Jorgensen set to writing his response.

Haskell asserted mental restraint to avoid snapping at the lord and lady for wasting his time. Just say, yes, I'll take the orphan girl, sign the letter and be done with it.

Lady Jorgensen said, "Mention how well the roses are doing that he gave us on his last visit to Oak Ridge."

"Oh, yes. The yellow roses are particularly beautiful this summer."

He finished the letter, and placed it in the envelope. Then Carl placed a yellow candle near the wax, and let the wax drip to seal the envelope.

Lord Jorgensen pressed his ring into the wax. He let it cool a moment, and then he placed the letter into the document pouch. He struggled a moment to tie it precisely, and finally inserted it into the original pouch Haskell had carried.

"Here you are, young man."

Haskell snatched the pouch from Lord Jorgensen. "Thank you both. I'm sure Gadiel will appreciate your quick response." He bowed and raced out the door.

CHAPTER 25

It was a hot day and the doublet made it even hotter. Haskell stopped running to take off the jacket. He jammed it into the pouch and slung it over his shoulder. As he ran through Oak Ridge, two bells sounded. He was too late to save the princess.

He didn't care. Haskell increased his speed, because maybe the princess had come to the marketplace later than normal this day. He might still have a chance to rescue her.

When he reached Whiterock Grove the village gates were locked, and the village guards weren't letting anyone in or out of the village. Haskell raced to a couple of areas he knew to be loosely patrolled, and he thought he might sneak in under the wall. A guard watched each entry and exit point. That meant one thing to Haskell, the princess was gone and he had failed to save her.

# # # #

It took Haskell two days to get inside the village gates. He slept in the forest and he was happy he had the doublet, because the nights were chilly. He considered throwing the doublet into the river but then remembered he might still get some money for it, so he used it as a blanket at night.

He dreamed of Princess Noreen screaming in the forest. In the dream, he'd search but couldn't find her. What must the girl be thinking? Kidnapped, probably shoved into a box or stable somewhere. There's no way Gadiel and the team could have gotten her out of the village before the village gates were locked, which meant they kept her in the village. But where?

Haskell assumed the castle guards had done a house-by-house search to find the missing girl. Where did Gadiel stash her? Had he already sold her, in which case she wasn't even in his hands anymore?

The following morning, he gained access into the village. Before entering, he waited for a wagon with blue sides and an empty bed to exit through the gates.

He thought it might be difficult to get into the village based on other people in his social status being hassled at the gate. It appeared that wearing the blue and silver doublet allowed him easy entrance. He raced back to Gadiel's and hurried to the box. The same box Gadiel used to punish Haskell. If Gadiel had kidnapped the princess, he thought Gadiel might hide her in the box. Maybe Dakarai could make it disappear so the guards wouldn't see it.

He reached the box and stopped. The box was locked, which meant Gadiel had stuffed someone in the box. Was it the princess? Haskell found the key for the lock.

Dakarai asked, "What ya doing?"

"Checking to see who's in the box."

Dakarai laughed.

Haskell fumbled with the lock and key; his heart raced in his chest. He released the clasp and threw open the lid.

Lenny lay curled in a ball in his small clothes; bruises covered every inch of his body.

"Lenny didn't listen to instructions and we almost lost our score. Shut the box Haskell."

"Is he still alive?" Haskell poked the body, but Lenny didn't move.

"Don't know and don't care."

"Where's the princess?"

"Ah, now we understand your interest in the box." Dakarai walked over to Haskell. "The transaction is complete, so quit fantasizing about her."

Heat rose to his face. "I'm not fantasizing about the princess."

Sims strolled into the area. "Princess Noreen was soft, pretty, and smelled like roses."

"Shut up." Haskell prepared to throw a fireball.

Dakarai jumped in front of Sims. "Don't do it, he's not worth it, and Gadiel will put you in the box with Lenny. Go see Gadiel. You have something for him, right?"

Sims smirked. "Oh, look at the pretty boy in the fancy doublet."

Haskell walked into the house, his nostrils flaring. He knocked hard on Gadiel's door.

"Come."

He entered. "I have a letter from Lord Jorgensen." Haskell handed the messenger pouch to Gadiel.

"Excellent."

Haskell stared at Gadiel as the old man read Lord Jorgensen's letter. Gadiel glanced at Haskell then dismissed him with a wave of his hand.

His heart felt like it was shrinking as Haskell wandered the marketplace. He shuffled in and out of businesses, not seeking anything, his mind not really registering where he was. When he reached the tailor's shop, he waved at the tailor who stood outside his shop watching people. The tailor grabbed his elbow. "That's a fine doublet you have there."

Haskell didn't understand the tailor's comment. The tailor shook the front of the jacket. Haskell looked down. "What about it."

"You need to have it re-sized. It's large on you. Do you want me to re-size it for you?"

The doublet reminded him of his missed opportunity at saving Princess Noreen, and he clutched his arms across his chest.

"With a couple of minor adjustments, people will think you're a lord from a neighboring village."

"Who cares?" He weaved side to side.

The tailor steadied Haskell. "Look. You helped me when I was short of money, and you didn't let that thug hurt me. Let me fix the doublet for you. No charge. You'll look like a prince if it's sized right."

"Yeah, whatever."

The tailor rubbed sizing marks on the jacket and helped Haskell remove it. "Come and see me in a week. You'll look great."

CHAPTER 26

"How come you're not wearing your new jacket?" Sims asked two weeks after Haskell retrieved it from the tailor's shop.

"Don't feel like it." Haskell said with a flat monotone voice. He didn't feel like playing games with Sims today.

"Then I'll wear it." Sims grabbed the jacket off the hook.

"Put the doublet back on the hook." Heat rose behind Haskell's eyelids. "It won't fit you, because the tailor sized it for me. Don't rip it."

"You're never going to wear it."

"I don't care, now put it back." Haskell scanned the room and hallway for Dakarai. If the other wizard wasn't there, then it was time to teach Sims a lesson. He didn't anyone.

Sims held the jacket to his chest. "Yeah, you're a little runt, aren't you? This won't fit me, because it's for little runts like you."

Haskell's extremities felt twitchy, the same way they had felt when he gained extra magic at the volcano. The couple of times he felt this before, the magic knew what to do before Haskell thought it. It happened once within the thief house, when he threw Sims against the wall. What did that mean? This ability worried Haskell because it controlled him, instead of Haskell controlling the magic. He rubbed the back of his neck.

Sims wasn't a large boy, but bigger than Haskell. Sims thrust his right arm into the sleeve. The doublet's sleeves were loose and baggy in the arms, but narrowed at the wrists.

"If you rip the jacket, I'll throw a fireball at you."

"Hah, you don't have the guts. Gadiel will put you in the box."

"He might reward me for killing you." Haskell frowned and crossed his arms. Was he ready to kill Sims over a jacket? It wasn't about the doublet. Sims had been a thorn in Haskell's side since Haskell showed up at the thief house. The older boy criticized Haskell daily, did things wrong during business operations on purpose when Haskell was in charge, and Haskell knew the boy had information on Princess Noreen, but wouldn't tell him.

"Gadiel's like a father to me. Hurting me might upset the old man, and he'll throw you in the box."

"I don't care about the box anymore. You know I can get out of it anytime I want."

"That'll anger Gadiel." Sims pulled a knife from the sheaf he wore across his chest. "How will the tailor's threading hold up to a sharp knife?"

"Drop the knife and throw the jacket over here." Haskell clenched his hands tight.

"Oh, you're going to fight me?" Sims worried a button on the jacket with the knife.

Haskell realized the doublet meant Princess Noreen to him. Every time he saw the doublet he thought of her.

A button fell to the floor. Sims sneered, "Oops."

"Don't oops me. Throw the jacket over here, before you make it non-repairable."

Sims sliced the thread on a second button and the button bounced to the floor and landed near Haskell's feet.

Lenny entered the room. "What's going on?"

"Stick around and watch Haskell cry."

Sims edged the knife toward a third button.

Haskell held his hands so tight, they cramped. He felt tenseness in the back of his throat. "Enough!" he shouted.

Sims smirked and ripped off a third and fourth button.

To Haskell, each time Sims played with a button, he saw Sims putting the knife to Princess Noreen's throat. Haskell threw a fireball at Sim's hand holding the knife and it exploded on his hand causing Sims to drop the knife. Haskell moved closer.

Sims used the doublet as a shield and backed to the wall. "Leave me alone."

Haskell shot a fireball at Sim's left foot and his pants burst into flames.

Sims threw the doublet at Haskell. "Stop it." He ran from the room.

Haskell sent a fireball over Sim's head which exploded on the hallway ceiling.

Lenny laughed.

Haskell lifted the doublet from the floor, and brushed dust off the dark blue back. He hung the doublet back on the hook. Then he dropped to his knees and searched for the missing buttons. How much money would the tailor charge him to re-sew the buttons?

Gadiel stormed into the room, with Sims close behind. "What's going on in here?"

Haskell stared up at the old man. "I'm gathering buttons that fell off my jacket."

"Did you throw a fireball at Sims?"

Haskell studied the smiling Sims hovering behind Gadiel. "I don't know what you're talking about, sir. I dropped these buttons and I'm picking them off the floor. Don't know how they fell off the doublet."

"Sell the doublet." Gadiel said.

Haskell took a sharp intake of breath and became lightheaded. "Impossible."

"Ten days in the box," Gadiel said. "You know better than to disobey me."

Haskell stared at his palms as if they held the answer to his problems.

Sims said, "I'll put him in the box, sir." He ambled toward Haskell.

Haskell pointed his hands at Sims. "Take one more step, and I'll burn you and this whole building down."

"I told you sir, he's irrational ever since we kidnapped Princess Noreen."

Gadiel pivoted to Sims. "You're never to say those words to anyone ever again, or I'll cut out your tongue. Do you understand?"

"Yes, sir."

Haskell wanted to smile, but he didn't have it in him. He ran a hand through his hair and shook his head. "I'll go in the box, but I'm not giving up the doublet."

"After I put you in the box, I'll burn the jacket myself." Gadiel said.

Haskell stood and moved toward the jacket, fiddling with the three loose buttons in his palms with his fingers. "No sir. The jacket stays and if Sims ever touches it again, I kill him." There he said it. It's time to ascertain Gadiel's magic strength. Did Gadiel have more power than Haskell, or was Haskell top dog in this building?

Gadiel studied Haskell.

Haskell watched the old man's black eyes. A red spot grew in his left eye, transforming from a spot into the shape of a scorpion.

"You're better than this Haskell. I don't expect you to be a fool like Sims. You have intelligence and can run this organization someday. Do you want to throw your future away over a silly jacket?" Gadiel pointed at the jacket.

Haskell threw up a shield protecting him and the jacket. Then he saw the thin thread of magic from Gadiel moving toward the jacket, but it stopped when it struck the shield.

"Who taught you that?"

He wondered how he knew what to do, and at his ability to prevent Gadiel penetrating the shield. The old man wasn't expecting it. Haskell shook his head and hunched his shoulders. He didn't know how he did it, but it happened. "The jacket's mine. I'm going to be a lord, and I need a good jacket."

Sims laughed behind Gadiel. "You, a lord? That's the dumbest thing you've ever said."

Gadiel sent a magic thread at Sims and the thread twisted around Sims lips like a tailor sewing his lips shut. Sims eyes widened when he tried to talk, but he couldn't open his lips.

"A lord?" Gadiel asked.

Haskell watched Gadiel as he stood pondering the comment about becoming a lord. Haskell could almost see the gears operating in Gadiel's brain determining a way to profit from Haskell's plan. "Yes. A lord and someday king." Haskell stood straight sucking in his stomach and raising his chest. He might be small, but someday he'd be powerful. He stared at Gadiel's eyes.

The old man stared back, and then crossed his arms. "Are you sure about this?"

Haskell's heart pounded hard. Would the old man kill him in his sleep, throw him in the box and let him die, or did he have another fate for Haskell? He stared in defiance.

"The last two boys that thought they were smarter than me are dead in the ground. Is that the fate you seek?"

"I seek power and to leave this small-time thieving den. I'm destined to be king, and you're standing in my way old man." Haskell thought of ways to injure or kill Gadiel, but was reluctant to take action. What would happen to the group without Gadiel's management and financial knowledge?

"It's time to take the Fire and Ice challenge," Gadiel said.

Haskell shook his head. "I refuse to take the challenge." *I'm not ready to die.*

CHAPTER 27

"Come on, tell me," Haskell said. He thought getting Lenny alone, without Sims at his shoulder telling him what to say, Lenny might tell him what he wanted to know.

Haskell and Lenny strolled to the tailor's shop, the doublet held carefully in Haskell's hands and the buttons in his pockets. Dark storm clouds threatened on the horizon as lightning flashed in the distance. The smell of rain hung in the air.

Gadiel hadn't pursued the Fire and Ice challenge after Haskell said no, but when Gadiel didn't persist, Haskell grew wary. The old man pushed, planned, and punished a subject until he accomplished his goal. Why did the man pressure Haskell about the Fire and Ice experience? What would Gadiel receive from the experience? Haskell knew he'd be taught more advanced magic from Dakarai, but he wondered what was in it for the old man.

Lenny said, "You know I can't. I won't go back in the box again. I almost died."

"At least a hint. Tell me what happened that day and why you ended up in the box."

Lenny shook his head. "Do you promise you won't tell Sims?"

"Absolutely." Haskell wanted to see Sims dead.

Lenny scanned the marketplace. They were alone. It was still early in the morning, and the craftsmen and farmers were busy with their chores. He lowered his voice.

"The princess was late getting to the marketplace." He studied his surroundings. "My responsibility was to pull a cart into the road to block it after the princess' entourage passed." He stopped talking as two guards exited the blacksmith's shop.

The boys continued their walk to the tailor's shop without speaking as the guards fell into step behind them.

When they reached the tailor's, Haskell went in with his doublet and buttons. The tailor sat on a stool at a large table, cloth spread before him as he joined two pieces of the cloth with needle and thread.

He lifted his head when Haskell entered. "Ah, how may I help?"

"I'm sorry sir, but some buttons fell off."

He looked surprised. "Fell off?"

"Oh, they . . . had help. Your sewing was fine."

The tailor looked at Lenny standing behind Haskell.

"We're just here for the buttons sir, I promise."

He sniffed. "Let's have a look. Buttons are easy to repair, but will this happen often?"

Haskell felt like a fool returning the jacket to the tailor's so soon after the tailor resized it for him. He hadn't even worn it since the adjustments were made, just another pinprick under the skin by Sims. He shook his head. "No, I'll protect it better in the future."

"I see."

"I'll pay you sir. I have money." He dug a handful of coins from his pocket.

They agreed on a price and Haskell relinquished a couple coins to the tailor.

"Will three days be okay?" The tailor asked.

"Yes, sir."

They left the shop and headed north for a project Gadiel requested. Lenny continued his story about the kidnapping. "So, the princess is running late, but I see them and I prepare to move the cart. My cart was a decoy. The princess wasn't going in it, but I needed to be right behind her entourage to block traffic and break up visibility of the castle guards."

The boys took a right turn and Lenny said, "It was time to move, and I pulled on the cart, filled with a little hay, not heavy, but when I tugged it, the cart didn't move."

"It's up here on the right." Haskell pointed at a shop.

Lenny stopped his story. "What are we getting here?"

"Gadiel called it a financial transaction."

"What kind of place is this?"

"Not sure." Haskell opened the door.

Three men sat on the bench along one wall. A long counter separated the back of the room from the front of the room and a wooden counter blocked off the rest of the room on the sides and the wall behind. There was a small, closed door on the wall behind the counter. A tall man dressed in black stood behind the counter.

The three men took an interest in Lenny and Haskell as they entered. The men were of varying sizes, but all looked trained in combat in wars serving the king. Haskell had no interest in skirmishing with these men.

The clerk behind the counter asked, "Can I help?"

Haskell glanced at the men one last time, and then opened his pouch. "I'm here to retrieve an item for Gadiel." He removed a leather envelope from the pouch and handed it to the clerk.

The clerk un-wrapped the string tying the leather envelope and pulled out another envelope sealed with Gadiel's crest. Using a knife with a bone handle the clerk stripped the seal and removed a parchment. He read the paper and nodded his head as he read. When he finished reading the letter, he regarded Haskell and Lenny.

"Nicolo, come here," the clerk said.

The largest of the three men sitting on the bench went to the side of the wooden counter, lifted a portion of the counter and stepped inside the room. Then they opened the door behind the counter and stepped into another room, closing the door behind them.

Haskell didn't know what the men did in the room, but Haskell waited and in a few minutes the men returned to the wooden counter. The big guy asked, "Where's Dakarai? He normally does this job."

Haskell shrugged. "Don't know. Gadiel asked us to do it, today."

"I'd feel more comfortable if you were a bit taller," Nicolo said.

"I'm the same size my father was."

Nicolo inspected Haskell. Studied Lenny and then nodded to the clerk. "Gadiel knows the risk, let him have it."

The clerk had wrapped the package in brown leather, tied with leather straps and sealed with wax in four spots on the package. He slid it across the counter to Haskell.

Haskell moved to lift the package and place it in his pouch.

The clerk said, "Wait. You have to sign this log book first." He obtained a leather-bound book, and turned to a page with writing in it. The man wrote a few words, Haskell couldn't read, and he didn't know what it said. Then the man turned the book to face Haskell. He handed the quill pen to Haskell and said, "Sign here, where Jorgensen's name is."

Haskell's ears went hot as he gritted his teeth and pressed his lips tight. "I can't write my name."

The clerk asked, "What's your name?"

"Haskell."

The clerk wrote something in the journal and handed the quill back to Haskell. "Make an 'X' right here." He pointed at the last entry.

Haskell dipped the quill in the ink jar and made an 'X'.

"Okay, make sure this gets back to Gadiel, if it doesn't, then you're responsible. Got it?"

"Yes, sir." Haskell stuffed it in his pouch, the leather package was heavier than he expected, since he thought he'd be returning with just a letter.

They left the building and headed back to the thief house. The clouds arrived before they left the building and the rain began, slowly at first, but then it pounded the boys on their way back to the house.

Haskell wondered what he carried in his pouch. It was heavy, so not a letter, but was it gold nuggets, silver or even bronze bricks? Why would Gadiel need so much of the material? What would he do with it?

Lenny said, "So I tugged on my cart and—"

"What?"

"The kidnapping."

"Oh, yeah, what happened?"

"I tugged, but the cart didn't move. I yanked hard, but it rocked forward and fell back. I checked the wheels and someone had placed a large rock in front of one of the wheels."

They both said, "Sims."

"Well, I didn't see him do it, but I know he did. Who else would do that?"

"The . . .," Haskell scouted for nearby people and finding none, said, "kidnapping was an important project, why would Sims do something like that? If Gadiel found out the truth and the project failed, he'd kill Sims."

"I've known Sims for a long time, and he's always done tricks like this. He's not normal," Lenny said.

"So, you removed the rock, were you able to get into position?"

"I was late to reach the point where I was supposed to be, which caused the well-timed process to suffer. Dakarai managed to make the girl disappear, which helped, but Sims got caught up with traffic we weren't expecting. When we got back to the house, Sim's blamed me for the error."

"Where did Dakarai put the girl?"

"He threw her in a farmer's wagon with blue sides. It was empty and when Dakarai kidnapped the girl, he tied her with air, and placed her in the empty wagon. It was brilliant, the wagon was empty, and the guards couldn't see her. They walked by the wagon four times and checked underneath, never saw the girl."

"A wagon with blue sides? Where'd they take her?"

"Don't know and wouldn't tell you anyway."

Haskell adjusted the pouch on his shoulder.

CHAPTER 28

Haskell struggled with dreams that night. He kept seeing Princess Noreen with Sims kissing her, and each time it happened Haskell wanted to throw a fireball at Sims. But Dakarai held Haskell's hands behind his back while Gadiel punched him with magic. The poor sleep didn't help his jangled nerves. He thought yesterday's outing with Lenny would help him determine where Princess Noreen was shipped, but he didn't think he knew any more than before.

Dakarai walked into the room and addressed the boys, "Nothing's on the list today, so go off and have a day to yourself. Looks like a nice day for a swim, so I'm going to the bridge to see if a couple of women from the castle might show up."

Sims said, "Yeah, that ugly cook might be there for you."

Dakarai hit Sims hard on the upper arm. "Keep your trap shut, Gadiel taught me how to thread lips to keep you quiet."

Sims lowered his head and rubbed his arm. That would leave a bruise.

Lenny asked, "Are you guys going to the river, too?"

Sims nodded.

Haskell said, "I might come by later in the day. I want to walk around a little, maybe find a shade tree to take a nap." Some key information tugged at his mind, but he couldn't tease out the answer. He hoped time alone, walking in the marketplace or even out of the village gates, might give him clarity.

"Did you find another girly-girl to become your princess?" Sims asked.

Haskell snarled at him.

There were normal daily chores the boys did around the house, and it wasn't until ten-bells that Haskell left the thief-house.

He wandered the marketplace, watching the blacksmith do his work as he thought of his dad and mom. The blacksmith sweated in the heat of the forge and the summer heat. Haskell enjoyed pounding on iron and bronze, and producing an object or holding the horses. He missed doing those tasks with his father.

An hour later, he walked through the village gate heading nowhere specific. He thought about when he had wanted to return to Velidred, but now with a price on his head as a wizard, that was the last place he could go. Instead, he wandered in the opposite direction on the road that led toward Oak Ridge. Oh, he didn't plan to go that far, but on a sunny day, it felt good to take in fresh air on a long walk.

He thought about the princess' kidnapping, Lenny's mistakes and the blue-sided wagon. He'd seen a blue-sided wagon not too long ago, but where? He'd hoped Lenny would share Princess Noreen's location with him, but wondered if Gadiel even told Lenny that information. If Sims knew it, Haskell assumed Sims would have said something by now, if nothing more than bragging, "I know where she is."

He'd do that to irritate Haskell; everything the boy did irritated Haskell.

He lost track of time and distance thinking random thoughts, of being a lord, what it's like to be king, what King Bryce might bestow on him if he found the princess and rescued her, where she was now, and he wondered if she ever thought of him.

Haskell stayed on the road and before he realized it, arrived in Oak Ridge at one-bell, hungry and thirsty. He stopped in the nearest tavern and ordered a bowl of stew and bread. After finishing the meal, he thought about visiting Lord Jorgensen's manor and thanking them for the doublet. They might be disappointed he wasn't wearing it, but he could tell them he left it with the tailor to be re-sized.

It only took an hour to reach the manor, and he found the gardener weeding the vegetables. "Oh, you're back."

"I wanted to thank Lord Jorgensen for the doublet he gave me."

"I see."

"Can you tell me where he is?"

The gardener raised his nose in the air. "Knock on the door, and Carl can help you."

Haskell went to the door and knocked.

Time elapsed and no one came to the door.

He knocked again. He remembered Carl moving slowly and deliberately when he was here the first time, and waiting impatiently to leave. Haskell waited. He wasn't really in a hurry, so it didn't matter.

Did the man forget that he heard the door? Were they gone from the manor and the gardener didn't want to tell Haskell? He knocked louder and thought about entering anyway, but waited. Maybe Lord Jorgensen could give him tips about being a lord, and he didn't want to make a serious social mistake and not be given a chance to learn.

When Carl still didn't answer the door, Haskell thought maybe they were around back and he should just wander back there. He wondered what the social etiquette might be for entering a lord's back yard.

He decided to knock one more time, and if no one answered, he'd head back to Whiterock Grove. Haskell knocked long and hard on the door and waited. He admired the size of the door, the silver door latch, the hardwood porch and whitewashed railings. It was a beautiful entryway. He could imagine sitting on a porch like this someday waving at the nobles as they passed his manor.

Finally, the door opened, and a servant woman answered the door. The woman was young, her hair covered in a white coif, and she wore a simple, dirty linen tunic and a stern expression. "What do you want?" She asked.

The woman looked familiar, yet her face was splotched with black marks, probably from cleaning a black pot or a fireplace. She showed no recognition of Haskell.

"I'm here to see the Lord and Lady. I want to thank them for a recent kindness."

"I see."

She didn't move.

"Can I see them?" Haskell asked.

She peered back at him with green eyes and rubbed her black, smudged hands on the back of her neck. The skin bunched around her eyes, and she gave a pained stare. The servant didn't move or say anything. Then her eyes focused on the garden.

Haskell turned toward the garden where the gardener stood staring at the door. What was going on he wondered? Had the gardener beaten the servant, and if so, for what?

He rubbed his chin and did a slight head shake. "Maybe now's not a good time for me to see the Lord and Lady Jorgensen."

The servant stared at him as if not understanding the words he used. She shut the door.

He blew out his cheeks and rubbed his hands together. Haskell walked to the gardener. "I guess they aren't home. She didn't say much."

"Not surprised, she's new to the manor."

Haskell meandered back to Whiterock Grove feeling haunted by the tight, under-fed servant's face and her green eyes.

CHAPTER 29

In the middle of the night Haskell bolted upright in bed. Was it a dream? No. Realization hit him as to who Lord Jorgensen's new servant was, Princess Noreen. He hadn't recognized her because she was smudged like a servant girl, so he saw only a servant girl. It had to be her. They must have cut her long beautiful black hair for it to fit beneath the coif. Haskell could have rescued her, right then. They probably weren't even home, and he could have grabbed her and run. If the gardener followed, he could have shot a fireball at him.

Then what? They would call the local constabulary and find Noreen with Haskell and charge Haskell with stealing a servant, a crime punishable by death. He'd found her, by accident, but now he needed to find a way to bring her back to Goodwin Castle. How?

King Bryce might say, "Thank you for rescuing my daughter. Where do you work, I'd like to reward you?"

"I work for Gadiel, the man who arranged to kidnap your daughter, and sell her to the highest bidder."

"Cut off this boy's head, before nightfall."

How could he rescue her? He needed to get back to the manor and save her. Who knew how long she could last at the manor? She didn't look in good health. Plus, they might plan to take her to a second home in the mountains or somewhere else. Maybe they were training her and planned to re-sell her to another lord in another province. Would she be punished for answering the door? How much control did the gardener have over her? They should be feeding her, why did she appear so gaunt and underfed?

Haskell didn't sleep the rest of the night as he thought of ways to rescue Princess Noreen. He had tasks on the schedule for that morning and the next day. Were the lord and lady at the manor, or were they visiting another village? Haskell had met Carl, Lord and Lady Jorgensen, and the gardener, but were there others at the manor such as unseen guards he needed to elude? He imagined taking Princess Noreen's hand, and running out the door into the forest. He envisioned Princess Noreen smiling at him once more and kissing him.

The next morning Sims stood over him. "What'cha thinking about, runt?" Sims asked.

"Nothing." Haskell glared. If Sims knew what was on Haskell's mind, the boy would blow a gasket. If Princess Noreen magically showed up at the castle, what would Gadiel do? Would he know Haskell had rescued her? He needed to become a lord or even a king if he wanted to marry Princess Noreen, and Gadiel would work hard to stifle any attempt Haskell made to make his life better. Was it time for Haskell to leave Gadiel's employ?

"Breakfast is ready," Lenny shouted from the kitchen.

Haskell felt a lightness in his chest as possibilities exploded in his mind. He patted Sims on the shoulder. "Let's get some breakfast, Buddy."

"Don't Buddy me." Sims threw Haskell's arm off his shoulder.

Haskell smiled, but his arms trembled.

After breakfast, Dakarai talked about the day's tasks. Easy tasks, they'd done them a hundred times, and they required little thought and effort. Most of the work was keeping Sims from doing something stupid.

Haskell daydreamed of saving Princess Noreen, and what their first kiss would feel like. He'd take her in his arms and spin her around. He strategized rescuing her at night, but he didn't know where she slept. Maybe he could locate her in the kitchen during the day and sneak her out the back. Haskell ran a scenario in his mind of sneaking around the manor and rescuing the princess without being seen. Could he pretend to have a task atthe Jorgensen's manor, and grab the princess and run like crazy?

The gang of thieves took their spots in the marketplace, but Haskell noticed more castle guards than normal occupied places near the shopkeepers.

He nudged Dakarai. "What's with all the castle guards?"

Dakarai shook his head, his lips pressed tight in a slight grimace.

"Should we call off today's action?"

Dakarai pulled on his ear, something he did when unsure, a clear sign to Haskell that his boss was confused.

Haskell said, "Call it off. Look at Sims."

Sims bounced on his toes, gazing at the two guards nearest him, which meant he was anxious, and about to do something stupid.

"Call it off."

Dakarai turned toward Haskell, "I call the shots, shut up."

Haskell stepped back, and noticed their target traipsing down the road. Their target was an older lord, who shopped in the marketplace twice a year. He was a wealthy man with ties to King Bryce. The man appeared older and less healthy than usual. Is that why the guards were in the marketplace, to watch out for the man and to prevent an incident?

"Abort the project," Haskell whispered louder than he wanted, but Dakarai needed to hear it. This project would land them all in jail, and make it more difficult for Haskell to rescue the princess. "Come on man, abort. This isn't our day."

Dakarai either ignored Haskell or had his own ideas of the possibility of success. He gave the signal to proceed.

Haskell didn't have much to do on today's mission. He was supposed to trip in front of the lord, and make the old man fall. The old man was already unsteady on his feet, he might fall on his own without Haskell's help.

Dakarai stared at him and blinked his eyes.

Haskell needed to begin the operation. He didn't want to go back in the dungeon, wondering if he'd eat or die the next morning. His major concern was having to spend time in the dungeon instead of rescuing the princess. What would Dakarai do to him if Haskell didn't move? Easy answer, back in the box, and days wasted, unable to help the princess.

Haskell walked toward the old man. Every guard near the old man had their eyes on Haskell and the old man. If Haskell fell in front of the old man, every guard would poke him with a lance in five seconds. This project couldn't survive first contact.

Then Haskell had a wonderful idea, he puffed air in front of the old man, and the wealthy gentleman fell to the ground. Haskell was far enough away that it was obvious it wasn't his fault, and close enough to be the first to help. He stepped next to the lord and bent down to help him up.

The gang was upon the old man in a heartbeat. They did their job flawlessly. Sims acted like he knew what he was doing, and Lenny provided back up for Sims. Haskell released the old man's purse, which was tied to his inner belt. Lenny stepped down, lifted it and stuck it in Sims' pocket.

Guards ran to the scene of the crime as they yelled incoherent words. Haskell didn't know if that was from the blood rushing through his ears or the guard's excitement at seeing something happen to the old man. Dakarai never left his position watching the transaction from the sidelines.

Sims and Lenny ran away, and Haskell helped the old man to his feet. The guards grappled with Haskell, but he didn't struggle. They grabbed his arms and pulled them behind him. Another guard helped steady the old man.

Haskell waited patiently for the guards to check on the old man and Haskell asked, "Are you all right, sir?"

The old man gazed at Haskell, but the old man didn't even see the boy. Haskell wasn't sure if anyone but him realized the old man was blind.

The guards checked the old man for injuries, and then the guard holding Haskell said, "Is this the boy who attacked you sir?"

Haskell waited for the answer. The man could say anything and the guards would believe him.

The lord stuttered, "yes . . . ss. He's the one. Stole my money purse." He checked his robes for his purse.

"I did not. I saw you fall and I helped you back to your feet. Check my body, I don't have your money purse."

The head guard said, "Throw him in the castle dungeon."

It was difficult for Haskell to breathe, his chest restricted and tight, he gaped at the old man and slumped forward.

CHAPTER 30

Haskell made up his mind during his first hour in the dungeon. Something was up and Dakarai knew this would be the outcome for Haskell. Had he tipped off the guards himself or did Gadiel? No one planned to come and release Haskell from the dungeon. Not today and not in a week's time.

Somehow, they knew he had visited the Jorgensen's manor, recognized Princess Noreen, and he suspected they planned to transplant her to another location in a few days.

He saw this as an opportunity. If Haskell was at the thief house, it'd be difficult leaving, as there were always tasks for the boys. But if he escaped the dungeon, then Gadiel and the others wouldn't even know he'd left. Then he would have time to rescue Princess Noreen.

A problem he might encounter though was how to deliver her to the king, with the guards expecting him to be in the dungeon. Every idea he thought of ended with the princess realizing he was a common thief and a blacksmith's orphan, instead of the lord he wanted to be to impress her.

The best solution was to rescue her with his doublet on, but that required him to re-enter the thief house at night which was a perilous task during the day and even more hazardous at night. Gadiel might expect this behavior from Haskell and already have a plan to prevent it.

At eleven bells, Haskell unclasped and dropped the chains attaching him to the dungeon walls. He checked the guard on duty and was happy the man slept like he had during his previous imprisonment. Haskell opened the door and re-locked it. He didn't bother securing the guard, he didn't plan on coming back tonight. Let them figure it out.

It wasn't a simple escape, but he thought getting out of the castle was easier than snatching the doublet from the thief house. Haskell hadn't yet learned Dakarai's ability to match a background and be invisible, but he had learned to place dark clouds around his person allowing him to hide at night in the shadows. This technique left him concealed in the shadows. He encountered three guards in the castle hallways, but hid in rooms or in corners and made it to the front doors.

Haskell hadn't considered how to open or escape through the front doors. He needed to go through the kitchen, where he had a better chance of escape.

When he reached the kitchen, two guards were scrounging for food. He didn't want to wait for them, so he walked into the kitchen and said, "Did you find any food tonight?"

The first narrowed his eyes and said, "Hey, what are you doing here?"

Haskell levitated two solid metal pots simultaneously and clobbered both guards on the head with the pots. They collapsed to the kitchen floor. Then he hurried to the kitchen door and opened it with caution. He was relieved when he didn't find guards at this entrance. He slipped into the courtyard.

He thought about escaping through the hole in the wall Max had suggested, but he wanted the doublet, so he hurried to the thief house. Haskell snuck between buildings, staying in the shadows and keeping the shadow cloak spell functioning. No need to alert night-watchmen to his presence.

When he reached the thief house, the building was dark. Gadiel kept a magic spell encircling the building each night to keep out intruders that might want some of the treasures he'd accumulated over the years. The old man kept a low profile with most of his work, realizing the less people who knew of his influence the better he could get away with his thievery.

They hadn't done a lot of night work; for some reason Gadiel liked his men doing their work during the day. There was one entrance left unprotected by the magic security system. It involved coming in through the same area where they kept the box. On a night like tonight, Haskell wondered if they might have prepared a trap and if Dakarai and the others planned to ambush him there and seal him in the box.

Haskell came into the thief house through the back door. He continued his shadow spell to reduce exposure. Sims and Lenny might miss him entering with the shadow spell, but they'd be sure to notice him without it. Dakarai and Gadiel had magic to reveal Haskell's presence, so he so he was prepared to fight.

Upon reaching the box, the yard was quiet, and it appeared he was by himself. But he knew Dakarai could be hiding Lenny and Sims in the shadows or even in the light. Haskell was wary and slithered along the walls. A single candle flickered in the yard near the door. He'd be exposed when he reached that point and he knew opening the door tripped the alarm, but he had to enter the house to retrieve the jacket.

Haskell estimated it would take him fifteen seconds to unlock the door, causing the alarm to sound, race into his room, grab the doublet, and return to the yard. Fifteen seconds before capture by Gadiel's team or a chance to rescue the princess. Adrenalin pumped through his body as his heart pounded in his chest. He stayed in the shadows taking slow calming breaths. Did he want to rescue Princess Noreen and become a lord?

Haskell stepped into the light of the night candle and manipulated the door lock. Even if the other thieves stood in the yard, hiding and waiting for him, he didn't care; he would maintain his resolve and retrieve the doublet. The door unlocked, and Haskell stepped into the house. He crept through the hallway barely breathing to prevent detection. Haskell opened his room door. The room was dark, but he knew its size and the objects in it, and he headed straight to the wall hook where the doublet hung.

He touched the wall and the doublet wasn't there, so he waved his hand across the wall seeing if he was off a step, but no doublet.

Sims said from behind Haskell, "Are you looking for this?"

Haskell pivoted in the direction of the voice and lit a globe of light.

Sims sat on the bed, the doublet in his hands and a smug expression on his face. "I knew you'd be stupid and come back for the jacket."

Haskell felt disoriented for a second as he shuffled back, breathless, and surprised. Then in a raging fury, he discharged magic at Sims. Not a fireball, he didn't want to kill the boy, but a flurry of silent, hard punches of air, to the boy's head, stomach, and back.

Sims' head bounced forward and backward with each punch, as blood and spittle splashed against the walls. With a final flurry to the head, the doublet dropped from Sims' hands to the floor, and the thief fell back into the bed.

Haskell seized the jacket off the floor, and returned to the hallway, his breath coming in huge gasps. He struggled to calm his mind and body, as he slithered back to the door and out into the yard. He was sure Dakarai and Lenny heard the exchange. Pumping blood pounded in his ears. Without care about being seen he raced through the yard out of Gadiel's compound and into the shadows of night.

CHAPTER 31

The last hurdle Haskell needed to clear to escape from Whiterock Grove was sneaking through the village gates or one of the holes found in the village walls. He darted through the village, finding areas of shadow, and he developed a plan as he ran. Wear the doublet when he reached the gates, and pretend he was a lord heading out of the village. It'd be difficult since he was young, but in the darkness and by candlelight, he might be able to accomplish the feat.

Haskell listened for sounds of yelling from Gadiel's thugs and thieves. He guessed they would try to catch him, or have the guards capture him. He heard only his heavy breathing.

He stopped at the last building before the village gate, and collected his breath and dignity. Nothing he did slowed his beating heart, but he took the time to put on the doublet, verifying that Sims hadn't ripped a button or sliced a hole in the jacket. He inhaled and exhaled and strolled to the gate. The only way to convince the guards he was a lord required him to act the part, arrogant, aloof and adventurous. Only a young lord would be stupid enough to leave the safety of the village gates at two bells.

"Open the gates," Haskell commanded.

"Who says so?" A guard picked up a spear and approached Haskell.

"Lord Haskell."

A second guard came from the shadows. "Late to be going for a journey. Don't you think you should wait till morning, my lord?"

"Who are you to tell me when I can go for a stroll?" Haskell's muscles quivered so much, he had to hold his left arm with his other hand to keep it from shaking. He worked hard to sound confident.

"But my lord, it's dangerous. There are wild animals in the forest and thieves on the roads at night."

"Do you think I don't know the dangers of the highway?"

The second guard studied Lord Haskell, and then nodded at his guard mate. "Open the night door for our little lord."

The guard led Haskell to a small door in the village wall next to the guard house, opened the door, and stepped through ahead of Haskell. "It's safe my lord." He bowed.

Haskell stepped through the gate and into the night. He struggled to continue to act confident and sure, not looking behind him for castle guards who might be chasing him or Gadiel's crew following.

It took a mile of walking, but he finally relaxed and thought about how to rescue the princess. Where on the manor property did Lord Jorgensen keep his kidnapped servant? Did servants have their own room in the manor; did they stay in the village or in another building on the property? It made sense to Haskell that she'd be sequestered in the manor so someone could keep a watch on her. Would they chain her or lock the room to prevent her running away each night? He figured she'd stop fighting to escape at some point, but she'd only been gone a month.

When he found her, he imagined she'd jump into his arms as her rescuer and protector. His biggest concern about getting her out of the manor, would be to stop her from kissing him too much.

Two moons shone their light on the road, enough for Haskell to see fairly well in the darkness. No traffic passed by in either direction, which made him happy, as the fewer people who noticed him the better chance he had to succeed.

Three miles ticked off, and the chill of the night air made it comfortable walking while wearing the doublet. He identified the night constellations, the wolf, bear, the archer, and the fish. His favorite was the tea pot, a constellation low in the sky at this time of year. He remembered as a child his mother showing him the constellation, holding his hand while she traced the stars that formed the tea pot.

Those good times were years ago, and he wondered how Mom and Dad would feel about his thieving and pretending to be a lord. Mom would be proud if he became a lord, but he saw Dad shaking his head and saying, "I didn't teach you to be a thief."

No Dad, you didn't, but you taught me to survive.

Horses galloped on the road behind Haskell, and he scurried into the forest. Had the castle guards realized he'd escaped the dungeon, and sent a contingent to bring him back? Did they send guards in all directions to find him, or did they get lucky in coming this way?

They were still far away and he wasn't able to make out how many horses there were from this distance. He considered Gadiel might send his thieves after Haskell, but he wasn't aware of Gadiel owning horses or the boys being able to stay on a galloping horse. Haskell smiled thinking of Lenny and Sims bouncing up and down screaming for the horses to slow.

The horses covered a lot of ground fast, and Haskell considered the advantage of having a horse when he rescued the princess. He hadn't ridden a horse in years, but thought he'd manage one well enough. A horse would add an extra measure of flamboyance to the rescue, and he imagined the princess holding tight to his waist returning to the castle. He thought of a plan to steal one of the horses, but first he needed to know if it was an army or only one or two guards, and he'd have to wait until they drew closer.

The horses thundered down the road and Haskell knew enough about horses to consider it dangerous to ride that fast in the darkness. Castle guards couldn't care enough about Haskell to ride in such a dangerous and foolhardy manner, but Gadiel's team might be bold, because they didn't have the knowledge and experience of owning horses. Haskell had handled horses since he was eight-years-old and heard stories of lords landing on their heads after their horse fell in a ditch riding hard at night. Sure, you want to get somewhere fast at night, but a smart guard wouldn't ride a horse that fast. These weren't guards.

Fifty yards away and Haskell made out the number of horses, three. Haskell wanted a good look at the riders before he played out his plan. If it were

Gadiel's men, he'd have to act differently than if they were just any thieves in the night. No way had Gadiel sent the boys out after Haskell on horses. They must be other thieves or just merchants in a hurry. It didn't matter, because he wanted a horse for the princess.

When the riders reached within twenty yards of Haskell's position, he threw a fireball into the sky causing a loud explosion and lots of light. He knew the rider's eyes would follow the fireball, and the explosion would scare the horses. Unless they were excellent horse handlers, at least one rider would end up on the ground. Haskell didn't watch the fireball trace its arc into the sky, he wanted to survey the riders. Who were they, and could he take a horse from them?

The fireball exploded a hundred feet in the sky in bright reds and yellows, followed a second later by a loud ka-boom. The horse riders reined hard on the horses at the sound. One rider's horse rose to its back legs and the rider tumbled hard to the road.

"Not excellent riders," Haskell muttered. He examined the rider's faces.

Sims maintained his hold on his horse's reins. Dakarai's horse shifted back and forth as he tried to regain control. Lenny sat on his butt in the road yelling for his horse to return.

Sims shouted, "He's over there. Dakarai tie him up with air."

Dakarai was too busy managing his horse to notice Haskell leaving the safety of the forest that lined the road.

Haskell liked Dakarai and thought of him as a friend, but what he felt for Noreen was love, and

Haskell couldn't let Dakarai capture him and hinder Princess Noreen's rescue. He tied Dakarai with air. His friend wrangled with the horse, but Haskell restricted his hands and arms, and Dakarai fell off the horse to the road.

Sims pulled a bow and arrow from the side of the saddle and nocked an arrow. Haskell blasted the arrow out of Sims hands with air.

Lenny yelled, "Come on Haskell, we're your friends. You should come back to the thief house with us."

Haskell took short, fast breaths trying to maintain control as he adjusted the jacket lower on his hips. "You won't take me back to the thief house. You'll kill me, or send me back to the dungeon. Well, I'm through with you all. You attacked an old blind man and left me to take the blame for it."

Dakarai said, "Let's talk, Haskell, release me and we can act like civilized human beings and not animals. Release the magic shield you threw around me and we can talk."

"No, I like having you tied up and shielded. I told you to halt the robbery today, and you knew it, too, but you set me up. Well, I don't approve of being set-up anymore. I own you boys now, and you'll do my bidding."

Sims kicked his horse in the side and galloped it at Haskell. "I'm not taking orders from a little runt like you."

Haskell threw air at the horse causing the horse to rear. Sims fell off. The horse realized it was free and bolted.

An animal roared in the darkness somewhere in the forest. Haskell realized he wasn't afraid of the animal, Sims, Lenny or Dakarai. He'd grown tonight, and he planned to save the princess even if it killed him.

Sims pulled a knife from its sheaf and ran at Haskell who blasted Sims in the chest with a fireball. The older boy was eight feet away, a second from killing Haskell, but he didn't make it another step. The fireball exploded on Sims' chest, pushed him backwards and his tunic caught on fire. The thief fell to the road roaring in pain.

Haskell didn't know Sims' story, other than like himself Sims was orphaned. But Sims had become a bully, and a know-it-all. He made mistakes, big mistakes that cost Haskell, Lenny and probably Gadiel time and money. Haskell was done with the drama and Sims' obstructing behavior. He sent fireballs at Sims' feet. "Run Sims, to Velidred or Kalluri, but I better never see you in Whiterock Grove or I will not spare you next time. Run."

Sims nostril's flared as he shook his fist at Haskell. "You're gonna pay for this, runt." Sims took off running as Haskell pelted the ground behind the runner with fireballs that kicked up dirt and rocks that landed on the fleeing thief.

Haskell went and checked on Lenny. "Are you okay?" He reached out to Lenny, but Lenny hit his hand.

"Don't touch me. You're in big trouble."

"You don't know the half of it, my friend. My trouble is just beginning."

Haskell let Lenny sit on the road. He checked on Dakarai.

"Do you think you'll be safe if an animal comes out of the forest?"

Dakarai blew out his cheeks and then relaxed. "Gadiel will be furious with you. The deal for the princess is complete, and if Lord Jorgensen knows you took her then he'll want his money back."

Haskell said, "I'll add a spell, so this clears in an hour, Lenny can protect you until then." The horses had stopped fifty yards away and were eating grasses that grew along the road. He left the two thieves and sauntered to the horses.

CHAPTER 32

Haskell walked the stolen horses for a mile. They needed rest and he expected to run them again after rescuing Noreen. When he crossed a creek, he allowed the horses to drink. He wanted them strong and fresh. Of course, the way Sims and Dakarai had been galloping, the horses might be of no use at all. At least he didn't have to worry about the thieves notifying Lord Jorgensen about the rescue attempt.

By four bells, Haskell arrived at Lord Jorgensen's manor. He tied the horses to a tree next to a meadow. He hoped they wouldn't be there long.

Haskell stared at Lord Jorgensen's manor. He hadn't appreciated its size the last two times he had visited. He counted fourteen windows on this side of the building. Wooden shutters were closed on three of the windows on the east end. He guessed that one of those rooms with the closed shutters was where the lord and lady had stashed Noreen. Haskell decided to start his search in one of those rooms.

Did the lord employ guards or use dogs as a warning system on the property? They lived far from the village and had no fence to protect their family from thieves.

Haskell knew elementary spells to search for traps or warning systems. He tested for magical traps, and found none. Were unseen guards in the nearby forest? Haskell transmitted a magic thread to discover the proximity of nearby people. The thread took a few minutes to return. The magic identified five individuals hiding in the woods about two hundred yards apart surrounding the manor. He stood less than fifty feet away from one, and was surprised the man hadn't noticed him.

Haskell wrapped the guard with air and then trotted to the man to check.

The guard wore a uniform of dark colors with a white stripe down the pant leg. Haskell had seen the uniform on guards he passed on previous visits through the Oak Ridge village. The guard was asleep and wasn't worth any money the lord paid for his service.

He weaved his way toward the manor, staying in shadows and using his cloaking cloud as much as possible. He hoped most of the guards slept. A guarded manor wasn't worth the hassle to a trained thief.

The moons in the sky threw sharp shadows, and Haskell used the gloom beyond a tree to his advantage. Haskell snuck to the back of the manor and crept along the wall.

A dog growled. Ten feet away stood a mostly black pit bull with a white stripe running down his snout. The dog barked, a loud piercing noise that could awaken the deepest sleeping guard.

Haskell didn't have any food on him to satisfy the dog, and he suspected the dog's barking had already alerted the guards. He was sure they were now awake and fully prepared to do their job. He quieted the dog with magic, and scampered to the back door.

Did the dog wake the people in the house? Dawn wasn't too far away. Maybe the dog woke the cook, gardener or butler, who would now decide it was close enough to normal waking hours to get up for work.

Haskell used magic to pick the back door lock. He entered the manor and found himself in the kitchen. He'd come in through the back door so he'd have to go left to find the rooms he suspected the princess to be locked in. If she was being held against her will, they might lock her in an upper room to make it more difficult to escape.

He snuck up the stairs, and on the fifth stair the floorboard creaked. He stopped and listened. In one of the rooms on the next floor, a bed frame groaned. Was that someone getting out of bed or just rolling over? He had to hurry.

At the top of the stairs, he turned left and counted doors as he walked. On the fourth door, he examined the lock. The room was unlocked, so he decided not to enter the room.

His heart beat faster the closer he thought he was getting to the princess' room. He was really going to save her and get his first chance to hold her arms and kiss her cheek. He passed two more doors and then found a locked door. He used magic to unlock the door and prepared to enter. The sounds of feet shuffling on a wood floor drifted through the silence. Were the guards in the house already, or was it just the staff?

Haskell lifted the door latch and eased the door open, happy the door didn't squeak. He'd always thought about holding the princess in his arms, but never what he'd say to her when he found her. The bed was empty and a cabinet stood in the corner of the room. This wasn't her bedroom.

He hoped it would be the next room. Four times the stair case creaked as people mounted the stairs, presumably to capture him. He didn't have much time. Haskell closed the door and rushed to the next room, also locked. He unlocked it and lifted the latch.

A man whispered in the hallway behind him, "You two go that way and we'll check this way. Be quiet and don't awaken the lord."

Even if he found Princess Noreen in this room, they'd have to fight their way out of the manor. Haskell snuck into the room, shut the door and locked it with magic. He figured he would make them work for it.

Someone lay on the bed, unmoving, but with labored breathing. In the dark, he couldn't tell if it was Princess Noreen. He magically produced a globe with soft blue light and examined the girl in the bed. In the dim light, he couldn't determine if the girl was the princess or not. He didn't know how many servants Lord Jorgensen had in his manor, and he needed to see if her eyes were green. Now what?

Someone jiggled the latch of the room next door, and Haskell expected the person to check this room next. The guards might not have keys, which meant they'd assume an intruder couldn't have gotten into the room. Would an intruder lock the door?

He extinguished the blue light and waited in the darkness. The soldiers were pretty noisy as they scraped their feet checking the door across the hallway. He heard one guard enter the room across the hall and say, "No one's here. How about that room?"

The voices must have awakened the girl in bed, or at least upset her sleeping, because she rolled over onto her side.

The guards wiggled the door latch and realized it was locked.

Haskell focused on the door waiting for it to open. "Nope this one's locked, too."

Haskell exhaled, not realizing he'd been holding his breath. They would continue on down the hall, he was safe.

The woman in the bed screamed.

CHAPTER 33

When the woman screamed, Haskell's adrenaline spiked and he froze to his spot on the floor.

Someone in the hallway battered on the door. "He's in here."

Many footsteps pounded down the hallway.

The girl kept screaming.

Haskell said, "Stop screaming, I'm here to rescue you."

She stopped screaming a moment, caught her breath, and released another loud, ear-splitting scream.

He didn't know what to do, so he sent a magic weave of air and stopped her screaming by muffling her.

"Stop screaming, I'm here to help." Haskell sent up the globe of light and peered at the woman he had come to rescue.

Her eyes were feverish and over-bright. Haskell couldn't determine the eye color without more natural light. Her face was drawn tight like she hadn't eaten for days, and her eye's black pupils were so big there was little color visible in the irises. Was this Princess Noreen?

The guards pummeled the door trying to break it down.

A man's voice in the hallway yelled, "Stop. Don't break it down. I have a key."

Haskell looked at the girl. "Shake your head, yes or no. Are you Princess Noreen?"

The girl didn't move.

"What's wrong with you? Are you Princess Noreen?"

Her eyes darted left and right.

Was this the wrong room, and he had found a different servant girl? Maybe another girl kidnapped from another village, or even another girl kidnapped by Gadiel that Haskell didn't know about?

A key went into the lock and a man said, "On three we charge into the room. One of you snatch the girl, and the other two grab the intruder. Knives at the ready."

They're coming in with knives? Haskell was going to become a pincushion for some over-ambitious guards who normally slept the night away in the forest for a few extra coins. Haskell stared at the door latch.

The latch lifted.

The servant girl touched Haskell's shoulder with her finger. Haskell turned toward her.

She nodded her head vigorously.

Three guards entered the room, one with a torch and the other two with knives drawn.

Haskell cast a shield around himself and Princess Noreen.

The guards bounced off the shield, and three other men, one of which was Lord Jorgensen, caromed off the guards.

Lady Jorgensen ambled into the room and said, "Oh, it's that nice little orphan boy. The doublet looks good on you."

Haskell felt his face, neck, and ears become impossibly hot and his breathing rushed. His first full introduction to Princess Noreen and it's that nice, little, orphan boy. He stared at Lady Jorgensen, and then stared with open mouth at Princess Noreen.

She grimaced, and her eyes blinked rapidly. She seemed to be gagging on the air in her throat which had stopped the screaming. Haskell released the spell. She placed her hands on her knees and gasped raggedly.

They all seemed at a deadlock. The guards couldn't get through the shield, and Haskell wasn't sure how to get past the guards. Now they knew who it was that wanted to rescue the princess. He turned back to Noreen to check on her.

Princess Noreen slapped Haskell upside the head, causing his ears to ring.

He shook his head and said, "I'm here to rescue you."

"Daddy didn't send the king's guards?"

Haskell gazed at the floor. That would have been a better idea, to tell the king and let the king handle the rescue. The king might have given him a reward or something. He shook his head. "No, just me."

The leader of the guards said, "Is this the missing princess?"

Lord Jorgensen said, "No, she's a simple peasant, orphaned in the last two years. I arranged for her to be a servant in our household. She isn't very good."

"How dare you deceive the guards, sir?" Princess Noreen said.

The guard said, "And who's the boy?"

Haskell straightened his doublet and stood as tall as his small frame could handle and said, "Lord Haskell of Velidred here to rescue the fair Princess Noreen." He reached out his hand to the girl.

She touched his hand detonating the tingling of a thousand nerves throughout his body.

Lady Jorgensen asked, "Rolf, is this the missing princess?"

"No, it's a lie, she's an orphan."

A guard said, "The door was locked from the outside. Did she try to escape?"

"Every night," Lord Jorgensen said. "She told us she was of noble birth, but I didn't believe her."

The guard leader, a wide man said, "Lord Haskell, release the princess to us, and we'll make sure she gets back to Goodwin Castle unharmed."

Haskell realized he couldn't let that happen. He had to walk her to the king himself so he received credit for rescuing her. These lazy buffoons would accept the credit, and he was sure a sizeable reward as well. He'd receive nothing, not even acknowledgement from the princess for his role in saving her.

"I can manage taking the princess back to the castle on my own. I brought a horse to transport the beautiful princess home to her father. Now that she's free of these evil people, she'll be safe with me."

"Don't do something stupid, kid. We're constables in these parts, and I'm sure the mayor of Oak Ridge wants to be a part of this special occasion of us finding the princess and returning her."

"Hah, without you guys, I'd have had her halfway home by now."

"Be reasonable. There might be thieves on the highway. We have the numbers to transport the princess safely to the castle."

Thieves on the highway? Yeah, at least two and they'd definitely want to get their hands on the princess. Haskell could use the guards' help, but he wouldn't let Princess Noreen out of his sight until she kissed her father.

"Don't you think it wise to take Lady and Lord Jorgensen to the village mayor and see about putting them in the dungeon for kidnapping the princess?"

Lord Jorgensen shouted, "We didn't kidnap the princess. We didn't know her title."

Haskell glanced back at Princess Noreen. She planted a kiss on his cheek.

CHAPTER 34

Haskell and Princess Noreen rode the horses through the Whiterock Grove gates side by side. They were followed by a detachment of forty Oak Ridge guards, which Haskell imagined comprised all the guards in the village. Oak Ridge's mayor rode beside Haskell and the princess. Lady Jorgensen gave Princess Noreen a dress to wear, though it was baggy on the princess because of all the weight she'd lost from not eating during her confinement as a servant. They allowed her time to clean up while the mayor and the guards assembled. And for some unknown reason she insisted on a something to cover her hair. Lady Jorgensen found a hooded hairpiece trimmed with pearls.

The contingent passed Dakarai and Lenny walking home. Dakarai, a thick vein pulsing in his neck, raised a fist at Haskell but didn't push his luck with the parade of guards.

They entered Whiterock Grove, and as soon as the gate guards recognized the princess, they allowed the parade of guards into the village. The villagers appeared confused at first as to whom the parade was for, but soon raised their voices in cheers for Princess Noreen.

Haskell felt lightness in his chest as he enjoyed the cheering villagers, and sat straighter on the horse. He straightened to gain full height. Princess Noreen waved at the crowd that formed along the way to the castle. *I'm returning home a hero for rescuing the princess. Is this how it feels to be king?*

Possibilities rushed through his head. How big a reward would King Bryce Goodwin bestow on Haskell for rescuing his daughter? If the riches were big enough, Haskell might be able to purchase his own land and manor. Would that be enough to ask for Princess Noreen's hand in marriage?

At the castle gates, the guards hesitated only a moment, recognized the princess and allowed Haskell and the Oak Ridge mayor into the castle bailey with five guards.

Haskell let out a full belly laugh at riding into the castle on a horse after escaping from the castle dungeon under cover of night less than a day before. They reached the castle keep and a stable boy held his horse as he stepped down. He stood next to Princess Noreen and held her hand. The guards opened two huge wooden doors allowing Haskell and the princess to march into the main foyer.

Servants wearing castle colors of blue and yellow welcomed them. Two female attendants reached Noreen and rushed her away, leaving Haskell and the mayor standing alone. A tall servant invited them to follow him up the stairs. Haskell knew the way to the dungeon but this stairway was foreign to him. He smiled at not being whisked back to the lower reaches of the castle. He watched for guards that might recognize him from his stay in the dungeon.

They climbed to the second floor and took a left into the hallway. Standing near a door were the two guards Haskell bopped on the head in the kitchen. Haskell felt his chest tighten, and he gazed at tapestries on the other side of the hallway. He rubbed his hand over his temple attempting to hide his identity.

They reached the next set of stairs, and ascended to the third floor. This hallway contained busts of kings and queens. Haskell examined large paintings of King Bryce Goodwin and the Queen. Haskell stopped at a painting of the royal family, where young images of Princess Noreen and Princess Carol smiled at him from the canvas.

The mayor and Haskell sat on a bench in the hallway next to a set of double doors. The mayor asked, "Lord Haskell, have you ever met King Bryce?"

Haskell thought of the times he'd seen the man riding through the streets on a horse surrounded by guards and knights, but no, he'd never had an audience with the king. He shook his head.

"It can be overwhelming. The king in all his finery sits on his throne while we little people try to speak to him as if we're his peers. Everyone in the room knows we aren't."

Haskell's mouth dried and he couldn't work moisture into his mouth. He planned to meet the king and tell him of his role in rescuing his daughter, but his mouth wasn't cooperating. *What if I say something and it comes out like a squawk or if nothing comes out at all? I can't let the mayor take credit for the rescue. I need to be strong and confident, even if I feel like running.*

He thought of the king sitting on his throne and wondered how to interact with a king. Was he supposed to bow, and was there a time limit within which the bow must occur? If he made a mistake with the bow, the king might not take him seriously as Lord Haskell. *The doublet has to sell me to the king. What if Princess Noreen isn't there to corroborate my story, then what will I receive?* He closed his eyes and took a deep breath, concentrating to keep his left leg from trembling.

"Let's work together on telling the king our story of rescuing his daughter, then we both get the credit for saving her."

"What?" Haskell asked.

"This is a serious matter," the mayor said, "and we need to word our comments in the proper manner to make sure the king understands the effort taken to rescue his daughter. But we also need to acknowledge our role as humble servants."

"I understand the need to be humble in the presence of the king, but you didn't have anything to do with the rescue. I only allowed you to accompany me to provide extra support on the journey back to Whiterock Grove." He leaned close to the mayor. "We'll agree on this version of the story, won't we?"

The mayor leaned away from Haskell.

Haskell didn't plan to let the mayor take credit for the rescue. "We're agreed then?"

The mayor nodded.

"Okay, then. Why won't they let us in?"

"You don't know the royal way. The princess has to take a bath and be attended as she is dressed in beautiful clothes. Then the king talks to her and gets her side of the story. If she's honest and can tell her father the story, then they might talk for a few minutes or a few hours."

"A few hours?" Haskell asked.

"They might have a meal before talking with us."

Haskell lowered his head to examine his pants and brushed at some dirt with his hand. A couple of servants walked by. They wouldn't recognize him, but those guards on the floor below, could they come down this hallway and get a good look at Haskell? How much time could he spend in the hallway before someone noticed him and they threw him back in the dungeon? There'd be no reward for Lord Haskell if they had him back in manacles before he talked with the king.

"Do we just sit here?" Haskell asked.

"What else do you want to do?"

Haskell thought of ten things he wanted to do. Find something to eat. Locate the king and talk to him immediately without waiting for all the things the mayor said might occur. Discover the princess' location and embrace her, grab the reward, and leave the castle before anyone recognized him. He'd rather do pretty much anything besides sitting exposed to all who walked by in this hallway.

"Relax boy, this is what it means to be in the royal court. When the king meets you, he'll reward you for your effort on his daughter's behalf. Where's your manor?"

His manor? He snorted. Haskell didn't have a manor, but he couldn't tell the king that. A good lord like Haskell needed to live in a manor. Oh, all these lies and deceptions would land him back in the dungeon or worse hanging from the gallows, or he'd find his neck beneath the sharp edge of a guillotine. He cleared his throat and raised his chest and back straight and said, "My manor is between Velidred and Whiterock Grove, a little place out in the country, I'm sure you've never heard of it.

    The tall servant returned and addressed the mayor. "The king will accept you at the next bell."

    Haskell grinned, he could do this. He stood and adjusted his doublet.

    A person dressed in black walked toward them and clapped Haskell on the shoulder.

CHAPTER 35

Gadiel whispered in Haskell's ear, "You're in trouble for this, boy."

Coldness settled in Haskell's core as adrenaline sent a prickle of angst through his body. He stiffened his posture tightening his muscles. *Gadiel is here and will ruin everything. The old man will secure the reward and leave me with nothing.*

Had Dakarai and Lenny returned already and told Gadiel what Haskell had done? Haskell wanted his audience with the king to occur before Gadiel learned of the rescue, so he could escape from Gadiel's influence. Now he was sure Gadiel planned to accompany him into the king's presence.

"What do you want, Gadiel?" Haskell asked his voice hard and commanding.

"I want to share in the celebration with you for your service to the king and his family. You'll want someone with you to speak on your behalf to make sure the king doesn't take advantage of you."

Haskell snorted. He knew Gadiel and the old man's ability at taking advantage at every opportunity. If Haskell received one gold coin, Gadiel would want ten for being there with him to help. "I'll be fine on my own. You may head back to the manor for now."

Gadiel fingered the fine scrolling on Haskell's doublet. "This jacket doesn't make you a lord, boy. I'll be happy to share with the king where you slept last night, and how you procured your spot there."

Haskell ground his teeth, thinking of ways to gain an advantage. He glared at Gadiel and cracked his knuckles. Did he want to get into a magic fight against Gadiel moments before his audience with the king? He couldn't let Gadiel enter the king's great hall with him. A quick slip of air around Gadiel, tell the old man to stay in the hallway until his audience with the king was complete, and then they could return to Gadiel's house. Did the mayor think Gadiel a father figure or Lord Haskell's servant? He wondered if Gadiel knew the king. It wouldn't surprise him to find they were close friends.

"What do you want?" Haskell asked.

"To make sure you get the reward you deserve. I'm here as your advocate, the king can be quite generous or stingy, depending on who you are. There are traditions and family names that show how you aid and support the king."

"I rescued the king's daughter. That shows my commitment to him and his family."

"Finesse, boy. I can teach you to be the lord you aspire to, but it requires subtlety."

Haskell shook his head. Cooperation with Gadiel landed him in Gadiel's box, and a number of times in the king's dungeon. *Will Gadiel train me to be a lord or force me to continue his servitude and thieving? How do lords earn money to support a manor, servants and guards?* He sighed, "What's the price?"

Gadiel sneered, "I'll help you with the king to ensure you receive the proper reward for your rescue mission. Plus, long term, I'll ensure the Council of Nine doesn't identify your whereabouts. I'll tutor you to be a lord, won't tell the princess your origins as a blacksmith and—you'll take the Fire and Ice challenge."

The Fire and Ice challenge again. The man is relentless. Haskell stared at his hands. A single word from Gadiel in the presence of the king and Haskell's neck would stretch on the chopping block before dusk. He weighed his options. *I need someone to teach me the duties and behaviors of a lord, and it'll help me secure Princess Noreen if I act the part. But the Fire and Ice challenge might kill me; the same way it killed Max.*

Haskell stared into Gadiel's black eyes. The red scorpion scurried from the corner of the old man's eye into the iris, and beckoned Haskell to acquiesce to Gadiel's commands.

The king's servant opened the great hall's doors. "The king is prepared to receive you."

Gadiel grabbed Haskell's wrist.

Haskell chewed on his lip. He glanced at the king's servant. Then he studied a painting of a younger Princess Noreen that hung on the wall across from his bench. Was he willing to sacrifice his life for Princess Noreen? He nodded at Gadiel.

The old man smiled.

CHAPTER 36

Haskell entered the great hall with the mayor, and he was prepared to match any social etiquette to ingratiate himself to the king. Gadiel entered the room behind Haskell, but close enough for him to feel his presence.

King Bryce Goodwin sat on his throne, a high-backed, wooden chair, upholstered in blue and yellow fabric in a diamond pattern. The chair sat on a wooden floor raised three steps higher than where Haskell stood facing the king.

In a lower chair, to the king's left sat Princess Noreen, her hair comb and entwined within a diamond studded tiara, enhanced with five crystal stars pointing to the ceiling. She wore a dress with a tight-fitting bodice of royal blue and a flowing skirt of a darker blue lined in a ribbon of gold trim from the waist to the floor. Long sleeves covered her arms and hands. She smiled as Haskell entered the room.

Haskell's heartbeat quickened, and he felt his throat growing thick and dry.

King Bryce stepped down from the throne and walked toward the mayor and Haskell.

The mayor bowed, a deep bow from the waist. "Your Majesty."

Haskell watched the mayor and imitated the movement. "Your Majesty."

"Is this the young lord that rescued my daughter?"

Haskell didn't say anything.

Gadiel poked Haskell in the side.

Haskell glanced at Gadiel.

"The king asked you a question, Lord Haskell."

He needed water or something to drink, his mouth felt dry and clogged. He peered at the floor while attempting to push moisture into this mouth. Then stuttered, "Ye . . . ss."

Gadiel jumped in. "I'm sorry, Your Majesty, the young lord doesn't get out of the manor often, and I've never taught him the etiquette of meeting royalty."

"Think nothing of it." The king came to Haskell, and put his arm around Lord Haskell's shoulders. "We're friends here today, and I can't tell you how happy I am to have my daughter returned to the castle. Princess Noreen tells me you're a brave man, and held off a large group of armed intruders to save her from her captives."

Haskell gulped as heat rose to his ears. He gazed at Princess Noreen and watched her emerald eyes sparkle. She kept his stare, and displayed a brief smile. Then she brushed her hands over her dress.

The king studied his daughter and said, "I see this has taken an unexpected turn. Where is your manor, Lord Haskell?"

Haskell peered at Gadiel, then the floor, a quick glance at Princess Noreen, and then settled on the King. The one question he hoped wasn't asked, yet here it was. A lord's manor, but where? "It's a . . . small . . . estate—."

Gadiel said, "The manor is south of Whiterock Grove, Your Majesty. The young lord is being humble. The manor sits on an estate of many acres of prime farmland, and is a perfect location for grazing."

"What animals do you graze on the property?" King Bryce asked.

"Lord Haskell owns hundreds of sheep." Gadiel said.

Haskell snapped his head at Gadiel. He worried his own deceptions might spoil the deal and cause him certain death, and yet Gadiel added to the distortions of truth.

King Bryce brought his fingers to his lips and said, "I see." He studied Gadiel for a few moments. "And what is the young lord's title?"

Title? Isn't lord a title? What more could the king be expecting?

Gadiel spoke, "The young man is a minor lord, Your Majesty."

The king nodded, turned and walked back up the dais. He clasped his daughter's hand and lifted her to her feet. They strode back to Haskell.

Haskell's face burned, being this close to the beautiful Princess Noreen, and he felt sure his hair would start on fire from the heat in his face.

King Bryce said, "I had heard that Lord Haskell was a local orphan boy that found a lord's jacket, and then pretended to be a lord. But your servant's poise and wisdom gives me a second thought about the young lord."

"Thank you, Your Majesty." Gadiel bowed to the king. "He is an orphan, both parents died when he was ten, and I've tried to raise him as a son. When he comes of age, he will be a powerful lord, and will desire to help Your Majesty with questions of state. He'll be open to helping the kingdom on your behalf as needed."

"I see." The king appraised Haskell.

In the back of Haskell's mind, he heard the king and Gadiel talking, but he focused on Princess Noreen. She must have taken a bath after returning to the castle, and she smelled of lavender. Her cheeks were rosy, a light green eyeshadow enhanced her emerald eyes, and her lips shone the color of red wine.

"Lord Haskell, is your manor taxed or have you given feudal aid to the Goodwin kingdom?" King Bryce asked.

Haskell returned his attention to the king.

He didn't know how to answer that question. The manor was imaginary and the king couldn't tax it, because it wasn't on the map. Would the king expect Haskell to provide taxes to the Goodwin kingdom? Where would he get the money for that expense? This façade about being a lord was becoming a farce of great significance. Haskell swallowed.

Gadiel answered, "The lord's manor is located between Goodwin castle and Velidred castle, and over the years we've given our service to Goodwin castle and sometimes to Velidred. We currently report to the Velidred king, because their kingdom has the Council of Nine and Lord Haskell has wizard skills. He desires to enhance those skills."

The king nodded his head, but frowned when Gadiel mentioned the tax. Then a slight smile fell upon his lips at the mention of Haskell wielding magic.

"I have a tutor helping him with his magic, and I have it on good authority that the Council of Nine is interested in Lord Haskell and his abilities."

Gadiel seemed to read the king's expressions and say the words the king wanted to hear. *Yes, I need training to become lord and king someday, but how am I going to acquire this imaginary manor?*

The king didn't say anything, but stared at Haskell for a long time.

Haskell feared breathing. All these lies and untruths, did Gadiel really think they could pull off this scam? Haskell's collar felt like it tightened around his neck. He expected the king to all of a sudden laugh out loud, and order the guards to take them both to the guillotine. He should say something now and tell the king it was all a lie. Maybe, if Haskell asked the king for a gold piece, then he could leave Whiterock Grove and never come back.

King Bryce said, "You were a brave young man to rescue my daughter." He snapped his fingers and the tall servant rushed to his side. The king whispered in the servant's ear and nodded. Then the servant left.

There. The king recognized the scam, and sent the servant to fetch the guards. Should Haskell run? He'd escaped from the castle two times already, but did he have enough luck to elude capture a third time? Haskell examined the room for exits. He'd never make it out of the room through the large double doors, so he eyed the doors behind the dais. Where did that exit lead?

The mayor spoke, "Your Majesty, I don't want you to forget the part played by the Oak Ridge guards. Without their service your daughter might not have made it home."

"I heard you brought forty of Oak Ridge's finest guards into the castle grounds, and yes, I applaud your efforts to keep my daughter safe after her rescue. I won't forget your service to the kingdom, both today and in the past. Tell me, what is to become of Lord and Lady Jorgensen?"

The mayor cleared his throat, and grabbed at his tunic collar. "They have served the king for many years, Your Majesty. I'm sure this divergent behavior can be explained."

King Bryce raised his voice, "I don't want explanations. I want punishment worthy of the crime of kidnapping."

Haskell wondered how much of the kidnapping was triggered by Lord Jorgensen, or was he someone that fell into Gadiel's machinations of the truth.

"I want to see the Lord and Lady Jorgensen hanged for their crime."

The mayor's mouth fell open and he brought his hands to his lips. "But Your Majesty, surely it's just a mistake, they wouldn't kidnap the princess."

"The facts in the case don't support your beliefs, Mayor. Is it time for Oak Ridge to receive a new mayor for their village?"

"No, Your Majesty. We'll prepare the gallows tonight and hang the lord and lady first thing tomorrow morning."

Haskell felt dizzy at the sudden and firm judgement of guilt. The king had that much power, to send people to their deaths with little evidence, Haskell could never be that hard on people. He'd listen to their side and gain more evidence before making such a substantial decision. The king was sure to command the same or similar judgement on Haskell in just a moment. He studied Princess Noreen, and wondered if he'd ever see her again after today.

She winked at him.

King Bryce said, "Mayor, you're dismissed."

The mayor lowered his head and his shoulders dropped. With a heavy sigh he bowed, and exited the great hall.

Haskell wondered how the mayor felt not receiving any reward for his efforts. The man must have considered coming here with Haskell a done deal for coins for himself and his small army of guards. Yet, now he's leaving the king's presence with nothing to show for his efforts. Should Haskell expect the same? He'd be happy to leave right now without being returned to the dungeon, and then he'd only have to deal with Gadiel's anger.

Gadiel and Haskell stood in the great hall.

King Bryce led Princess Noreen back to the dais, where they both sat.

This is it. Now comes the part of the audience with the king where the guards march into the hall and lead them either to the dungeons or to their deaths. What would it be like on the chopping block with Gadiel?

The room was quiet as they stood waiting for the sentence of death. Why didn't the king just say the words and be done with it? What was he waiting for?

The entry doors opened, but Haskell kept his eyes on Princess Noreen, wanting to remember this scene of her royalty and splendor. The sounds of shoes on the floor filled the room as someone marched toward the king. Haskell anticipated a large contingent of guards lined the hallway ready to pounce on them if they tried to escape or leave. It was time for the king to pronounce his judgment to send Haskell to the gallows alongside Lord and Lady Jorgensen.

The tall servant had returned bearing a large bag in his hands. He stopped and stood at the bottom of the dais.

King Bryce strolled toward a guard standing on a corner of the dais and withdrew the sword from the guard's sheath. He approached Haskell and Gadiel.

This is it then, Haskell thought. No need for public humiliation, the king would whack their heads off right here in the great hall. He wondered if Princess Noreen would avert her eyes or sit smiling as the king wielded the weapon at Haskell's neck. Haskell's neck stiffened and he wobbled his head back and forth to loosen the tension he felt.

"Please kneel, Lord Haskell."

Haskell knelt, and gazed into Princess Noreen's eyes. Her pupils were large and black, but her face held a soft expression. She ran her hands across her jaw and pushed back a wisp of hair that escaped her tiara. Haskell wished it could be his hand caressing her jaw, but today and forever that would never happen.

The king lifted the sword and touched Haskell's shoulder with the blade.

What if Haskell created a magic shield to prevent the king from lopping off his head? That'd surprise both the king and princess. Haskell grinned.

"I, King Bryce Goodwin, King of Whiterock Grove, Goodwin Region and high king of mountains, rivers, meadows and villages, do so pronounce to all present and not present, that today in Goodwin castle, I command that Lord Haskell, landowner and king's man, is this day, Baron Haskell. I do decree that no man except the king may remove this title from him. In honor for his marvelous deeds, I bequeath to him one-hundred gold coins and Lord Jorgensen's manor." The king tapped the sword on Haskell's left shoulder and then his right shoulder.

Haskell's heart froze, and then pounded in his chest, as blood rushed to his face. His eyes went wide, and he sucked in a quick breath. He couldn't believe it. Had he hit his head and all this was an unbelievable dream? Baron Haskell?

The tall servant commanded, "Baron Haskell, please rise."

Haskell smiled and rose.

Princess Noreen smiled and stood.

Gadiel said, "Bow."

Haskell bowed.

The servant handed the gold coins to Gadiel.

Haskell said, "Thank you, Your Majesty."

King Bryce said, "We must have a ball and celebrate your new status." He pivoted to assess his daughter. "And to give you a chance to dance with my daughter."

CHAPTER 37

Haskell stood on the back porch of his new manor, worrying about what he had heard at breakfast. He'd hoped Gadiel had forgotten the date, but at breakfast Gadiel had told Dakarai and Lenny to prepare to travel to the mountains. There's only one thing it could mean—the Fire and Ice Challenge. Haskell thought about running as far from Gadiel as possible, but he realized that would mean he'd have to forget about Noreen, and these days she was in his thoughts all the time.

All but Sims had taken residence at Lord Jorgensen's manor, now Baron Haskell's manor, and Gadiel had moved his operations to the manor. They had responsibilities to the local community, and Gadiel had sunk his grip into the local mayor and created an income stream from the local economy. Haskell didn't know what or how the old man had made the arrangements, but now the manor had money coming into the coffers.

Gadiel hadn't expelled Sims from the group, but Haskell demanded that Sims stay in Whiterock Grove, instead of living in his manor in Oak Ridge. Gadiel had arranged it, and as long as the disruptive thief wasn't around to harass him, Haskell felt all was fine.

The bag of coins from King Bryce had gone to Gadiel, and he told Haskell that he had invested the coins so they would provide revenue into the manor regularly.

Gadiel had set a date for Haskell to take the Fire and Ice Challenge after leaving the Goodwin castle, and Haskell's stomach had been in knots for days thinking about it.

He still didn't know how to manage all these titles and arrangements, though Gadiel had arranged for Carl, Lord Jorgensen's old butler, to educate Haskell on royal etiquette by spending time with him each day. Carl arranged for one of the young servant girls to work with Haskell on dances he might engage in as a baron. Princess Noreen was on his mind when they were practicing dancing, but as soon as he left the practice sessions, the fear of taking the Fire and Ice Challenge weighed heavily on his mind.

At ten bells, Gadiel placed a hand on Haskell's shoulder. "It's time."

# # # #

Snow blanketed the mountains as they laboriously trudged the last few miles through the early fall snow drifts. They reached the spot where Max had taken his fatal Fire and Ice Challenge, and Gadiel called a stop to the caravan's progress. Haskell thought back to his friend's last days and shuddered at now taking the challenge himself.

Lenny and Dakarai got busy prepping the area and then a third person showed up, Sims.

Haskell pointed at him, "What's he doing here?" Haskell's chest hitched. He worried what questionable activities Sims might engage in to ensure Haskell failed.

Dakarai answered, "He knows the process. It's easier to have someone familiar with the procedure. He's one of the best at cutting the ice for that portion of the test." He touched Haskell on the shoulder. "Don't worry, it's going to be okay. Look I survived."

Haskell thought back to Max's challenge. What had gone wrong? He looked at Sims, who sneered back at him. A heaviness developed in his gut, and his face tightened as doubt weighed heavily on his mind. He wasn't happy that the trial might put his life in the hands of someone who would be happy to see him dead.

Darkness settled upon their camp as the sun set over a distant mountain range. Thirty feet away, coals glowed a dark red, a three foot by twenty-yard line in the snow.

Gadiel said, "It's time. Come into the tent."

Haskell's heart pounded in his chest. He tried to come up with reasons that might dissuade Gadiel from continuing the initiation. Fear gripped his guts, and Haskell couldn't think of any strategies to change his mentor's persistence to take the challenge.

Dakarai pushed Haskell in the back and forced him toward Gadiel, who sat near a small fire. A hooked pole stood over the fire where a tea kettle warmed over the flames.

Gadiel motioned to a bench. "Have a seat."

"Can't I just stand?" Haskell was too nervous to sit while contemplating his death.

Gadiel again pointed at the bench.

He sat heavily and grabbed the bench seat, his fingers gripping so tightly his knuckles turned white. It was all happening too fast. Nervously, he snuck a peek down the mountain path, searching for an escape route. Maybe it wasn't too late to make a run for it.

Gadiel smiled, almost a sad, grandfatherly type of smile when you have to force your grandkid to do something unpleasant. He grabbed the teakettle and poured a small amount of hot liquid into a wooden mug. After setting the tea kettle back over the fire, Gadiel pulled three pouches from his long black jacket and sprinkled their contents into the cup.

Finally, he poured honey into the cup.

He offered it to Haskell, who reluctantly held it.

"Drink this. It will help you relax."

Haskell eyed it suspiciously. "What's in it?"

"A concoction I have found to help the Fire and Ice participants relax. You have a powerful spirit. You'll be fine. Now drink."

Haskell didn't believe the old man. If he died, would Gadiel keep the manor? Without the young baron, would King Bryce still allow Gadiel to live there? Haskell sniffed the mixture in the hot water. A pleasant scent of tea, lavender, and honey wafted to his nose.

Haskell scrutinized the men that stood around him. They had been his companions for the last three years. He had learned a lot of magic from Dakarai, and if he survived this challenge, he could learn even more. Lenny had been a friend and treated him with respect. But then there was Sims.

He blew on the hot water and took a sip of the liquid. It tasted pretty good on the first sip, but then it had a bitter aftertaste that Haskell didn't like. Haskell spent a few moments waiting for it to cool some more as four sets of eyes watched his every move.

In another five minutes, Haskell had downed the liquid and felt more relaxed. His vision seemed a little blurry, but overall, he felt less reluctant to continue the procedure.

Gadiel said, "Lenny, go to the end of the fire walk. Haskell will walk toward you. Make sure he keeps moving. Dakarai, stay with me and be his guide if he runs into trouble."

Despite feeling tranquil, Haskell heard the word trouble and thought back to Max and his walk across the coals. He tried to stand, but stumbled. Sims laughed as he caught him before he fell into the fire. A hint of fear returned to Haskell and his blood pumped furiously through his veins, leaving his hands shaking.

Gadiel said, "Sims, walk with him to the coal bed."

Sims grabbed Haskell's arm tight and pushed him toward the coals.

Haskell tried to shake Sims' grip, but couldn't. He just knew that Sims was walking him to his death as he glared at the thief.

He reached out for his magic, but Gadiel stopped him with a touch and said, "No magic. Any conjuring during the challenge puts you in extreme danger."

Haskell stumbled in the snow, but Sims held him upright. He could barely stand, and yet Gadiel expected him to walk twenty yards over burning hot coals without incident.

When they reached the edge of the coals, Gadiel told him to remove his shoes.

Haskell stared into Gadiel's eyes. The scorpion stood in the center of the pupil, daring Haskell to do or say something stupid.

Haskell removed his shoes.

Gadiel raised his hands over Haskell and placed them on his head. "The first test is fire. This will rid you of sins you have committed against others."

Gadiel motioned to Sims, and the thief released his grip on Haskell. Gadiel said, "Focus on Lenny at the end of the coals. Keep walking toward him, no matter what."

Haskell remembered how Max had just stopped while on the burning coals. Is that why he went crazy? He repeated to himself, "Keep walking, keep walking, keep walking."

Gadiel gave Haskell a gentle push in the back and Haskell stepped forward onto the red-hot coals.

CHAPTER 38

As Haskell stepped onto the glowing embers, a searing heat surged through the soles of his feet, urging him to quicken his pace across the fiery path. He stared straight ahead at Lenny, fixing his gaze on the thief. He continued his chant, "Keep moving, keep moving . . ."

Ten feet into his journey, the air turned thick with smoke, which seemed to have blossomed from nowhere. He lost sight of Lenny and his fast pulse raced even harder.

The landscape seemed to change before his eyes. No longer was he in the mountains walking across coals, but he stood back in Velidred, transported to a time before Gadiel kidnapped him. He was a young, newly orphaned boy, hungry and cold, looking for someone to help him, someone to feed him.

Haskell huddled against a building; the snow blew fiercely against his exposed skin. With a firm grip, he adjusted his thin tunic to help cover his head from the falling snow. He desired an invitation into the building he leaned against, but the owners had refused him.

The scent of apple pie blew on the breeze, and Haskell peered through a small hole in the tunic. It looked like another young orphan boy walked in the snow with something in his hands. Did he carry a fresh pie?

Haskell moved to get a better look. He adjusted his tunic to re-cover the now unprotected parts of his body.

The teen with the pie hurried past him.

Haskell followed, his stomach rumbling as desire grew within him for a piece of the pie. The piercing, wind-blown snow made it difficult to track the kid, as Haskell had to keep his eyes almost closed against the biting icy snowflakes.

The boy didn't seem to notice that Haskell followed.

Haskell hurried. No telling where he was taking the pie. Maybe it wasn't all for him. It definitely wasn't something the boy had purchased; he had stolen the pie, and Haskell wanted a piece of it. He needed to get it sooner rather than later.

He turned right at the next building, and the structure provided relief from the fierce wind. Snow swirled around Haskell, blowing off the roof, as he stalked the boy with the pie. He stopped to adjust his tunic, a difficult task while holding the pie with one hand.

Haskell stopped next to the boy and asked, "Would you like me to hold that for you?"

He gazed at Haskell in surprise. He put two hands under the pie and said, "Go away."

Haskell said, "I only want one piece."

The teen examined him. "Do you have money?"

Haskell didn't have any money. If he had money, he'd have better clothes, shoes that weren't too small for his feet, and he wouldn't be so hungry. He shook his head.

"Get away from me then." The boy quickly adjusted his tunic, shook the accumulated snow off his head, and moved away from Haskell.

Haskell followed and grabbed his shoulder. "Only one slice. It doesn't even have to be a large slice." A whiff of the pie wafted up and Haskell breathed in the aromatic bouquet.

The boy moved his shoulders, and Haskell lost his grip. The kid moved on.

"Stop." He ran after the boy.

"Get away from me or I'll call the guards."

Haskell knew the street urchin wouldn't call the guards. In weather like this, the guards would be at the castle as far from the street as possible. No. They were alone. The noise from the whistling wind would prevent any sound the boy made from traveling very far.

Haskell reached out and grabbed the pie.

The teen reacted by pulling it back toward him.

Haskell hit the kid's jaw with his hand. His hand was so frozen, pain traveled up his arms from the punch.

The boy didn't hesitate. Taller than the short and scrawny Haskell, and he had definitely eaten better than Haskell. With one mighty jab, he knocked Haskell to the ground, secured the pie in both hands, and hurried away from his attacker.

Haskell landed hard on the frozen snow. He struggled to rise, and he rolled his arm on a rock as he rose to his feet. The boy with the pie was hurrying down the street. Haskell snatched up the rock and ran after him. He didn't feel the cold or numbness in his limbs. Striving for the pie seemed to have warmed his body.

The teen had almost reached the end of the street when Haskell caught up. Without thinking, he brought the rock down hard on the boy's head and heard a crack as the rock contacted the victim's skull.

He crumpled to the snow-covered lane like a dropped sack of potatoes. The pie bounced off the snow, but remained un-spilled.

Haskell stood perfectly still as he pondered about what he had just done. The boy lay motionless in the snow. Haskell poked him with a shoe, but he didn't move. Guilt gnawed at his conscience as he grappled with the consequences of his actions, while a surge of fear and uncertainty clouded his thoughts.

The wind whistled around the buildings. Haskell studied his surroundings, although he could see little through the whirling snow. He searched the snow-covered lane, looking for witnesses, but he saw no one. Blood oozed from the boy's head into the snow.

Haskell sat down in the snow and took a slice of pie from the pan. He smelled its sweet apple and sugar fragrance and ate the slice in three quick bites, barely taking time to chew his new found food source. The pie was still warm, and it tasted like the best food he had ever eaten.

In no time at all, Haskell had finished the pie and sat numbingly satisfied in the blowing snow. Then he looked at his fellow street urchin. The kid hadn't moved since Haskell had struck him. He wondered what he should do. If the blow had killed the kid, then the authorities would find him dead in the street and might come looking for Haskell. He would end up in the gallows like his father.

As the realization of what had just happened slowly sank in, Haskell found himself frozen in shock, his trembling hands clutched his stomach which now hurt from eating so much pie so fast. His heart pounded in his chest as panic overtook his senses.

He had to get rid of the body, but he had done nothing like this before. The frozen ground would prevent him from burying it. How else could he hide the body? He had to move fast before the snow stopped blowing and people exited the comfort of their homes.

Tears welled up in his eyes as he took in the sight of the lifeless body before him. Maybe if he shook the boy, he'd wake up. Just injured. He jostled the body, tentatively at first and then with more force and intention, he pushed and pulled the cooling corpse. He never responded. His eyes didn't open, his fingers didn't move, and he made no noise.

Haskell wanted to run from the scene, but he couldn't risk being caught for murder. With a glance around at the buildings puffing out smoke from their chimneys, he made a decision. The river was maybe two hundred yards from his current location. He would have to pass houses and buildings, but in this weather, he hoped no one would see him. With icy hands, he grabbed the boy's feet and dragged the body toward the river. A trail of red followed the trench the body created in the piling snow.

The body became heavy, but Haskell hauled on, stopping briefly for breaks and to verify no one was watching his movements from the shuttered buildings he walked beside. He wished he could turn back time and talk the boy into giving him one piece of pie, but it was too late.

Eventually, he reached the river. The river had frozen on the sides, but it flowed swiftly in the middle. Now came the hard part, getting the body into the fast-moving section. He could probably push it while lying on his stomach, but he couldn't risk having the ice break beneath him. Falling into the river in this cold weather with no place to get warm would mean certain death. Haskell had to be smart.

Haskell pushed the body onto the ice. Then he went to his hands and knees, still on the snow piled on the river bank. He pushed the lifeless corpse across the ice. When he couldn't reach it any more, he edged his own body onto the ice, first just his upper torso, enough to push the street urchin a little further.

Three more times, he edged farther onto the ice and pushed. The sound of the fast-moving river and his own fear of being caught pounded in his ears. It had stopped snowing and Haskell worried someone might exit their home to run a delayed errand and catch him as the murderer he was, ditching the body in the river. By this time, Haskell's body was five feet from the bank. The dead kid's legs dangled in the moving water, but not enough to drag the body into the deep.

Sweat poured off his forehead as he pushed a little more. The body swung around as the legs caught in the water, and it seemed the body sat up for a moment. Was the kid still alive? Then the ice underneath the body cracked, and the river swallowed it as it disappeared from Haskell's view.

Haskell lay panting on the ice and cried, and an overwhelming wave of sorrow crashed over him. A thought entered his mind—*keep moving. Don't stay here on the ice, I have to keep moving. Keep moving.* Why was that thought so insistent in his mind? *Keep moving.*

CHAPTER 39

Haskell moved off the ice and walked toward the buildings. The voice in his head still told him to keep moving. A heavy fog clouded his vision. He couldn't stay in Velidred. The authorities would find the boy's body, and they would find out that Haskell had killed him. He had to keep moving. As he walked on, the fog grew less dense. The snow beneath his feet turned into red-hot coals. Sweat covered his body, and he saw a figure less than three feet before him. His eyes cleared as he recognized Lenny.

Haskell gripped Lenny's outstretched hand and his friend pulled him off the coals. He fell to his knees and his whole body shook with giant weeping sobs; his intense grief squeezed his heart to bursting. His whole body wracked with the grief of his actions so many years before. He had just relived a memory he had buried deep in his subconscious, a memory lost to that time of his life when he struggled just to stay alive.

He remembered being carried back to the tent, where Gadiel offered him a hot beverage. Haskell wrapped his hands around the wooden mug and held the steaming liquid close to his face. He thought back to that experience in Velidred as the point in time where he transitioned to Whiterock Grove.

Gadiel took a bowl from his trunk and walked over to Haskell. He dipped his thumb into an oil in the bowl and rubbed it onto Haskell's forehead. "You have completed the fire experience. You may wish to take a different path in life, but life controls you. This oil absolves you of any sins you may have committed in your previous years on the planet."

After that, Haskell lay on a bed for an hour, resting, and not resting. Thinking of the little street urchin he used to be, and knowing that the experience had haunted him these many years in his dreams. He hoped he could make better decisions in the years ahead.

Dakarai came to Haskell and said, "It's time for the next challenge."

Haskell sighed, and in an unemotional tone said, "Yeah, and what's that?"

"For me, it was a lot better than the first one."

He raised his head and stared into Dakarai's brown eyes, "Promise?"

"Promise. Now get up. Gadiel is waiting for us."

He felt exhausted, and didn't know how he could finish two more of these challenges. He trudged up the hill behind Dakarai. Gadiel sat in the night glow of a fire where two logs burned a soft orange color. Sims and Lenny sat on large logs next to their master.

Gadiel stood when Haskell arrived. "How are you doing, Boy?"

Depression held tight to Haskell's chest as he wobbled on unsteady feet. He wanted nothing more than to stop this ordeal and go home and sleep for a month. He answered, "I'm fine. What's next?"

Gadiel's black eyes seemed to bore into Haskell's. He grabbed Haskell's chin and said, "Look at me. Be present if you want to survive this next test. I usually lose most of my students during the smoke challenge. Are you up for it?"

Haskell bobbed his head. *No, I'm not up for it. The old man is right, and I'm not ready for any of this.* A shiver ran down his spine, sending a chill through his body despite the warmth of the nearby fire. He was through with this process. Why bother going on? He would probably just die anyway. "We should have waited until I was older."

"We can't stop the process now. You either finish it or you die."

"Just let me die."

Gadiel slapped Haskell across the face.

Haskell snapped to attention. "Why did you do that?" Blood trickled from the corner of his mouth and dribbled down his chin.

"Listen. It's important for you to survive this process. Our futures are entwined, and if you die, then I will die."

Haskell laughed, "Then you better not kill me with these stupid games you play." What did the old man mean their lives are entwined?

"They aren't games. This is an age-old tradition, handed down by wizards for hundreds of years. You will grow stronger and use your magic more successfully by finishing the challenge. Do you hear me? You must finish."

Haskell raised his hand to block another anticipated strike from Gadiel, but the old man didn't move. He relaxed as a sense of resolve settled over him. "Okay. What do I do?"

Gadiel directed a studied gaze upon Haskell and then finally said to the others, "Prepare the smokers."

Sims took two pieces of coal from the fire and placed them on an incense burner. Lenny retrieved a leather pouch from his tunic pocket and poured a healthy mixture of the bag into the hot coals on the incense burner. A dense, sweet-smelling smoke drifted from the burner.

Gadiel fingered a small vial and poured its contents into a mug, which already contained heated water. He let it sit for a moment then handed it to Haskell. "Drink this."

Haskell placed his nose near the mixture and took in a waft of floral tea. He tilted his head back and chugged the mixture in one large gulp. The liquid was a little hot, but it went down smooth until the very end. He gagged and tried to spit it out, but to no avail.

"Ugh. Is that sour milk?"

Dakarai laughed. "Yeah, that's what I thought it tasted like."

Haskell slapped his fingers across his tongue, but the taste lingered in his throat.

Gadiel grabbed the incense burner from Sims and stood in front of Haskell. He swung the censer side to side. The incense wafted toward Haskell; the potent scent filled his nose.

"Breathe deeply and think of those people who are still alive that you care about."

There was only one person in Haskell's life that he cared about, Princess Noreen. He thought of her laughing green eyes and pictured her flowing red hair. He felt a little dizzy as the smoke enveloped him. The landscape seemed to rotate around him; he saw the fire, then the mountains, and then a castle. He recognized the Goodwin castle in Whiterock Grove. The scene spun around him again: fire, mountains and castle. Haskell took another deep breath. Once more fire, mountains and castle. Then the spinning stopped. Haskell stood at the steps of the Goodwin castle.

He donned a brown doublet, featuring large gold stripes across the arms, and intricately woven gold threading across the chest, embellished with white pearls at each intersection of the diamond pattern of the fabric. A frilly lace collar encircled his neck with a lace cuff. His pants were the most extravagant pants he had ever seen, brown puffy material with gold stripes that ran vertically down the legs. *What kind of madness is this?*

Gadiel, dressed all in black, stood by his side. He touched Haskell's arm, "You must go inside the castle, Baron."

Castle guards lined the ten stairs to the castle entrance doors. This felt like a dream to Haskell. It couldn't be real. Another nudge from Gadiel and Haskell stepped up the stairs and into the castle foyer. It was like another world, different from all the times Haskell had been in the castle. Great drapes of fabric ran from the enormous staircase twenty feet to the foyer floor. The strips alternated the Goodwin colors of green and white. Five golden chandeliers with fifty candles each hung from the ceiling, lighting up the floor of people.

Many people stood in small clusters, and the sounds of everyone talking made it difficult for Haskell to even make sense of what he was seeing.

Gadiel leaned close to Haskell's ear. "I have to spend time with the servants tonight and I won't be able to be by your side. This is Princess Noreen's party. Mingle with the lords and ladies in the room, be sure to address the king the way Carl taught you, and dance with Noreen. Remember, you are no longer an orphaned street urchin, you are Baron Haskell, and you need to impress the young princess. For both our sakes. Can you do that?"

Haskell rubbed his face with both hands. He didn't think he was ready to dance with the princess. He wished for a few more days of practice. He nodded at Gadiel.

A bell sounded and Gadiel drifted away.

Following the king's guests through a hallway, Haskell patiently waited in line for his turn to be presented to the king, queen, and their daughters. He worried that the other guests would see the scared street urchin instead of the mighty Baron Haskell.

In a few minutes, he stood next to the courtier, who waited a moment and said, "I present Baron Haskell of Oak Ridge."

Haskell's mind went numb. All the practice and education that Carl had taught him flew from his head. He just stood next to the courtier, unsure of what to do next.

The courtier pushed him slightly in the back toward the king, and Haskell's legs moved on their own. He reached the king and remembered to bow at the waist and to look into the king's eyes. "Your Majesty."

King Bryce turned to his wife, the queen. "This is the young boy that rescued Noreen."

Blood rushed to Haskell's face as he relished the kind words the king said. He next turned to the queen, bowed, and said, "Your Royal Highness." He noticed the queen's green eyes and immediately thought of Princess Noreen.

They talked to him, but he truly didn't hear a word they said as fear of making a mistake numbed his mind. Eventually, they passed him down to the king's son and the two princesses. First, he met Princess Carol, a blue-eyed blond, who favored her father's complexion. She said nice things to him, but he kept trying to sneak a peek at Noreen.

"Okay, Carol, you've bored him enough." Noreen said, "There are others that need to go through the line."

Carol smiled at Haskell and he moved over to the most beautiful woman in the kingdom, Princess Noreen. He almost forgot to bow, and when he did, she stuck out a hand toward him. What was he supposed to do with that? Carl didn't warn him about this behavior. He looked questioningly at the princess, who puckered her lips.

Did she just blow me a kiss? Was that a message? Suddenly, it hit him. He again felt his face go red. He tenderly touched the girl's fingers, lowered his lips to her hand, and kissed the back of her hand. This was the most exciting moment of his life. When he looked back at Noreen, she had a silly grin on her face, which was as red as Haskell's felt.

He looked longingly into her emerald eyes and wanted to hold her in his arms. Princess Carol cleared her throat and motioned for Haskell to move away from the royal family. He smiled once more at Princess Noreen and stepped into the grand ballroom.

He found a place out of the way of the other guests where he could see Princess Noreen and still watch the interactions of others within the room. Every once in a while, she would glance in his direction and smile.

He felt lightheaded at these intimate moments. It seemed like forever until a small contingent of musicians commenced playing. At first the king and queen danced, just the two of them. Then a tall gentleman asked Princess Carol to dance, and an olive-skinned man asked Princess Noreen to dance. Haskell thought the man was a few years older than the princess.

Haskell's body heated with jealousy. This man wasn't supposed to dance with her, she was only supposed to dance with him.

A small group of three men and two women stood next to Haskell. He asked, "Who is that dancing with Princess Noreen?"

One woman said, "Oh, that is Prince Jordan of Kalluria. Isn't he a talented dancer?"

The other woman whispered rather loudly, "And good looking."

Haskell murmured, "Yeah, I suppose." He watched the prince twirl and waltz with the princess. The man had impeccable form, and Noreen seemed to truly enjoy the experience. She smiled and moved effortlessly with the music, staring at the man's eyes the whole time. The man was tall and muscular, all the traits Haskell didn't have. *I can't compete for the princess' hand with someone like that.*

The two of them danced three dances before other men lined up to dance with the princess. She would steal a glance at Haskell now and then, but he was too afraid to step up to dance with her. He hadn't practiced nearly enough. He always pictured just him and Noreen, alone in a room, with no one else to watch them.

The night grew late, and a serving girl stopped by Haskell. She said, "Your servant man wants to see you." She pointed to the doorway where Gadiel stood.

Haskell bowed his head. Gadiel wouldn't be happy.

When Haskell reached Gadiel, the man said, "Have you danced with Noreen?"

"No."

"Why not?"

"I'm not good enough."

Gadiel squeezed Haskell's arm. "Look at me."

The red scorpion floated across Gadiel's eye. Haskell stared at the little creature. He felt a presence within, and then a voice. "You must dance with the princess. We are running out of time."

When Haskell returned to the ballroom, he noticed that some of the royalty had retired for the evening and the room was less crowded. He searched for Princess Noreen. She was dancing with Prince Jordan again and appeared to be enjoying every second of the dance.

He heard Gadiel's voice in his head. "Dance with the princess."

The music stopped and before the next song started, Haskell walked over to the princess and prince. He tapped the prince on the back. "May I have the next dance?"

Prince Jordan looked down his nose at Haskell and then looked at Noreen. The princess nodded, and the prince moved away.

The music started up and Haskell took Princess Noreen's hands. He took the appropriate pose for the dance as the music began. If he looked at his feet, then he didn't have any problems, but any time he wanted to look at the princess, he lost his count and stumbled. She smiled as if nothing was wrong.

It was a complicated dance and required them to change partners four times as they sashayed around the dance floor. Of all the dances for him to dance with the princess, this was the worst choice. He moved, not in any kind of rhythm, and he suspected Prince Jordan stood against a wall laughing at him.

The song was coming to a close, and Haskell suspected when he grasped Noreen's hands that this might be the last chance he would have this evening to impress her. Carl had taught him to forget his feet and look into his dance partner's eyes. So, he concentrated on her eyes and ignored his steps and the count of the song.

Her skin was smooth and beautiful. She smiled at Haskell and her green eyes beckoned him. He lost count of his steps, moved out of rhythm, stepped on Noreen's right foot, at which point he stumbled and fell, brought her to the floor, and she fell on top of him.

The music stopped as the crowd gasped. Prince Jordan walked toward them.

Haskell repeated over and over, "I'm sorry. I'm sorry."

"Oh, it's nothing. It happens all the time." She smiled at him.

Prince Jordan arrived and helped her to her feet.

He said, "We don't normally allow vagabonds to dance with Kalluria's princesses. Let's get you a drink, my princess, and make sure you're all right." He escorted Princess Noreen off the dance floor, but she turned her head to Haskell, winked and smiled, then continued with the prince.

Haskell slowly got off the floor and brushed off his pants and doublet with his hands. He tried to get a glimpse of Noreen, but the prince had firmly escorted her somewhere else, somewhere safer, away from the bumbling street urchin in fancy clothes.

Another song started and Haskell moved to the doorway. It was time to leave the castle and forget about ever being with Noreen.

A heavy smoke encapsulated him and when it cleared, he stood in front of Gadiel, who gently swung the censer back and forth. He smiled. "Good, you returned. I was worried."

Haskell hung his head. "It was the most humiliating experience of my life." The experience had felt so real to him. *Certainly, I won't act like that at an actual event with the princess.* In the back of his mind, he wasn't so sure. He grappled with feelings of embarrassment, guilt, and self-doubt, questioning his worth as the Baron of Oak Ridge.

Gadiel handed the incense to Sims, and Lenny handed Gadiel a small metal tin. The old man pulled the lid from its base dipped his thumb into the red cream, and made three marks on Haskell's face. One long mark across his forehead, another beneath his right eye, and the third across the beard on his chin.

"Let the goddess of Velidred heal you from your sins. May you learn from your mistakes in the present day to guide you to a better future."

CHAPTER 40

Haskell sat on a bench next to the fire, reliving the smoke experience over and over in his mind. He couldn't believe he had tripped while dancing and pulled Princess Noreen to the floor. Did this show an actual future, or a future he could control if he prepared better? Assuming he survived the last challenge, he planned to take his dance lessons more seriously than he had before. But more than that, he wondered if he was worthy of dancing with royalty. The comments Prince Jordan made had struck home, reminding him he was nothing more than a thieving, lying blacksmith's son.

Gadiel came and sat next to Haskell. "Are you ready for the last challenge?"

Fatigued wracked his body, and he hated that all the challenges so far ended in tragic circumstances. Haskell didn't know if he could handle another challenge that showed his true nature and ineptitude. "Is there any chance this last experience will be better?"

Gadiel gave a flat smile. "There is no way to predict what the challenge will show the participant. It is in the hands of the Velidred moon goddess."

Haskell looked at the full moon of Velidred, casting its red glow over the mountain snow. He silently whispered, "Make this last one a pleasant one, please."

"Is the ice ready?" The old man looked over at Sims.

"Yes, Sir."

The old man sprinkled powder on Haskell's head. "The ice challenge is the last test and allows you to foresee a future sin against your fellow man. Strip to your small-clothes."

Haskell sighed. It was already cold and now Gadiel wanted him to take off his clothes. This can't be good, he thought. He was already shivering when Gadiel handed him a hot tea infused with honey. He held it close to his body for warmth before taking a sip.

Haskell drank half of the liquid, his gut tying itself in knots.

Gadiel proclaimed it time to proceed to the ice.

They hurried down a path that led to a meadow lake. Haskell saw his breath in the moon's red light and wondered what might be next on Gadiel's torture campaign. When they reached the lake, Lenny and Sims tied a rope around his waist.

"What's this for?" he asked.

Gadiel answered, "To help you out of the water in case . . . you run into problems."

Haskell shivered at the implication. "I thought the second challenge was the one that caused death and physical problems."

"They all cause death, so be careful, and keep working your way back to the surface."

Haskell looked at the lake and noticed the hole that had been cut in the ice. He grabbed Gadiel's arm.

"You can't be serious. You're gonna push me into the freezing cold water?"

Gadiel ignored his question. "Is he secured?"

Sims and Lenny nodded.

"Submerge him."

Sims and Lenny both took hold of one of Haskell's arms and threw him in the opened hole in the lake ice.

He hit the water hard and at a strange angle, and the water stung his face. He gasped at the cold temperature of the water and bobbed up for air. When he breached the surface, Sims pressed his head under the water. He struggled for as long as he could against the hand that held him firmly underwater, but finally succumbed to the water.

Dizziness overwhelmed Haskell as he realized Gadiel planned to kill him. Of course! Haskell should have seen it coming. The old man must have known that Haskell had more magic than his mentor and Gadiel would die once Haskell knew more about the business, so that he could run it himself. It was too late now. The time had come for him to join his parents in the shadow of Velidred, the resting place of the dead.

Haskell stopped flailing. Bubbles surrounded him in the dark water and when they cleared, he found himself in a room. Had he reached the shadowland so soon? He sat on a richly appointed throne that he recognized. Yes, this was the Velidred Castle's throne room, where King Stonegate sat on the day he sentenced Haskell's mother to the dungeon. He wondered if he was allowed to sit on the throne.

Lenny, Dakarai, and Sims stood before him.

Haskell realized he was king now, and said, "I've learned that my wife plans to leave the castle tonight with my daughter and Cugbert, the priest."

Dakarai said, "Where did you hear that, Your Majesty? We've no news of that."

Haskell pounded his hand hard on the chair arm. "I have my sources."

"Let us check our own sources. Maybe your sources heard wrong."

Haskell rose. "My sources are not wrong."

Sims asked, "Do you want us to kill Queen Noreen, Your Majesty?"

Haskell yelled, "No, I don't want you to touch the queen. Cugbert is the troublemaker. Capture him, hurt him, and throw him in the dungeon where he can rot and die." Haskell studied Sims. He had that look that he always got when he planned to do something stupid.

Haskell turned his attention to Dakarai. "Do you understand the task?"

"Yes!"

"Then you're responsible for any actions Sims takes to disrupt my direct orders."

Dakarai stared at Sims for a moment and then sighed, "Yes, we will follow your directions to the letter, Your Majesty."

Haskell talked them through the plan, as described to him by his young daughter, before dismissing them. He rubbed his hands across his face as he saw

Sims leave with that stupid look he always wore. He trusted Dakarai to get it right.

####

Haskell waited by the castle window. He had extinguished all the candles in the room so he could see outside and watch his men take down Cugbert. The carriage had arrived, and they had convinced the driver to park it in a different place than originally planned. The new location would allow him to watch everything unfold as they stopped Noreen's escape and captured Cugbert.

He couldn't understand why she thought it necessary to escape. They had been married for several years and he thought she was happy. What had happened to their relationship?

Haskell saw movement below and recognized the three figures scurrying along the castle wall. Cugbert led Noreen and his daughter toward the carriage. They stopped at the wall's edge surprised that the carriage wasn't in the planned position. Haskell smiled. *You won't escape easily from me, my love, and especially with my daughter.*

Suddenly, he saw Noreen and the child run toward the carriage. A figure stood up behind the carriage and nocked an arrow. It looked like Sims planned to take the shot. That was okay, he was skilled with a bow and arrow.

Haskell couldn't wait to see the look on Noreen's face when the arrow sliced through Cugbert's body, and the next day, when the guillotine finished the priest with a thwack.

The scene played out in slow motion. Noreen ran and their child worked hard to keep pace. Sims released his shot, and the arrow reflected the little light from the moon in the sky as it flew toward its target.

Haskell took his attention from the arrow and stared at Cugbert, waiting to see the priest fall to the ground. He heard a scream and expected Cugbert to fall, but the man still stood. The scream came from a woman. His stomach dropped as if he had thrown himself off the tower.

He glanced back at his wife, who lay prone on the ground, his daughter standing over her. Cugbert ran away from the woman he was helping to escape.

"No, this can't be happening! This is wrong." Haskell hurried down the stairs, half-way down, he tripped, fell over several stairs, and hit his head on the landing below.

Haskell gained consciousness as someone hauled his body out of the icy water and dragged him ten feet across the ice using the ropes tied around his waist. He struggled to get his breath and finally expelled water and took a deep gasp of oxygen, filling his lungs.

Gadiel stood over him.

Haskell said, "Will any of it come true?"

While Haskell was still wet and cold, Sims and Lenny dragged him over to the fire. Haskell thought it was to help warm him up before he put his clothes back on, but instead they pushed him face down to the cold, wet, muddy ground.

Gadiel pulled on a pair of leather gloves and yanked a branding iron from the fire. He asked, "Leg or back?"

Haskell sucked in air, dumbfounded at the question. "What does that mean?"

Sims laughed. "The brand, you fool. Where do you want the brand?"

Haskell's eyes went wide as he realized what was about to occur. The iron Gadiel had pulled from the fire glowed a bright orange and yellow, sizzling in the frigid mountain air.

Haskell shouted, "No! You can't brand me like an animal. That's inhumane."

Gadiel said, "As long as you're already on your stomach, I'll put in on your shoulder."

Haskell struggled, but Sims and Lenny pinned him tight.

Gadiel pressed the hot iron into Haskell's shoulder.

Haskell screamed as the smell of burning flesh wafted into the air.

Sims laughed.

Anger filled him, as he struggled to get to his feet, to show Sims how it felt to have the hot iron against your body.

Gadiel said, "You have survived the fire and ice challenge. You are ready for more responsibility and are now a member of a small and powerful group of wizards. Your brand marks you as one of us. Now bow before your master."

Haskell found himself in a state of confusion. He was glad the challenge was over, but who was his master? He struggled to stand.

Sims kicked him in the gut. "Bow before Gadiel, you fool."

Haskell realized the reality of the challenge. The brand showed that he belonged to Gadiel, just like the sheep and cattle of the iron brands made by his father. Well, it wouldn't be for long because he had plans to escape Gadiel's evil ways, become a respected king, and marry the princess.

Haskell raised a hand before Sims could hit him again. "Okay, let me get to my knees." He negotiated the muddy terrain, moving his wet and stiff body to kneel before Gadiel. He bowed his head in allegiance.

Sims laughed. "The great and mighty orphan king is now sealed to Gadiel, his master."

CHAPTER 41

Three days after the fire and ice challenge, Haskell still felt the pain of the branding. Haskell was practicing his dancing again, under the watchful eyes of the manor servant, Carl. Since he returned to the manor, Haskell had worked hard to learn how to dance, hoping that he wouldn't disappoint Noreen if he ever danced with her. It was imperative that he didn't trip or stumble when he had the opportunity to win her heart. For the moment he remembered back to his fire and ice challenge and his failure at dancing.

Haskell came out of his reverie when Carl said something, "What?" He had become so lost in his thoughts that he wasn't paying attention to the moves Carl had been teaching.

"You didn't make the right move after you dipped her under the outstretched arms of the others. You must concentrate."

"Yeah, yeah. I understand. Let's do it again."

The servant girl seemed to enjoy the chance to dance with him, but he gave her no reason to think that it was any more than a business encounter to help him reach a goal.

Sims walked into the great room Haskell had commandeered as a practice hall. "Ooh, the mighty Haskell is learning to dance like a proper member of the royal ruling class."

"What are you doing here?" Haskell asked in a near shout.

Sims said, "Oh, your master won't be happy if he finds out you're yelling at me."

"I don't care what he says. I'm the baron here." Haskell marched from the room and shouted, "Gadiel."

He walked three doors down the hallway and found Gadiel sitting at his business desk. Gadiel looked up when Haskell entered the room.

Haskell slammed the door shut. "I want him gone from here. Like I told you before, I don't want Sims anywhere near me."

Gadiel smirked. "I need the young fellow for a project I have planned. You'll want him to be with you for this venture."

Haskell leaned over Gadiel's desk until he was in his face. "I want him gone."

Gadiel leaned closer to Haskell and said, "He stays. You may be a baron, but in my eyes, you're still a boy."

"As baron, you bow to me, not the other way around."

Then what felt like a million strikes of lightning struck at Haskell's core. He shook for three seconds and then dropped like a rag doll to the floor. Haskell lay on the floor wondering what had hit him. He took in huge gasps of air as he evaluated the situation.

Gadiel came and stood over him. "I had been looking for an opportunity to test our connection. It appears very strong. Very strong, indeed."

Haskell didn't move, but just stared up at Gadiel. "What did you do to me? How?"

"It's our connection from the fire and ice challenge. We're . . . interconnected, so to speak. I have a connection to make sure you understand who the master is in our relationship. Now, get off the floor, and let's talk about a project I have outlined for you."

Gadiel opened the door and said, "Lenny, Sims, get in here."

Sims quickly entered the room as if he had been standing just outside the door. "Boss."

"You and Haskell have a job to do. We need to raise the taxes on the local businesses."

Haskell asked, "Why should we do that? The local tax structure has worked for quite a while, according to Carl."

Gadiel quietly said, "It was enough for the Jorgensen's, but we have a bigger need than they had."

"What do you mean, we have a bigger need?" Haskell asked.

Gadiel said, "He was a minor lord. The services required of the minor lords are less than what the king expects from a baron."

Haskell rolled his eyes. "What do you think the king expects of us? Of me?"

Gadiel changed his voice as if he were talking with someone that wasn't very intelligent, "To begin with, you have the ability to take land from the landowners who don't pay their taxes. You need men who will administer those taxes. You, my young baron, are expected to contribute to the king's financial needs."

"The king's financial needs? He has more money than I have. Why should I give him some of mine?"

Sims snorted a laugh. "When you tax your landowners, the king is owed part of that money. It's all a business decision and part of the contract."

Haskell felt like an idiot as Sims talked about his obligations to the king. His face heated as Sims berated his knowledge of being a baron. He wanted to throw a bolt of fire at him. If anyone else had told him this information, it wouldn't bother him nearly as much.

Gadiel went on with Haskell's education. "The king will expect you to build and finance a small military service and supply soldiers to him as necessary."

Haskell thought back to the village mayor who had arranged Princess Noreen's escort from the Jorgensen's manor. Did that military group now come under his jurisdiction? He wondered what they might expect from him. He pictured himself riding to the castle to see the princess with fifty to a hundred men escorting him, riding horses and carrying shields and swords. They'd all wear the same uniform, representing his colors. He wished his parents could see him riding before a military escort, the people admiring him and his position of power.

Gadiel must have noticed Haskell consuming the information, and he waited a moment. "You'll tax these people. I've looked over the Jorgensen's books and we have rents to collect for some lands. We'll have to talk with the mayor to see if you'll be responsible for maintaining order and making decisions on legal matters between the people."

Haskell looked at Gadiel and smiled. "I'll be delivering justice to the people." He stood a little straighter as he imagined townspeople coming to him to settle disputes.

Gadiel said, "You now see the need to bring more revenue into the manor. Lenny and Sims will help us collect and administer the accounts; they've practiced the same techniques back in Whiterock Grove."

Sims pounded his fist into his hand. "I love collections."

Haskell didn't like the idea of having Sims around in the manor. He didn't know why Gadiel kept the thief around. It seemed he always did the wrong thing at the wrong time. *When I take the real power in this operation, Sims will be gone for good.*

Gadiel held up a sheet of paper. "Here is a list of the people that pay taxes to you. I made two columns. One column shows what they used to pay Lord Jorgensen and the other column the amount they will now owe you. It is your responsibility as Baron of this land to introduce yourself to all the landowners and tell them their new taxes. Take Lenny and Sims with you and you won't have any problems."

# # # #

Haskell dressed up in his finest outfit that he felt would reflect his new position as baron. He had thought that now he was baron, he wouldn't have to force other people to give him money, like he had when he worked Gadiel's extortion gambit on the local businesses in Whiterock Grove. He realized now that the taxes the king enforced on his kingdom really were a form of legalized extortion of the kingdom's people.

Haskell mounted his horse and Lenny and Sims joined him as they threaded their horses between rows of bushes to reach Haskell's location near the barn's entrance. With a wave of his hand, the two thugs followed him down the road to collect the king's taxes and tell all the businesses about their new tax rates. It was a conversation he wasn't excited to have with the locals.

The first stop they made was at the blacksmith's shop. The day had warmed, and cirrus clouds streaked across the sky in long white lines in sharp contrast to the blue background. Stopping at the blacksmith's brought back memories of Haskell's youth growing up in his father's smithy.

They dismounted and stood in front of the small hut-like structure. The blacksmith's shop was less than half the size of Haskell's father's place. This far from the kingdom's castle, the man didn't get any royal business and had to depend on his income from local farmers and the small army the village could roust when needed.

The blacksmith noticed them standing near the building's entrance and looked up from his work. He straightened his spine and then knuckled his back. A move Haskell had seen his father make a hundred times a day. Smudges blackened the man's face, and his leather apron had experienced a lot of wear over the years.

"What do you need?" he said as a way of greeting.

Haskell cleared his throat and said, "I'm here to introduce myself. I'm the new baron in the village, Baron Haskell."

The blacksmith snorted and took a metal ladle hanging from the edge of a barrel, dipped it into the barrel, and brought the ladle filled with water to his lips. Some water spilled onto his chin as he drank.

After the blacksmith finished a long drink, he stared at Haskell. "I'd heard that Lord Jorgenson had legal problems, and they executed him. I expected the village to get a new lord." He turned back to his forge. "Mighty young to be a baron. The boy's father must be the king's brother," he muttered under his breath.

Haskell wondered if he should tell the man that his father had been a blacksmith? He decided the man didn't need to know that bit of information. It seemed better to let him believe he had arrived at his position by birth.

Sims spoke for him. "It doesn't matter how Baron Haskell became baron. We need to talk to you about money."

Haskell's chest tightened as he looked at Sims with a stern, disapproving glance. If he was baron, he couldn't let a low-life like Sims take control. He shook his head in anger. "Shut up, Sims."

Sims turned as if he was ready to beat up Haskell right there in front of the blacksmith. His face reddened, and the thug tightened his fists.

Haskell's lips pressed tight. Sims didn't know how to act around real people.

The blacksmith sighed. "Well, I'm guessing you're not here to ask me to dinner. What can I do for you?"

Haskell had never found it easy to ask people for money. It seemed to come easy to Sims and Lenny and they never tired of using force to get Gadiel's ill-gotten coins. Haskell tried to reason with people, but Sims would just come out and beat them until they gave him the money, and sometimes he asked for a little more.

Haskell explained, "Like you said, Lord Jorgenson is no longer in the manor. King Goodwin has appointed me baron, and I take the responsibility seriously. As baron, the king is asking us to give him more money than he asked of the lord." Haskell looked at the smithy's dirt floor and scratched the dirt with his recently polished boot. "We'll have to raise your taxes to meet the king's demands."

The blacksmith pulled the metal rod he was heating out of the fire and examined it.

Haskell pulled out the scroll Gadiel had given him, and laboriously ran his finger down the paper until he found the name Richardson. "You're Richardson, right?"

The blacksmith said, "At your service, My Lord." He bowed at Haskell, but it seemed in mockery not respect.

"It says here that you will be responsible for . . ." Haskell looked once again at the figure and read it to the blacksmith.

A desperate look crossed Richardson's face. "That seems excessive, My Lord. I assure you, I'm an honest, law-abiding citizen. I pay my taxes and follow all the regulations. I cannot afford to give additional funds. Please reconsider."

Sims stepped forward. "You don't worry whether or not it's excessive. The baron has told you the amount, and we want the money right now."

Richardson backed up closer to a table where several tools lay ready for use. He placed his hand on a hammer's handle. "There's no need to threaten me."

Sims moved closer to the blacksmith.

Richardson picked up the hammer and stood his ground.

Haskell felt his body tense and his body sweated in his fancy jacket. In every situation, Sims managed to make it worse than necessary. "Sims, stand down."

Sims withdrew a sword from the sheave that hung from his belt.

Haskell shouted, "Sims, stand down."

Sims raised the sword.

Haskell chanted a spell, "Ut telum ab invasore." The sword flew from Sims' hand and landed behind Haskell, sticking in the dirt. "I told you to stand down. Get over here. Now."

Sims scowled at Haskell, shot a threatening stare at the blacksmith, but returned to stand next to Lenny.

Richardson smirked and said, "It's difficult to find good help these days, My Lord."

It seemed like a heavy iron block balanced on Haskell's head. This situation was already stressful and Sims' aggressive behavior increased the tension in the hot hut. He thought back to the pain Gadiel had caused him earlier in the day and realized he needed to get this money.

Haskell said, "I give you two days to get the agreed-upon amount."

Richardson shook his head. "I'm a king's man and I will pay my fair share. It's just I haven't budgeted to be taxed at that amount. I need a week to come up with the money."

Haskell knew if he gave the man a week, Gadiel would punish him. Even the two days might cause him to be punished. The blacksmith would come to realize that he held the title of a baron and was not a child of some wealthy lord who could be pushed around. "I will send Sims to retrieve the monies in two days. I suggest you have it."

CHAPTER 42

Six months later, Haskell stood in Gadiel's office watching the old man count the day's collected taxes. His mind was only partially on the coins and precious metals that littered the man's desk.

Gadiel reached a stopping place in his counting and entered numbers into the opened scroll. The businesses had agreed to the higher taxes, and it seemed to Haskell that the manor had plenty of income coming in for both the king and the manor's needs. Gadiel, though, made sure Haskell saw none of the money.

Sims came into the room with a leather pouch that clinked with coin. He smiled and said, "The baker and the miller had worked together to not give us the extra money due to the baron."

Gadiel looked up from his note taking.

Sims said, "It seems after refusing to pay the new taxes, that the baker's eldest son had an accident that broke his arm. It looked pretty bad to me."

Gadiel only grunted.

Sims clinked the pouch in his hand. "After the accident, they decided to pay after all. I also found out that the miller has a couple of attractive daughters."

Haskell shook his head. "You can't go on beating up all the hard-working people that owe us money. If workers can't work because you cripple them, they can't make their goods, and then they can't pay us."

Sims sneered. "We're doing your job for you. Be thankful we can secure the taxes as outlined by law."

Haskell rolled his eyes. The man was a no-good thug. "Gadiel, is there any way to teach this low life better ways to get our taxes?"

Gadiel held out his hand to Sims for the leather pouch.

Sims handed it over.

Gadiel weighed the pouch on a scale and noted something in the scroll. "It looks like his methods are quite adequate."

Sims derided Haskell, "You heard the man. My methods are quite adequate."

Gadiel added, "It's a proven method for getting payment from your subjects. Look at what happened to Lord Jorgenson. He tried to do something illegal and lost his manor and his life from his mistake."

Haskell responded in disbelief, "His mistake? You're the one that sold the princess to him. If it wasn't for you and your kidnapping of the princess, he wouldn't have died."

Pain rippled through Haskell, dropping him to his knees as Gadiel sent a low-level punishment through his body.

Gadiel calmly replied, "We agreed to never mention the kidnapping."

When Haskell got his breath back, he stood, bowed to Gadiel and said, "I'm sorry."

"That's better." Gadiel poured out the contents of the pouch and verified the coins were proper for the owed taxes. "You see that we have doubled the amount of income into the manor. You are becoming quite the successful little baron."

Sims said, "I forgot to mention some important news I heard in the village. Princess Noreen has a special male visitor in the castle for the next two weeks." He turned toward Haskell and grinned. "Do you want to know who it is?"

Haskell's heart pounded just hearing the princess' name, and it doubled in beats per minute when Sims mentioned a male visitor. He tried to maintain a calm exterior, but when Sims baited him like this, he normally lost the control he wanted.

Sims asked, "Well, do you?"

Haskell smirked and tried to act casual. "Just tell me."

Sims waggled his eyebrows twice. "The male visitor is the very eligible Kallurian bachelor, Prince Jordan. His whole family is at the castle, and rumor has it a marriage certificate is being drawn up during their stay."

The news almost sent Haskell to the floor. He felt just as devastated as when Gadiel struck him with the awful shocks through the connection with his branding. *This can't be happening. The princess cares nothing about Prince Jordan. She loves me.*

Haskell said, "I've got to get over to Goodwin Castle."

Sims laughed at Haskell. "You're like a lost puppy. 'I've got to get over to the Goodwin Castle,'" he mocked.

Haskell opened and closed his fists as he tried to contain his anger with Sims and the devastating news. He had to do something.

"You're nothing to the princess," Sims said. "She doesn't even know who you are."

Haskell knew that wasn't true. If he could get over to the castle and see her again, then they could get to know each other better. "Come on Gadiel. I can take our taxes over to the king and he can see what a great job I'm doing as baron."

Sims scoffed. "Job you're doing? I'm the one collecting the money. Without me, you're nobody. The local businesses would kick you into the mud if you collected the money. I have a better chance with Noreen than you do."

Haskell launched himself at Sims, but before he made contact, Gadiel sent the pain of a thousand pins and needles all throughout his body. Haskell fell to the floor. His breath came back slowly and in huge gasps. He couldn't expect to go through life with this pain any time he did something Gadiel didn't like.

"Have a seat and we can discuss this like reasonable adults," Gadiel ordered.

Haskell struggled to his feet and staggered to the chair. "I've got to get over to the Goodwin castle and see the princess."

"It's time for you to sit down and listen to the facts of life between you and royalty." Gadiel sat back in his chair. "You're young and don't realize how these relationships work. The reason the king is pursuing a member of the Kallurian royal family is because a marriage between the princess and the prince will provide value to King Goodwin."

Gadiel moved the coins on his desk to a lockbox that sat on the floor.

"Prince Goodwin has always been afraid that King Stoneforge of Velidred might attack him and try to take over his kingdom. A real possibility. Velidred has a powerful army, the power of the Council of Nine, and King Stoneforge is known for his aggressive behavior to surrounding kingdoms. An attack by Velidred might spell doom to the Goodwin kingdom."

King Stoneforge's name made Haskell's blood pressure rise. The man had killed his father for no good reason and Haskell planned to get revenge for his father's and mother's death someday.

Gadiel rubbed his dry, parched hands together as if they needed warming. "Now, if Goodwin could form an alliance with King Kalluria, they would make a formidable opponent to Velidred. The black castle of Velidred would be between two kingdoms that have an alliance. It would be difficult for the king to fight on two fronts at once." He leaned forward on his desk. "You're a baron, Boy, and you're already a member of the Goodwin kingdom, which means you can offer nothing new to King Goodwin."

Haskell's ego deflated, and his shoulders slumped. "But we have tax monies for the king. If I show him the money, then he'll realize I'm a big help to him, and worthy of having his daughter's hand in marriage."

"The king has a man like Sims in his employ," Gadiel said. "In fact, if we didn't give the king his fair share of the money we collect, then he would send an army to collect the money from us. How will you stand up to an army, Boy?"

Sims parroted Gadiel, "How would you stand up to an army, Boy?"

As waves of frustration rolled over him, Haskell shouted, "Shut up, Sims!"

Gadiel raised his voice, "Both of you. Relax."

Haskell couldn't give up and pressed his point. "Is there anything I can do to make King Goodwin want to wed his daughter to me? I can raise an army to protect the king from the evil king at Velidred. In fact, I'll raise an army and take over Velidred myself."

Gadiel smirked, "Do you remember that the Council of Nine is searching for you and wants to either execute you or take away your magic? If it wasn't for me, they would have already found you."

Haskell had forgotten that. He practiced his magic every day with Dakarai but hadn't actually used the skill outside of the manor, except that one time when he wanted to keep Sims at bay with the blacksmith. He had magic with knowledge now, but he wasn't as skilled as he needed to be with the master wizards at Velidred Castle.

Haskell hung his head. "What can I do?"

Gadiel said, "You're a baron of the land, and if the king has important visitors, then normally a baron is welcome to visit and meet the visitors. There are parties and other social events, and maybe you can talk with the princess."

"Yeah, that would be great." His face lightened with a smile as hope bloomed in his chest. "We should do that."

Gadiel raised his hand. "Stop! Don't get your hopes up." He stared with unfeeling eyes at Haskell. "You have nothing to offer the king. The girl may have affections for you, but she will marry whomever her father tells her to marry."

CHAPTER 43

Haskell's nerves worked overtime as his body tingled in anticipation of seeing Princess Noreen once more. Gadiel had used his influence to get an invitation to the Goodwin Castle while Prince Jordan and his family were being entertained at the castle.

He had worked extra hard on the dance moves the last two days, while Gadiel worked his contacts to get the invitation. Now he wore his finest doublet, the one that had a red background with yellow scrolls of needlework that added color and interest to the jacket as he waited to see Princess Noreen.

The young baron had one more door to enter, and he would again see the beautiful princess. His heart raced in his chest; it beat so hard he was sure it would break his ribs. He rubbed his sweaty palms once more on his black pants.

The line moved forward, and Haskell entered the great room. Two couples were ahead of him and had to be introduced before he received his chance. Forest green and white banners were draped across the walls of the great room. The chamberlain introduced the other couples, and then Haskell stepped next to the man and handed him his invitation.

Before the man could say anything, Haskell looked through the room to find Princess Noreen. He wanted to witness her reaction when his name was announced. She stood in a group of five people. Her sister and brother stood beside her with two men and a boy younger than Haskell. The darker skin tone of the males led him to believe that they were part of the Kallurian contingent. He recognized Prince Jordan from his Fire and Ice Challenge. A flash of jealousy raged through his body.

The Chamberlain made the announcement, "Ladies and gentlemen, honored guests and esteemed nobles, may I present to you Lord Haskell, Baron of Oak Ridge. A beacon of courage and honor. Let us extend our warmest welcome to this illustrious guest, whose presence adds to the splendor of this gathering."

A smattering of applause rang through the great hall as some of the older guests standing along the walls clapped at the introduction.

Haskell didn't care about them, as his eyes were focused on Noreen. She never looked up at Haskell or the Chamberlain. She smiled at something Prince Jordan had said, while others in the group guffawed at the comment. Noreen leaned closer to the prince and whispered something into his ear, which brought a smile to the prince's lips.

She hadn't even noticed the proclamation of his arrival, but he didn't have time to worry about her reaction, he had a duty to perform. As the young baron approached the king and queen, his heart raced with excitement and trepidation. He cleared his throat and offered a polite bow, just as Carl had taught him.

Haskell said, "Your Majesties, it is an honor to be in your presence."

King Goodwin smiled warmly and said, "The honor is ours, Baron Haskell. Welcome to our court.

We've heard many good things about your achievements in Oak Ridge and are excited to have you here with us tonight. How was your journey?"

Haskell's nervousness crept up his throat, and he struggled to speak. He rushed the words, "Thank you, Your Majesty. The journey has been quite uneventful, but arriving here is a momentous occasion for me."

Queen Olivia took his hand in both of hers and said, "It is a pleasure to have you here with us tonight. Please, relax. This is a celebration. I know the weight of a such a gathering can be overwhelming the first time you're at court with the royal family."

He tried to sneak a quick peek at Noreen, but couldn't find her quickly.

The king must have caught the quick look, and he leaned over to the queen. "This is the young man that rescued Princess Noreen."

"Oh, I regret not having the opportunity to personally thank you for your courageous rescue of our daughter," Queen Olivia said. She squeezed his hand in hers. "I can't thank you enough. I'm sure Princess Noreen will want to thank you again herself."

Haskell felt the heat rise to his face. That was exactly what he was hoping to hear. "Your kind words are appreciated, Your Majesty." He pulled on the collar fastened around his neck. It felt like it tightened each time he thought of Noreen.

"You must meet some of the other guests in the hall tonight." Queen Olivia raised her hand slightly to the elders in the room. "I'm sure they are eager to meet someone as chivalrous as you. And later, we'll make sure Princess Noreen dances with you to show you her appreciation for your noble actions."

The stress of meeting with Noreen's parents made Haskell think he might pass out, but he managed to say, "I would be honored, Your Majesty."

King Bryce clapped a large hand on Haskell's shoulder. "Excellent. Remember, tonight is about camaraderie and celebration. Our court is like our family."

Haskell said, "Your words have eased my nerves, Your Majesties."

Queen Olivia laughed softly, "Good. Now, go and enjoy the event."

Haskell nodded, "Thank you, Your Majesties. I look forward to it." He felt taller and stronger as he walked away from the king and queen with his chin high and chest thrust forward. He knew what Gadiel had told him about the wedding being about alliances and political posturing, but with this interaction with Noreen's royal parents, he knew that he would be the one marrying Noreen and not Prince Jordan. Tonight, he could do anything, even conquer the world.

He spied Noreen's group and walked toward them. Older people stood in small groups between him and Noreen, and they all made an effort to greet Haskell. Carl had coached him that this might happen, and he paused to introduce himself and talk with them as he passed. Carl had told him that if he ever became king, he would have to make alliances of his own. Taking the time to learn people's names would help him in the future to build those alliances.

He stopped a number of times to interact with the older generation, taking what he thought was forever, but probably lasted less than fifteen minutes, shaking hands and making small talk and eventually worked his way over to the king's daughters. His stomach roiled uncomfortably from nervousness. He tried to think of something clever to say when he introduced himself to Noreen, but his mind had gone blank.

Haskell smoothed his doublet, stood tall, and squeezed between Noreen's sister and brother, who listened attentively to Prince Jordan. In this group of people, the other Kallurian men were more than half a head taller than he was, except the prince's youngest brother and Noreen's sister, who were both smaller. He hoped the strategy worked in his favor. He looked at Noreen and smiled.

Noreen focused her attention on Prince Jordan. The man was talking about horses and Noreen seemed transfixed by the conversation.

Haskell wanted to grab Noreen's chin and have her look at him, but fear and what he thought might be royal etiquette stopped him from taking such drastic action. *Relax. It'll be a long evening. She'll see me and speak with me.*

The prince droned on and on for the next five minutes, and Haskell waited patiently. At one point, Princess Noreen nodded in his direction, but must not have recognized him.

Finally, the prince stopped talking, and he looked at Haskell. "Oh, who is this?"

Princess Noreen's sister, Carol, said, "Oh, you two haven't met. This is Baron Haskell of Oak Ridge." She winked at her sister.

Princess Noreen's face turned bright red as she moistened her lips. There was an awkward moment of silence as she stared with her beautiful green eyes at Haskell. Then she grabbed Haskell's hand and stood him in front of the prince.

She said, "Your Highness, may I introduce you to my hero, Baron Haskell? This is the white knight that rescued me from those horrible people."

Haskell wanted to shout, "*I love you*," to the princess, but he managed what he thought was an appropriate bow before he shook the man's hand. "It is my pleasure, Your Highness."

Prince Jordan held Haskell's hand in a firm grip. "Thank you for rescuing this lovely princess." He nodded at Princess Noreen. "It is brave and loyal lords like you that make a kingdom strong." Then he released Haskell's hand and turned to the others. "These are my brothers. My eldest brother, Prince Kiran, and my youngest, Prince Krunal."

Haskell bowed and shook their hands.

They spoke for an hour. Well, Prince Jordan spoke, the rest of the group mostly listened. As far as Haskell was concerned, the prince was a windbag, talking about himself and his accomplishments.

Haskell kept his attention on Noreen, but she listened with rapt attention to Prince Jordan's monologue. He wanted to yell at the prince to just shut up so he could converse with Noreen himself. She would occasionally glance at him with a slight smile on her lips, but then return her attention to Prince Windbag. Haskell desired to grab Noreen's hand and find a corner so they could talk intimately without the others nearby, but Carl had assured him the royal court would frown upon that behavior.

A sharp noise of wood striking against the marble floor interrupted the conversations about the room. Haskell looked up to see the chamberlain striking the bottom of his staff against the floor.

Everyone in the room stopped talking. To Haskell's amazement, even Prince Windbag stopped speaking.

The Chamberlain waited a moment longer and then proclaimed in a loud voice, "Hear ye, hear ye! All noble lords and ladies, pray give heed, for a distinguished guest of our gracious king has joined us this evening. I present to you King and Queen Goodwin to make a special announcement.

The gathered assembly clapped as the king and queen stepped onto a small dais. The king waited a moment as the people quieted. He said, "Thank you all for joining my wife and me for this special celebration." He looked around the room, his eyes sparkling. "Princess Noreen, please join us."

Princess Carol squealed with joy as Princess Noreen smiled at her sister and they embraced. The princess touched the hands of the small group of people surrounding her. She stopped a moment as she grasped Haskell's hand. She looked into his eyes, smiled, and gave a quick wink. Her green eyes spoke volumes to Haskell of desire denied because of royal duty. She squeezed his hand tightly, and with a look of sadness and regret, turned toward the dais.

The king said, "I now present to you Prince Jordan of the Royal House of Kalluria who graces our castle with his presence this evening."

Prince Jordan went around the small group shaking hands and when he reached Haskell, a scowl replaced the haughty smile that had been there the entire evening. He took Haskell's hand and squeezed so tight, it hurt. Like a warning, thought the young baron.

Prince Jordan stood next to Princess Noreen on the dais.

The king smiled. "If you two would please join hands."

Princess Carol squealed with joy once more.

Princess Noreen blushed a bright red as the prince took her in his hand and looked into her eyes.

The king continued, "I am pleased to announce the engagement of my daughter, Princess Noreen of Goodwin, to Prince Jordan of Kalluria."

The assembled guests clapped, cheered and whistled. All except for the baron.

Haskell felt devastated as a burning sensation grew in his chest and the blood drained from his face. They had signed the marriage contract. He clenched his fists in anger.

The king put his hand on his daughter's shoulder. "Let us celebrate."

Prince Jordan held out his hand toward Princess Noreen, and she blushed as she extended hers to his. They moved to the ballroom floor and other court members stood near them and prepared to dance.

The Chamberlain signaled the musicians and they began playing the music for the dance step known as the pavane, a slow and elegant dance that combined graceful arm and head movements and intricate footwork.

Haskell recognized the music and saw the dancers prepare for the procession in the formal court dance. He wished he was dancing with Noreen but felt fortunate he didn't have to risk embarrassment on this complicated dance. His stomach hardened as he watched the engaged couple perform the dance. Prince Windbag's hands touching the lovely Princess Noreen's.

He stood with folded arms as he tried to think of some way to break up the marriage or, at the very least, break up the dancers. There must be some way to dissolve this horrible contract. How was this any better for Noreen than having Lord Jorgensen kidnap her and sell her off as a lowly maid? *King Goodwin should have given Noreen's hand in marriage to me. I rescued her from a life of drudgery and pain.*

They danced a few dances Haskell had practiced, the galliard, branle and the allemande. Haskell watched, hoping for Prince Jordan to fall, or step on Noreen's toes, but he did neither. Instead, the man was a master of the dance, his movements flawless and his smile nothing short of royal. Haskell thought about putting his foot out and tripping the prince, but decided against that tactic.

Carl had taught Haskell to approach the prince and ask to dance with the princess after an appropriate amount of time, but each time another man at the party beat him to it. A song was just ending and Haskell's confidence at being with Noreen had eroded almost to the point he was ready to go back to Oak Ridge. As the song ended, Noreen disengaged with the prince and approached Haskell.

She smiled at him and pushed a strand of hair behind her ear, her face glistening from the effort of dancing. Noreen said, "I have promised you a dance, my hero."

Warmth radiated through his core as he held out his hand. She smiled, blushed, and placed her hand in his.

Joy ran through Haskell's body, scattering his thoughts and making him unable to think. He walked with her to the dance floor, his stomach doing a little dance all its own. The musicians opened with the music for the cariole, a dance that was performed in a circle with many people. He held onto Noreen's hand with his right hand and another woman's hand with his left.

Haskell stumbled once as he tried to remember the steps of the dance and quickly found his rhythm. He wanted to be confident and smile at Noreen the way Prince Windbag had done, but he needed to concentrate on his steps to keep from falling. Haskell felt carried away in the moment of the dance and found it ended way too fast for his satisfaction.

He felt disappointed that the dance didn't allow him to embrace the princess, but he was happy for the opportunity to dance with her. They stood together a moment, breathing hard and smiling at each other, when the musicians playing the lute and harp started up the next song. It was the music for the lovely stately dance called the Basse Danse, a dance that would allow Haskell the opportunity to be alone with Noreen. He could prove his ability to dance and try to talk her out of marrying the prince.

Haskell lined up his hands in the appropriate manner with Noreen's and thought about which foot he should start with.

A hand touched his shoulder.

Haskell looked over to see Prince Windbag. With a hardened stomach, he prepared to dance with Noreen despite the prince's presence, but he felt Noreen's hands loosen within his own. He smiled once more at the princess, who smiled back and winked at him. He dropped his hands, which quickly turned to fists. With a scowl at the prince, he bowed, and in a strained voice said, "Your Majesty."

Haskell watched them dance another few dances and saw no new opportunities to be with the princess. He retired to the room prepared for him at the castle, slamming the door as he entered. There had to be a way for him to stop this marriage. Noreen was his. She must know it was a mistake to marry Prince Jordan. He didn't trust the prince. Something about him led him not to like the man, and he didn't think it was just his feelings for Noreen that made him feel that way.

CHAPTER 44

The early morning sunrise streamed through the window and struck Haskell in his bloodshot eyes. The sleep he got overnight was restless and inadequate. His anger about Princess Noreen marrying Prince Jordan had increased, and he had no way to release his fury. He rolled out of bed and dressed, putting on green quilted breeches and a matching padded doublet made of velvet. He needed a walk to clear his head and help him find a solution to his problem.

Haskell stormed out of the castle and into the village of Whiterock Grove, scowling at anyone who so much as smiled at him. Many men and women crowded in the market square, where tents were setup for artisans, farmers, and traders to hawk their wares. He almost smiled, remembering how easy it was to pick-pocket a lord or rich manor owner in the square.

A woman holding a couple of pieces of painted pottery approached him and extended them toward Haskell.

"My gracious Lord, would you like to sample my exquisite pottery? If you would like one of my unique pieces, I can have your coat of arms applied, making it a one-of-a-kind treasure for your household."

Haskell sneered at the woman. It hadn't been that long ago that shop owners like her would shout for the castle guards when Haskell stood anywhere near a shop owner's tent. Now she practically salivated because he looked like he had money. He hated these people and wanted to trample all of them under foot.

Without looking at the tents, he walked onward, staying near the center of the path. He didn't want to talk with these people, he just wanted to walk and think. For a moment, Haskell considered going up to the tree where he used to talk with his friend Max, but decided it wouldn't be a proper baronial activity.

A farmer approached Haskell with vegetables in his hands. "Greetings, my lord! I hope your day is wonderful. Allow me to introduce myself. I'm Thorson, a local farmer from this village, and I grow the tastiest fruits and vegetables. Very fresh produce."

Haskell dismissed the farmer with a wave of his hand. He had no responsibility to purchase fruits and vegetables for his manor house. The crowds and pushy salespeople became too much for him. He needed peace to think about his dilemma. He continued on toward the river.

The river was flowing fast, and the handful of anglers along the banks didn't make an effort to sell him anything, so he stood and watched the water and considered his options about the princess.

Someone tapped him on the shoulder. "My lord. If you have a minute."

Haskell rolled his eyes and turned with the thought he would send a fireball at the person who thought it appropriate to interrupt his train of thought. He turned and realized that he recognized the man.

"My lord, I have a treasure that you might want to consider for yourself." The man began his spiel for whatever useless knick-knack he might be selling.

Haskell smiled for the first time that morning. "What useless rubbish are you pushing on the rubes this morning, Jasper?"

"My lord, my goods are first class." Jasper squinted his eyes and tilted his head right and left, his lips pursed slightly suggesting by his facial expressions that he didn't recognize him.

Haskell enjoyed his current anonymity with the former Gadiel thief. Jasper was a goof-off and made so many poor decisions that Gadiel had to let him go. The man used too much force, tried to pick-pocket the wrong people, and ended up in prison too many times for Gadiel to leave him on the team.

"What are you selling, Jasper?"

The thief still didn't recognize Haskell and his face bunched up, trying to determine Haskell's identity. "Should I know you, my lord?"

Haskell smiled at Jasper. "Not necessarily."

Jasper bent closer to Haskell and whispered, "My Lord, I have something of great value. Quite possibly the most sought-after magical object in history."

Haskell shook his head. The man had taken to selling magical objects, which he suspected had no magical capabilities at all. Find an unsuspecting person with money and try to convince them you have a rare magical artifact. It was the oldest trick in the book.

"And how did you acquire this scarce resource?" Haskell's smile grew bigger, realizing Jasper still hadn't figured out who he was speaking to. Jasper had grown over the last two years and now stood at least six-foot-two and was eating well.

"I can't reveal my sources, my lord."

If the item was real, then Jasper had probably found a way to steal it from a wizard, possibly after his ale had been drugged. It was possible the item was just a useless carved piece of wood, or a lady's pendant that he had lifted in the marketplace.

Haskell decided he would feign interest until Jasper finally recognized him. "I'm a powerful wizard and I might be interested in this unique item. Let's look at your wares."

Jasper stealthily looked around to see if anyone stood nearby. Convinced it was safe, he reached into his tunic and pulled out a long wooden stick.

Haskell looked at the stick, realizing the possibility it might actually be a wizard's wand, but did it have any magical properties?

Jasper said, "It's a wand."

"I figured that was its function."

Jasper lowered his voice even more. "A rare and valuable wand, My Lord."

"May I touch it?"

Jasper again looked around him. He hid the wand next to his wrist and moved his arm toward Haskell.

The man definitely had improved his presentation skills. Make the object appear valuable by making sure no one else knew about this transaction. Haskell was familiar with this technique and received it just as covertly. He took a moment to study the wand, a piece made by combining woods of maple, pine, and mahogany. Actually, a very nice-looking piece of carving, but did it have any magical power?

As Haskell examined the wand, he felt Jasper's eyes on him. A studying stare.

"Excuse me, My Lord. Have we met before?"

Haskell glanced up at Jasper. "Have you been to my manor home, perhaps?"

That comment threw Jasper for a loop and the man stammered, "Uh, I don't think so. Is the home close by?"

There was no way Haskell would let Jasper know where he lived. The thief would find a way to rob the house of all his valuables.

"I'm not from this area. I'm visiting the King in celebration of his daughter's forthcoming nuptials."

Jasper nodded. "Yes, of course, the lovely Princess Noreen. Lucky for her that baron had saved her."

"Lucky indeed." There was no luck involved. Haskell had risked his life and his future to save the princess, and she should marry him, not Prince Jordan. His gaze returned to the wand, and he rubbed his hand across the wood. He delved into it with magic and was surprised to discover that he indeed held a magical artifact.

"Tell me again which wizard has decided to part with this fine object?"

Jasper took off his hat and wrung the hat in his hands. "An older wizard from the mountains. He passed away suddenly and his widow is trying to get a little money to live out her life the best way possible. I assured her I would do everything possible to get a fine price for the object. She claims the magic in it is first rate and powerful."

Jasper's story was obviously fabricated to enhance the wand's value, but Haskell thought that the wand indeed had value. It would need testing to verify how valuable it really was.

Jasper said, "You would do well to have this unique wand. Legends are declared of its magnificent capabilities."

"Oh? Can you tell me one of them?" Jasper's capabilities did not extend to verbalizing grand sales pitches, and Haskell hoped to trick Jasper into telling him who he really stole the item from.

Jasper waggled his head back and forth. "I'm having trouble remembering any of the stories the old widow told me right now. But it's a superb piece of—"

He suddenly stopped talking.

Haskell looked up.

Jasper scrunched his face and smiled. "You're that little runt, Haskell, aren't you? What are you doing dressed up in finery and pretending to be a baron? Who are you scamming?"

So, the big lug had finally figured it out. Haskell smiled. "You're standing next to Baron Haskell."

"No!"

Haskell nodded. "In the flesh. I was the young baron that rescued the beautiful and magnificent Princess Noreen."

Jasper just looked in disbelief at Haskell.

"What kind of price were you thinking on this worthless stick?"

Jasper looked around him again. "Five crowns."

Haskell laughed. "I could buy an entire store of wands for that price. How about half-a-crown and I won't tell the castle guards you stole it?"

Jasper leaned in. "Listen, you little runt. I didn't like you when I worked with Gadiel and I like you even less now that you're pretending to be a baron. Give it back to me." He grabbed at the wand, but Haskell quickly put it behind his back.

"Jasper you were never a very good negotiator which is why Gadiel let you go. You're supposed to make an offer and then I make a counter-offer. Then you come back with another offer until we find a price we can agree on."

"Five crowns! A big hot shot baron like you should be able to afford five crowns."

"I don't think it's worth that much, unless there's something you aren't telling me about where it came from. I can get one just as nice in Crossroads for less than a crown." He paused a second and pursed his lips. "I'll be generous and offer two crowns. It's not worth it, mind you, but I know a low-level thief like you could use the money."

Jasper drew his hands into a fist.

Haskell brought the wand in front of his body and threatened Jasper with it. "Careful, my friend. I do indeed have magical capabilities."

Jasper scowled and looked around. "Hey, be careful with that thing. I've been told it has a tracking spell on it and the authorities might find you if you use it."

"Ha, so that's the first honest thing you've told me. Whose wand is this?" A shiver of worry scurried down his back."

"Give me three crowns, and I'll tell you."

"Two crowns." Haskell bargained. He dug into his money purse and flashed two crowns at Jasper.

Jasper's eyes went big and hungry.

Haskell closed his fingers over the coins. "Do we have a deal?"

The thief took a deep breath. "Okay. Hand me the money."

He dropped the coins into Jasper's hands. "Whose wand?"

"Have you ever heard of the Imperium Wand?" Jasper pocketed the coins.

Haskell snorted. "The greatest wand ever made? No way is this the Imperium Wand. The last I heard, it belonged to the Grand Master."

Jasper pointed his finger at Haskell. "Bingo."

"You sold me the Grand Master's wand?" Haskell palmed his hand over his face. "I'm a dead man if I'm found with it in my possession."

Jasper grinned like a fool. "Easiest two crowns I've ever made. Be careful using it, Lord Baron." The thief dragged out the words and sneered. "I'm confident about the tracking spell on it. Use it once and you'll have the Grand Master's hounds after you." He laughed and ran towards the crowded square.

Haskell stuffed the wand, no, the Imperium Wand, into the inside of his doublet. He took a quick look around him to see if anyone had watched the transaction, adding an extra bit of caution to see if the Grand Master's men had followed Jasper and were about to apprehend him. With a sigh of relief that he was safe at the moment, he decided he'd best not stay in his current location.

He walked along the river, working out his options. It might be Jasper just talking nonsense when he said it belonged to the Grand Master. Maybe the story about the old widow was the true story and Jasper said it belonged to the Grand Master to get back at Haskell for being a baron. The thief had to know that Haskell wouldn't be able to sleep, knowing that at any minute guards from the Council of Nine could pick him up and take him back to Velidred.

Haskell had felt strong magic emanating from the object when he first touched it, but now fear and reluctance taunted him about testing the artifact. The Imperium Wand, the most powerful wand known to humans, and he now owned it.

He continued his journey along the river until he came to the tree where he and Max used to meet up. This would have been a good day to talk with Max, who had always given him sage advice. Despite the urge to climb into the tree and examine his new wand, he knew that was an inappropriate activity for a proper baron and servant of the crown.

Haskell rolled his eyes at the thought. Then his eyes went wide when he thought about Gadiel's reaction to him owning the Imperium Wand. A shudder of fear traveled along his spine. He had to do everything in his power to make sure Gadiel never found out he owned it. With a slight touch to his doublet, he felt to make sure he still had the wand. He had to talk with people to see what the Imperium Wand looked like, but do it in a way no one knew he owned it. Just thinking about it sounded impossible.

Maybe a visit to the Goodwin castle library would be in order. Maybe there was a written record about the magical artifact. Yeah, that was a good idea, and a task he could do without drawing much attention to himself.

He would have to ask Dakarai if there were a way to shield the wand so he could practice magic without notifying the Grand Master of his usage.

A noise sounded behind him, startling him, and he turned to find Sims. Since obtaining the wand, every little sound seemed magnified. He worried a big sign pointed at him, letting everyone know of what he carried.

"What do you want Sims?"

"What're you doing way out here, lover boy?"

"It's none of your business." He rubbed his chest where he had concealed the wand. "Shouldn't you be applying your trade in the market this morning? Your master will be upset with you if you don't bring in your day's thieving."

"*Your* master is wondering where you are. He has a task for you. It looks like he's angry that he can't find you."

Haskell grimaced. Now holding the object that could get him killed, Gadiel had been looking for him. He hoped he wouldn't be punished for not being at the castle. He tried to come up with a laissez-faire attitude when he said, "Tell him I'll be in when I'm ready."

"I suggest you find Gadiel quickly. He didn't look happy you weren't in the castle."

Haskell waved his hand in a no care flourish although his heart thumped in panic. "I'm going back to the castle right now."

Sims smirked, "You don't know, do you?"

"Know what?"

"It appears the lovely Princess Noreen has requested your presence."

Haskell felt his face grow hot, and he wondered what she might want. Finally, a chance to spend time alone with the princess. His chance had arrived to tell her how he really felt. Now, they could hold hands and convince her father that she wanted to marry Haskell instead of Prince Jordan. He turned and hurried toward the castle with Sims in hot pursuit.

CHAPTER 45

When Haskell reached the castle, he had to catch his breath before asking to see the princess. He stopped in his room a moment to freshen up and then went to the second-floor royal audience chambers. There, the princess had a formal space to hold court and receive guests. He had never been in the room, but knew its location within the castle.

Gadiel waited outside the chamber door, a sour expression laced his lips. "Where have you been, Boy?"

Haskell stood straight, with his back strong, a slight panic forming within his chest as he thought about the wand just inches from Gadiel. "Walking the marketplace." The old man didn't need to know what his real purpose was for leaving the castle.

Gadiel grabbed Haskell's doublet and pulled him close. "Don't get flippant with me. I need you to stay on the king's good side, or you'll be waving from the gallows. Do you understand me?"

Haskell nodded. He didn't know if he should fear Gadiel's power over him or the risk of losing his life in the gallows. Wait until Gadiel found out that he held the Imperium Wand. That wouldn't make the old man happy.

Gadiel straightened Haskell's clothes. He tapped Haskell's chest with the flat of his hand and paused a moment as a frown crossed his lips in a look of uncertainty.

Haskell was relieved that he'd worn a quilted doublet which prevented Gadiel from feeling the wand. He asked, "What is this about?"

"I don't know, but be on your best behavior, and don't do anything stupid."

Moments later, the chamberlain opened the door and peered at them. "Oh good, he's here. Come in."

Gadiel and Haskell both approached.

The chamberlain stopped Gadiel. "No, just the boy."

Haskell was both frightened about going in by himself and happy to be going in alone. He took a deep breath and entered the chamber, his heart pounding up and down a hundred beats a minute. Finally, his moment to be alone with his princess. This would give him a chance to discuss his concerns about Prince Jordan and tell her why he didn't trust him.

His gaze found the princess immediately, and he smiled.

Her radiant smile welcomed him into the chamber as she stood on the dais.

Then he noticed three other people in the room with her and his heart thudded to a stop. Prince Jordan, King Bryce, and Queen Olivia also sat in their royal chairs on the dais.

Haskell walked with the chamberlain to a spot on the floor fifteen feet from the dais, where the man held up his hand and they both stopped. He bowed appropriately to all the royals as sweat beaded on his forehead.

King Bryce spoke, "Thank you for joining us, Baron Haskell. It's a pleasure to have you join us at this joyous celebration. Prince Jordan has asked for a moment of your time."

Prince Jordan, standing on the dais, made their difference in height seem even more intimidating. He stood regally, and Haskell detested him for it. The man was tall, smart, and charming. He hated to admit it, but the man was the perfect match for the princess.

The change from talking to Princess Noreen to Prince Jordan concerned Haskell. Had the man somehow read his mind?

Prince Jordan said, "I spoke to Princess Noreen about you."

Haskell went hot in the face. Did the man know how much he loved her?

"Your rescue of her from the hands of her kidnappers was simply astounding. I don't believe any knight of my kingdom would be as brave."

Haskell nodded and bowed, as Carl had taught him. At the very least, Princess Noreen should see him as a proper and loyal subject.

"I have spoken to my father about your bravery, and we both concluded that we wouldn't have had the opportunity for this celebration without your gallantry. So, with my father's blessing, as a token of our appreciation, I am rewarding you with property within the Kallurian Kingdom, property that used to belong to me, along with a small manor house, and a group of twenty soldiers. With great honor and respect, I present to you this golden shield, which used to be owned by one of the kingdom's favorite wizards. Upon learning you also are a wizard; we were delighted for the opportunity to award it to you."

Two guards, standing in a corner, went to a table and returned with a golden shield and a large bag of coins. The one-foot-diameter round shield had a large golden eye that protruded from the face of the shield. Haskell stared at it with an open mouth, his eyes wide in astonishment.

He felt surprised and humbled by the coins and the magical object. He looked at the prince with curiosity at the gifts. But Haskell realized his good fortune and thrust his chest out, straightened his shoulders, and felt his lungs fill with deep, satisfied breaths of pride.

"I am humbled at your generosity, Your Majesty." He bowed with his best taught flourish. When he rose, he glanced at Princess Noreen, who made firm eye contact, and her face flushed.

Prince Jordan stared at Haskell, looked at his betrothed, and raised his eyebrows. The prince stepped down from the dais. He motioned to a guard. "May I borrow your sword?"

The guard pulled it from its sheath and handed it to his prince.

Haskell's heart jumped to his throat, and he knew the prince had found the secret in his heart about Noreen. The quickest move from baron to death in the kingdom's history. The prince planned to kill him right this moment for looking with lust at his soon-to-be bride.

Haskell placed his hand over his chest, feeling the wand. He could use it right now to save himself and kill the prince all in one swift move.

The prince said, "Please kneel."

Haskell closed his eyes, wondering what spell would be most appropriate. He went to his knees despite his fear. He would die with honor.

Prince Jordan placed the sword blade on Haskell's shoulder, very near his exposed neck, the cold sharp steel scratching his skin. "As prince of Kalluria and representative of the crown to our trusted friend and ally, King Bryce Goodwin. Baron Haskell, in recognition of your steadfast commitment to my betrothed, it is with great pleasure and honor that I bestow upon you the title of Viscount of Kalluria."

He tapped Haskell with the sword on his left shoulder, and then his right. "This title is a testament to your glorious service to your princess and the trust I place in you. May you serve Kalluria Kingdom with the same commitment and abilities as you now show Goodwin Kingdom. I honor you as our ally and friend and confer the title of viscount with pride and honor. May your service to both kingdoms flourish and your dedication be rewarded with good fortune."

Relief flooded through Haskell. Not death, but another title. One more chance to be seen at the same level as royalty.

The prince handed the sword back to the guard and helped Haskell to his feet. The prince took Haskell's wrist, and they shook to seal the deal. Prince Jordan gave Haskell a warm smile.

King Bryce was first to step from the dais and shake his hand, followed by Queen Olivia, and finally the lovely Princess Noreen extended her hand to Haskell. He felt his head might go up in flames with the heat across his face. He dropped to one knee and kissed the back of her hand.

Haskell thought his knees would drop out from under him and he felt light-headed with what had just occurred.

Prince Jordan said. "We must celebrate with a small feast. Join us, young Viscount."

CHAPTER 46

Later that evening, after the celebration, Haskell practically danced down the corridor holding his new treasures in his arms. Feelings of excitement and power coursed through his body. He had the Imperium Wand tucked in his doublet, carried his bag of coins, and held a magical shield. His thoughts wandered back and forth from the magical objects in his possession to his conversations with Princess Noreen during dinner.

When he opened the door to his castle room, he found Gadiel sitting on a bench in the corner of the room. Gadiel stood and quickly said, "Shut the door, Boy, we need to talk."

Gadiel's tone dampened Haskell's excitement about the evening. He closed the door and turned to him.

The old man's forehead held deep creases, and he kept clenching and unclenching his fists. He had never seen Gadiel looked so stressed.

Haskell remained quiet, wondering what the old man's concerns were now. The man looked like one of the veins in his neck might pop any minute.

Gadiel pointed to the bench. "Sit down."

Haskell raised his eyebrows, but acceded to the man's command.

"Do you realize the purpose of the gifts Prince Jordan presented to you?"

Haskell looked at the treasures in his arms and smiled. "Everybody likes me because I saved the princess from a life of toil and drudgery."

"No! You fool." Gadiel slapped him hard across the face. "These gifts are a bribe. A request. A command. The purpose of these treasures and new title is to ensure that you do not pursue the princess anymore. You were supposed to beg off dinner and return to your room or maybe the kitchen if you were hungry, but by all means, not to engage the princess in conversation."

Haskell felt the welt forming on his cheek from the slap. Then his face twisted in confusion and anger. He stood and stepped closer to Gadiel.

"Are you suggesting that I forget my feelings for the princess and let that . . ." His fury grew. "That poser of a prince wed the woman I love?"

"Yes! You are to forget any feelings you may have for the princess. The prince is concerned about the strength of your affections. He fears that your love for the princess might compromise his own relationship with her. And you reward those fears by flirting with her all night during the feast. His irritation is such that I imagine there is a knight being directed right now to eliminate you as a rival."

Haskell shook his head in disbelief as he replayed the night's events in his mind. "He can't do that. He told me himself that we are allies. Friends and partners sharing the duties of the crown."

Gadiel snorted and looked even angrier than when Haskell had arrived. "The prince knows you have feelings for the girl, but he can't have you sneaking off to be with her behind his back. He has given you those gifts to stay away from her. I suggest you listen to my words."

Haskell didn't need to hear this, and felt his muscles quivering in rage. Gadiel had robbed him of what he felt was the happiest moment of his life. He had made a real connection to the princess tonight. They had laughed at dinner and when he left, he made sure to kiss the back of her hand once more. She had giggled and blushed. He had no intention of giving up the woman he worked so hard to rescue to a prince he didn't trust. He cracked his knuckles and his nostrils flared. For a moment he thought of the wand and using it to eliminate Gadiel in one swift move.

"You mean to deny me the one thing I desire most in the world?"

"Pack up your stuff, Boy," Gadiel commanded. "We leave tonight, before the prince finalizes plans for your murder."

"Plans for my murder! He'll rue the day he wanted to marry Princess Noreen. I don't plan to just run from the prince. If he wants a duel, I'll happily comply."

Gadiel touched Haskell's shoulder and Haskell flinched, expecting one of Gadiel's magical surges of pain, but nothing happened.

"I understand your pain at losing the woman. As a viscount, you'll have opportunities for other women in the kingdom."

"I don't want other women." Haskell tried to control his emotions of not being able to be with the princess. He had saved her from a cruel life, from Gadiel and his cronies, and he thought she deserved the opportunity to choose him as her beloved.

Gadiel sent a surge of pain through Haskell's shoulder, forcing him to the floor. "This is part of being a royal. Sometimes you don't have a choice in these matters."

Haskell's face felt hot and his chest tightened. He placed his hand on the wand. Surely there was still time.

Gadiel moved his arm. "Let's pack. I have our horses waiting in the courtyard."

Haskell picked up the shield and tossed it across the room. He didn't care for the prince's bribes anymore.

The golden shield hit the stone chamber wall, emitting a ringing clang that reverberated within the room. When it bounced off the floor, it landed in a final clatter of metal against stone, creating a cacophony of metallic resonance.

"What's a title and gifts when you can't have what you really want?" Haskell stood staring at the shield.

Gadiel gently touched his back. "It's part of growing up. You need to learn that don't always get what you want."

Haskell spun and glared at the old man. "I never get what I want. You're always pushing me to do things I don't want to do. Well, I'm done. I'm leaving you and the titles." *I'll show the old man. He can't control me. I'm my own man, he can find another puppet.*

Gadiel stepped closer, unfazed by Haskell's threat. "Before you get worked up, there's more you need to know." He pointed at the shield now lying face down on the floor. "The shield that you accepted as a gift to stay away from the woman is charmed."

"Who cares?"

Gadiel smiled his crooked little grin that meant that things were going to get worse. "Have you thought of why the prince gave you a magical shield with an eye? Think for a minute about what that might mean."

Haskell tried to think of what it might mean, his curiosity opening to possibilities as he looked at the shield's eye and etchings.

"The shield is charmed with an enchantment that will reveal any attempt you make to defy the condition to stay away from the princess," Gadiel said.

Haskell's eyes widened in disbelief. He took a step away from the shield, as if it might spring to life and look into his very soul, accusing him of the things the prince paid him not to think.

"You mean the prince gave me the shield to spy on me? Will it expose my every action and thought?"

"We will have to get more information about the magic, but yes, the shield's enchantment ensures that you uphold your promise to stay away from the princess."

Haskell stood dumbfounded. "I didn't agree with any of this. If I had known of this deal, I would have killed him on the spot." In his anger, he pulled out the Imperium Wand from his doublet. "Let me go to him right now. I'll show him what love means."

Gadiel grabbed Haskell's forearm that held the wand. "What do you have there?"

He stared at the wand in his hand as his brain realized the mistake he had just made. "Nothing. A magic wand I bought in the marketplace."

"Which is it, Boy? Nothing or a magic wand? Let me see it."

Haskell felt so stupid. Why did he let his anger get the best of him? Now Gadiel knew about the wand and it wouldn't take the old man long to figure out who it belonged to. The man knew things. He felt his throat close up as Gadiel extracted the wand from his hand.

Gadiel examined the magical object. "Where did you get this?"

"Like I said, I bought it in the marketplace."

"Don't lie to me, Boy."

"Stop calling me, Boy. I'm a viscount. Call me Lord." Haskell moved back from the old man and prepped his hands to create a shield. He didn't know what Gadiel would do with the wand, but he was glad it was out of his hands if his master planned to use it.

"Lord," Gadiel's voice dripped with disdain. "You're a nobody pretender, and now you're going to be the ruin of all of us. Do you know whose wand this is?"

Haskell hung his head. "I've been led to believe it belongs to the Grand Wizard."

Gadiel rubbed his right eye with his free hand. "You are carrying—" He glanced at the shield. "A powerful magical object. One use of this and you'll have us all hanging from the gallows at sunrise. You have to be the dumbest person I've ever trained."

Kenneth Brown

    Haskell's heartbeat felt sluggish, and he thought his legs wouldn't hold as shame and humiliation galloped through his body. What would the old man do to him? He felt trapped, as if his entire life was collapsing all around him. He turned away from Gadiel, his hands trembling with helplessness.

CHAPTER 47

A week later, Haskell sat on his horse, awaiting Lenny and Sims to finish loading the wagon. They were going to visit his new manor in Kalluria for a month or more. This trip would give them the opportunity to check out the surroundings, the viscount's small army, and the money they might profit from as the new owners.

At Gadiel's suggestion, Haskell had hidden the wand, securing it with magic traps. He felt fairly confident no one would find it where he hid it. He just hoped there was some way that he could make use of it in the future without it killing him.

They traveled for three days, leaving Goodwin castle, the princess, and all its inhabitants far behind. Haskell had resolved to forget about Princess Noreen, though he felt numb at not being able to tell her goodbye.

When they reached the little village of Crossroads, they stopped. Gadiel had sent the others to get supplies and took Haskell with his magic shield in hand to the little village Magic Shoppe.

The ornate wooden door creaked slightly when they opened it. One window at the front of the shop allowed a little light to enter the room, but candles next to mirrors brightened small sections of the shop.

When the young viscount entered the shop, he felt an enchantment surround his shoulders and a prickling of his scalp. A light blue mist seemed to infuse the room with a slight fragrance that Haskell couldn't identify.

He stopped for a moment and admired all the amazing items in the room. Three bookshelves held leather-bound books and one shelf kept a disordered mass of scrolls. Other shelves contained jars of dead insects, multi-colored powders, crystals, and bones.

Haskell touched a trinket in the shape of a stegox hanging from the ceiling and pulled back his hand quickly when the animal snapped at his fingers. Other trinkets, also hanging from above, seemed to move and change color as he passed them. Twelve staffs stood in a cylindrical container at the end of one aisle. He stopped for a moment to admire the workmanship of the wooden staffs and wondered if they were all magical.

An elderly gentleman greeted them. "Gadiel, it's been a long time since I have seen you. What brings you to my poor corner of the kingdom?"

Gadiel engaged in some weird handshake with the shop owner. "I have a magical object that needs to be interpreted." He snapped his fingers. "Bring it here, Boy."

Haskell rolled his eyes. The old man should be showing him more respect, especially when they were in public. He hurried to the counter, dug into the leather pouch that hung from his shoulders, and removed the shield from the bag. He lay it on the counter.

The shop owner's eyes lit up when he saw it. "Ah, the Eye of Vigilance. I just sold this recently to a certain prince that came through here. Interesting that it should end up in your hands." He looked down at Haskell disapprovingly.

Haskell raised his hands shoulder high. "A gift to me from Prince Jordan. He just made me a viscount and gave me some property, too."

"I see," the man said, as he continued to stare accusingly at Haskell.

Gadiel asked, "Can you tell me more about the inscription? It's written in language, I'm unfamiliar with."

The shopkeeper took the golden shield and held it close to a nearby candle. He made some muttering noises as he read the inscription and then dipped a quill pen into a jar of ink and translated what he read onto a nearby piece of paper. It took a couple of reads because the man went back and crossed out some words before replacing them with what Haskell figured was a different interpretation of the script.

"If you sold it to the prince before, don't you already know what it said?" he asked.

The shopkeeper shook his head. "The prince wanted an object to spy on a friend. He wasn't too particular about the other details of the artifact."

"Is there any way I can make it stop spying on me?"

A smile lifted on the old man's face. "Do you want the rich prince to stop bringing his business to my small shoppe? I think there is no way to prevent its purpose."

Haskell groaned in disappointment. "I figured as much. So, what else is it good for? I want to use it as a shield."

"Well, I translated the ancient script, which I might add, hasn't been around for three thousand years, the best I could. I might be a little off in a translation here or there, but this is a close interpretation."

He raised his scrap of paper to the nearby candle and read:

> *Through the eye's watchful gaze, the truth shall be revealed.*
>
> *By its magic, secrets concealed, and destinies unsealed.*
>
> *Bearer of the shield, your path is a mystic quest,*
>
> *Unlock the powers within, and put them to the test.*

Haskell snorted. "That tells me nothing. It's gibberish. If you don't want to tell us what it says, just say so. Don't be making up pleasant sounding poems."

Gadiel gave Haskell a stern stare which quieted the viscount. He looked back at the shopkeeper. "Can you elaborate at all?"

"It has more power than just a way to spy on people you don't like. It contains a secret, but the ancient script isn't forthcoming about what that secret might be. I think it might be a riddle, a clue, and possibly a promise all in one."

"Now I have to solve a riddle. Give me a break," Haskell moaned.

The old shop keeper looked at Haskell for a few seconds. "It's more powerful than the prince realized. The shield in the hands of a competent wizard—" a look of derision and disdain filled his eyes, "could be a shield, possibly an oracle, and may have a connection to one of the moon goddesses. I can't tell which of the three moons it might be linked with."

That news caught Haskell's attention. He had experience with the Velidred moon. Might this object also have a connection that would allow him to use its power for himself?

"I suggest you test its power a little before walking into a battle expecting it to protect you from harm. I am *not* saying it's a powerful shield that can defend its owner from a magical attack. Do you understand what I'm saying, Young Man?"

Haskell's mind went racing to possibilities. Moon goddesses were sometimes known as protectors and guardians. His mom had read him the stories as a kid, of the magical protectors that came to the defense of the legendary figures of yore. This shield, his golden magical shield, might make him undefeatable in a battle against other wizards. Maybe even protect him from the outrage of the Grand Wizard of the Council of Nine.

The shopkeeper looked at Gadiel. "I suggest you keep an eye on the boy if you think he might do something stupid with the shield."

Gadiel exhaled a long breath. "The boy is shortsighted and foolish every day."

Haskell said, "Is there a chance the shield can prophesy about people's lives, reveal future truths, or provide insights into complex events?"

"I can only tell you what I've shared with you." He shrugged as if he had no other answers. "Would you like to buy a wand or a staff? They're very popular with the boys."

Haskell's eyes lit up but Gadiel's scowl snuffed out his desire for either of those items.

Gadiel gave the man a coin, and they did their secret handshake before he led Haskell from the shop.

Haskell thought about the Velidred Moon, due to be at full moon status in just a few days. This might provide him with certain insights and opportunities for testing the shield's power. He stuffed the shield back into its pouch, a little more enthusiastic about its properties.

####

A day later, the small party of travelers arrived at the Viscount's new property, and Haskell found himself quite impressed. The manor house stood behind a six-foot tall brick wall and the entrance into the courtyard required traveling between two guards at the wall gate. The guards greeted them at the gate and they stayed there until someone from the house was informed of their arrival. Then, when the house steward arrived, the guards allowed them into the courtyard.

Haskell walked his horse toward the house, admiring the trimmed landscape, statues, and the water fountain, which he assumed worked by the use of magic. It was all very opulent, with a small section of yard in front of the wide front door worked in a herringbone pattern of white and red stone. After he dismounted, a stable groom took his horse while Lenny and Sims followed the groom with their wagon of supplies. Gadiel and Haskell were escorted through the front door.

The steward gave them a tour of the new home. The house had a room that was big enough to hold a royal dance in and Haskell imagined standing in the room welcoming guests with his bride, the Goodwin princess.

The house had a reflecting pond in back, more statues of people Haskell didn't know, and another water fountain that made a pleasant sound, like standing near a small stream's waterfall. Stables had been located east of the manor, so the prevailing winds would force the stable smells away from the house. The steward told the viscount about the smithy on the property, though the village blacksmith only used it at the commands of the prince.

He thought the manor a magnificent place to call home. Maybe he could convince Gadiel to send Sims and Lenny to the other property and Haskell could manage this property without them. Then he thought back to the tasks Sims and Lenny performed on the other estate. Collecting taxes, intimidating the locals, and helping bring much needed money into the estate's coffers.

Haskell whispered, "How are we going to pay for all this?"

Gadiel spoke to the steward, "Tomorrow, we'll want to examine the books."

"Of course, sir," the steward replied.

He saw Gadiel sizing up the paintings and art collection that hung on the walls, probably wondering what he could get for them in the open market.

Haskell spent the afternoon on the back terrace admiring the landscape. They were still in a mountainous region and the house stood on the top of the ridge. The view opened up into a valley below, flanked by other mountain ridges. He wondered how far his new property extended into the valleys and ridges.

The steward brought out drinks for the new viscount and an hour later returned with a message that broke Haskell's enjoyment of his new home. He handed a card to Haskell but before he could read it, the steward proclaimed, "Prince Jordan hopes you find the accommodations to your satisfaction. He has requested an opportunity to visit with you in five days and hopes that the two of you could find time to go hunting in the forest."

The news left a sour taste in Haskell's mouth and a tingling in his chest because he didn't want to visit with his benefactor so soon. He looked at the card in his hand without reading it. How could the prince already know they had arrived? Did the shield provide this information? With a heavy sigh, he said, "Let the prince know that we look forward to his visit." He stood and walked down the hill away from the house, deep in thought, wondering if he had time to learn the powers of the shield, and if it was too soon to kill the prince.

CHAPTER 48

Over the next two days, Haskell tried to tease out the golden shield's secrets, but it was a difficult task. He wished Dakarai had traveled with them. His magic knowledge was better and he had more experience than Haskell. He didn't know how much the shield's magic eye could see and share with the prince. Did it just transmit information about him when he thought about the princess, or was it watching him now? He still hadn't determined if it could read his thoughts, though he figured the prince would have had him killed already if the shield had that capability.

Haskell tried to pick apart the verses the shopkeeper had given him. He decided the first line just told what the eye could do and wasn't of interest to him other than if it could read his mind.

Through the eye's watchful gaze, the truth shall be revealed.

By its magic, secrets concealed, and destinies unsealed.

The second line led him to believe there were more secrets of the shield that he needed to unveil. Destinies unsealed seemed exciting, as he wanted to believe the prophecy of him becoming a king that Forest River Blossom had given him those many years ago on the Velidred Volcano. He had a lot of magic, but his knowledge of how to use it to his advantage still eluded him. If he could tease out the shield's magic, then maybe his destiny could come true.

Bearer of the shield, your path is a mystic quest,

The third line held possibilities. A mystic quest seemed to be something fun to get him out of Gadiel's sight for a few months, but he had to determine the path and object of his quest. These words he decided were just gibberish until he knew more. Then he read the last line about unlocking the powers within.

Unlock the powers within, and put them to the test.

He tried to imagine what powers the shield contained, but he feared that putting the shield to the test in random sequences would probably hurt him and possibly kill him. He needed wisdom and knowledge to direct him.

Haskell thought of a few tests he might attempt on the shield, with the last one on his list the one he considered the most dangerous. He hoped the early tests would be enough to find the magical item useful.

The first idea in his mind was to do an elemental analysis, a simple test to see what types of magic the object contained. He held his hands over it and chanted a spell Dakarai had taught him early on to analyze objects.

He perceived ethereal wisps of current emanating from the shield. Elemental energy showed itself through his magic, each with its own distinct qualities corresponding to water, air, earth, and fire, allowing him to judge the amount of each elemental magic the artifact contained.

The shield contained a minor water element, a slight air element, and strong earth and fire elements. Dakarai had shown him earth-based enchantments, and he decided to test the shield's capabilities. He grabbed dirt off the ground, sprinkled it on the shield, and chanted.

After waiting a minute, nothing happened, so he figured it didn't respond to dirt. He found a couple of pebbles and, saying the words taught him, bounced the pebbles off the shield that lay on the ground a foot away. The ground suddenly rocked, pitched, and rolled. Haskell held out his arms to stay on his feet as large boulders sprang from the ground and surrounded him. The process surprised him, and he found himself enclosed in a small claustrophobic space. His breath came in rasping gasps with panic and fear filling his mind as the large structures encased him.

Then he noticed something strange. He could see through the boulders. They had a translucent component that he determined as a one-way process. He could see from inside the boulders, but he thought someone outside wouldn't be able to see him.

Haskell ran his finger along the surface of one boulder, marveling at its simplicity and its power of deception. This form of the shield could prove useful for protection sometimes or at the very least, to hide him.

His breathing became more relaxed as he contemplated its potential and a growing excitement at the wonders his new found artifact contained. It took a couple of tries, though, to get the magic to release him from this encompassing barrier.

The next experiment was to find out if it could act as a shield against magic. Why would they make it into a shield if they didn't have expectations that it could actually prevent another wizard from hurting its owner?

He leaned the shield against a tree trunk and then retreated fifteen yards away and prepared a magic fireball. He imagined Prince Jordan had his eye against the other side of the shield, and one fireball from Haskell would permanently blind the prince and make him so ugly that King Bryce would call off his daughter's wedding.

Haskell smiled at the thought and then released a fireball at the shield.

When the fireball neared the shield, a shimmering blue wall of light formed in front of the shield and the fireball just hovered near the magical object without touching it. The fireball didn't move forward, it didn't rebound off the shield, or even dissipate. Haskell had never seen anything like it. He wondered if he had been holding the shield, if he could now manipulate the spell and throw the attack back toward its sender.

Since he was the sender, he didn't know quite what to do at the moment with the hovering fireball. After a minute, the fireball began to dissolve and when its energy fizzled out, the shield's blue wall of light also burned out.

The result of the test definitely seemed interesting, even though Haskell wasn't sure exactly what he could do with the hovering spell once it got caught up in the shield. He considered putting its magic to an overload test, sending a large continuous magical attack against it to see at what point its ability to protect its owner would break down, but he didn't feel comfortable with its characteristics yet to take that chance. The barrier overload spell had been known to ricochet excess magic back at its creator, leaving the wizard dead or injured to the point of uselessness.

After a few tests, Haskell determined that the golden object had favorable properties to make it worth his while to use as a wizardly shield, despite its ability to spy on him.

The last test he wanted to perform on the artifact would be to see its reaction to water. Even though his initial analysis showed the device to be a poor water elemental object, he felt it important to test. He walked to a nearby stream carrying the shield in his hand. He reached his cupped hand into the mountain water and drew it up above the shield. With a slight turn of his wrist, he dripped water onto the shield and stepped back, just in case it did something he wasn't expecting.

Nothing happened at first as the water splashed onto its golden surface, but then its eye and golden skin seemed to shimmer, turning a bluish gray fog-like color. Haskell moved farther from the object, afraid of what might be happening.

A thick fog lifted from the shield, creating a cloud in the shape of a six-by-four-foot oval door. As Haskell looked at the cloud, wondering what might happen, shapes formed within it. He prepped a magical shield in case the shapes might attack him. His heart beat harder as he felt adrenaline kick in, and he maneuvered to the side for safety.

His eyes narrowed in confusion as the shapes became more pronounced and looked to be Prince

Jordan, his brother Krunal, and possibly an aide. He heard them speaking.

Prince Jordan said, "What did you find out?"

"You won't believe it, My Lord," the aide said.

Haskell marveled at the cloud and the ability to see people within it. There was no indication they could hear him or see him through the clouds. He lifted his chin and moved around the box to get a better look at the speaker. He appeared to be a truth catcher that his father had known in Velidred, a person skilled at teasing information from people. Prince Jordan had hired the man to dig into Haskell's past.

The truth catcher smiled and his narrow, beady eyes seemed to glow with anticipation. "The little baron is a blacksmith's son."

What would that mean to Prince Windbag's opinion of him? He had never tried to hide his past, but he hadn't been forthcoming either.

"The little bugger that I made a viscount is a lowly smithy?" Prince Jordan laughed. "Does King Goodwin know this?"

"I could find no sign that he knows about the boy's heritage."

"Heritage! A smithy has no heritage. He's a commoner."

Haskell's nostrils flared, and he bared his teeth as he shouted at the figures in the box of clouds, "I'm not a commoner. I'm a lord. A baron. A viscount!"

He couldn't let Princess Noreen find out about this. She wouldn't understand. Sure, in the past, he had been a blacksmith's son, but not now. Surely now, she saw him as the viscount. A true and powerful lord of the Goodwin kingdom.

"Fine work." The prince tossed a bag of coins at the man. "A commoner can never escape their roots, can they? Once a laborer, always a laborer. There is no path for the average man to rise above his family."

Prince Krunal asked, "What are you going to do? After all, you made him a viscount."

Haskell felt light-headed and overheated as his frustration built. He leaned closer to find out what the prince planned. He couldn't allow the king or princess to find out this news. Knowledge of his background might ruin everything.

The prince picked up a goblet from a nearby table. "We should have noticed his calloused hands and called him out at the Goodwin castle when we were there. Well, his little secret won't last for much longer."

The prince knocked back a goblet of wine. He wiped his lips with the back of his hand and said, "We have a trip planned with the young blacksmith, don't we? Grab your weapons, my brother. We're going on a hunting trip. I suspect when we return, the manor will be restored to my possession. Once the mettlesome viscount is dead, I'll marry the princess, kill the king and queen, and I will sit on Goodwin's throne."

CHAPTER 49

Haskell had less than two days to come up with a plan to protect himself from the prince. The royal had a brilliant plan. Nothing like a hunting accident to get rid of your rivals. But Haskell now knew about the threat and he would be prepared. He could walk around with a magic shield surrounding him the whole time the prince was at the viscount's residence.

Though that wasn't a bad idea, it was difficult to hold a spell for more than a day. He'd eventually have to release it. Plus, holding a spell for that long pulled magic from its user, depleting his reserve of magic to use for other purposes.

He needed something else, not only to be defensive, but to turn the tables and remove the prince from his life. Maybe the prince would be the one to have the "hunting accident." Then his problems would go away and he could pursue the princess once more.

He sat on the terrace looking out over his little kingdom. Thinking. It was difficult, though, because every time he thought of the prince's words about him being the son of a blacksmith, he'd get angry. He would remember and regret the actions he had taken that caused his father to be executed by King Stoneforge, the Velidred king. He hated King Stoneforge as much as he did Prince Jordan.

"A blacksmith!" he shouted and pounded his hand on the table.

A servant came to him. "Is there something I can help you with, my lord?"

"No!"

"Yes, sir." The man turned and walked back toward his station.

An idea came to Haskell. "Wait."

"Yes, sir?"

"Where is the smithy on this property?"

The servant pointed toward one of the outlying ridges in the distance. "It's about a mile in that direction, My Lord. Should I have someone find the village blacksmith to help you with your project?"

"No, that won't be necessary." He *was* the son of a blacksmith. He didn't need help with what he had planned.

"Is that all?"

Haskell waved his hand to dismiss the servant, but then said, "Do you ever have guests from the Velidred Castle here?"

"Yes, My Lord. Is there someone in particular that you are thinking of?"

"No, but can you tell me, does the manor have Velidred guard uniforms stored here in case there's a need for them?"

The man nodded.

"Good, have one brought to my room."

"My Lord, that is very irregular."

Haskell smiled as his plan took shape. "Do it, man. And have someone saddle my horse. I plan to visit the smithy."

"Of course, My Lord."

####

He looked at the smithy. It wasn't much, not like the spacious place near the Velidred Castle where his father worked. This building was no more than a lean-to with an uncovered fire pit outside. A creek ran near the hut to provide easy water for the smithy's quench process.

Just as he had hoped, he found arrowheads and shafts. He rummaged through the hut looking for painting supplies and found what he needed—a small jar of paint in the color used by the Velidred soldiers. The prince had unwittingly given Haskell exactly what he needed to defeat the arrogant royal at his own game, and further Haskell's career.

Haskell got a fire going in the pit and found a sharp pointed tool to do some etching into the arrowhead. His father had made so many of these that Haskell knew exactly how the volcano symbol used by the Velidred crown looked. No one would know that the blacksmith's son had created these.

Sims entered the smithy. "A viscount doing blacksmith work. That's not a good look. You might smudge your fine clothes, My Lord." Derision dripped from Sims' lips.

The peace and calm that Haskell had felt working the forge heated at the sound of Sims' voice. "What are you doing here?" He asked between gritted teeth.

"I heard a rumor that you were coming out to the smithy and I wanted to get a look at the place."

"Well, I don't want you here."

Sims pouted his lips. "I'm hurt that my Lord doesn't like me."

Haskell didn't need this irritation. He had hoped to keep his plan to himself. The fewer people that knew, the better chance he could succeed and get away with it.

Sims picked up one of the painted arrows. "Interesting. This looks like a Velidred arrow. Have you decided to renounce your viscount title and go back to working for the king of Velidred?"

"Never mind what I'm doing. It's none of your business." With Sims' ability to mess things up, he couldn't reveal his actual plan.

Sims walked closer to Haskell. "But My Lord, you have a smudge on your nose right here." He touched Haskell's nose with his forefinger.

Haskell swiped the irritating thief's finger away from his face. "Leave me alone."

"But I came down here to give you something that you accidentally left back at the manor." He nodded his head in the manor's direction, its roof line visible in the distance.

"I left nothing at the manor." Haskell growled.

Sims reached into a leather satchel that stretched across his chest and hung next to his hip. He removed

Haskell's golden shield. "I thought you might want this. It looks pretty important, and I wanted you to know it is safe."

Haskell's throat tightened and his stomach hardened in frustration at the irritating thief. He formed a spell on his lips and raised his hands, prepared to eliminate the irritant in one magical moment.

"I wouldn't do that, my lord." Sims wagged his finger at Haskell. "Gadiel wouldn't be happy if he found out."

"There wouldn't be anything left for him to find." He scrubbed a hand through his hair and realized that his hands were full of soot. Sims was right, of course. The prince wouldn't have a chance to kill him, because Gadiel would do it for him.

"That's better, my lord." He stuffed the shield back into its leather pouch. "So, tell me what you're planning for the prince."

Haskell looked at the leather pouch. If he said anything to Sims, the prince would be listening and would know his plans.

Sims noticed his glance. "Gadiel tells me that there is a low-level spell on the pouch. The eye won't release any information to the prince." He walked over and put a hand across Haskell's shoulders. "Now tell me your plan, I might be able to help."

Haskell knew Sims wouldn't help, but would do everything in his power to prevent his plan from succeeding. He had to come up with two plans. One that he told Sims and another that would actually eliminate the prince.

CHAPTER 50

Haskell escorted the prince and his hunting party through the forest. Five guards encircled the prince and two of the manor's guards walked with Haskell. The prince's younger brother Krunal had joined the hunting party along with five more of the prince's friends, dukes, barons, and lords from the surrounding area. With the way the prince's soldiers ringed him, Haskell thought that his chances were poor of succeeding with his plan.

The sun showed it to be mid-day and played hide-and-seek between large fluffy cumulus clouds. The royal hunters held bows and arrows in their hands, all excited to kill a deer or stegox.

Birds chirped merrily in the trees, flitting from limb to branch. Squirrels ran along the forest floor either looking for nuts or burying nuts they had found. Dappled sunlight filtered through the leaves onto the forest floor.

The prince, an experienced archer, exchanged jests and friendly competition with the Viscount and others in the group.

Haskell carried the golden shield along with a bow and quiver of arrows. When they were a hundred yards from Haskell's trap, he prepared a magical shield to cover himself. A light wind rustled the summer leaves, and one duke guffawed at a joke told by another lord.

Suddenly, a series of shouts and panicked cries shattered the tranquility. The guards closed rank around the prince as one soldier walking with the group cried out in pain.

Haskell faked surprise and shouted, "What happened?"

The soldiers raised their weapons and scanned the immediate area. Tension filled the group as the soldier on the ground screamed, "Get it out! I've been shot with an arrow."

Several soldiers rushed into the forest in search of the perpetrator of the incident.

The prince's lead guard pulled Prince Jordan back from the soldier on the ground. "It's time to return to the manor, Your Majesty. We can't protect you out here."

Prince Jordan didn't move. "I need more information. If it's a lone person who is angry with the crown, or a poacher, then we can continue the hunt."

Haskell laughed to himself. He had planned for the arrow trap to release when he and the prince were closer, but Sims had managed to alter his plan. Luckily, he had anticipated Sims' involvement. "Are there people who are angry with the crown, Your Majesty?"

"A handful of troublemakers," the prince waved a dismissive hand, "don't like the amount we ask them to give to the crown. There are others that feel offended by some action the crown has taken."

"Will I be safe when I walk in my local forest?" Haskell asked.

The prince glanced at one of his guards. "Yes, I'm sure they're angrier with me than you. Mostly because they don't know you yet."

They stayed where they were for five minutes, waiting for the soldiers to return with information. When the soldiers returned, their leader spoke, "We weren't able to find anyone, Your Majesty. I suggest we return to the manor."

"Nonsense. We're having fun." He pointed to the soldier on the ground who had stopped struggling as someone pulled the arrow from his shoulder. "Is he okay?"

"He'll be all right. I will send him back to the manor to be treated."

"Very well. Let's continue the hunt." The prince smiled and continued down the path.

Haskell felt relieved that the prince didn't accuse him of the attack. *There might still be time for an attack that Sims doesn't know about. I have to kill the prince before he kills me.*

As they walked through the forest, a deer came into view. All the hunters became still as the prince nocked an arrow. His guards cleared space to give him the best chance to hit his target. The deer stopped eating and looked at the men, but didn't move. The prince took a deep breath and then slowly released it. A moment of quiet and then a twang sounded from the prince's bow as he let go of the string. The arrow flew toward the deer, who stood still watching the men.

The arrow struck its target and the men cheered. They all watched the deer move a short distance and then fall to the ground.

What they failed to notice, though, was a second arrow released from the trees fifty feet from the group. The arrow flew past the soldiers, lords, and dukes without being noticed, as they turned to congratulate the prince.

With a loud thwack that startled birds out of the trees, the second arrow struck the prince in the chest. Prince Jordan's head jerked back, and he spread a hand over his chest. His eyes bulged in shock as he looked at Haskell.

Haskell shook his head, wanting to smile at the brilliance of his plan, but knew now was his moment to begin the second part of his strategy.

"The prince has been injured!" he shouted.

The prince stumbled backward into Haskell's arms as his mouth flew open. His eyes held a dazed expression as he looked down at the offending shaft. The arrow's feathers had almost penetrated his body from the force of the attack.

"I've been hit!"

The guards ran to his side, while lords gasped and looked at the surrounding forest.

Haskell used magic to send a wave of sound through the forest, as if two or more people were running from the scene.

The prince's captain pointed to three soldiers and shouted, "After them!" The soldiers dashed through the forest in pursuit.

Prince Krunal shoved Haskell from his brother. "Stay away from him. You did this." The prince stumbled and Krunal supported him.

Soldiers ran through the forest shouting and chasing an imaginary enemy.

"How dare you accuse me of this atrocity? I stood right here next to your brother the whole time," Haskell replied.

The shock of the moment had passed and some of the older lords in the group came to the prince's side and helped lay him on the ground. Younger men stood watching the forest for enemies, their arrows set in the bows ready to release.

Haskell undid a cloak object spell, that exposed pieces of cloth in the forest, not far from what might be the direction the arrow originated. He knelt next to the prince's side, feigning concern. "Is the injury bad, Your Majesty?"

"Yes." The prince gasped as blood trickled through his lips.

Prince Krunal glared at Haskell. "I told you to move away from him. Guards. Arrest Viscount Haskell."

CHAPTER 51

Haskell stood in the manor's great room where three soldiers had bound him and now stood guard to make sure he didn't escape. They had taken the prince upstairs to his room and had found a local healer to examine the wound.

An empty feeling sat in the pit of his stomach. The prince's younger brother would like nothing more than to execute Haskell right here. He was happy that he made it back to the manor alive, though he wasn't too concerned since he believed his magic could overcome the others' man-made weapons.

Gadiel came into the room trailed by Sims and Lenny.

Could Haskell trust Sims to stay quiet? He calmed his fast-beating heart and worked hard to show an innocent expression.

Gadiel poked a large bony finger into Haskell's chest. "What did you do? You fool."

"I did nothing," Haskell said. "We were on a hunting trip and an arrow came from the forest and hit the prince."

Gadiel's black eyes stared back at Haskell.

"You can ask anyone that was hunting with us. They'll tell you that I was next to the prince nearly the entire time and at no point did I nock an arrow." Haskell wanted to put his hands up in surrender, but they were tied behind his back.

"Well, you might find yourself on the gallows by nightfall if Prince Krunal has his way. He's convinced you planned this murder."

"He's wrong," Haskell shouted. "I have no need to murder the prince. Especially, after the prince's kindness and largess." his eyes took in the house's luxuries.

Prince Krunal stepped into the room followed by a dozen guards.

The guard's captain came in a moment later.

"What did you find?" Krunal asked.

The captain opened his hand to reveal three pieces of cloth. "Every clue leads to Velidred soldiers initiating this attack." He motioned to one guard. "Give me the arrow."

The guard opened his hand for the captain.

"This is the arrow we extracted from the prince. It has the Velidred sigil on its point. There's no doubt the arrow came from Velidred."

Prince Krunal grabbed the arrow and examined its point. He stared at Haskell. "It's not true. This man killed my brother." He motioned at the guards holding Haskell hostage. "Prepare a tree for hanging. This man doesn't deserve to live. My brother planned to kill him anyway. We'll take a life for a life."

Haskell's stomach roiled, his bravado faltering as he felt the icy fingers of death on his neck. "Your Majesty, have mercy on me. The evidence supports the fact that Velidred soldiers are responsible."

"I'm just finishing up my brother's business here."

"You can't be serious. I'm an innocent bystander," Haskell pleaded.

"You've lied to us since we first met you. We have proof that you aren't of royal birth. You're nothing more than a blacksmith. Your lies are your downfall, even if you didn't have any involvement with my brother's attack."

Haskell pleaded with his eyes for Gadiel to do something. The man stood there silently. Sims had a big smile planted across his face.

Haskell argued, "Your Highness, one's family background does not define their worth. It's my character and actions that matter."

Krunal smirked. "That may be true, but a commoner can never escape their roots, can they? You attempted to reach the ripe fruit, but your deceit has caused you to fall, rotten, back to the ground."

Haskell's jaw tightened, his frustration with the young prince building. He tried to respond to Krunal's false accusations with as much dignity as he could.

"My father's profession as a blacksmith was an honorable trade. I'm proud to be a blacksmith's son. At no time have I denied my heritage. It is my willingness to risk my life to save Princess Noreen that has placed me in my current position."

The prince continued his attack on Haskell's family background in a voice that leaned toward mockery. "Ah, yes, an honorable blacksmith's son. How noble. Tell me, Viscount, do you still have calloused hands to prove your previous trade?"

Haskell feared the prince might actually inspect his hands, which for the moment were indeed blistered, cut, and slightly burned from his time in the smithy earlier in the week. But the prince didn't really want to see his hands.

"I don't think that the prince needs to continue to insult my family's trade. A blacksmith's occupation requires skill, dedication, and integrity. Don't belittle my dead father's profession. He served the Velidred king for years." Haskell's face turned red with heat as he thought back to how his father had died.

"Your father served the Velidred King? Then you would know how to make an arrow with the Velidred colors and royal symbol. Look at this. Did you make this arrow?" Prince Krunal jammed the arrow near Haskell's eyes.

"I would never hurt the prince. Tell him Gadiel."

Gadiel stood across the room, no expression on his face that Haskell could read. His plan centered on Gadiel standing by his side. The old man had to know if they killed Haskell, they could murder the rest of his associates, including Gadiel and Sims.

"It doesn't matter. My brother planned to kill you today. We both saw you flirting with and pining for the princess at the Goodwin Castle and her own desire to be by your side. And now we know you're pretending to be of royal blood when you're nothing more than a lowly blacksmith's son."

Gadiel looked more intensely at Haskell.

Haskell rolled his eyes. "The princess is a lovely woman, but I understand who she is engaged to, and it's not me."

The guard's captain pulled Krunal over to the side of the room where they had a whispered conversation Haskell couldn't hear.

Haskell glanced out a window where two men struggled to throw a rope over a large tree limb on the manor property. He wondered if he could survive this makeshift trial and stay a viscount to the Kallurian crown. Honestly, he was happier in Oak Grove Village. He hoped with Prince Jordan injured, he saved the princess from having to marry the creep. For now, he had to keep from getting his neck broken.

A soldier stomped down the stairs to Prince Krunal. He whispered in the prince's ear.

The prince reeled toward Haskell and marched over to him. His face contorted with anger and grief. "You had a chance if my brother had lived, but now I'm carrying out his original wishes when we came to the manor. You will be hanged for killing my brother."

Haskell strained against his bindings.

Prince Krunal said, "Take him outside."

The guards manhandled him toward the door.

"Wait, Your Majesty. Hear me out." Adrenaline rushed through Haskell's body as he wondered if he should fight or use his magic and run from the manor.

The prince pointed at Sims and Gadiel. "Take them, too."

Gadiel's actions surprised Haskell because his boss still didn't put up a fight. What game was the old man playing at? It wasn't like him to let events unfold without being in charge. He hoped he didn't expect

Haskell to save him, because he would be happy to let the old man die.

The guards pushed Haskell through the door and down the front stairs. Halfway down, he stumbled and ended up planting his face in the dirt.

The guards jostled him back to his feet, pulling his arms in opposite directions.

"Your Majesty, it wasn't me. I wished no harm to your brother. The evidence surely points to the Velidred King."

The prince pounded his forefinger on Haskell's chest, emphasizing each word. "You. Don't. Understand! We planned to kill you today, no matter what."

"But you're going to want my help." Haskell tried to maintain his balance as the guards pushed him closer to the tree.

"For what?" The prince's face was red and anger folded the skin on his forehead.

"I swear on my honor and the lives of my family—"

The prince screamed, "You have no family."

"It was a misfortune. An enemy attack," Haskell pleaded. "Your guards tried to tell the prince to return to the manor, but he refused."

"Misfortune?" the prince shouted. "My brother is dead, and you will gain by his death. I claim you as his murderer."

Haskell knew he had to reframe the conversation away from him being killed, to how he could help the young prince and his family to avenge his brother's death. He needed to start the second part of his plan to save Princess Noreen and King Goodwin. He was the only one who could stop Kalluria from taking over the Goodwin Kingdom. This part of his plan would help cement his power and allow him to use this tragedy to his advantage.

"Your Highness. Ever since your family's marriage contract and treaty with the Goodwin family, there have been rumors of tensions with the Velidred kingdom. You can't blame them. By themselves, the Goodwin kingdom couldn't defeat Velidred, but together now, you have become dangerous. The Velidred king has a reason to kill your brother. They must show that they have power to defeat you, despite King Goodwin's support."

With a flick of Prince Krunal's wrist, the guards continued walking Haskell toward the tree. They lowered the noose.

"Here's a chance for Kalluria to take down the evil king that sits on the throne of Velidred. He's threatened you in the past. Now's your opportunity. Your brother's death needs to be avenged."

Prince Krunal raised an eyebrow. "We can defeat Velidred without your involvement." He stared angrily at Haskell.

Haskell suspected the young prince had never actually commanded someone's death and hoped he'd lose interest before Haskell lost his head.

"I have magic. Powerful magic." Haskell pulled his hands in front of him as the ropes binding him magically fell to the ground.

Two guards immediately tackled him, pushing him to the ground.

Haskell struggled to get back to his feet. He didn't want to hurt the guards, but he had to have a conversation with the prince.

"How will one wizard defeat the Velidred army and the Council of Nine? Are you saying you're more powerful than the Council of Nine?"

Haskell levitated the men that lay on top of him, and they flailed their arms and hands in the air in surprise. He stood and brushed off his doublet.

"I'm not a complete idiot." Prince Krunal stepped back. "Any average wizard can perform that feat."

"What if after we defeat King Stoneforge, your father put you on the throne of Velidred? You'd be the youngest king ever in the Velidred kingdom. With the treaty with King Goodwin and your father's backing, you could combine your kingdoms and it would be the strongest kingdom in the region. Think about it. King Krunal of Velidred."

Haskell let the guards float back to earth. They grabbed his arms, and he didn't resist.

The prince paced back and forth, clearly torn between grief, anger, and the possibility of becoming king.

Haskell hoped he had said enough to convince the prince.

"One wizard won't be enough. I don't care how powerful you think you are."

"I have tremendous powers, Your Majesty, but I agree we need more than just me. Give me a few months to recruit several wizards to work in tandem with me, and we can form an army of wizards."

One guard said, "I have a friend from my village that is a wizard and he claims that all wizards have to honor the code that they won't form an army of wizards. It would produce chaos if they did."

Haskell's eyebrows raised in surprise. His plan hinged on him creating a group of wizards to support his uprising.

He thought for a moment and then came up with a lie to pacify the guard and any doubts the prince might have. "True. I misspoke about an army of wizards. I don't mean that we would terrorize towns and villages. We would talk to the Council of Nine and let them see the wisdom of overthrowing the current king and putting King Krunal on the throne. It would take several like-minded wizards to convince the council and the Grand Wizard about this plan."

Prince Krunal stopped pacing and looked at Haskell. "You think you have the power to do a bloodless coup at the Velidred Castle?"

"Absolutely, Your Majesty." Haskell hoped his facial expressions showed his belief at overtaking the castle. At the moment, it was nothing but bluster. "Or should I address you as King Krunal?"

"Don't get ahead of yourself. I have an older brother who might be interested." Krunal crossed his arms and placed a finger on his lips. "The evidence is strong that Velidred had a hand in my brother's murder. I see possibilities in your plan, but my father might have other thoughts." He moved his finger, and the guards released Haskell's arms.

Haskell rubbed his wrists. "Your father will see the obvious aggression from our enemies and will want to avenge his son's death."

"Don't be so sure about that. He's always been a peaceful ruler and is more likely to ask for compensation rather than engage in a war."

Haskell hoped to convince the Kallurian King of Velidred's danger to his kingdom.

Prince Krunal turned to go back into the manor. "Viscount Haskell, make no mistake. Your fate is still uncertain. Throw him in the dungeon for now."

CHAPTER 52

Four weeks later, Haskell walked up a treacherous mountain path, along a steep and winding trail of rocks, gravel, and dangerous drops to the valley below. He walked in the darkness, afraid to light a lantern for fear of being seen. He hoped to reach the Weary Wanderer tavern soon. Despite climbing high into the mountains, the summer heat held its tight fist in the sweltering night. Sweat glistened on his brow as he took the next bend on the path. He wiped the moisture with a trembling hand. He thought maybe his goal of convincing other wizards to join him in his attempt to take the Velidred castle was a foolish dream of a young inexperienced boy wizard.

Since Prince Jordan's death, Gadiel had kept a close eye on Haskell, monitoring his every step. Haskell had created a well-rehearsed plan of action and snuck out of the manor a few hours earlier. He hoped to be back before Gadiel found out he was missing.

Haskell thought back to the days of Prince Jordan's death.

Two days after being thrown into the dungeon, Prince Krunal had released him. It was really just a dark and dank basement that Haskell knew he could get out of at any moment he wanted. Despite the guards at the door and small basement windows, the cell couldn't hold him if he really wanted to escape.

Before setting him free, they had a lively conversation, as Haskell worked hard to get the young prince's consent on his plan to overtake Velidred.

"Your Highness, I understand that my presence here may stir up your suspicions. What happened to your brother was a tragedy," Haskell had trouble speaking, because of his parched throat. "But I assure you, I had no hand in his demise."

The prince sneered. "How can I trust your assurances when my own eyes witnessed the events that led to my brother's death? You were there, with powers beyond mortal capabilities. How can I believe you had no part in it?"

"I cannot blame you. I was there, but by your brother's side. Your Highness, I was at risk just as much as your brother. Another two feet to the left and that arrow would have struck me instead of your brother." Haskell knew beyond a doubt the arrow was not meant for him. "I swear to you, my intentions have always been to serve the greater good. In fact, I seek to right the wrongs that now plague your kingdom and prevent further bloodshed from Velidred."

"And yet, I cannot shake the feeling that you are trying to manipulate me, to use me as a pawn in your schemes." Prince Krunal stared with golden brown eyes at Haskell. "Why should I believe that your offer to help me ascend the throne is anything but a ploy to further your own agenda?"

Haskell took a deep breath. "As you say yourself, I'm a blacksmith's son. I never tried to hide that, and I understand your reservations, Your Highness. If I desired power or control, I would not approach you with an offer of partnership. You show the potential for true leadership, for a reign built on justice and compassion. Let us work together for the change our kingdoms desperately need."

"You speak of partnership, but how can I trust you won't betray me? What assurance can you offer me that your intentions are pure?" The prince moved in closer.

"Your Highness. I will pledge myself to you, to swear an oath of loyalty and service. Let us forge a bond based on mutual respect and shared goals, and together we can overcome any obstacle that stands in our way. I will earn your trust by my actions."

"I've only met you twice. Your words sound sincere, but I have been trained to watch other's actions, not merely the pleasant things they say."

The prince gave off a vibe of having been trained well in the ways of court. Haskell felt certain he could learn from the young boy on how to rule a country.

The prince continued, "Proceed with caution, for if I detect any hint of betrayal, there will be consequences."

Haskell dropped to one knee and bowed before the prince. "I will do everything in my power to earn your trust and prove the sincerity of my intentions."

The prince left the room and his entourage left the manor later that morning, as they took his brother's body back to their castle.

Now Haskell worked to bring about the change he desired, getting revenge for his father's death by defeating King Stoneforge. He continued his walk to the tavern high in the mountains. The scent of pine hung heavy in the air and his heavy breathing barely covered the incessant loud buzzing of the cicadas. He stopped for a breath and to take a drink of water. Even more important, the other wizards he invited had better be there.

One more bend in the road and the welcome glow of the tavern's candlelit windows flickered through the trees. Anticipation and dread rushed through his body as he tried to catch his breath before entering. His informant assured him that the quaint, remote tavern would meet his needs.

Haskell searched the darkness for people who might have followed him or planned to do him harm. He pulled his cloak from his pouch and tossed it over his shoulders settling its hood over his head to hide his identity. He continued toward the thatched roof building.

The sound of laughter and muffled voices drifted on the wind before he reached the door. Conversation mixed with the occasional clink of glasses almost overpowered the enchanting melodies of a fiddle playing in the background.

His heart raced, knowing that beyond those doors, three other wizards awaited, their intentions as nefarious as his own. He'd either leave with the approval of solid co-conspirators or be a young wizard with a target on his back.

Drawing a deep breath, he pushed through the heavy wooden door. Its hinges creaked softly. The sweltering night grew sultry in the crowded room, as the smell of stale ale, smoked tobacco, and burned meats forced him to stop just inside the door. A simple wooden candelabra hung from the wooden beams with ten candles providing dim light.

Haskell waited for his eyes to adjust to the room. Despite the man on a small dais in the corner playing a fiddle, it appeared the tavern's patrons were busy in conversation, ignoring the tune.

He examined the men at each of the tables, and his eyes lit upon three figures in a corner, their cowls hiding their faces. He approached the rough-hewn wooden table. The men didn't look up from their conversation. One's hands cast shadows on the table as he talked. Haskell's heart pounded in booming beats as he prepared for this clandestine meeting. He hoped, among the shadows of the tavern, he could find the people he needed to defeat the king of Velidred and alter the course of his life forever.

The conversation stopped as Haskell reached the table and sat on the empty bench. Two men sat across the table, the elder with a hunched back and frail frame. The man ran his hand through his long, tangled beard, a dirty mis-match of black and gray, and a polished oak staff leaned against the wall next to him.

The one beside him looked more middle-aged, and he had an air of authority about him. Unlike the first, his well-groomed hair and trimmed black beard revealed a sense of power. A wand with a gold handle peeked from the top of his tunic.

The middle-aged wizard nodded in Haskell's direction. "Are you the one that called this meeting?"

Haskell stared back at the man's piercing blue eyes, trying to determine if he was friend or foe. The next words out of his mouth might get him killed tonight. His letter to the wizard had discussed a signal he would give so they would know that they were meeting the right people.

He rubbed his right finger down his nose and touched his left ear. The men at the table all followed his lead. They leaned closer to Haskell.

Haskell looked over his shoulder to make sure no one stood close and might be listening to the conversation. "I'm looking for friends to help me with a project."

The middle-aged wizard, wearing dark, finely crafted robes, shook his head. "We aren't your friends."

The old wizard sighed and rubbed a hand across his wrinkled face. "Don't be pedantic, Garrick. He knows we aren't friends. Let him talk." He looked deeply into Haskell's eyes. "Don't waste our time. These are dangerous times and we don't want to spend much time here together."

Haskell glanced at the wizard beside him. He was younger than the other two with long curly hair that cascaded from the back of his cowl. He was hidden so well within the cowl it would be hard to identify him. Everyone in the room probably knew him.

Haskell whispered, "I need some wizards to help me take down a king."

Garrick laughed, a loud raucous sound emanating from within his cowl. "Are you a fool, or just too young to understand life? I'm out." He stood.

Haskell grabbed the man's arm. "Wait. Hear me out."

Garrick looked at the old wizard, who nodded for him to sit.

Once he was settled, Haskell continued, "I want to take down the King of Velidred."

The old wizard smiled, his crinkling eyes deepened the lines in his face. "King Kaelen Stoneforge is a mighty force to be trying to defeat." He eyed Haskell up and down. "Especially for a wizard still wet behind the ears, like you."

Garrick smiled at the older wizard. "Ambrose, are you not interested in the project?"

Ambrose said, "I've run into the king and his cronies, the Council of Nine. I'm not keen on having my magic extracted forcefully while I cry out in agony for hours. I've seen their methods." The old man stared once again at Haskell. "I recommend you give up this dream. You won't win and you'll find yourself hunted by the council."

"He's already on the council's watchlist." The youngest wizard at the table joined the conversation. "This is Haskell. He's the boy wizard who stole all the magic on Velidred during the eclipse. The council wasn't happy."

An uncomfortable look glinted in Garrick's eyes. "If that's true, then we can turn him in for the reward. They've been searching for him for a while. I'm sure they'll be delighted when we deliver him to their door."

Panic seized Haskell. He hadn't expected the meeting to go like this. *Should I flee now, before they capture me?*

The wizard sitting next to him on the bench, grabbed his wrist.

Haskell struggled.

The youngest wizard said, "Relax, kid. Despite what these other men might think, I am your friend.

Let's have an ale and talk about your plan. If we don't like your plan, then maybe we'll turn you into the council."

Garrick threw back his head and laughed once more. The room quieted for a moment, and many of the tavern's patrons looked in their direction.

Ambrose touched Garrick on the shoulder. "Let's hold it down a bit. The tavern is becoming curious about our conversation. I'm of a like mind with Mortimer." He nodded at the younger wizard. "Let's hear your plan and decide on its merit. First, with your consent, I will encapsulate us with a spell that makes it impossible to be heard. It's a little enchantment that makes it appear we're having a conversation about cards and dogs."

For the next several minutes, Haskell outlined his plan. Finally, he finished with, "As a small wizard army, we could defeat the council's wizards and force the king to his knees."

"It'll take more than a handful of wizards to defeat the council." Garrick took a drink of his ale. "They are a powerful group of wizards with at least a quarter of them full mages."

"Not just the four of us. I suggest we have twenty or more." Haskell said.

Ambrose touched his staff that leaned against the wall as if he might pick it up and leave, but then he returned his hand to the table. "The laws clearly state that any wizard who creates an army of five or more or is involved in a wizard army will face death."

Mortimer shook his head. "Those laws are outdated and unnecessary. If we created a group of wizards that worked for the good of the land, they'd be clamoring for us to help the small villages that have roving gangs that loot and destroy their villages."

"This boy," he nodded in Haskell's direction. "Wants to kill the king, not necessarily for the good of the land." Garrick took a sip of ale and wiped his mouth with the back of his hand.

In the background, the fiddler took up a slow sad dirge.

Mortimer leaned across the table. "The king has been ruthless to the people that owe him taxes. I've seen families killed because they didn't have the money to pay."

"The king is ruthless, petty, and trouble to the weak, but twenty wizards, despite the laws preventing their banding together, won't be enough to pull him down." Ambrose fingered the staff once again.

Haskell wondered for a moment why Ambrose kept his hands so close to the staff.

"Where do you plan to rustle up these twenty wizards all excited to put their necks to the guillotine?" Garrick asked.

"Always thinking logically, aren't you, Garrick?" Mortimer asked.

"I'm a practical man."

Haskell said, "I plan to meet with others, and," he looked sheepishly at Garrick, "hoped you would help me recruit the numbers we need."

Garrick smiled, "Ah, a leader willing to shove me off the cliff to get his way. And who will you put on the throne after our beloved king is dead?"

Haskell made eye contact with each of the wizards individually. "I plan to be king."

Garrick brayed once more with his laugh. "You're a brave man, for one so small." He placed both hands on the tabletop. "The wizards you plan to recruit for this project are just as likely to kill you after they finish storming the castle."

"I hoped to get their assurance that they wouldn't kill me after we achieved our aim."

Ambrose's eyes crinkled once again. "Unless you plan a blood oath for your followers, you will die. Either in the attack itself or afterwards."

Haskell had expected these wizards who King Stoneforge had publicly dishonored would gladly join his rebellion. Yet, they were asking questions about subjects he didn't have the answers for. "Is a blood oath difficult?"

"The oath itself is easy, but if one of your followers were to be captured before your surprise attack on the castle, then the oath can be used against you to identify you as the instigator. Are you sure you want to do this?" Ambrose asked.

"Are there any other ways to force them into my service?"

"Not unless you have access to the Corruption of Evil. Let me look at your eyes to see if control the power of the goddess of Velidred." Ambrose raised his eyebrows.

Haskell thought, *I don't have the Corruption of Evil but I might be able to convince Gadiel to help me with my plan. He'd love to have the power of the Velidred Castle at his fingertips.* "I don't have that power, but I might work out something to my advantage."

Mortimer jumped in, "And what advantages will we gain for following your ill-conceived plan?" He touched his leather gloves that lay on the table, the pair etched with intricate sigils, showing his mastery of spell craft.

"What do you want? Money? Power? Girls?" Haskell asked.

Garrick shook his head. "I want my life back. I've seen the dark side of our society's rigid rules and exclusivity to wizards. My younger brother, a budding wizard, had his spirit killed because the established wizards refused to extend their help or resources to him. His potential, squashed and wasted. Now he sits in a little cell at the house rocking back and forth, drooling all day long, and saying nonsensical words."

He finished his glass of ale and raised it toward the barmaid for a refill. "I'm interested in your vision hoping no one else is forced to endure my brother's fate at the hands of the ruling class."

Mortimer added, "I've been searching for a way to teach the council of the consequences of their actions. Your vision of wizard warriors might help me in my personal quest."

Haskell lowered his voice to almost a whisper. "I've carried the burden of a grave injustice to my family for many years. The king falsely accused my father of a crime he didn't commit. They sentenced him to death because the king's favorite horse bucked when he was being shoed. They tossed my mother into prison where she died of an illness she suffered in the dungeon."

"Revenge for your father's death? You want me to risk my life for you to gain revenge?" Mortimer sneered. "I understand your pain and the injustices you and Garrick have received at the hands of the king. Ambrose, sorry to say, is an old man and has nothing to lose. But look at me. I'm young and handsome and all the world is at my fingertips. Why would I engage in this losing battle?"

Ambrose touched the staff once more. "And what do you envision, young Mortimer with the flowing hair and fair face that women swoon over?"

"Just the talk of a wizard army would escalate tensions with the Council of Nine. They wouldn't hesitate to draw wizards to the castle and use magic to gain information about our plan." Mortimer argued his case.

"That's why it's important we keep it quiet." Haskell responded.

Ambrose moved his hand toward his staff once more.

Mortimer raised his hands above the table. "If you touch that staff one more time, I'll turn it into ashes."

Ambrose grabbed the staff and released a firebolt toward the door, striking a man who had just placed his hand on the door. At the same moment, he stopped Mortimer's planned attack on his staff with a visual display of the dispel magic spell.

The man at the door fell to the floor. By the looks of it, dead. His clothing smoldered.

Mortimer sat frozen in the same spot, unable to move because of Ambrose's spell.

Garrick laughed his garish laugh once more. "Who was the man at the door?"

"A troublemaker that's been following me for the last month. I tricked him into coming here tonight. No one in this room will say they've seen or heard of him. I suspect he won't follow me home."

Haskell touched Mortimer, but only his eyes moved. He looked at Ambrose. "I'm impressed by your speed and precision. I would love for you to join our little group."

Ambrose placed his staff back against the wall. "The Council of Nine has powerful allies and resources. They'll be prepared without us knowing who told them of our plan. They won't go down without a fight, and the innocents in the kingdom will suffer the consequences." He chanted some words and Mortimer's stiff body loosened and the young wizard dropped his hands.

"Once we build the army of wizards, we can let it serve as a deterrent to potential aggressors." Haskell felt it was time to leave. He had been here too long and Gadiel would wonder where he had been. "There must be other wizards that the King has wronged or whose lives were disrupted by the Council of Nine. We start with them. At the very least, we find enough wizards to form a formidable force and put pressure on the council to oust our corrupt king."

He stared into Garrick's eyes. "It's about taking control of our destiny and ensuring that injustices like what happened to your brother don't go unanswered. By standing together, we can confront challenges and adversaries in a way that maintains peace, rather than allowing the kingdom to fall into chaos."

Garrick placed his hand on the table. "I'm with the boy." He glanced at Ambrose.

"I haven't had this much fun since I was your age, Garrick." With a quick glance at the men that hauled the man he had killed out the tavern door, Ambrose stuck his hand on top of Garrick's. "I think it'll be exciting."

Mortimer looked at the others. "No, I don't think so."

Ambrose raised his eyebrows. "What would your sister say?"

Mortimer raised his hands once more as if to throw magic at Ambrose, but then stopped. "What do you know about my sister?"

"Join our group and I can help you locate her. She's still alive."

Mortimer's mouth opened wide and his posture stiffened. "How do you know?"

"I know. Now, join us so we don't have to kill you."

Mortimer frowned and bit his bottom lip as if he needed to think about this new information. Finally, he asked, "Do you promise?"

Ambrose said nonchalantly, "If we live."

Mortimer raised his hand over the other's hands on the table as he stared at Haskell for a long moment. He placed his hand on top of Ambrose's.

Haskell smiled as he slapped his hand onto the top of the other's.

CHAPTER 53

After speaking with the other wizards, Haskell hurried home. His senses were sharp in the darkness and he felt a lightness in his chest. The meeting with the wizards at the tavern had been successful. They had completed the blood oath, and he knew his plan to be king of Velidred was in motion.

Haskell had to sneak into the Kallurian manor late at night hoping that Gadiel didn't realize he hadn't been there for the last few hours. He planned to slip through the back door, which had a squeaky hinge. With a flick of his wrist, he chanted a spell to quiet any noises that he might make as he opened the back door and entered the kitchen.

There were no lights on in the kitchen, and Haskell snuck through the dark room into the hallway. Candlelight from Gadiel's office shone through the partially opened door, but Haskell moved quickly past the room. His heart thudded as he hurried through the hallway to the steps.

He placed his hand on the stair's handrail and put his right foot on the first stair when a voice shouted from Gadiel's office, "Haskell! Get in here."

Haskell felt his heart drop into his stomach as fear gripped his chest. He shuffled away from the stairs and tried to control his breathing as he moved back to Gadiel's office. He wondered how much information he should give him. The old man would know if he lied and his punishment for lying would be more intense than if he just told the truth.

When he reached the partially opened door, he closed his eyes a moment before pushing the door open. Gadiel sat behind his desk, while Sims sprawled on a bench.

"Where have you been?" Gadiel asked. His nostrils flared, as he bared his teeth.

Haskell had a sour taste in his mouth. He suspected the old man already knew where he had been and wasn't happy about his decision to go there.

"I went up into the mountains to talk with three wizards." There he said it, now let Gadiel punish him and be done with it.

"What did I tell you about your poor judgment in building a wizard army?"

Haskell's shoulders curved forward. "That it was a stupid and would get us all killed."

"Do you have a death wish? Because if you do, I can kill you right now." Gadiel stood, walked over to Haskell, and touched the viscount's shoulder, and the young wizard dropped to his knees in pain.

Haskell felt the pain, but tried to struggle through it. The old man had delivered punishments to him so many times over the last few weeks that he had learned ways to minimize the pain or at least cope with the torment until it dissipated. He rocked back and forth on his knees, riding the pain, his teeth gritted in agony. Gadiel seemed to find that right level of continued torture just until Haskell felt he'd empty his stomach and then the discomfort would subside.

"Who did you speak with? Maybe I can minimize our risk."

Haskell knew that meant Gadiel would probably try to kill the wizards. But his own life would be horrific until he spilled their names. "I met up with three wizards—Garrick, Mortimer, and Ambrose."

Gadiel grunted, "Ambrose is powerful and mean. He could be problematic."

"We don't have to kill them. They're our allies." Haskell thought he would try to get ahead of Gadiel's oppositions to his idea. "I signed a blood oath with them."

Gadiel closed his eyes and shook his head. "You know nothing, Boy. A blood oath means the target on your back is even larger than it was before. Hasn't Dakarai taught you anything about magic?"

"I have more power in magic than he does."

"Yet, you have the brain power of a squirrel. All the magic power in the world won't protect you from doing stupid things. Signing a blood oath shows your ignorance."

If he lived through this night, Haskell intended to show the old man his ability to do the right thing and reach his goals.

Haskell said, "Ambrose mentioned there was another way to force them to our will."

"You will not tie me up in your schemes."

"Hear me out." Haskell leaned toward Gadiel. "You and I would have total power at Velidred Castle." *I need to make him want to take over the castle as much as I do. He wants power. I'll offer him more power than he ever dreamed possible.*

"You can't just walk into the castle and say you're king. There's a process. Even if the current king were to die, his descendants are in line for the position by birth." Gadiel threw his hands up in exasperation. "Do you plan to kill all his descendants, too?"

Haskell hadn't considered the problem with the descendants.

Sims piped up from his seat on the bench, "Did you know that your girlfriend's mother is in line for the Velidred throne? Though she is on a family branch that will probably never see the title."

Haskell clenched his fists in frustration. That meant that Princess Noreen was in line for the throne. How could he have not thought of this development? It wouldn't do to kill the princess in the process of making her marry him. Stupid. Stupid. Stupid.

Gadiel stood next to Haskell and placed his arm across the boy's shoulders. Haskell flinched at the touch, but no torture emanated from the old man. Instead, he guided the young wizard over to a bench on the other side of the room, away from Sims. They sat together as Gadiel spoke, "Do you see what I mean when I say you don't know enough to plan this grand coup of Velidred.?"

"Any time a king is assassinated, the kingdom will lean toward chaos and anarchy, even if you do everything right. Only powerful leaders can quell that rising tide of discontent. Your power struggle may lead to all the little villages falling into instability. How will you quell these pockets of strife?"

Haskell shook his head. His plan was simple and perfect as it was. All he needed was to have Gadiel help him. Now the old man just complicated the very fabric of his strategy. Maybe he could come up with an idea to salvage his scheme. He wanted the princess, and she was in a line to the king's throne. There must be a way.

Gadiel droned on next to him, "We have it good here and at the manor in Oak Ridge. We're making good money, and growing in prestige."

"You don't understand. I don't care about prestige. I want justice for my father and a chance at marrying the girl." Haskell tried to think of other solutions that would allow him to take over the Velidred Castle, but in his current state, his mind was blank at formulating plans to convince Gadiel to help.

Gadiel stood, grabbed the front of Haskell's tunic and pulled him close. "I've been around a long time. The girl means nothing in the grand scheme of things. Forget the girl. If you keep pursuing this, I'm going to re-implement the box just for you. Your father made a mistake, and the king killed him. Get over it."

Haskell's ears burned as blood rushed to his head. "You don't know how I feel."

Gadiel pushed him against the wall and Haskell rebounded off it, struck the bench on his way to the floor, and crumpled in pain.

Anger flooded through him, and he prepared to throw a fireball.

Dakarai stepped into the room. "Don't do it, Haskell. I have Gadiel shielded."

Haskell felt like a little child wanting something so bad that he had to resort to a temper tantrum. Gadiel would never let him have his way. A fireball formed in his hand.

"Haskell!" Dakarai warned.

I'm stronger than Gadiel and Dakarai combined. Let the old man have the manors. I can waltz into Goodwin castle and the princess and I can elope. We'll go to a foreign land where no one knows us. It'll be perfect.

Gadiel said, "I don't know what you're thinking, Boy, but if it includes the girl, give it a rest. You can't have her. That's life and sometimes life is tough."

He wondered if he could forget Noreen. With a gentle roll of his shoulders, he let the fireball dissipate, and released the tension in his back muscles. He struggled to his hands and knees, crawled to the bench, and clumsily got himself into a sitting position. His muscles twitched in pain from the strain he had put on them in his anger.

His neck which felt sore on one side. "You know we wouldn't have to use a wizard army. We could use your little eye juju to make the king relinquish the crown to me."

"That juju you reference isn't a lucky talisman that I can wave around to force people to obey me."

Haskell said, "But I've seen you change people's minds. Imagine if you were in court and some noble came along looking to make trouble in the kingdom, we'd just have him talk with you and the problem would disappear."

"It doesn't work like that."

"Well, there has to be some solution. I'm supposed to be king."

Sims guffawed. "Are you still delusional about that foolish prophecy from the young spiritualist on the volcano? She's a con artist using visions of grandeur to take money from gullible people like you."

Haskell didn't think the woman was conning him. He thought she looked as surprised as he was at what she saw.

Gadiel said, "Even if her vision was authentic, it takes many years and decades to make a king. Maybe when you're fifty years old, you might have a chance. You're not even twenty. The populace won't support a young boy as king, especially if he didn't rise to power organically. If you start a war, people will die and will dislike you."

He wondered if the old man was right. No doubt Haskell's age might play a part in who supported him. But he promised Prince Krunal that he would build the wizard army and take down the Velidred King.

Haskell decided it was time to visit the spiritualist. He could confront her directly and see if she was just conning him. Maybe she tells everyone they will be king, and he wasn't wise enough to see her for what she was.

Gadiel gazed deeply into Haskell's eyes. There appeared to be a mixture of wisdom and concern on the old man's wrinkled face. "I will repeat this once more. Listen, there's a truth you must understand. Following the desires of your heart, as enticing as they may be, may not always lead to the best outcome. The dreams of youth, with their glittering allure, can sometimes mislead us."

Haskell rolled his eyes and shook his head. What did this old man know about the dreams of youth?

"I understand you have a great desire to avenge your father's death, achieve your dream of being king, wear the crown, and have the young princess on your arm. But remember, there's a price to your ambitions."

Haskell stared back at Gadiel, and through gritted teeth he said, "I know there's a cost to becoming king. You aren't listening to me. I'm willing to pay every penny of that fee."

Gadiel's eyes narrowed. "You aren't the only one that will pay the price. Your pursuit of this dream will affect everyone in this household. Challenges you can't imagine will be forced on you, and each decision you make might make us richer or kill a friend."

Silence cloaked the room for a moment.

"You're a viscount before age twenty, without royal blood, and the son of a blacksmith. If you keep your nose clean, you can live better than a king for the rest of your life. King's lives are always at risk because there is always some snot-nosed little toad like you that thinks they can defeat the king and take over."

Gadiel pointed at Sims and Dakarai. "Your friends are happy and comfortable and it's all because of you. Your happiness is already within your grasp. Don't let your ambition, desire for revenge, or a girl," his voice dripped with derision, "be your downfall."

CHAPTER 54

Haskell trotted his horse out of the manor a few days later to take a trip to Tanuku to see Forest River Blossom. He needed answers to some questions, and it was time for the spiritualist to tell him the truth. It hadn't been easy, but he had decided that whatever information he found out from the woman would define his course of action about defeating King Kaelen Stoneforge of Velidred.

It had been a long ride on the horse and his bottom hurt from being in the saddle for so long. He had been honest with Gadiel about where he was going and the old man had agreed to Haskell's desire to see the woman. The ride over to Tanuku had given him time to formulate his questions, and he hoped to get answers that agreed with his desires. He wasn't sure what he would do if he found the woman to be a fraud.

When he reached the small hamlet, he heard dancing and singing coming from the far side of the village. Haskell rode his horse under a canopy of ancient trees with leaves of gold, orange, reds, and yellows. The centuries-old trees let in late afternoon sun that dappled the path with light and shadow.

As he reached the village green, he found women in white dresses dancing around a large, gnarly oak tree in the center of the large space. Four men on the edge of the green played flute, drums, mandolin, and violin.

Haskell stood watching the women, aged from girls his age to women he thought might be older than his mother would have been. An aroma of roasted meats, freshly baked bread, and soups and stews filled the air. Men lined up to a small shed where townspeople poured ale and cider into their wooden cups.

He didn't know what to make of all this celebrating, but he worried he wouldn't be able to find the spiritualist. After a few minutes of watching the dancers, he made his way around the square. Small huts lined one side of the green where he saw local craftspeople displaying hand-carved wooden figurines, textiles, and painted pottery.

Haskell picked up several of the figurines, representing the great legends of hunters, soldiers, and kings of the past. He didn't need any of those, he was going to be a legend himself someday.

A cheer erupted off to his left, and he headed in that direction to see what might be happening. Teenagers were attempting to climb a log that someone had placed vertically into the ground. As he watched, a boy older than himself planted his feet next to the log and grabbed it with two hands.

Something looked strange about the twenty-foot log. It seemed to be coated with a white coating, but not a paint or whitewash.

Haskell asked a man who stood next to him, "What is the pole covered with?"

"Huh?" The man looked at Haskell. "Ah, a stranger to our autumn festival. The town fathers rub copious amounts of pig grease onto the log."

"Why are they so excited about climbing it?"

"You might not be able to see from here, but there are five gold pieces on top. The person who climbs the log gets the gold."

This news made Haskell smile as he watched the teen climb about five feet up the pole, and then his progress stopped and he slid back down to the ground. The crowd erupted with another cheer. He watched multiple attempts. Some didn't even make it five feet, while older kids managed eight feet, but they all slid down to where they began.

After a while he tired of watching the boys, and continued his search for Forest River Blossom. He thought she might have a small hut of her own, where she told people their fortunes for a coin or two, but he couldn't find her.

The sun continued to drift lower, and the smoke seemed to settle over the village, enhanced by a slight fog as the temperature dropped.

A man called from a small wooden platform on the north side of the green. "Hear ye, hear ye. Come one, come all. Ladies and gentlemen, gather round. Boys and girls, it's time to hear wondrous tales from the realm of imagination and splendor. Our storyteller has traveled from the coast to the mountains and has fought against giants, mages, strange animals, and unbelievable spirits. He stands here today to share stories that will transport us to distant lands. Let's welcome to our humble village the grand master of verse, fable, myth, and saga—Eldric the Enchanter.

The crowd had stopped whatever frivolous activity they had been involved in and pushed closer to the stage.

A short, man with a beard that extended to his mid-chest stepped upon the platform.

The crowd cheered and whistled in anticipation.

Haskell had heard of storytellers, but he had never listened to one before. He snuck through the crowd to get near the front so he could see the man.

Despite his small size, Eldric's deep voice boomed over the crowd. His first words were powerful enough to quiet the people. He started a story about an evil dragon that terrorized the lowlands. The monster's teeth were sharp and its stomach hungry. With amazing adventures and with a voice that dipped to a whisper and shouted loud enough to hear in the nearby mountains, the man enchanted the crowd. For twenty minutes, he told a story that ended with a young villager defeating the dragon and saving the village. The storyteller finished with a flourish and a bow.

The villagers cheered their approval.

Eldric called out, "What other story would you like to hear?"

People shouted, "Tell us the story of the cliff dwellers."

"Let's hear the legend of the sword of Velidred."

"No, I want to hear of strange lands and strange peoples."

Haskell got caught up in the process and shouted out, "I want to hear the story of an orphan boy who married a princess."

Others continued to shout until Eldric raised his hands.

Kenneth Brown

The crowd grew silent.
Eldric started his story softly.
"In a land where dreams and legends intertwine,
A man with hope and courage, his heart aligned,
He yearned for a princess, fair and bright,
To be with her, his guiding star of the night.

Upon a path that led to a mountain's crest,
He set forth on a journey, a valiant quest,
With each step, his love's flame burned so bright,
He'd climb any mountain to win her delight.

Beneath Velidred's moon's fiery embrace,
He reached the summit, his heart in its place,
The mountain whispered secrets of truth and lies,
As stardust sparkled in the depths of his eyes.

On the peak where the gods landed on earth,
A wise sage sat, sharing wisdom of great worth,
With beard as white as snow and eyes of blue,
He held a key, the seeker's love still true.

"Brave traveler," *the sage said with a smile,*
"To win her heart, you must go that extra mile,
A princess's love, a treasure so demure,

Requires a great courage and a mind so pure."

The sage handed him a key, to the prodigy
Its hope came from the inheritance of progeny,
The kingdom of her heart, your dreams will sway,
Be brave, be true, and love will never betray.

With the key in hand, the man began his descent,
His heart filled with joy, his spirit content,
For in that mountain's secret, he'd come to peace,
That love's true journey can never cease.

He returned to the kingdom, his heart so sure,
To find the princess, a love so pure,
The key from the gods, felled him like a dart,
Love's true magic within his heart."

    Haskell stood, mesmerized at the words and the man's rich, sonorous voice. The tale told his story. This wasn't fiction or the story from times of yore. This was Haskell and Noreen's saga. Two lovers from different worlds, but their hope to be together would not be denied. Did he have to find the sage and go on a quest to find the key?

    He pushed his way out of the crowd, his heart beating fast and hard in excitement and expectation. It was now imperative that he talk with the spiritualist. He believed that she would confirm his suspicion that

Kenneth Brown

the story was related to him, and it wasn't just chance that the storyteller had chosen his suggestion and the tale he wanted to hear. Maybe she was the sage he needed to visit. No one and nothing could deny him his goal. He would have the throne and the princess by his side, no matter the cost.

CHAPTER 55

The fall festival lasted long into the night and Haskell finally had to resort to asking about Forest River Blossom. Fog had settled thickly onto the village green and he couldn't see across the square. The crowd had diminished, and he asked one of the crafters where he might find the spiritualist.

The man smiled, "On a night like this when the fog is so thick that it's hard to see the Velidred moon in its heavenly abyss, you can find the woman in the hollow of the great oak tree." He pointed to the center of the village green.

"The hollow of the oak tree?" Haskell repeated.

Two women approached the man's booth, and the man waved his hands at Haskell. "Go. I have paying customers."

Haskell shrugged and moved in the direction he thought led to the center of the green, where he remembered seeing the majestic tree. He didn't quite understand what the hollow of the oak tree meant, but he'd find the woman. When he reached the tree, he stared at it for a moment. It looked fine from where he stood.

As he walked around the tree searching for the hollow in it, he sensed someone watching him and checked behind him for others in the area. The fog had thickened even more, and he saw no one. He had walked around the tree a couple of times during the day and he didn't remember seeing a hollow in the tree near the ground.

He looked up higher in the branches, but still saw nothing. An icy coolness settled around his shoulders. He wished he had a candle with him so he could see the tree better. With a shake of his shoulders, he moved closer, and he noticed a slight glow on the tree at about his eye level. The light emanated from a carving within the tree. He hadn't noticed the carving before. Again, he searched behind for someone watching. The fog had dampened the reveler's voices in the village green.

Feeling satisfied that he was alone with the tree, he cautiously ran his fingers over the glowing carving, feeling a sensation of ancient magic radiating from the wood. As his fingers brushed over the intricate image of a woman in a forest staring up at the moon in the sky, he heard a slight whisper.

A woman's voice, soft and ethereal, said, "Come closer, my friend."

Fear told him to run as the hair on his neck stood up and his skin prickled. But curiosity beckoned him to learn more about this phenomenon. With a slight hesitation, his muscles tensed and he cocked his head in confusion, stepping forward. One step. A second step. He was close to the tree, and he had no room for a third step. Suddenly, a hand reached out from within the tree, grabbed his wrist, and with surprising strength, pulled him inside.

He braced his hand in anticipation of smacking into the tree's rough bark, but instead he stumbled through an opening that wasn't there a moment before.

Despite the tree being solid on the outside, he found himself inside it, in a space larger than the tree's trunk could possibly contain. A woman stood by his side. The spiritualist from the volcano. She wore a full-length silk gown of forest green, with yellow butterflies stitched into the fabric.

Even with finding the woman he sought, his heart beat rapidly in wariness and his eyes were fully opened in surprise at being drawn into the interior so forcefully.

"What took you so long to find me?" Forest River Blossom asked.

"I looked for you all day. Why would you be hiding inside the tree?"

Her eyes shimmered, and she used a hand with silver rings on each finger to brush her hair from her eyes. "My mother birthed me under this tree and she said it would always protect me and share its ancient wisdom if I protect this hidden sanctuary from harm."

Haskell thought it sounded a little weird, but everything the woman did seemed strange.

She asked, "What brought you to me? The tree's ancient knowledge is poised to discern answers to all your questions."

He smiled at that, because he hoped the woman could help guide him to win the princess' hand in marriage and take revenge on King Stoneforge. Haskell talked with Forest River Blossom about her prophecy on Mount Velidred during the eclipse.

She nodded, "I remember it well, because . . ." she hesitated, "you didn't appear to be king material." After a moment where she examined him from head to toe, she said, "You appear to have come up in the world."

Haskell stood a little taller. "Yes, I'm the new Viscount of Kalluria."

Forest River Blossom frowned. "You also murdered Prince Jordan."

He backed away and shushed her. "Not so loud. I didn't do it; the Velidred soldiers killed the prince."

She shook her head in almost imperceptible micro-movements. With a jangle of bracelets, she raised her right hand to her head and touched her forehead with two fingers. "No. This action has hurt your chances of becoming king."

He moved closer. "Tell me more about becoming king. Assure me I can still be king."

The woman was even smaller than Haskell and she waved her hands in front of her head. "No, stand back. The forest and the tree are upset."

Haskell grabbed her left wrist. "Help me. I need to be king."

She tried to back away, but he held tight.

"I need answers. You can help me find the answers I seek."

"Easy, your Lordship." Her eyes shone bright in the dim candlelit space. "I am here to help you, but your behavior troubles the ancients. Let me go." She shook her arm.

Haskell looked around the room, but still grasped her wrist. "I need clarification on your previous foretelling."

She looked him in the eyes. "You have come for a reading, then." She shook her arm once more, and he released her from his grasp. "Come to the table."

He studied the tree's interior. In the middle of the space stood a wooden table with four chairs. A plaid, green and red tablecloth covered the table, and in its center glowed a pale-green crystal globe.

Forest River Blossom sat on one chair and beckoned for Haskell to join her.

He sat cautiously at the table wondering if he made a mistake coming to her, realizing for the first time he might not like her answers.

The spiritualist placed a laced fabric over her hair with a sparkling, green opal resting on her forehead. She hovered her hands over the crystal and began a ritual. "The first step in the process is to awaken the crystal's energy, so I may speak with the ancients."

She closed her eyes and chanted.

> *"O crystal of wisdom, ancient and bright,*
>
> *I call upon the forces that dwell within,*
>
> *Awaken now, reveal the hidden truth,*
>
> *In harmony with nature, may your powers enlighten us."*

The crystal's colors brightened and its interior fog swirled in the light.

"Tell me, young viscount, what question do you have for me?"

Here it was then, finally, he could have his questions answered. He felt excitement build within his chest. The woman seemed to be a professional and not the con artist Sims thought she was.

Haskell took a deep breath, "Will I become the king of Velidred?"

Forest River Blossom frowned and her forehead creased in consternation as her lips straightened into a line. "I've already told you the answer to that question. It is as predicted on the volcano."

He smiled in triumph. "Do I need to build a wizard army to defeat the current king?"

She opened her eyes and stared at the globe. It seemed an electric current flowed from the crystal and the opal on her forehead. Her demeanor became serious and with a voice devoid of emotion, she said, "There is a price for you to become king. A price that wasn't there originally. You have broken the agreement with nature and the moons . . ." Her voice trailed off, as she appeared to be listening to someone or something. "Your desire to force your destiny to achieve your own wicked ambition will require you to sacrifice a great personal treasure."

She stopped talking and closed her eyes again.

"What is that price? Maybe I don't want to pay that price?"

Forest River Blossom gave him an understanding nod and a sad smile. "The moon goddess of Velidred has already affixed the price to the bargain."

"What bargain? I didn't agree with any bargain. Tell me what I will sacrifice." He felt his throat closing in frustration and concern. He had already lost his best friend and his parents, what more could he lose?

"What is your third question?"

"You haven't answered any of my questions." His lips were pinched tight as he rubbed the back of his neck. He had trouble concentrating on the third question on his list. The woman was irritating him by not giving him proper answers. He wanted to shake her so she would cooperate.

She stared at Haskell. "I'm waiting."

He took a few quick deep breaths and exhaled noisily through his nose. He bared his teeth as he stood on the edge of anger.

"Okay, okay. This is the most important question and the only real reason I'm here." Just thinking about the question had his heart pounding. "Will I marry Princess Noreen?" He felt the vein in his neck throbbing in anticipation of an answer.

The spiritualist closed her eyes once more and hovered her hands over the crystal. The fog inside the crystal became dark and angry, and sparks of lightning flashed within the globe. She moaned as her body swayed side to side.

He couldn't believe what he was seeing. This couldn't be good. *I shouldn't have come. I just know she will give me bad news.*

The lightning within the globe dissipated and Forest River's body stopped swaying. She abruptly sat up straight.

He waited expectantly for her answer in anticipation of a positive response.

A rush of red flushed her cheeks, and she leaned away from Haskell. "It seems my advisor cannot answer that question. You have set your personal goals over letting the organic, natural life lead you to your destiny. Your behavior has disrupted the future."

Haskell felt overheated by what he was hearing. He wiped a sheen of sweat from his forehead in agitation. "The prince planned to kill me. What was I supposed to do?"

"Nature would have found a way past your desire for the woman. You have changed the path of your destiny. And furthermore—"

"What more do you have to tell me? I'm just a kid. You told me I would be king. I'm just trying to make that happen. Why do you torment me, woman?"

"I saw a new prophecy. No matter what happens in the future, this will occur." She closed her eyes once more and placed both hands on her forehead, gripping the opal with her fingers.

"In realms where destiny's tapestry unfolds,

Beware the teenagers, both young and bold.

A portal they possess, a key unknown,

To disrupt your plans, your purpose overthrown.

Their curious minds, a force unbound,

May breach the gateway, chaos confound.

The threads of fate may fray and tear,

With consequences dire, beyond compare.

In shadows cast by fate's enigmatic game,

A dissatisfied daughter, a soul aflame,

She lingers near, a tempest in disguise,
Her discontented heart, a silent cry.

Guide them, thwart them, the choice is thine,
For in their hands, a power undefined.
The path ahead, uncertain, veiled, and vast,
In this cryptic dance, ensures your fate is cast."

She leaned back in her chair in exhaustion, her eyes still closed.

Haskell shook his head in confusion. "What does all this mean?" He leaned closer to the spiritualist. "Tell me more." He grabbed her arm.

Her eyes opened in terror. "We are done. Never touch me again or you are doomed." She quickly raised her arms over her head and quickly spread them apart. "Be gone!"

Haskell found himself outside the old oak tree, the fog still thick as soup. He walked around the tree searching for the glowing carving, but found nothing. His brain ached from the experience within the tree's interior. The woman had told him nothing, though she reiterated that he would become king someday.

But when?

He pounded on the tree screaming out, "Let me back in, I still need answers."

Nothing changed. He sat on the ground in front of the mighty oak hoping that Forest River Blossom would step outside and he could ask additional questions or she might invite him back into its hollow. The temperature dropped, and he finally gave up hope of seeing her once more.

His original plan was to come into town, spend a couple of hours and then return to the manor, but it was too late to be traveling on the road, which could be unsafe at night. He searched for a room, but the tiny village was full of visitors who had come for the festival leaving him outside where the cold penetrated his jacket.

He sat next to a fire on the village green with men who had drunk too much ale who were either singing or sleeping. Thoughts soon rambled through his mind. *The spiritualist didn't say I wouldn't marry Princess Noreen, but who are these teenagers that threaten my future? Forest River Blossom said I would become a king.* He spent the rest of the night trying to decipher the cryptic message.

CHAPTER 56

Haskell rode his horse toward his manor home in Oak Ridge. The journey had been long, and he looked forward to a good night's sleep in his own bed. The full moon of Velidred provided enough crimson light on the path for him to feel comfortable continuing at night.

As he neared the village, he had to pass a graveyard. He always felt uneasy passing cemeteries at night. Tonight was no exception, and the red glow of Velidred made him more restless as he traveled by the crypts and gravestones. About halfway on the journey past the graves, he heard a voice. A single male voice that sounded like he was having a conversation, but Haskell could only hear one side of it.

He stopped his horse and stepped closer to the graveyard stone walls. The cemetery had been there for centuries and the walls had lost a few stones over the years. He tied his horse's reins to a nearby tree and jumped over the wall, curious about the conversation because the voice sounded familiar.

As Haskell stepped cautiously between the graves, the moon's red glow cast strange shadows and shapes around the headstones, making them dance as if to an evil tune. A chill ran down his spine. He stopped fifteen feet from the man who kept talking and gesticulating at the moon.

"If we allow the boy to continue to his goal, we'll all face the punishment when he fails. And the foolish boy will surely fail. Lives hang in the balance."

Haskell gasped, recognizing Gadiel's voice. He couldn't hear or see the other person to whom Gadiel spoke, but he was afraid to move closer.

"Is the power to be gained worth the price? There must be another way. At the very least, let me find another person to become king. He is too inexperienced for the position." Gadiel dropped to his knees and screamed in agony.

Haskell looked for the source of pain, as he hid in the shadows, but still couldn't find another person in the cemetery to be causing Gadiel's pain and stress. He wished he could get a better view of who the old man argued with because he had never imagined there was someone that caused Gadiel the same grief the old man caused him.

"Do you really want to overturn the ancient prophecies that put King Stoneforge on the throne?" Gadiel stayed on his knees as he begged with his advisor. He opened his palms toward the moon as if pleading for the moon to listen to him.

"There's knowledge at the castle that I don't want Haskell to find. The boy is powerful in his magic and he has access to the wand."

A wolf on a distant hill howled at the moon as a breeze blew leaves across the ground.

Haskell couldn't understand why he couldn't hear the other side of the conversation. They obviously didn't know he was near. The other person had to be close to whisper in such a way that he couldn't hear.

"If he finds the scroll, he could unleash chaos in Velidred and for miles around. I beseech you to let me find another candidate, someone we can control."

A scroll to unleash chaos. That's exactly what I need to take over the Velidred Kingdom, thought Haskell. He needed to get Gadiel to reveal the scroll's location.

"I know the wheels are in motion and I understand your power to make this happen, but what if something goes wrong? He is a loose stone, just as likely to foul up the waterwheel, as to crush the wheat at his feet. We can't trust his judgment."

Gadiel struggled back to his feet, still gazing intently at the Velidred Moon. Haskell thought the old man would look at the person he was speaking to, but for some reason he couldn't look the other man in the eye.

Haskell went to change his position behind the headstone and stepped on a branch which broke with a reverberating crack. He dropped to the ground. He couldn't afford to be seen until he learned more.

The cemetery went quiet. The wind stopped blowing, and Haskell held his breath. He couldn't see anything in his current position and worried that Gadiel was stalking in his direction. The man would make his life miserable if he knew he listened.

The wind blew once more, and an owl flew over Haskell's head, hooting as it passed his position. He hoped it wasn't a portent of trouble. It wouldn't surprise him if Gadiel controlled the beasts of nature.

Gadiel spoke once more, "I understand your determination to make the viscount a king, but I cannot condone further meddling with his destiny.

The path we've set him on is fraught with danger, and I fear it may be his undoing. He needs guidance and nurturing, not manipulation and interference. Pushing him further towards this destiny could have dire consequences for us all."

Silence once more. Darkness enclosed the graveyard as a cloud passed between the moon and the land.

"I'm not blind to his potential. He is powerful, but we must tread carefully. If we push him too hard or too fast, he might break under the pressure. Give me time to nurture, educate, and train him for the task at hand. He's not there yet. The boy killed a prince, and I fear the power of the throne might make him too hard for us to handle."

The conversation continued, as Haskell stayed hidden.

"And what if I refuse?"

He heard the old man scream in pain once more. Haskell delighted in seeing Gadiel punished in the same way he punished others.

Nothing happened.

Haskell heard nothing for several minutes. He wondered if the conversation had run its course. His horse whinnied in the distance and he froze. Gadiel would do horrible things to him if he found him listening in on the old man's conversations.

He peeked over the headstone and tried to determine if anyone was still there. A body lay next to the grave marker. Was it Gadiel's, or had the old man snapped and killed the person he spoke with? It wouldn't surprise Haskell for that to happen. His mentor was as capable of snapping as anyone.

He wondered if he should check to see if it was Gadiel's body. If he checked and it was Gadiel, and the old man still lived, then Haskell's life might be over. Unless the other guy truly desired Gadiel to assist Haskell in taking over the Velidred kingdom, Gadiel would throw him in the box for the rest of his life. Despite his brain screaming to leave the cemetery and go home, he felt it was necessary to check.

With small steps and watching each foot fall, he edged closer to the headstone. Whoever lay there hadn't moved in quite some time, and Haskell became more nervous with each step. When he reached the headstone, the clouds cleared enough for the Velidred moonlight to filter to the ground. Gadiel lay in a heap.

Haskell checked for a pulse. The old man still lived. He had mixed emotions about that, but despite a voice in his head screaming at him to leave, he helped get Gadiel sitting with his back against the gravestone. He had him drink some water from his waterskin. Eventually, he got the old man to his feet and assisted him back to Gadiel's horse, which he found not far from his own.

Gadiel said nothing as they walked to the horse. Concern of punishment for listening into the conversation nagged at Haskell.

Once on their horses, they directed them to the manor.

Gadiel asked, "How much did you hear?"

"I heard a man scream in the cemetery and came to see what happened." Haskell lied.

"She saw you there, so don't lie to me, Boy."

Haskell looked down at the ground moving below him, as the horse's hoofbeats pounded rhythmically over the hard dirt road. "Something about you helping me to be king, even though you don't think I should be king. Who was the woman?"

He glanced at Gadiel, and the moon's red glow cast an evil glow around his body.

"That's none of your business, but she controls things around here. You heard what was said back there. It's time to prepare you to be king."

Adrenalin pumped through Haskell's body, and he suppressed a smile that still curled the corners of his lips. Gadiel's attitude had changed about him being king. With the old man's backing and support, they could win this battle.

"I will help you build your wizard army," Gadiel continued. "The Council of Nine will fight us every step of the way, and many good wizards will die because of your impetuousness. But the Lady of the Moon has spoken and I can't sway her."

"Who is this lady?"

Gadiel looked at the moon for a few moments. "That isn't any of your concern."

It wasn't any of his concern before tonight, but now he would find out who the woman was that wanted to make him king. Maybe he could thwart Gadiel and just work with the lady without the old man's interference.

The horses trotted through a dense forest. Fall leaves still clung stubbornly to the trees, as moonlight danced on the forest floor as if enchanted with mischief. Night animals scurried across the road to avoid the approaching men.

Gadiel moved his horse closer to Haskell's and whispered, "In the morning you will contact your new wizard friends, and we will meet. We have a lot of work to do to be ready to spring this trap."

CHAPTER 57

With a flick of his wrist, Haskell guided his horse to the Lonely Tankard Inn in the small village of Stillbarrow. Gadiel and Dakarai rode next to him and they all dismounted when they reached the meeting place. The time had come to introduce Haskell's co-conspirators to Gadiel. Haskell had concerns about how the meeting might turn out. His old mentor, Gadiel, didn't get along with everyone.

Stillbarrow had a population of less than a hundred people and Haskell hadn't seen anyone as they rode into the village. Two horses were hitched in front of the tavern. He took a deep breath and entered the small building with Gadiel and Dakarai at his heels.

Ambrose and Garrick sat next to each other at a table and one other patron sat across the room on a bench with a table all for himself.

Haskell moved into the room, removing the cloak he wore in the cool night air. It was now necessary to get commitment from the others, and the fact that the youngest, Mortimer, hadn't arrived, concerned him.

He sat at the bench across from the others and introduced Dakarai and Gadiel.

Ambrose straightened when Gadiel sat. "It's been a while since we last conversed. It doesn't look like you've aged in the last sixty years."

Gadiel smiled slightly. "The gods have favored me with good health."

"I see they are by your side." Ambrose took a drink from his cup of ale.

Gadiel said, "Are we missing someone?"

Garrick looked at the door and answered, "We're still waiting for our young friend Mortimer. He seemed to be a little spooked at our last meeting. I hope he shows so we don't have to kill him." He laughed as if he had told a joke.

"He'll show." Ambrose brushed his hand over his beard, making no difference in the tangled mess it had become.

The new arrivals all ordered a drink and some food from the man behind the counter. It appeared there was just the one person who wiped the tables, served the drinks, and prepared the food.

Gadiel said, "This is definitely a quiet place."

"It has other advantages that I will explain in a few moments." Ambrose raised his hands and wriggled his fingers. "In the meantime, I will secure our conversation from any who might want to know more about our purposes for tonight." He glanced at the other patron and the barkeep.

Haskell felt the same spell Ambrose had used in their first meeting to prevent others from listening to them.

The door opened and Mortimer rushed into the room, breathing heavily. He looked at the others at the table and placed his hand back on the door knob.

Ambrose's eyebrows creased as he stared at Mortimer.

The young man at the door seemed to be having an internal conversation, then released the door knob, and approached.

"How's your sister?" Ambrose asked.

Mortimer placed his cloak on a wall hook and sat at the table. "She's well, as you said she would be. How did you know and not me?"

"When women get that disease, they make a point to hide from family and friends, as it embarrasses them."

"I tried to get her to return home, but she refused."

"Visit her a few more times and maybe she will be more likely to return to her family."

Mortimer pointed at the food in Haskell's hand. "What's good here?"

Dakarai shook his head. "Nothing. The ale isn't bad, but the food isn't spicy at all."

Gadiel took control of the meeting, "Let's begin. Haskell tells me that you are on board with his plan. Is that true?"

Ambrose nodded. "He was persuasive."

Mortimer shook his head. "I changed my mind. It's too risky for me, and now that I've reunited with my sister, I decided to do other things with my time."

"You can't opt out now." Haskell felt a rush of panic and frustration as he countered, "You know our plans; you'll be a risk for us."

"Doesn't matter. Things have changed, and I want out."

"It does matter my young friend." Ambrose leaned close. "You have agreed to do this deed with us."

"I had too much to drink that night and didn't realize what I was agreeing to. Now I understand the folly of this endeavor." He assessed the others. "You don't need me."

"Listen, young one," Ambrose spoke with a deep calming voice. "There is a bigger purpose at play here. We are saving the kingdom with our actions and bringing peace to the wizards in the region which hasn't happened in a hundred years."

"There must be another way." Mortimer furrowed his brows, "I don't want to be part of a conspiracy and use magic to harm others. We must trust in the greater good to bring about the change we seek."

Ambrose spoke, "Your magical powers are unique, and they could be the key to tipping the scales in our favor. Consider the consequences of inaction—the lives of other wizards that will be lost if we fail to take action. Can you truly turn your back on the fate of fellow wizards?"

"He's just a boy." Mortimer pointed at Haskell. "Surely we can do better than him."

Haskell scowled and wished he had brought the Imperium Wand with him. He'd show Mortimer that he wasn't "just a boy."

"Ah, here we come to the crux of your problems with our plan." Garrick smiled. "It isn't so much you don't want to help; you don't like our choice of king.

Are you going to offer another candidate for the throne? Such as yourself."

Mortimer raised his hands. "No, no, nothing like that."

"It's written all over your face. Why should we put the boy on the throne when it should be you?" Garrick grabbed Mortimer's wrist. "You're just a lady's man. You don't have the leadership abilities to be ruler."

Mortimer wrestled his arm from Garrick's grasp. "I should smite you right now."

"I wouldn't try that if I were you." Garrick drew forth an ornate wand, its tip shimmering with arcane energy, and leveled it at Mortimer.

"You all know I would be a better choice, with my magic, and don't forget I have a little royal blood running through my body." Mortimer pushed his shoulders back and thrust out his chest and pointed at Haskell. "He is the son of a blacksmith. We'll never get the other wizards to agree to that."

Haskell squirmed on the bench raising his hands to release a fireball at the wizard. He would show Mortimer who should be king. Gadiel silently placed a hand on his shoulder and gave Haskell a deadly glare—a silent reminder to be quiet and let the others talk.

Ambrose said, "We all know his history, but he started this movement, so let's see it through. I believe it will be interesting."

"Well, I have no plans to be a part of it." Mortimer stood to leave.

Gadiel grabbed his hand. "Sit."

Mortimer struggled but Gadiel held firm. He leaned in toward Gadiel. "You don't scare me old man."

Haskell saw the scorpion move across Gadiel's eyes and watched as Mortimer's eyes tracked its progress. Mortimer didn't move as Gadiel opened his eyes wider, controlling him with his ancient power.

"Your aspirations are commendable, but a primeval force that you will never understand has chosen the boy. I sense the greatness welling within you and your destiny has been secured, but it isn't as the Velidred King."

Mortimer continued to struggle. "You can't use your ancient voodoo on me. I'm aware of your powers of manipulation and I won't be swayed."

"Relax. You are part of a greater tapestry, woven by threads of fate and destiny. But you won't realize your greatness unless you remain a part of this group. Embrace this role which will lead to the destiny that awaits you." Gadiel's focus on Mortimer never wavered.

"Release me from your evil influence, Gadiel, and let my decisions be my own," Mortimer cried out.

"You have a resilient spirit, but remember, your choices shape the destiny we all share." Gadiel turned Mortimer's arm so that it was palm up. He outlined the symbol for the Velidred Moon of a moon rising over an active volcano on Mortimer's wrist. As he drew the symbol it turned into a tattoo of reds and blacks. "Choose wisely, for the threads of fate are delicate at this time and may still snap. Your future and ours hang in the balance of your decisions."

Mortimer looked outraged as Gadiel placed the magical tattoo on his arm, but then he watched his arm as the image disappeared. A questioning look appeared on his face. Something changed in Mortimer and he relaxed and sat.

Gadiel released his grip but still stared at Mortimer whose gaze seemed unfocused.

Haskell wondered what just happened. Just when he thought he didn't need Gadiel, the old man would apply his own distorted magic. To his surprise and relief, someone else bore the brunt of Gadiel's wrath, sparing him from the usual torment. Would it be enough for Mortimer to stop his whining and stay a part of the group to overtake the castle or would the wizard become a loose end that needed to be handled?

"Now that we have removed a source of irritation to our cause, let's talk about our needs." Ambrose took a drink and set his cup on the table. "We'll need to make sure we have a broad mix of wizards skilled in elementals."

Everyone at the table nodded.

Haskell took out a scroll that he had prepared before coming to the meeting. He could write on the scroll, but to everyone else it looked like a recipe to prepare a stegox stew. He made four columns and wrote Fire, Water, Earth and Air for each of the elementals.

Haskell continued, "Of all the wizards we recruit we should only need a fraction who specialize only in water. We will be fighting in the Velidred mountains, where it will be difficult to work with water. Let's find wizards that are competent in one of the other skills, but who might have a propensity to also work with water as needed."

Ambrose nodded at Haskell. "You've given this project a lot of thought,"

He smiled. "I'm committed to sitting on the throne and correcting injustices that have occurred in the past."

They talked into the night about using fire wizards to launch fireballs and create walls of flame for offensive and defensive maneuvers. The water wizards could be utilized to snuff out the fires if needed or to deflect enemy attacks. Since the battle would occur near the Velidred volcano, the earth elementals could manipulate the ground beneath their opponent's feet with seismic disturbances or reshape the terrain for their own battlefield benefits. Those wizards capable of shaping air and deploying wind to disrupt enemy formations would help overwhelm their opponent's ground attacks.

Haskell wrote furiously, trying to keep up with everything Ambrose, Garrick, Dakarai, and Gadiel discussed about the future battle plans. The information was so new to him, and he realized that Dakarai still had a lot to teach him about working magic with the different elements. Up to this point he had used what seemed right at each moment, but could see more power in being conscious of the magical decisions you used.

Then the talk turned to recruitment measures. How would they find the wizards to join their team? Their most likely candidates would be wizards who were currently dissatisfied with King Stoneforge.

Garrick thought for a moment and said, "We might find a kingdom such as the Kallurians that will be willing to help us take down the king of Velidred."

Gadiel gave Haskell a sharp look. "We are in negotiations with them at this moment. Aren't we Haskell?"

Haskell looked down at the table. He was supposed to have already gotten their buy-in, but King Kalluri still seemed dissatisfied with what Haskell did to Prince Jordan and he hadn't given Haskell a positive response yet. "It's not a problem. I'm working on it, and he'll join us." He hoped that was true.

"When the nobles begin marching through a kingdom, the odds are good that discontented commoners will take up weapons against their king." Ambrose raised his hand for another ale.

"Do we have money to hire skilled mercenaries?" Garrick asked. "I can send out a call to some friends of mine that have connections to these groups."

"That would be good, a couple hundred trained combatants can go a long way toward discouraging the king's guards." Ambrose took the cup that the tavern owner handed him. He took a swig and looked at Gadiel. "And here is an important point that I think you can handle, Gadiel."

"Yes, what is that?"

"There must be men and women in the king's court that we can turn to our side. I'm thinking with a little manipulation on your part, they'll be happy to help us in our quest."

Gadiel nodded. "I have contacts that might prove useful in this part of our strategy."

Mortimer spoke for the first time, "You all say we need all these skilled wizards. How do you plan to find them? They aren't just going to tell you they hate the king."

Garrick smiled. "That's my role. Tomorrow we will meet at the Veils Gate Nexus, which is close to this location. It's a known portal to other worlds and is not only a means of transportation but also a mystical sanctuary that provides protection from prying eyes and ears. Few know of its power to send messages to wizards that meet certain criteria. You'll see and be amazed at its power."

CHAPTER 58

Six wizards left the Lonely Tankard Inn the next morning and followed Garrick as he led them up the mountain. Haskell hadn't slept well. The bed was lumpy, the blanket pocked with holes, and wind whistled through the gaps in the walls. Last night's meal hadn't settled well with his stomach either, and he wondered if this was an omen for the day's coming attraction, Veils Gate Nexus.

They walked for about fifteen minutes and the ground leveled, before they came upon a meadow. Granite stone walls shot into the sky to the north of the meadow. Garrick proceeded toward the walls of stone. Late summer grasses still covered the meadow and there was no path, so they walked through the grasses on uneven ground.

"Where are you taking us?" Haskell asked.

"You'll see soon, my young viscount," Garrick responded.

As they neared the stone wall on their left, Haskell sensed a change in the environment. It began as a disturbance to his ears, a slight ringing and pressure buildup in his head.

Garrick stopped. "Do you hear that, gentlemen?"

All the wizards except Garrick were tugging at or pressing on their ears.

"I can't hear much of anything," Mortimer said.

"Exactly." Garrick raised his hands and spun slowly in a circle. "We are standing in Veils Gate Nexus. A portal to another world is nearby, and this area is a powerful link to strong magic of mythical proportions."

The ringing in Haskell's ears made it difficult to hear Garrick, but he could feel the magical energy of the area.

"Only those who have been granted permission or possess a specific magical attunement can perceive the Veils Gate Nexus and utilize its power. This selective attunement ensures that the node remains a well-guarded secret." With a sly smile, he said, "I will provide you all with the key to this power."

Haskell pulled on his ear and opened his mouth wide in an attempt to clear his hearing.

Garrick continued his introduction to the nexus as he pointed at the symbols etched into the rock. "These signs allow us to protect ourselves from shorting out our magic by using too much. They act as a protective barrier to burn-out." He raised his finger. "If you know how to use the codes."

Dakarai held his hands over his ears, scowled and yelled, "And you'll teach us how to use these ancient cryptograms?"

"Of course." Garrick waved his hand. "But let me tell you more about this area so you can understand how we can use this for our purposes."

He pointed to one wall etching shaped like a clock. "This, my friends, will allow any of you skilled in time-based magic to enhance your magic and play with time, showing other's future events or past events as your abilities enable you. If you aren't a master of the magic of time, then I suggest you not touch this symbol, or you might find yourself in a dimension of time not of this world." He laughed his loud, obnoxious laugh.

"What do you have that will stop this blasted ringing in my ears? I can't hear a thing you say," Ambrose shouted.

With a quick smile, Garrick moved to his right, stepping past six of the stone etchings and touched a symbol that was shaped like a ram's horn. The image showed a man who held the horn in his hands, the smaller portion in his mouth, and the larger part of the horn curved out to the sky.

"Sonus Tacere," Garrick said.

Immediately, the ringing in Haskell's ears stopped. The ringing was replaced by birds singing and the scurry of small mammals in the grass. "Finally. Relief."

"As you can see, this is a special place with great potential for enhancing the magic we'll need to defeat the king." Garrick raised his hands overhead and spun slowly to indicate the symbols and the mountainous region they were in. "This is a magical focusing region, and to my knowledge, there is no other like it in the world."

"How many wizards know of this area?" Haskell asked.

Garrick wavered a little, as if he counted people he knew while he pictured them in his mind. "Fewer than ten."

"Are we here so you can teach us how to use the magic and symbols?" Dakarai asked.

"Not today. That will come. Today, I wanted to introduce you to the place, and we will send out our first message to a handful of potential candidates to join our wizard army."

Mortimer spoke, "If we meet everyone here, then everybody will know about this nexus. We can't have that."

"It won't be a problem. This is a place for us to send out a magical message." Garrick looked at Ambrose. "Where do you suggest we meet this first round of applicants?"

"Hmm." Ambrose started, then said nothing as he placed a finger on his lips. "Let's start in Whispering Woods."

"No. That's an awful choice." Gadiel said, "The woods won't be private enough. At any time of the year or day, there might be other groups using the woods for their business. Pick someplace else."

Mortimer spoke, "How about Blades-Sorrow? It's hard to get to, secluded, and few people travel there this time of year."

Haskell had never heard of the place and he looked to the others for their reactions.

Garrick and Ambrose nodded in agreement. Dakarai shook his head as if he didn't like the idea, while Gadiel paused a moment before agreeing to the plan.

"No, it's a dangerous location." Dakarai voiced his opinion of the meeting location. "Thieves inhabit the place and I've heard of people going in and never returning."

Garrick grinned, "Exactly. It's the perfect place to make those who won't join our army to accidentally disappear, never to be seen again."

"Oh, I see." Dakarai nodded in approval.

A smile creased Haskell's lips as he saw the value of a place where people who didn't agree to the plan would just disappear.

"I don't suspect we'll have problems with thieves and the like." Garrick started to walk back to the symbols. "How many new candidates should we meet for our first session?"

Gadiel said, "Ten or under."

"So, there is a limit to the number of people you can manipulate with your powers." Ambrose leaned on his staff for support. Haskell thought the old man's hips seemed stiff or sore this morning, based on his movements or lack thereof.

"No, I'm concerned about growing too fast and not being able to control the growth of the group. We need committed wizards that aren't afraid to die for our cause, but can bring us the different levels of skill needed to make this insurrection succeed."

"Fair enough." Garrick studied the etchings. He ran his hand over a symbol shaped like a bird in flight. "Yes, this is the one we seek. I will send a message to ten wizards who have expressed disappointment with the king. We'll meet in Blades-Sorrow in five days."

####

Five days later, the same six wizards traveled toward the center of the ancient city of Blades-Sorrow. Haskell was amazed as they walked through the city ruins. Many stone walls had collapsed over the years leaving a rubble of rocks, while other structures stood nearly intact. There must be some danger here, he thought, as Ambrose held his staff so tight that his knuckles were white.

Garrick was acting as a tour guide as they traveled through the city. "Fifteen-hundred years ago, the city had over two-hundred-thousand inhabitants. It was the largest and most populated city in the world. They had the fiercest soldiers, over fifty-thousand strong, and had never been defeated."

"What happened to them?" Haskell asked.

"That's the strangest thing. No one knows. We don't know if they abandoned the city or were driven out by another army. There is no record that tells us of their fate."

Haskell looked ahead and stared at a pyramid that rose ten stories high in the center of the city. "What was that used for?"

"Researchers claim the wizards used it for human sacrifices to enhance their magic."

Haskell wondered if the people being sacrificed were skilled in magic, and their magic transferred to the wizards. He had so many questions on his mind.

Within two blocks of the city center, Garrick turned right and led them down a narrow alley. Crumbling buildings blocked out most of the sunlight and the sky seemed to darken. The alley twisted and turned. They reached an intersection, turned right, walked five steps and turned left into a smaller alley.

Haskell heard whispers of conversations around him. They were walking in single file and he wasn't sure if the conversations he heard were from his companions or from the buildings they passed. A person laughing loudly sounded behind him and he knew it wasn't Garrick. Checking behind, he didn't see anyone else in the alley. He hurried his pace to stay close to Dakarai, who was ahead of him.

Haskell then heard a flute and lute playing in the alley and he noticed the others searching for the source of the music as they walked. "Are we close?" He shouted to Garrick, hoping for some indication of how much further they needed to walk.

Garrick stopped and the others behind him stopped.

Ambrose asked, "Is there a problem?"

"This map I'm using is rather bleached out. I'm not sure if we were supposed to turn at the last intersection or the next. There is a fading magical residue that is disrupting my directional incantation."

"Let me see." Ambrose stepped next to Garrick and pulled the map closer. "Hmmm. Okay, we are here, right?"

"We're supposed to be, but there should be another alley right here that intersects with the one we're walking on, but you can see there is a building here."

"Are you sure it's not the next intersection twenty yards ahead?" Ambrose leaned in closer to the map as if his eyes weren't very good.

"That should be a different intersection. See, it's marked here." Garrick pointed at the map with a long, bony finger.

Dakarai stepped close. "What's the name of the intersection you're looking for? I'll run ahead and see if I can determine the street name."

"That's what makes the situation difficult. Most of the intersections don't have names." Garrick shrugged. "But it should be named . . ." He studied the map for a moment. "Rustica or Ruista. I can't quite make out the smudge."

"I'll be right back." Dakarai hurried to the next intersection where he stopped. He looked at the walls on the intersection, first one side and then the other. After searching for names on all the corner walls, he turned toward the others.

Haskell noticed a foggy, almost ghostly shadow behind Dakarai. Then the wizard suddenly disappeared. A shiver ran down Haskell's back.

"Did you guys see that? Dakarai just disappeared." Haskell asked the others. "Should I go after him?"

"Wait a second. That happens sometimes in certain sections of the city." Garrick returned his attention to his map. "He might reappear."

Haskell thought that the word *might* wasn't very reassuring. Did these guys really know what they were doing? He looked to Gadiel, who didn't appear worried. *Okay, I'll wait. Maybe they really do know what's happening.*

They waited a minute, but Dakarai didn't return. After three minutes, the remaining five still stood in the same spot.

"Should I go look for him now?" Haskell asked.

"Take Mortimer with you." Ambrose said.

"I'm not going in that death trap." Mortimer raised his voice. "I'm happy back here with you guys. Unless you know exactly where he is, I'm staying."

Gadiel leaned toward Mortimer. "You will go with our young viscount, keep him safe, and stop complaining. Do you understand?"

Mortimer stepped back and raised his hands. "Okay, back off. I'll go with the kid."

Haskell didn't know if having Mortimer with him was going to be much help. He didn't seem like the kind of guy that liked dangerous situations.

They walked toward the intersection where Dakarai disappeared. When they reached it, they stopped. Haskell looked down the alley as far as he was able. The dispersed sun light threw strange shadows against the walls and it seemed darker in the opposite direction.

"Which way should we go, Boy Wonder?" Mortimer sneered.

Haskell didn't have a clue. "Let's walk left until the next intersection and see if we see him. Then we can walk back in the opposite direction if we don't find him. He has to be around here somewhere; people don't just disappear." Haskell thought the wizard hadn't disappeared so much as someone or something had grabbed him.

"Wait a sec." Mortimer stopped Haskell before he got too far. "I have a spell that can find residues or traces of a person. It will allow us to track him if it hasn't been too long." He raised his hands and mumbled an incantation.

It didn't seem to Haskell as if anything had happened, and then he saw it. A faint blue line went to the right. "Is that the trace?"

"That's our man."

They headed off, tracking the glowing line. At the next intersection, they turned left, moving a block before the line veered again. Another left, they traced the magical trail for another block until the line began to fade, leaving them in the dim uncertainty of the labyrinthine streets.

"Is this a problem that it's fading?" Haskell asked.

"Sometimes it means the person you're tracking is dead."

"Dead!"

"Relax. Sometimes it means you're close to finding them."

"Well, which is it?" Haskell hurried along the line hoping to find Dakarai before the line completely disappeared.

The line and alley came to a dead end.

Haskell ran his hands through his hair. "Now, what do we do? He has to be alive; we have to find him." Haskell studied the alley and the buildings. The red brick walls went up four stories all around them. The nearest door was fifteen feet from their location, but the residue from the tracking spell ended right here where they stood.

"This is a conundrum." Mortimer spun slowly in a circle as he examined the walls.

"I don't think your spell worked. You don't know what you're doing."

"My spell worked just fine. Your friend is nearby. I can feel his presence, though I can't tell if he's still alive."

Haskell shook his head. Despite Mortimer's proclamations, he didn't know where Dakarai was and he had no confidence in Mortimer. "Show me."

Mortimer started pushing bricks. "Help me look for a concealed door in the vicinity."

Haskell rolled his eyes and cast a spell that would identify hidden doors. An outline of a door appeared in an area where there was nothing more than a solid brick wall.

"Oh!" Mortimer exclaimed. "That's one way to find it."

Maybe Mortimer wasn't a person they needed in their core group, Haskell thought.

It took only a moment before Haskell opened the door. As the stone door groaned open, shadows danced across the wall. A flickering torchlight cast eerie shapes on the walls, filling the air with tension. He crept forward, his footsteps echoing in the dimly lit corridor. The air grew colder with each step, a foreboding chill seeped into his bones.

Not knowing if Dakarai was in trouble or with others, he whispered his friend's name, but received no answer. His eyes adjusted to the poor light in a long hallway.

Haskell prepared a shield, afraid of what might lurk behind the opened door ten feet away. A noise sounded from the opened door and Haskell prepared a spell to kill whatever beast might be prowling in the room.

CHAPTER 59

Haskell walked cautiously toward the opened doorway and heard a voice mutter. "Yes, this is the room we're looking for."

Dakarai walked out of the doorway, and Haskell recognized his friend moments before he launched a fireball at him. A moment of panic raced through his body at what might have happened if Haskell had fired.

"Hey guys," Dakarai said. "Whoa. Put your hands down. I found the room."

They wandered back to the others and brought them to the room.

Garrick cried out, "Eureka! This is it."

Haskell looked around the spacious chamber. Faded murals adorned the walls, showing women frolicking near pools, soldiers steadying rearing horses, and two wizards sending out a magical blast against an invading force.

Garrick raised his hands and intoned, "Ignis Lucis." The candles within four candelabras in the corners burst into flames, lighting the room. Dust kicked up by the six wizards danced in the soft glow of the candles.

Haskell stopped at the doorway and examined the two statues that stood as guardians to the door. He couldn't identify the dark stone the statues were carved from, but he recognized the two characters from stories his mother had told him.

On his left stood the woman known as the Enchantress. Her eyes seemed real in the candlelight. In one hand she held a staff of bronze, and in the other hand, an orb that the legends say allowed her to predict the future. Haskell figured that ability wasn't enough to save the city.

The statue on the right represented the Warlock Guardian, another mythical person from a bygone era. His expression gave off feelings of being stern and resolute, though Haskell couldn't tell why the warlock emanated those vibes. The statue wore ancient armor that appeared uncomfortable.

He walked to the center of the room where the other wizards stood around a simple stone table. The table wasn't quite circular, seeming to follow the natural flow of the cut rock. He questioned why Garrick and Ambrose chose this chamber. It was difficult to find, and he figured half of the recruits wouldn't find the room. Dakarai was right, this city wasn't the best place for these meetings.

"Excellent, the Stone of Wisdom still operates in this chamber," Ambrose announced.

"What is all of this, Ambrose?" Mortimer asked.

Ambrose smiled and leaned on the staff at his side. "This stone table isn't any ordinary rock. It comes from the heart of the Celestial Quarry in the nearby mountains. When the abandoned city began to disintegrate, a group of wizards attempted to move this special stone. They couldn't, so it has sat here for centuries, used by a small group of us to discern wisdom. People believe that it is infused with energy derived from a fallen star."

Haskell rolled his eyes at the story. The elder wizard had recounted many legends the last two days, and Haskell had learned to just nod his head at whatever Ambrose said, because there was no way that these outrageous legends could be true.

Ambrose lifted his staff and tapped the center of the table. "Transmuta Stella." A tone as if from a deep bell sounded from the table. A subtle metamorphosis occurred on the table as soft shimmering runes became visible on the stone's surface.

"Each rune on the table allows the participants at a meeting around this table to make better decisions. In theory, the table works with our two guardians at the door, using the alignment of cosmic energies to channel the essence of the star's remnants."

A sense of awe and wonder filled Haskell as he felt the energy from the table's magic. His heart quickened, and a shiver of excitement ran down his spine. It seemed to call to him, and his skin tingled when he lightly touched one of the runes.

Ambrose smacked Haskell's arm with his staff. "Don't touch the table unless you know what you're doing."

He quickly pulled his arm back and rubbed it. After touching the table, he realized this meeting would take on another level of intrigue. He felt as if the stone whispered his name and proclaimed him king when he brushed his hand across it.

Haskell looked back at the doorway as two men and a woman entered the room. He didn't recognize them, and he looked at the others to see if they were friend or foe.

"What's all this?" The tallest approached and greeted Garrick by grabbing his wrist in an embrace. "Could you make this meeting place any more difficult to find?"

"We are trying to keep out the riff-raff from our little group," Garrick responded.

The man took a quick look at the others and said, "I think the riff-raff are already here."

Garrick gave another of his donkey guffaws. "Come."

Within fifteen minutes, all the expected recruits had arrived. Their little band of potential recruits totaled ten, with three women wizards in the group. Garrick had them all stand around the table, and with a wave of his hand he lowered the light from the candles.

Garrick's theatrical capabilities impressed Haskell.

The glow from the runes gave Garrick an otherworldly appearance. He touched one of the luminous runes and spoke with conviction, "Esteemed colleagues and magical brethren, we stand here at a crossroads of destiny, where fate has woven a tapestry that demands our attention and action. It is time for us to re-shape the course of history."

All the recruits watched Garrick as he walked slowly around the table, touching each of them on the shoulder as he passed by.

"The king, once a beacon of hope, has succumbed to the shadows of tyranny. His reign has become a stain on the very fabric of our magical community. Everyone in the room has witnessed the suppression of our freedoms by King Stoneforge."

They all nodded, grunted, or agreed verbally.

Garrick stopped talking and took time to meet the eyes of each of the recruits.

"It's time to end the oppressive reign of the king. For the sake of our magical heritage, for the preservation of the values we hold dear, the king must be vanquished."

"Hear, hear!" One recruit blurted.

Garrick gestured toward the celestial table; its magical glow emphasized the gravity of their mission. "We gather around this table as witnesses and architects of change. It's time to usher in a new era of prosperity where our magical gifts flourish without fear of oppression."

No one moved, and Garrick waited.

Haskell wanted to say something, to agree with Garrick's words, but he held his tongue. The silence in the room almost choked the air from his lungs.

Finally, Garrick continued, "And in this endeavor, we have a beacon of hope. A young wizard, untainted by the corruption that plagues the current regime, stands among us. He is the embodiment of our shared values. Together, we shall not only remove the shackles that bind us, but also place this young wizard on the throne, a symbol of a brighter future."

The recruits looked at the wizards in the room, their gazes stopped on Mortimer and then Haskell, but then returned to Mortimer.

The other wizard smiled as he realized the same thing that Haskell felt. They saw Mortimer as the young king and had dismissed the smaller Haskell. His heart beat faster, and he wanted to shoot a fireball at Mortimer. He hated that no one seemed to take him seriously as a future king.

Garrick raised his hands, palms turned upward, invoking the support of the gathered wizards. "I implore you to join this noble cause. Let us unite our magical strengths, forge an unbreakable bond, and strive for a new realm where magic is revered, where our gifts are celebrated, and where justice prevails. Together, we shall rewrite history and bring about an era of enlightenment that will resonate through the ages."

One of the female wizards, introduced as Lyra Starwhisper, spoke first, "If Mortimer is your young wizard king, then I'm out. He's an uncouth, narcissistic, and womanizing outcast that I will not support for this role."

Another wizard said, "Agreed."

Haskell smirked at Mortimer, who just smiled and leered at Lyra.

Lyra turned to leave.

"Wait, Lyra," Garrick said. "Mortimer isn't the one we plan to put on the throne."

The tall wizard that had greeted Garrick earlier said, "Is it you?"

After a moment of his braying laugh, Garrick said, "Let me introduce you to the boy who will be king." He leaned over to Haskell and whispered, "Put your left hand on the rune shaped like a crown, right there." He pointed at the mark on the table.

Haskell followed the directions given him and immediately felt a power rush through his body. Magic, or was it celestial magic from the cosmos? He couldn't tell, but he definitely felt like a man that could change destiny. He straightened his posture and felt an innate sense of being capable of leading and inspiring the people around him.

The others looked to him and he confidently met their gazes, where before he might have stared at the floor.

"Three years ago, a spiritualist predicted that I would become the Velidred king." Haskell placed his right hand over his heart. "Today, we ask that you join our cause to remove the king currently on the throne and replace him with fresh blood. I propose a united front, a coalition of unwavering resolve. We will weave spells of solidarity and strength, standing as one against the looming tyranny. Our goal is not merely to dethrone, but to rebuild. Let us forge alliances, hone our magical talents, and become a force that cannot be ignored. Together, we shall not only dethrone the current king but usher in a reign of unity and justice."

A few of the wizards in attendance clapped, while the wizards with staffs pounded them on the stone floor, making a noise of acceptance.

Haskell smiled inwardly as he stood majestically and let the applause and accolades fill him with confidence.

Haskell absorbed the energy from the table and the praises of the other wizards. He could get used to this power and wondered how long this feeling and ability to inspire and move others would last after they left the table and this room. Maybe they should forget Velidred Kingdom and he should become king right here within this forgotten city.

The meeting lasted another few minutes, and toward the end of the proceedings, Garrick said, "It appears that you all have decided to join our humble group. Is there anyone here who disagrees with our plan or the person we have chosen for the throne?"

Haskell looked at the recruits. Without hesitation, they all shook their heads.

"At this time, we will need a blood oath from you. Is that a problem?" Garrick looked around the room.

Lyra said, "A blood oath could kill us all. It would only take one spy and we'd all have our throats slit in a moment."

Two other wizards pounded their staff on the floor in agreement.

The old man, Gadiel, said, "Can we talk over in the corner about this blood oath?" He motioned for the dissenting wizards to follow him to the corner of the room.

They were in the corner for several minutes before they all returned.

"They have agreed to the blood oath." Gadiel motioned for Garrick to finish.

"Come to the table one at a time." Garrick withdrew a small amulet carved from wood from his cloak. "You will squeeze one drop of blood onto the amulet, which is sourced from an ancient elder tree. I have embedded magical properties into the pendant to prevent the blood from spoiling."

They each came forward and pricked a finger, letting their blood drip onto the amulet.

"Now you, Haskell." As Haskell came closer, Garrick whispered, "Place your other hand on the crown rune."

Haskell followed the directions and then Garrick pricked Haskell's finger and squeezed ten drops of blood onto the amulet.

"Ambrose, if you will seal the covenant?"

The elder wizard at the table raised his staff, waved it over the table, and chanted.

"Sanguine nexus, soul entwined,
In life I bind, with heart and mind.
Through this blood, a secret bond,
Eternal pact, a covenant of magic beyond.

Whosoever dares to break this trust,
Evil shall befall, fate robust.
Darkness looms, shadow's strife,
Bound by unholy ties, a troubled life."

CHAPTER 60

In the early morning quiet at his manor house in Oak Ridge, Haskell took the Imperium Wand from its hiding place in the treehouse at the back of the property. He rolled it back and forth between his fingers, itching to use the powerful magical artifact, but he knew he must wait. When they attacked the Velidred Castle, then he would use it to take down the reigning Grand Master of the Council of Nine.

The previous owners had built the treehouse for their daughter. With people coming and going within the manor, townspeople, servants, and royals, Haskell never felt he could find the peace and quiet he relished. The tree house was far from the house and no one ever came looking for him there. Plus, he always had enough warning to know when someone approached so he could hide his precious magical treasure.

He wanted to concentrate this morning. They were getting ready to do their fourth recruiting meeting, and he was thinking about his speech that he delivered to the candidates. It had gotten a little longer each meeting and Garrick was allowing him more flexibility in what he told the recruits. Haskell loved the power he felt when they agreed to the blood oath and then knelt, proclaiming, "We support you in your quest, Your Majesty."

A few more meetings like this with an additional forty to fifty recruits, and he knew they could defeat King Stoneforge, allowing Haskell to become king of Velidred. Once king, he would resolve two problems. He would avenge his parents' murders at the hand of King Stoneforge, and he would ask King Goodwin for his daughter's hand in marriage.

A shout penetrated the early morning quiet, "Haskell get into the manor now. There's a problem." Sims didn't even bother to walk all the way to the treehouse, choosing to stand just outside the manor's back door and yell at the soon-to-be king.

Haskell imagined with glee his first command as king would be to eliminate Sims as the irritant that he had always been. "Coming," he called back. With a flick of his wrist, he hid the wand and scrambled down the tree.

All the others sat at the kitchen table eating breakfast. Haskell took his normal place as his mouth watered at the smell of bacon and pancakes.

Gadiel looked at him. "Good. You're here. Sims has returned from Velidred Castle and has heard rumors that might be bothersome."

"Such as?" Haskell asked tentatively. Things were progressing well. What were these rumors? If he knew Sims, the thug probably started the rumors himself, to cause trouble.

Sims looked up. "In my work at Velidred Castle as a spy, I overheard a couple of wizards talking. I couldn't actually see them from my hiding place."

Haskell nodded.

"Well, it sounded like they were both going to our next recruitment meeting. That's what caught my attention." Sims could never seem to get right to the heart of the problem and liked to drone on with nonessential information.

"Recruits from within the Velidred Castle itself. That's a win for us. Isn't it?" Haskell leaned closer.

"It might be, if that was all they said. But they couldn't keep their traps shut." Sims continued. "This is what I heard."

"One wizard said, 'I've heard whispers of wizards planning to overthrow the king.'

The other responded, 'We should tell the king.'

'No, not yet.'

'Why not?'

'I want to go to one of the meetings. Apparently, the group is recruiting wizards that are dissatisfied with the king and the way things are going here in Velidred.'

'That's crazy. It's terrific here.'

'Yeah, I agree. Anyway, I'm going over to the meeting tomorrow in the ruins at Blades Sorrow. I'll act like one of their new recruits. Get the lowdown on their activities and then I'll present the information to the king.'

'Are you going by yourself?'

'Yeah, why not?'

'Let me go with you.'

'If you want, but we need to be discreet. No one can know we're loyal to the king. We get the information and then turn it back on them. Nip this little insurrection in the bud. Might make for a little more power here in the castle for us, if you know what I mean.'"

Sims said, "Then I heard footsteps behind me and I had to leave. I'm pretty sure those two have plans to be at the next recruiting meeting."

Haskell's mind swirled with a mixture of anxiety and frustration as doubt gnawed at the edges of his resolve. He looked at Gadiel. "We'll be able to eliminate them, won't we?"

Gadiel took a bite of pancake and thought for a moment while he chewed. He swallowed and said, "We don't know what they look like. I'm concerned with how they heard about our group. We can't have the king expecting our rebellion before we're ready. Surprise is our biggest benefit to a swift defeat of the king. If he knows we're coming, he might leave the castle. We might succeed in conquering Velidred Castle, but if the king still lives, then we might not secure victory we seek."

"What do you propose we do then?" Haskell asked.

"This might be our last meeting."

"Can we win with only forty or fifty of us? That doesn't seem like nearly enough." Haskell felt his confidence slip at this news. Garrick and Ambrose seemed to think they needed at least one hundred wizards to defeat the king's army.

"We'll talk with the others. Maybe if we can identify these traitors before they get too much information, then we can continue to recruit." Gadiel drained his coffee cup, stood, and walked out of the kitchen.

Haskell sat at the table pushing his pancakes and bacon around on his plate as he contemplated the different scenarios that might occur without the proper number of wizards in his army. He felt their carefully laid plans were slipping through his fingers.

# # # #

Two days later, twelve recruits stood in the meeting room within the ruins at Blades Sorrow. Mortimer, Dakarai, and Ambrose weren't there for this meeting, as they were off securing other important resources for the insurrection. Sims stood at the door greeting the recruits as they arrived. The hope was he would identify the voices he heard at the castle.

When the last wizard entered the room, Haskell peered over at Sims, who shook his head. He hadn't identified the moles. They had only invited ten wizards to the meeting, so there was definitely two people that shouldn't be here.

Garrick started the same as he had the previous meetings, only this time because Ambrose wasn't there, he used his wand to ignite the table. With a light touch on the table, he moved around the room and touched the shoulders of all the recruits.

After Garrick's introduction, Haskell spoke, keeping his hand on the crown rune embedded within the table. He let the celestial magic infuse him and launched into his talk. He didn't know if it even mattered what he said. As long as he touched the rune, the recruits nodded and smiled.

When it came time for the blood oath, Gadiel and Garrick figured that the ceremony would flush out the king's men.

Garrick pulled out his elder amulet and set it on the celestial stone table. "Esteemed wizards, as we embark on this noble quest together, there is a sacred tradition that binds us further—a blood oath. A symbol of our commitment, unity, and shared purpose. Are there any here that are unwilling to share in this pledge to our cause?"

The air in the room grew tense, and Haskell scrutinized the reactions of the recruits. Which among them were the suspected spies? Some wizards gazed at the floor. The blood oath was a serious obligation, and many had doubts when presented with this part of the ritual. But Haskell searched for the two wizards that would look at each other before agreeing to this promise.

No one bowed out or said no. Gadiel waited in the corner to encourage any that were reluctant to take on this vow.

Garrick emphasized, "Everyone should know that this oath should not be taken lightly. It is a binding commitment, a pledge to the cause that goes beyond mere words. The blood you share with us today signifies your dedication to our shared resolve."

The recruits moved toward the amulet, ready to drip their blood on the bargain. Two wizards hung back, ensuring they were at the back of the line forming for the oath.

Finally, it came time for the last two newcomers to make their guarantee to the group. The first stepped forward as if he planned to do the blood oath, but then twisted on his front foot and sprinted for the door. It happened so fast Haskell didn't have time to attack with his magic. The wizard was fast, but Sims stepped in front of him with his ever-ready knife prepared to strike. But it wasn't enough. With a blast of magic air from the fleeing wizard, Sims flew against the Enchantress' statue. The wizard dashed into the alley.

The second spy didn't start soon enough, and Haskell raced after him. The spy shot forth a fireball blast at Haskell, which he avoided. Sims was down for the count, and Haskell realized he wouldn't be able to help.

As the spy reached the doorway, Haskell cast forth a magic stick that slipped between the man's legs causing him to topple to the floor. Haskell jumped on top of the man and grabbed his hands, preventing him from casting a spell.

A wizard that only moments before had taken the blood oath brought forth a rope that he had secured to his belt like a whip. "Tie him up with this. It'll keep him from using magic." He helped Haskell tie up the spy with the rope.

Haskell didn't know what to do next. Should he sprint after the first spy, finish the ceremony, or interrogate the captured wizard?

Gadiel walked over to the table from his spot in the corner. "Don't worry about the one that escaped. We'll manage that loose end later. Let's finish the ceremony. But first, let's take a little blood from our friend here."

The captured spy shouted, "No, I refuse to take the blood oath. I'm loyal to the king and will never join you in your rebellion."

"You will take the blood oath." Gadiel walked over to the spy. "And when your friend leaks to the king what he saw here, you will die with the rest of us."

The spy spit on the floor in front of Gadiel. "I will never follow your king."

"You won't have a choice. Bring him over here."

Garrick and Sims dragged their prisoner to the table and Sims took his knife and made a shallow cut in the wizard's neck. They let the blood drip onto the amulet.

When they completed that part of the ceremony, Haskell gave his eleven drops of blood to seal the deal, and Garrick finalized it with his incantation.

"Can I gut him?" Sims asked.

"No, he's still useful." Gadiel walked over to him and Haskell saw the movements of the scorpion across Gadiel's eye. "We need your friend's name."

"Never! There's nothing you can do that will make me. You'll have to kill me."

Gadiel smiled. "You will die. And before we're done today, I'll have your friend's name, and you'll wish you had never come to this meeting."

CHAPTER 61

Late in the afternoon, long after the meeting had dissipated, Haskell looked at the spy lying in a heap on the meeting room's floor. He had died two hours earlier, after Gadiel had teased his friend's name from him. There was no blood, just one minute the man lived and the next he was dead, as if from internal injuries. The interrogation had been painful to watch as the spy screamed in agony. Though the man exhibited no outside signs of injury, Gadiel had sent wave after wave of pain and suffering through the wizard until he caved under the cumulative effect.

An hour later, the other members of their core group returned. Garrick updated them on what had happened.

Ambrose was furious. "They've forced our hand before we're ready." He struck his staff sharply on the stone floor.

Garrick waved his hand as if shooing a fly. "It doesn't matter. We're ready and have enough for our purposes."

Haskell wondered if that was true. If it wasn't, then they probably all would die. He looked at Gadiel, wondering if the man regretted recruiting him years ago.

"What did you find when you were shopping?" Garrick asked.

Ambrose dipped his hand into a leather satchel. He pulled out five worn leather amulets. "These will allow their wearers to bond their magic with each other without being close. There will be a synergistic effect allowing them to cast more potent spells."

Haskell took one amulet and examined it. The amulet was made from a small stone with an interlocking symbol etched into it, which appeared to be multiple strands, forming a central knot with a small emerald stone in its center. The words, *"Through realms entwined, our spirits pledge bonded unity, for eternity,"* were inscribed on the amulet.

Ambrose placed the four amulets on the table. Two had leather lanyards allowing the users to wear them around their necks, while the others were to be worn around the wrist.

"This grimoire of battle spells might be useful." Ambrose placed a leather-bound book with yellowed pages on the table.

Mortimer laughed in response. "In the heat of battle, you're going to read a book?"

"No!" Ambrose snorted. "I'll study its contents and be ready to use it as a resource to shore up holes during the battle."

"You better get reading," Garrick said, "because we'll be going into battle soon."

"You don't worry about me. I'll be ready," Ambrose said angrily.

Ambrose held up an envelope embossed with the king's seal. "I also acquired an invitation to meet with the Council of Nine."

"And how will that help us?" Haskell asked. "I have no desire to meet with them, since they want to imprison me and take away my magic."

"It's a way for you and maybe a couple of others to enter the castle without having to fight your way in," Ambrose explained.

Gadiel appeared tired from dealing with the spy but said, "Did you find anything else that will be useful to us?"

"I purchased three moonstones that will provide us with a momentary period of temporal distortion."

Haskell asked, "What does that mean?"

"These stones," Ambrose dropped them on the table. "Will temporarily distort time and disable our enemies, allowing our wizards to move into strategic positions. The time the enemy is incapacitated will last anywhere from five to twenty seconds."

"Five seconds? How can that be enough time to do anything of value?" Mortimer picked up one stone and examined it.

"You have to make do with the time given you during the attack. It might be enough to save your life," Garrick answered.

Haskell grabbed a moonstone from the table. It had a cylindrical stone shape with carvings of lines etched into the center portion. "How do you activate it?" He hefted it in the air to understand its weight and size. "It's kind of heavy to carry around when you want to be quick."

"That's the beauty of these devices. We don't carry them. We'll plant them near the castle, allowing any of us to utilize them during the attack." Ambrose smiled. "By placing them in the shape of a triangle, we'll be able to chant the proper words when needed."

"What will keep our enemy from figuring out what we're doing and disrupt our plans?" Mortimer asked.

"We will attune them to our group and only members attuned to the moonstones will be able to activate and use them." Ambrose picked up the last stone from the table and rubbed his hand across its surface. He chanted,

> *"Warp the hours, twist the days,*
>
> *Guide me through a temporal maze.*
>
> *Rock of moonstone, with power imbued,*
>
> *Grant me passage, alter the mood."*

Haskell looked at Mortimer, who wobbled, became unfocused in Haskell's eyes, and then dropped to his knees. The whole room seemed to spin in front of Haskell and he couldn't focus on anyone. He closed his eyes, which didn't help, and he too dropped to his knees. The effect seemed to go on forever. Then, just as quickly as it occurred, it stopped.

He took a cleansing breath and struggled to his feet. A quick search of the room revealed that everyone but Ambrose was trying to stand, displaying different aspects of discomfort. Ambrose wasn't by the table. Where had he gone?

Ambrose called from the statue of the Enchantress, "Did you enjoy that experience?"

Mortimer was still on all fours, his face white and gaunt. He groaned, "Why did you do it to us for so long?"

"That was only six seconds. I could easily have gone another twenty or thirty feet by the time you regained your abilities or disabled you with ease."

"And if we are all attuned to it, then we won't be affected when it is engaged by one of our members?" Dakarai asked.

"That is correct."

Gadiel looked especially upset by the experience and he seemed eager to dispatch Ambrose, but held his anger in check.

"Then it's time to plan our attack." Garrick laid out a map of Velidred Kingdom across the table.

Haskell slipped one of the amulets onto his wrist.

They strategized for seven hours before deciding they had planned as much as they could at that moment. It was time to assemble their wizard army and prepare for the attack.

# # # #

Fifty-seven wizards and a handful of non-wizards stood within the meeting room in Blades Sorrow. Garrick had split the people into groups that represented their strengths, with groups strong in the ability for air, earth, water, and fire separated by their specific elemental. All the groups weren't equal in numbers, but the leaders in the room were confident that they had enough to do the job at hand.

Mortimer said, "We're missing six wizards. Should we wait for them?"

A tall woman with long, flowing, dark hair said, "They aren't coming."

Haskell said, "I thought the blood oath forces them to be at our command."

"No one can come to our meetings when they're dead," she replied. "King Stoneforge discovered their secrets and carried out their execution."

The room quieted. The wizards looked at each other with the realization of the consequences of their plans to overthrow the king etched into their faces.

"Stoneforge will kill us all if we don't follow through. He's an evil man that must be destroyed." Garrick said.

A pensive expression crossed their faces.

Ambrose raised his voice, "It's time to take action." He placed his hand on a rune that looked like a soldier's helmet, intersected by crossing a sword and spear over the helmet's face, as he separated the wizards into battle groups.

The first team consisted of two air wizards and a couple of wizards known for their ability at stealth.

Ambrose commanded the wizards, "I'm placing Norah in charge of this group. You are to sneak into the castle and disable their communication systems."

Norah, the tall woman who had spoken before, asked, "If they know we're coming, how are we to sneak in?"

"Unfortunately, I don't have an answer for that. Use one of the distortion moonstones if you have to.

But only once. If we use them too much, the members of the Council of Nine will expect it and they might have a way to combat a key part of our strategy." Ambrose looked truly sorry about that fact. "But I'm confident you will achieve your goal. They know we're coming, not you specifically."

Norah didn't look too pleased with the answer, but nodded, and huddled with her team.

"Next, we need a team to sabotage their defensive weapons and traps. Look for high-value targets that will enable the rest of us to get into the castle with the least number of casualties." Ambrose pointed at a short wizard with a gray beard that touched his waist. "John Joseph will lead this group. Choose your team."

John Joseph picked four from the fire, two from air, and two from the earth group.

Ambrose said, "Take one of the water wizards, too."

"I don't need a water wizard."

"You may not think you need that skill set on your team, but you will find their abilities surprisingly effective in battle." Ambrose encouraged the man to choose another wizard.

With an exhalation of air, John Joseph studied the wizards gathered in the water elemental group. "Okay, I will take her." He pointed to a short, albino woman.

John Joseph led his team to an empty corner of the room.

"We will assign two high impact commands to this next group of wizards. One, you will be on the outside of the castle creating diversions and coordinating attacks to keep the soldiers occupied." Ambrose pointed his staff at a woman in the water elemental group. "Aarna will lead this group. I suggest you choose some strong earth elementals to shake the castle and keep the soldiers unsteady on their feet."

Aarna was of average height with caramel-colored skin. Her black hair and dark brown eyes made her an attractive woman despite her bold nose. She quickly chose three of the earth elementals, an additional water elemental, four fire wizards and two from air. With a nod of her head, she led them to an open corner.

Ambrose seemed satisfied with her choices and took a moment before barking out his next command. "This next group will infiltrate the castle and neutralize high-value targets. You will be at high risk the moment you step into the castle. The Council of Nine is in session and you know there are always wizard fan boys in the castle when the council is active." He shrugged his shoulders a moment, as if tired from the stress of building an army to cause a rebellion and overthrow the king.

Haskell worried the elder wizard might not have the strength to attack the castle.

"Dakarai will lead this team. Haskell and Mortimer will be members as well as two members of the fire elementals and three of the air."

Haskell was a little perturbed at not being chosen captain of this team, but he realized that this was the group that would be most at risk against the strongest wizards from within the castle. If he wanted to be king, he would have to defeat the Master Wizard of the Castle of Nine and maybe other members of the council.

Ambrose said, "The wizards on the Council of Nine may not give you a battle. They shouldn't care who is king, but they may make it appear that they are fighting you. Unless they give the impression they want you dead, disable them, but don't kill them."

The wizards in the room grumbled about this decision. "If we really want to create change, we'll need a new Council of Nine. Otherwise, they will continue to bully us and force their ways on the rest of us, creating rules that are impossible to follow while they themselves ignore their own proclamations."

Ambrose touched another rune on the table as he said, "I understand your concerns, and we will either force them to change or oust them from their seats of power. But they may prove useful to us to certify our new king. We can't have King Stoneforge's family claiming their seat on the throne after our rebellion is complete."

Haskell still heard rumblings of discontent in the room, but it died down quickly.

"Gadiel and I will visit with King Goodwin and King Kalluri to tell them we have moved up our battle. But we aren't asking them to join us until two weeks after our own scheduled attack on the castle."

"Are you crazy, Old Man?" John Joseph shouted. "We're supposed to have them to overthrow the soldiers. How are we to battle the entire Velidred army with fifty wizards?"

Ambrose raised his hands to quiet the discussion in the room. "Relax. We are doing this for a purpose.

Once the spy made it back to the castle and told the king, his commanding officers decided they needed to train their soldiers better. The army is practicing in a meadow ten miles from the castle." Ambrose took a drink of water.

"When we confirm the time for our allies to attack Velidred Castle, this information will get leaked to the king and his commanders. They will feel they are safe within the castle without their full regiments because they know when the attack will occur."

John Joseph nodded in agreement with Ambrose's argument.

"With subterfuge and misinformation, plus we attack when they are least expecting. It means the king stays in the castle. We defeat the wizards within the castle, kill the king, and proclaim our young viscount as King Haskell." Ambrose struck his staff on the ground and others in the room clapped, stomped their feet, and pounded their staffs in agreement.

The remaining wizards formed a separate group that would be deployed as needed by the insurrections' central command. Garrick took charge of this last group, and nodded at Haskell, who placed his hand back on the rune with the crown symbol.

Haskell raised his voice and spoke confidently, "Today marks the beginning of a new chapter, a chapter written by the collective will of those who dare to dream of a brighter future. We find ourselves united by a common cause—the desire for justice and for a realm where magic flourishes without restraint."

"Know this, my comrades, we are not merely rebels; we are architects of a renaissance. The castle walls may tower above us, but they cannot contain the strength of our convictions. Today, we rise as one. We carry within our hearts the power to reshape the course of history. May we step into the shadows of uncertainty and may the blood oath that binds us be the beacon that guides us to victory."

    The room erupted in noise and the gathered wizards dropped to their knees and loudly proclaimed over and over, "Long live, King Haskell."

CHAPTER 62

Three wizards stood at the gate to Velidred Castle. There were many people trying to get into the castle, but because the Council of Nine was in session, the guards limited entrance to nobles, wizards, and those with an invitation. The crimson Velidred moon shone hazily through the thin night clouds, with a red, irritated appearance.

Haskell's heart throbbed as he stood beside Mortimer and Dakarai. This was the night they had planned for the last few weeks. The time to defeat King Stoneforge and claim the crown for themselves. With a smile on his face, he contemplated the impending chaos and destruction that would soon consume the castle.

He hoped his nervousness didn't show when they reached the guards. The Imperium Wand remained hidden in his tunic and he carried the Golden Shield in a leather satchel at his side. Haskell wore the bonding amulet on his wrist, as did Dakarai and Mortimer.

Dakarai leaned over to Haskell and whispered, "Relax, they'll let us through. We have the invitation. No one knows who you are."

It seemed everyone in line at the gate was looking at him and just waited until he reached the guards. Then they would all shout his name, "There's Haskell, the wizard wanted by the Council of Nine. Grab him." The guards would grab him and the plan to take the castle would fail. Waiting to get into the castle's inner walls might kill him before he ever faced battle.

Finally, they reached the gate. A guard asked, "Name?"

Mortimer showed him the card. "We have an invitation."

The guard took it and examined the card. "Okay."

Haskell released a silent breath and prepared to walk into the castle.

A second guard suddenly shouted, "Hold it! Check the leather satchel. We are supposed to be looking for weapons."

Two guards pulled the satchel off Haskell's shoulder and peered inside. "We have a pouch filled with . . ." He opened the pouch and his eyes opened wide. "Uh . . . pebbles."

"Rocks?" The captain asked.

Haskell said, "It's from my homeland, it makes me think of home."

"And how about this small vial of liquid? Filled with poison, perhaps?"

"No, it's not poison. Just water from my father's well. I was hoping to get it analyzed by one of the king's chemists. It smells a little funny." Adrenaline pumped through Haskell's body and he wanted to grab the bag and run. "You can drink it, if you want."

"No, that won't be necessary." The guard pushed the vial back into the satchel.

"Ooh. This looks interesting." The guard pulled the Golden Shield out of the bag. "This isn't a standard shield. It's smaller and has that strange eye on its face." The guard examined it more closely.

The captain said, "It looks magical. We are to confiscate all magical artifacts."

Haskell wasn't expecting this, and he felt his stomach churning. He wanted to throw a spell at the guards and retrieve the shield.

Dakarai must have realized what Haskell's reaction would be, because he touched the viscount's arm and said to the guards, "Yes. It's a magical shield. It is a gift from the Viscount of Kalluri to the Grand Master."

Haskell looked at Dakarai with wide eyes. He wasn't going to give the shield to the Grand Master. He was here to kill the wizard.

"A gift you say?" a guard asked.

"Yes." Dakarai bowed. "The viscount would be disappointed to find out that his gift was confiscated before he could present it to the Grand Master himself."

The guards looked at each other and then at their captain, who nodded. They handed the Golden Shield back to Haskell, and waved them through the gate.

Haskell breathed a sigh of relief. They had passed the first hurdle and were on their way to make him king.

As they walked through the bailey toward the keep, twenty or more soldiers practiced with swords, spears, and halberds. The clash of swords and other weapons echoed off the fortress walls. Knights on horses rode up and down the green, striking with their swords at straw men attached to wood poles.

Mortimer pulled the other two wizards to him and whispered, "I don't see barricades or additional fortifications set up. The king must not be expecting our attack tonight."

"More good news," thought Haskell. That meant the king was probably still on the castle grounds.

Dakarai looked up at the castle watch turret standing high above the walls. He whispered to the others. "John Joseph and his team are at work. A moment ago, there was a guard standing watch and now he's gone."

"I've heard he is a master of stealth," Mortimer said. "There won't be anyone to sound the alarm when he is done."

"Garrick told me the man has a way with shadows that rivals the moon goddess herself." Haskell pushed them toward the keep. "Enough chatting, get moving. We have our own job to do."

"The clouds are helping despite the brightness of the moon." Dakarai said.

"Yeah, it was unfortunate we couldn't stop the spy from leaving our meeting hall," Mortimer said. "Otherwise, our tasks would have been easier during a new moon phase. We're on a limited clock. Let's go."

Haskell and the others pressed forward. His next concern included getting past any guards at the keep's door.

A rather plain door adorned the castle keep. It was open at the moment as a group of ladies and lords stepped through to the foyer. They were laughing and pushing each other in playfulness. The wizards of the rebellion hurried to join the group. They planned their timing so they went in with the partyers and hurried into the foyer.

Haskell stopped and stared at the grand staircase and its highly polished wooden banister that ascended in a sweeping curve to the upper floors of the castle. He admired its beauty that reflected the light from the chandelier of candles directly above them as they stood on the tiled floor with its intricate fleur de lis pattern.

A pair of guards wearing chain mail stood by the staircase, keeping any uninvited guests away from the lords and ladies' private rooms.

Two large tapestries hung above the floor, adding a sense of grandeur to the space. One showed the king killing a wild boar and the other a portrait of the king and the queen.

Haskell and the others had memorized a map of the castle and where they might find the Grand Master and the king. Since the Council of Nine was in session, there were normally parties in the great hall and they were to look for the king there, but the expectation was the king was in an upstairs chamber with a wizard or two by his side.

They had dressed appropriately to blend in with the castle's royal guests, and made their way to the great hall, still following the partyers. All the while, Haskell searched for people that might recognize him or for threats that might affect their ability to find the king.

Entering the hall became difficult because of the number of people in the room. A band of musicians sat in a corner playing flutes, lutes, drums, and a lyre.

Clear, bright tones entertained the lords and ladies, and the music drowned out private conversations.

Many people congregated in the center of the room, performing one of the many popular dances that Haskell recognized from his practice sessions with Carl. He continued to keep his eyes open for the king or the Grand Master.

As he looked at the people enjoying the food, music, and dancing, his eyes were drawn to one of the women dancing. He couldn't believe his eyes. It looked like Princess Noreen. She shouldn't be here. Her father was supposed to be preparing to go to war with Velidred. Why in the moon goddess' name would she be here?

His face flushed in surprise and he didn't know if he should rush to hold her in his arms or leave the room before she saw him. This was a disaster. She could be injured in the battle. Then he saw her dance partner and it triggered his jealousy. A handsome young man he didn't even recognize danced with the woman Haskell hoped to make his wife.

Just as he prepared to run to her, Dakarai placed his hand on his shoulder. He stared at Princess Noreen, just as Haskell had. "You can't go to her."

"I must warn her of the danger she's in. She could die in the attack."

"That's beyond your concern. We can't afford to lose focus on why we're here."

"You don't understand." He couldn't imagine the heartache he'd feel if his actions killed her or injured her beyond repair by a healer. "I can't leave her without telling her to get out of the castle."

"You can't make that decision. If she notices you, our whole operation might be ruined. Don't you realize the risk you'd put us in by telling her of the attack?" Dakarai twisted Haskell to face him. "Look for the king. If you don't see him, we leave. Understand?"

Haskell stared at the floor and shook his head. "I can't abandon her. Not here, not like this, before our attack."

Mortimer must have realized something was wrong and stepped close to the conspirators. "Right now, our cause is hanging in the balance. We can't let this moment slip away for a silly romance."

A silly romance? Haskell wanted to shoot a fireball at Mortimer right that moment. "What if something happens to her while we are fighting the king?"

Dakarai touched Haskell's arm. "It's okay. The castle has healers. She's a princess. She'll be one of the first to be evacuated when fighting breaks out. We need your skills for the rebellion. We're already late. The king should be dispatched by now and we haven't even found him. Any second now, the distraction team will pummel the castle walls."

"I know. That's why it's important I warn her about the imminent attack. I'll make it quick and then I won't have to worry about her."

"I can't let you do that." Dakarai pulled him close. "The king isn't in this room. Let's finish what we started and when we're done, you can be there for her."

Haskell's chest tightened in concern for Princess Noreen as he struggled to find the right words to convince his co-conspirators of the need to save the princess from certain death tonight.

Dakarai pushed Haskell out of the room. "Let's find the servant stairs. It's imperative we locate the king. We're way behind schedule." They hurried past large vases filled with fresh flowers as they ran through the foyer.

Haskell looked back at the door to the great hall, still struggling to find a way to save Noreen, and almost ran into a servant carrying a tray of food. He stopped abruptly, the servant swayed back and forth as she balanced the tray in one hand. Haskell quickly sidestepped the woman and followed the other two wizards to the stairs used by the servants to service the royals without being seen.

They found the narrow staircase unguarded and ran up two flights of stairs to the floor where the king's chambers were located. If they couldn't find him there, then they were to look in the throne room.

They ran through a hallway and found a servant lying unconscious on the stone floor. Norah's team must have identified this person as a messenger between the king and others. She was being efficient and showed that they were behind in their schedule.

They slowed as they neared a corner. The expected chamber should be just around the bend in the hallway, and they needed to tread lightly in case his room was guarded. They stopped and Haskell sneaked a peek.

Two soldiers dressed in chain mail and holding halberds stood guard at the chamber door, making it plausible that the king was in his chambers at that moment.

Mortimer said, "I'll take care of the guards. Wait here."

"Make it quiet," Haskell whispered.

Mortimer stepped into the hallway and blasted the guards with air. It was a soundless attack until the wind picked up the guards and smashed them against the wall in a cacophony of metal against stone as the metal clad guards and their weapons bounced more than twice off of the floor.

Haskell shook his head in frustration. "You were supposed to do it quietly."

An explosion rocked the hallway, and the floor swayed.

"We have to hurry. Aarna has begun her attack on the outside walls," Dakarai ordered. "Everyone is going to be panicked, especially the king."

"He must be in the king's chambers. Let's get him." Haskell rushed to the room and found the door closed. He figured the amount of noise he made didn't matter as another explosion boomed from outside. With a blast of fire, the door exploded into the chamber.

Smoke filled the room and Haskell hesitantly peeked to search for the king. A fireball from inside the room pulsed past his head and exploded against the far wall.

"Careful, a wizard's in there." Haskell shouted as he backed against the wall for protection against additional attacks.

"Did you see the king?" Mortimer asked.

"There was too much smoke, I didn't see much."

"Create a shield and let's attack." Dakarai rushed to the other side of the door to give them visibility from both sides.

Haskell created a shield that covered them all. Just as he prepared to step into the room, it exploded in light, blinding him from seeing what was inside. He staggered back behind the wall for safety.

They waited a moment as they all blinked their eyes to restore their eyesight. Haskell hated waiting, but they couldn't risk rushing into the room blind.

His eyes cleared, and he got the nod from Dakarai to attack. Haskell stepped in front of the opened doorway, shield up, ready for an attack, but nothing happened. He looked into the room, still clearing from smoke, but it was empty. "There's no one here."

"What do you mean, 'no one there?' Someone just cast a flash spell." Mortimer rushed to stand next to Haskell. "A wizard has to be in the room for that to work."

"It's empty." No matter what Mortimer said, the room was empty of humans. An explosion outside shook the chamber's walls once more.

Dakarai said, "There must be a secret doorway. Totally makes sense, the king's chamber would have a secret door. Find it so we can chase after him."

CHAPTER 63

Explosions rocked the castle walls and screaming filled the hallways. Haskell used magic spells and his hands to search the walls in the king's chamber for a secret door. Nothing he tried identified the method the king used to exit the chamber. He even checked the empty suit of armor that acted like a guard in a corner of the room.

Mortimer asked, "Did you find anything?"

Haskell shook his head. "Nothing."

Concerned, Dakarai's lips were pinched tight as he declared, "Enough time has been wasted searching for the hidden door. We'll have to go through the hallways to find him. We can't allow him to leave the castle."

"Shield as we leave, because it sounds like the rest of the castle knows what we're doing." Haskell created a shield and stepped into the hallway, where a fireball unexpectedly struck his shield in a blast of reds and yellows.

"Get back! We're under attack." He pushed the other two back into the room. "There are two groups in the hallway on either side of the door. All wizards, though none that I recognized as members of the council."

"In that case, we're allowed to kill them. It's time to use the bond from the amulets on our wrist." Dakarai stuck his arm out.

Haskell bumped his amulet against Dakarai's.

"I wish we had more time to practice with these." Mortimer said. He took a deep breath and repeated Haskell's actions. Then they read the inscription on the back of their amulets.

A blue glow filled the chamber as the magical bond formed between the wizards, and Haskell felt a tingling sensation course through his veins, chased by a shiver that raced down his back.

Mortimer called out, *"Whispers of air, flames aglow, waters dance, let illusions grow. Elemental spirits, form and play, heed this call, come forth this day."*

Haskell didn't believe what he saw before his eyes. Two giant stegox, powerful bearlike creatures found in the mountain forests near Velidred, stood in front of the door.

Mortimer waved his arms, one to the right and the other to the left and the stegox charged out of the room.

Screams sounded in the hallways. Haskell rushed to the chamber doors, peeked around the corner, and the stegox and half the wizards waiting for them in the hallway had disappeared. The numbers were now more evenly matched between the castle wizards and Dakarai's team.

Mortimer laughed. "It works every time."

Haskell turned right and launched a fireball at the two remaining wizards on that side of the hallway. The charging stegox must have surprised them enough to force them to let down their shield. A fireball struck one wizard in the chest and erupted in flames. The wizard fell to the floor.

Dakarai turned left and Haskell could feel the magic flow around his partner wizards as if they were one attacking force. Dakarai sent the empty suit of armor flying toward the wizard on the left side of the hallway and knocked the wizard to the ground.

The remaining wizard on the right fled from the hallway.

"Which way?" Mortimer asked.

"Wait." Haskell said.

"We don't have time to wait. More wizards will be back in moments." Dakarai said.

"This will save us time finding the king." Haskell pulled out the golden shield and the vial of water. He removed the stopper and dripped a tiny amount of water on the shield. He hoped this command suggested by Ambrose worked.

A mist formed above the shield and thickened into a deep fog.

With determination in his eyes, Haskell spoke into the fog, *"Veiled whispers of the mystic mist, enshroud your secrets, let none resist. In shadows deep, where secrets cling, reveal to me the presence of the king."*

The fog shifted and swirled and coalesced into a small cloud riding near the hallway's ceiling. The cloud sat a moment in its spot and then moved to the right.

"Follow it," Haskell commanded.

As they followed the cloud, it sent out tendrils through different hallways, stopping for a moment, then re-congealing into a whole, and following one tendril's pathways.

They zigged and zagged through the corridors, dispatching unsuspecting wizards that didn't realize they were part of the group of insurrectionists. The searching cloud and the raging battles charged the halls with magical energy.

Then the cloud stopped at a dead-end corridor.

"Hello. What's this?" Mortimer asked.

Haskell watched the cloud dissipate first into a fog, a light mist, and then disappear.

"Did it run out of magic or lose the king?" Dakarai asked.

Haskell didn't know for sure. "I think the king is nearby." He placed his hand on the stone wall in front of him. He didn't see any way that wall could move or be hiding someone behind it. Was it possible the king was on the other side, but they chose the wrong path to get to him?

Dakarai pulled on a tapestry hanging on the wall to his right, exposing a narrow corridor. "This way."

The passage wound its way down a couple of staircases into a long, dark corridor. Doors and tapestries lined the hallway as it veered left and then right. They opened doors that seemed to be filled with castle supplies. Finally, they reached the end of the corridor where they found a locked door.

Haskell said, "We've found our king." This time he used fewer explosions and more cunning to open the door, ready to accept his destiny as king. He whispered, *"Whispers of shadows, silent and deep, unveil the way, let secrets seep. Gatekeeper's grasp, release your hold, in silence profound, the door unfolds."*

He could feel the magic touching the lock's small pins and pushing them into the position needed to open the door. It finished the lock, and the door handle moved to open.

"Be ready," Dakarai whispered. "Get the king first and then worry about anyone protecting the king."

The door opened to a larger chamber than Haskell expected. A number of people had crowded into the room, two that he recognized—King Stoneforge and the Grand Master. Seeing both of his foes in the same room took Haskell off guard, and the wizards protecting the king seized the moment of surprise.

Dakarai sent a blast of air from his fingers that hit a shield created by the king's force. The blast dissipated without effect.

The king's wizards set off flash chants, which blinded Haskell and his companions.

Haskell sightlessly lofted fireballs at the wizards, but didn't know if they landed.

Mortimer cried out in pain, obviously hit with a counterstrike that their shield couldn't stop. He shouted, "We have to move back. They have the advantage."

No! We can't retreat now. Haskell had both of his adversaries trapped in this room. It was a perfect time to eliminate them both and cheer in victory. He pulled the Imperium Wand from his tunic and locked eyes with the Grand Master.

The master wizard recognized the Imperium Wand and Haskell watched the old wizard's mouth open wide in surprise.

The Grand Master called for the wand to come to him. *"Wand of power, our magic aligns, come swiftly now, to the call that binds."*

Haskell couldn't believe it. The wand shook in his hand, trying to free itself from his grasp. *This can't be happening,* he thought. *It's my wand. My weapon. He can't have it.*

Pooling the forces of the amulet's bonding, Haskell tried to counteract the Grand Master's chant by releasing a spell at the wizard. He called forth the Glorious Halo. A luminous beam, glowing with a blend of golden and azure hues, leapt from the Imperium Wand. The halo spell cracked with raw magical power on a path toward the Grand Master.

The air itself in the small corridor hummed with raw energy, spectral sparks bounced from the walls. Energy pulsed from the beam pushing into the room and breaking through the king's wizard's protective shield. It headed straight to the Grand Master.

Once the halo of energy had beaten their opponent's shield, he knew that the Grand Master would die. There was no defense against that much magical power, especially since it originated from the Imperium Wand. They would win this battle and defeat the king all in one swift move.

The Grand Master raised his hands and formed a visible shield in a spot that would block the magic halo. If it held.

The attack struck the Grand Master's shield, and as it tried to get past the obstacle, the Grand Master moved his hands to the side and down, diverting the attacking magic's power to the floor. He stepped aside to prevent getting struck by any of the incantation's residue.

He called once more for the Imperium Wand, and Haskell, too shocked at the failed outcome of his attack, failed to take the steps to prevent it from leaving his hand. With shock and horror, he watched as the wand flew back to its master's hands.

Haskell yelled at the others. "We have a problem. We have to move. Now!" He pivoted away from the Grand Master and pushed the others back along the corridor.

An explosion pounded against the corridor right behind Haskell and stones fell from the ceiling. A voice yelled, "Don't destroy the corridor. We still have to get out of here."

They turned a corner, giving Haskell some relief from the fear of dying from a blast of magic against his back. The Grand Master had the Imperium Wand and Haskell and his friends were in serious trouble.

As they raced through the corridor, Dakarai stopped, pulled back a tapestry, and said, "We hide in here."

"That's crazy. They'll find us and kill us here," Haskell shouted. "Don't you think they'll look in here as they go past, the same way you just did?"

"It's a place where we can mount a defense."

Haskell snorted, "A defense with what? The Grand Master has the Imperium Wand. There's nothing we can do to stop him."

"Why did you have to give it back to him?" Mortimer examined his leg where raw, angry flesh blistered from a blast by the king's wizards.

"I didn't have a choice. The wand responded when he called." His mind raced, trying to find a solution to their current problems.

Dakarai said, "The king would be dead now if you hadn't been making goo-goo eyes over some skirt."

"Don't blame me, we found the king. You had a chance to kill the king, just as I had, and you let him get away." Haskell felt the blood rush to his head in anger.

Voices sounded in the corridor.

"Quiet," Dakarai whispered.

A voice in the corridor whispered, "There's a small room, about the size of a closet, just up ahead. I bet they are hiding in there. It's right behind the red and white tapestry."

Haskell felt all hope drain through his heart like a cannon ball dropping from the top of the castle tower. It was over for him and the rebellion. They had no chance against these wizards, especially if the Grand Wizard was with them, using the Imperium Wand.

Dakarai and Mortimer tensed as Haskell felt a shield form within the room. He didn't think the shield would last long, but they had no other options.

The tapestry was ripped from the wall exposing Haskell and the others. Five wizards stood on the other side, wands and staffs pointing at the insurrectionists.

A wizard said, "Give up and promise you won't use your magic or you'll never get out of here alive."

Haskell looked at the floor, noticing the satchel he carried holding the Golden Shield. They still had an option that he was interested in testing.

Dakarai said, "Okay, it's over. We're coming out."

Haskell touched Dakarai's arm and whispered. "Wait. I might have something that will prove useful." He hurriedly pulled out the golden shield once more and the pouch of pebbles. He untied the leather holding the pouch tight and tossed pebbles onto the shield.

Immediately, the stones holding the room and walls together seemed to converge and move, closing off the door between them and the king's wizards. After the rocks and stones stopped moving, the space within the room didn't seem to grow or shrink in size. There was now a barrier between them and their attackers.

A king's wizard launched a fireball at the barrier. Haskell ducked within the closet, but the barrier held and the fireball ricocheted back toward the wizard, blasting a hole in his chest. The other wizards took cover as Haskell sent a lightning spell, which struck two of the king's wizards and forced them to the ground. He couldn't tell if they were dead.

The remaining wizards raced down the corridor away from the attack.

CHAPTER 64

Haskell watched the corridor through their stone fortress, its magic allowing him to see through it as if a one-way window, as his friends bunched inside the little closet and waited for the Grand Master. They could see through the stone wall, but they didn't know what the king's wizards on the other side could see. Would the Grand Master pass them and they could surprise him by attacking him from behind?

A king's wizard crept up the corridor, noticing his fallen comrades on the stone floor outside of Haskell's location. He looked farther up the corridor for activity, but he failed to realize that the insurrectionists he searched for were holed up just a few feet away.

Mortimer recognized the wizard as the spy that had escaped their meeting place just days ago. "Let's kill him while he's searching the bodies."

"Wait," Haskell whispered. "They don't seem to know we're here. Maybe we should let him pass and then we'll be able to surprise the Grand Master."

"No! I'm not letting him live a moment longer."

"It's a mistake to attack now. We'll draw fire and lose our element of surprise." Haskell felt the magic well up as they were still bonded. Mortimer wasn't going to listen.

Mortimer conjured a small flock of hummingbirds, which he sent out into the corridor. They flapped their wings, and hovered where they were, drawing the spy's attention.

Haskell couldn't let the spy notify others of their position. He chanted a spell to disrupt the spy's speech. *"Words entwined, in a mystic dance, garble the tongue, disrupt the trance. Speech now twisted, a linguistic maze, a fleeting grasp in a cryptic haze."*

The spy went to chant a spell, but it came out as, *"Indfay izardsway, ouyay endway, osmay undergay ethay ockray ofway agicmay. Uncoverway ethay iddenhay, owflay otay eerclay, espray entway orway ethay owerlay, ollowingfay ethay ustray."*

"What did he just say?" Dakarai asked.

"Nothing intelligible. Now he can't attack with magic or tell others our position, because nothing he says will come out in words others understand."

Mortimer's spell struck the spy's leg and he tumbled to the floor, screaming in pain.

"Shouldn't we silence him?" Dakarai asked.

"No, we want the Grand Master to find him." Mortimer said. "Then we can attack with an upper hand, but the spy won't be able to tell him where we are."

Mortimer attacked again, this time disabling an arm, and the spy dropped the wand he was holding. The spy tried to back away, but the action was difficult.

Another wizard came up behind the spy. It was the Grand Wizard.

Haskell said, "There's our man. Finish the spy and the Grand Wizard."

"Yes, your Majesty," Mortimer said. With a final chant and a wiggle of his fingers, twelve knives flew from the corridor ceiling above the spy and the Grand Master. The spy had no way to stop the attack, but the Grand Master stopped where he was in the corridor, raised his wand, and created a shield to stop the attack.

Dakarai sent air at the Grand Master, but he blocked the strike with ease.

Mortimer created ten large hammers that descended from above their opponent, but did no damage to him.

Haskell thought of a rare spell he had seen in a book at the manor. He thought hard to remember the spell and its effects on those around him.

Dakarai asked, "How do we finish him?"

Mortimer shook his head slightly. "Don't know."

"I'm thinking." Haskell said. He really wanted the Imperium Wand back, but first they must eliminate the Grand Master.

The Grand Master shouted from the corridor, "I know where you three are. Give up now, and I promise we'll go easy on you. Tell us who your leader is and you can go free."

"We aren't giving up." Haskell looked at the others. "This is our best chance to kill him. I'm going to release a powerful spell. Be ready to shield for a second and then move on the wizard."

They all nodded.

Haskell hoped he didn't kill them all. He moved his hands, pointing his fingers at a spot above the grand wizard as he shouted, "Celestial Conflagration." He channeled the arcane energies, drawing a sigil in the air that glowed with an ethereal light. The energy within the fiery essence illuminated the corridor with its light, a radiant beam of white-hot energy.

"Are you crazy?" The Grand Master shouted. "You'll bring down this castle upon us."

The spell flooded the corridor with brilliant, blinding light. Intense heat scorched the stone walls and floor and a small fire formed on the clothes of one of the downed wizards. The scent of burning stone and seared flesh filled the enclosed space.

Haskell kept his hands raised as a shockwave crashed against him, sending dust and debris flying all around. The wave of energy forced him off his feet unto his back.

The Grand Wizard was also caught off guard but instead of falling, he staggered back as he raised a defensive barrier against the powerful, chaotic energy.

Haskell saw the wizard stumble and wanted to finish his adversary, but was taken aback when the wizard maintained his balance and sent a fireball at Haskell. "It'll take more than ancient magic to defeat me."

Haskell's stone wall blocked the blast, and he looked at the others, who looked just as dumbfounded as Haskell felt. Even in their collective knowledge and bonded magic, they didn't have the experience or skill of the Grand Master.

"I gave you a chance, but time's up." The Grand Master rotated the Imperium Wand just a small fraction of an inch, almost too minute to see, and pointed it at the floor.

"Don't worry, his magic can't get through our shield." Haskell told the others. At least he hoped it wouldn't get through the shield.

The Grand Master smiled as a small four-foot-long snake slithered from the end of his wand onto the floor. The red and black copperhead with hour-glass markings raised its head and slithered to the wall where the opened doorway used to be. It seemed to analyze the magical wall protecting the insurrectionists, and then pushed its head through the wall.

One second, the snake was in the corridor and the next moment it slithered into the closet toward Haskell.

He moved toward the back of the closet only to be pushed in the back by Dakarai, forcing him forward at the snake.

Mortimer shot a fireball at the snake, which didn't affect the creature because it had its own shield protecting it. The fireball dissipated into the surrounding stones.

The Grand Master somehow knew what was going on within the enclosed space and could be heard laughing.

Coiling itself and showing long fangs, the snake prepared to strike at the nearest wizard, which happened to be Haskell.

With a flurry of fear, Haskell placed the Golden Shield between his body and the dangerous snake. He watched the snake's movements, readying the shield to move where needed to protect himself.

Dakarai tossed a disperse earth spell, and the ground beneath the snake buckled and launched it into the air.

Haskell swiftly positioned his shield in the path of the snake that had been thrown towards him. The snake bounced off the shield and landed upside down on the floor. "Are you trying to kill me?" Haskell shouted at Dakarai.

"Don't just watch the snake, kill it." Mortimer cowered in the far corner.

The snake wriggled and squirmed back into a coiled position, its forked tongue licking the air as it hissed at its enemies.

Haskell commanded, "We must work together. Dakarai, throw your earth spell again. Mortimer, send down your knives at the snake at the same time. At the snake, not at the rest of us," he clarified as his blood pumped furiously through his veins. "I will see if I can alter its shield at the same time. Are you ready?"

The other two nodded.

"As soon as I finish my dispel shield chant, then attack." He prepared the Golden Shield to protect him in case the snake flew in his direction. "*Shield of magic, now unwind, release the ward, break its bind.* Now!"

The amulet bonds between the wizards crackled within the closet space in blues and greens as the smell of sulfur filled the room. With amazing speed, the snake flew into the air as the floor buckled beneath it. The force knocked it toward Haskell, but he was ready with his shield and bashed the snake to the ground. Twelve knives dropped from the ceiling. The first knife bounced off the snake's shield, but eleven others penetrated deep within its skin. It squirmed on the floor as its blood spilled onto the stone.

They stood over the snake, all prepared to send another killing incantation against the creature, but it squirmed just a moment and then went still.

"The bond worked." A smile crossed Haskell's face as he relished the victory over the magical snake. "It's time to use the same forces to defeat the Grand Master. Then the king will be ours. Apply your magic into my little tornado."

Haskell gathered additional magic from the amulet bond and channeled fire, water, and air into a swirling tempest of energy. *"Flames dance, winds entwine, waters weave, in cyclonic union, elements heave."* He released the magic tornado into the corridor, aiming it at the Grand Master.

With a wave of his hands, the Grand Master created a shield that buffeted the attack. His magic forced the cyclone's trajectory to change, and it bounced erratically off the walls, reducing its impact when it finally reached him.

In response, he conjured air and fire from the splintered tornado and blasted the shield that had protected Haskell and his co-conspirators. Their shield collapsed in a jumble of stones and dust.

Shivers of surprise and fear raced down Haskell's back as he realized their best defense had just dissipated into nothingness. They were now at the Grand Master's mercy.

"I don't want to die today," Mortimer exclaimed, and he raced out of the room and down the corridor away from the Grand Master.

CHAPTER 65

"Wait!" Haskell shouted after the fleeing Mortimer, but it was too late. Their partner didn't stop running. "We don't have any protection," Haskell yelled to Dakarai.

Dakarai said, "Apply your magic to me, and I'll create a new shield with harmonics and sound." He pulled a knife from his tunic and struck the wall as he shouted, *"Harmony's resonance, sing my shield, elements aligned, protection steeled."*

Moments after Dakarai set his shield, the Grand Master blasted them with another fireball, but Dakarai's shield held and the burst exploded on the shield in bright colors.

"We have to disable his wand if we want to win this battle." Haskell yelled over the explosion that rocked the corridor, forcing the Grand Master back a couple of steps.

Before they could provide an answer to the fireball, the Grand Master waved his wand in five giant circles and immediately Haskell saw four instances of the Grand Master.

"Which one of the Grand Masters should we attack?" Haskell asked.

Dakarai conjured a dazzling display of fire and water and fired it at the corridor's ceiling. He looked at the four illusions and said, "Target the second one on the right."

Haskell couldn't see enough differences between the apparitions to dispute Dakarai's decision. "Let me see if I can disrupt the wand's power." He unleashed a disruption spell at the end of the Grand Master's wand.

Without hesitation, the Grand Master on the corridor's left unleashed water and earth at Dakarai's shield, weakening its protection.

"Well, that didn't work." Haskell thought through the spells Dakarai had taught him over the months he had trained with him. What weren't they thinking of? Because of his actions at the volcano so long ago, Haskell thought he should have extra powers. Surely, there was a spell that could beat the Grand Master. If only he could figure out what it was.

Another blast from the Grand Master further weakened the shield and Haskell grew nervous they'd fail. The corridor became a battleground of illusions, elemental displays, and disruptive energies, as each side strove for dominance in this crucial confrontation. Each time Haskell thought he had his opponent beaten, a simple flick of the Grand Master's hand or a nod of his head proved him wrong, dissipating the spells. All the while, their own defenses gradually deteriorated. They were running out of time and depleting their capability for magic.

Haskell created an oval mirror that he placed in the corridor. The mirror allowed them to see the real Grand Master, who happened to be at the farthest position on the right side. The other illusions disappeared. He cast a spell at the mirror that bounced off its surface and caught the Grand Master unprepared for the hit. It was enough to weaken the Grand Master's shield.

Dakarai released a destroy shield spell at their opponent and the spell forced the Grand Master back in the corridor.

The Grand Master blasted the mirror with earth elementals and it shattered into a thousand pieces.

A whip struck out at the Grand Master from behind him, striking the unprepared wizard across his face. Haskell noticed Mortimer standing in the hallway behind the Grand Master.

Haskell felt through the bond that Mortimer had come, right when they needed him. It was time to finish this battle. Haskell whistled to the others, a sharp high-pitched sound that was their signal one of them would use the disruption spell. Once they cast the spell, they had to be prepared to move on their opponent. He hoped that the Grand Master's shield and magic had been drained enough for this to work.

He chanted the command to distort time, and the room fell silent. Haskell ran toward the Grand Master with Dakarai right behind him. Did they have five seconds, twenty seconds, or no seconds? He hoped the spell worked on the master wizard, or in a moment, they would all be dead.

Haskell scrambled over the debris and clutter within the corridor, hurrying to attack the Grand Master before the disruption spell dissipated. It took seconds to breach the wall of rubble and once he cleared it, he slipped on liquid pooled on the floor, falling on his face.

The Grand Master stood ten yards away, a grimace on his face as he tried to stave off the effects of the spell.

With a shove off the floor, Haskell regained his feet and rushed toward his opponent.

The Imperium Wand moved within the Grand Master's hand as if he still had some control over his surroundings, despite the disruption within the corridor.

Haskell didn't think he could reach his opponent before the Grand Master recovered enough to blast him with the wand. He had to think of a spell to hold the wizard in place. No spells to shackle an opponent's hands came to mind, but he thought of hands reaching up from the ground to grab and hold his adversary's limbs.

He shouted, "*From shadows deep, in realms untold, Tentacles of Dominance, let darkness unfold. Whispers of doom, in the void they swim, rise, ethereal tendrils, hold all limbs.*" He continued to race to the Grand Master, and as he ran, the floor buckled underneath his opponent and writhing octopus arms reached from the floor and latched onto the Grand Master's legs.

The Grand Master's face changed to a scowl as he stopped looking at Haskell and focused his attention on the action beneath him. Because he was still deep within the disruption spell, he appeared to be moving in slow motion.

Willing his legs to go faster, Haskell struggled through the cluttered corridor.

Tentacles had fastened their inky appendages around the Grand Master's waist while two other tentacles wriggled toward his arms. The realization of what was happening registered on the Grand Master's face as his eyes widened in shock and he struggled to point the Imperium Wand at Haskell.

Mortimer blasted the Grand Wizard with a firebolt and an angry red spot appeared on his skin where the hole penetrated his tunic.

The air within the corridor hummed with an eerie resonance as a ball of blue energy coalesced at the end of the Imperium Wand.

With another six feet to go, Haskell dove at the Imperium Wand as the tentacles clasped around the Grand Master's arms, pulling his hands toward the floor. The spell which he released discharged toward the floor, which warped and skewed the stones and dissipated in blue lightning.

Haskell was in the air as the spell released, and as he soared toward the Grand Master, he reached out his left hand and grabbed for the Imperium Wand, his right shoulder smashed into his opponent's midsection.

The Grand Master's grip on his wand was too strong for Haskell and the young wizard fell to the floor without the wand in his hand. He landed hard, and his shoulder hurt from crashing into the Grand Wizard. He looked up to see the Imperium Wand pointed at him.

A sneer formed on the Grand Master's lips as he looked at Haskell, but another two tentacles rose from the floor and wrapped around the master wizard's neck. The Grand Master sent a spell at Haskell and it blasted into his thigh, blood dripping from the wound.

Mortimer cast a spell to send knives from his hands and two knives planted themselves in the master wizard's upper chest.

Time had run out on the disruption spell and events in the corridor returned to normal speed within the room. Haskell trembled as he looked up at the Grand Master, realizing his plans to be king would end this day.

The Grand Master appeared about to say something, but he couldn't speak because the tentacles continued to grapple with him and wrapped around his neck. As his face turned blue, he dropped the Imperium Wand.

A set of tentacles snaked toward Haskell and he kicked his feet and wiggled his body to keep from being snagged by the magical beast. Each push with his leg caused pain from his injury. As he pushed away, he grabbed the fallen Imperium Wand and slid behind the Grand Master and away from the attacking limbs with their powerful suction.

Dakarai pointed his wand at the floor and called forth a storm within the corridor. It formed as a small tornado, picking up the debris and broken pieces of stone within the space. When it had filled the corridor, he pointed it at the Grand Master.

The tornado wound its way toward the Grand Master until it engulfed him, pummeling him with tiny bits of stone, dust and bone. In mere seconds it finished rounding up the debris and dissipated into the floor. The tentacles were gone. The debris had disappeared. The Grand Master had vanished.

Haskell sat on the floor; his breathing labored as he analyzed the battle they had just waged against the Grand Master. "Is he still alive?"

Dakarai shook his head. "No. In a small environment like this, the shrapnel from the stone would be too much. He was too weakened to block it."

Mortimer came and stood by Dakarai.

"Thanks for coming back, Mortimer. I don't think we could have won without your support." Haskell strained to rise from the floor with his injured leg. "Should we check to see if the king is still hiding?" He hobbled toward the king's hiding space.

The group outside the castle continued their battle as the castle walls shook and dust drifted from the ceiling. Haskell wondered if this battle would leave anything of Velidred Castle and the kingdom he hoped to rule.

Their shadows danced along the corridor walls as they approached the chamber where the king had taken refuge from the battle. When they reached the space, the door was open, and the king sat on a small throne with a single wizard standing by his side.

Haskell shouted into the room, "Resign your kingdom, King Stoneforge!"

"Never! Do you dare to challenge the king? You're a mere gang of immature cubs." The king motioned at his wizard, Ophir, a member of the Council of Nine.

A gust of wind flew from Ophir's fingers, failed to reach its target as it was blocked by the shield that protected the insurrectionists.

"We have been instructed not to hurt you, Ophir, because you sit on the council. We just want the king." Haskell was happy the shield held.

Ophir said, "The Grand Master will come behind you any moment now. I suggest you give up this foolish notion to overthrow the king and tell us the names of the leaders of this rebellion. You all are young and have nothing to fear. We're sure others are forcing you into this outrageous action."

"The Grand Master is dead." Haskell raised the Imperium Wand.

"Is that true?" The King asked.

Ophir looked at the king and shrugged, his confidence momentarily wavering. "He's holding the Imperium Wand, which is not a healthy sign for the Grand Master."

"I will never relinquish my crown." The king stood his ground against the insurgents. "You are merely pawns in someone else's quest for power. It's a foolish pursuit and you will all die unless you cease this action this very minute."

"We'll never stand down." Haskell raised the Imperium Wand, feeling its power surging within the depths of his body. He sent out a storm of pelting rain from the wand that pummeled Ophir's shield. He didn't really think it would take out the shield, but he wanted a feel for the wand he held and his opponent's magical power.

The king seemed emboldened when the shield held. "I am not just a king; I am the living incarnation that has weathered the storms of time. What legacy do you bring to Velidred Castle? Your rebellion is but a transient hill against the massive mountains of my reign, destined to be forgotten in a year's time."

"Ophir, stand down and let us take the king and we promise not to hurt you." Haskell ran his hand over the Imperium Wand, feeling its curves and minor imperfections.

"Your chants and incantations are but sparks compared to the permanent blaze of ancient magic that courses through my veins." Ophir stood taller and more confident next to the king. "My mother and her father were on the Council of Nine and I will still be on the Council after I dispatch your measly embers of magic."

Haskell took a deep breath. He wanted to give Ophir a chance to stand down and save himself, but he was getting anxious. There were still other wizards in the castle that might come up behind them at any moment and the king might get away. Plus, his leg was hurting, and he needed a healer to look at it.

"We are prepared to vanquish you this very minute. We have the power to destroy your shield and crush you both in a moment. Are you sure you want to die?"

Ophir stood defiantly next to the king. "Your understanding of magic is like children reaching for the stars on a dark night, unaware of the vast universe beyond their comprehension. My supremacy over magic was earned through years of experience and fine-tuning, not by the momentary whims of youth."

Haskell had enough of this talk and grew angry at Ophir's constant belittling their lack of knowledge and their youth. Combining the wand's magic with the amulets' bond he sent out a dispel shield spell at the king and wizard.

The shield fluctuated and flickered but held, which surprised Haskell.

The king's face showed his concern as the shield wavered, but when it held, he said, "In your effort to overturn an institution as old and solid as the

Stoneforge dynasty, you embrace anarchy. Tradition is the bedrock that supports a realm. Your rebellion, driven by a foolish hunger for change, will crumble into dust at the bedrock of the enduring pillars of Velidred Castle and its people."

With a turn of his head at his companions, Haskell nodded, and they fired a constant fireball attack at the shield protecting the king. Despite the onslaught of magic and fire, the shield held though it swayed and bowed.

They continued their assault and with a loud bang and the nasty smell of sulfur, the shield disintegrated, leaving the king and wizard unprotected in the chamber.

Ophir fell to the floor, shock registering on his face as his shield failed. "I surrender."

The king looked at Haskell in contempt and stood with an air of arrogance and scorn. "I am immortal. My legacy is engraved in the very building blocks of this fortress. Your feeble uprising is a mere glitch in my sovereignty."

Haskell turned to Dakarai and Mortimer with a question, "Should I finish the king?" They both nodded.

CHAPTER 66

Haskell stood victorious over the defeated king. He sighed in relief at achieving his goal of conquering the Velidred fortress and kingdom. He felt all powerful and his lungs expanded to their fullest, as he sucked in deep, satisfied breaths.

Haskell ordered Ophir to stand and to walk with them to ensure his safety until they could tell the other members of the rebellion to stand down. He sent Mortimer to the castle walls to send the signal that the king was dead and the insurrectionists had won the battle.

Despite feeling confident and happy, his heart pounded with concern as he navigated the castle's hallways, twisting, turning and quelling little skirmishes. There was a person on his mind and he didn't know where to find her. He called her name as he walked the halls that only minutes before were a battlefield.

He met his allies in the hallways and asked what happened to the people that were in the grand hall when they arrived, but these wizards didn't know the answer. If the princess had gone outside, she might have been in danger from the attacks on the castle walls. But inside the building, the battles were just as intense. Fireball spells from the combat had left debris and blackened walls everywhere he went.

For twenty minutes, he searched the castle without finding her. The previous moments when he had felt triumphant were now replaced with a tingling in his chest. He should have pulled her out of the hall when he first saw her and sent her home.

Smoke still rose from the tapestries where they had been hit by a stray fireball or flaming magic. The castle smelled of smoke and sulfur from the clashes.

Retracing his steps back to the grand hall, Haskell found eighty or more people had taken refuge in this one room while the battle raged within the castle. He searched the crowd within the room, asking if they had seen the princess, only to be told, 'no.'

Where can she be? She has to be hiding with someone from within the castle itself. He would have to check the private chambers to see if there were guarded sanctuaries where she might have sought refuge.

Haskell's leg seemed to be getting worse as he limped through the damaged hallways.

Dakarai said, "Forget the princess for now. You need to get that leg looked at before you bleed to death."

"Don't worry about my leg," Haskell shouted back at Dakarai, "If I don't find the princess, I might as well lose the leg." All the joy of victory had turned to dread that something might have happened to her.

They knocked on doors and Haskell had Ophir tell the room's inhabitants to open the door. Most times, the doors were opened with reluctance. Ophir's presence helped calm the mood of the people they met, and they lowered their shields.

They didn't find her in the lower level, so they moved up to the next floor. When the third door opened, there stood King Goodwin, Princess Noreen's father.

A light-hearted feeling pulsed through Haskell upon seeing the princess's father, and he realized Noreen had taken up shelter with her family. Haskell bowed, "Your Majesty, I . . . I came to ensure the safety of your daughter. Is she here?"

King Goodwin's nostrils flared, and he glared at Haskell. "What business does the son of a blacksmith have barging into my royal chambers? The princess' safety is of no concern to a commoner like you."

Haskell felt the heat rise in his face. "I beg your pardon. I only sought to ensure she is unharmed after the chaos that unfolded. The rebellion is over, and I wished to verify she was safe."

"Rebellion?" The king's eyes narrowed and two guards came to stand beside him. "Do you think I don't know your involvement in this travesty? Guards, take hold of this traitor and throw him in the dungeon."

"Your Majesty, I mean you and your family no harm." Haskell backed up into the hallway as the guards stepped forward. He quickly set a shield between him and the guards. This was a situation where he had to take Gadiel's advice about being a lord and using manners as opposed to just using magic to solve problems. "My concern now is for the princess. Please, let me see her."

Princess Noreen yelled from within the chamber. "Count Haskell, I'm safe here with my family."

Haskell wanted nothing more than to blast King Goodwin, charge into the room, and hold the princess in his arms, but he realized that if he wanted to marry her someday, he'd have to appease her father. He bowed to the king, "Your Majesty, I'm glad that you and your family are safe. I hope the insurrection did not distress your family."

The guards attempted to lay their hands on Haskell, but were unable to navigate through the shield.

Ophir approached King Goodwin, and said, "Your Majesty, the hallways are safe now."

"Ophir, were you part of this treasonous act?"

The Council of Nine member sneered at Haskell. "I was protecting the king, but these young wizards bonded their magic. They defeated me and the king."

King Goodwin said, "Well, we can help King Stoneforge win back his castle."

"He is dead," Ophir said in a bland voice.

"Dead! That's outrageous." The tension in the hallway increased as the king's face grew red and blotchy. He pointed at Haskell. "Leave my sight now, you traitor, before I decide to deal with you myself."

A painful tightness enveloped Haskell's throat at the king's words. Princess Noreen's father had labeled him a traitor. He shook his head in disbelief. He thought they had an arrangement with King Goodwin and King Kalluri and they were all on the same side. What had the man thought would happen?

The king slammed the door, and the guards took up a position beside the door.

Haskell stumbled back against the wall and stared at the floor. His goal of becoming king was to avenge the death of his father by King Stoneforge and win

King Goodwin's approval. Now it appeared he was no better in King's Goodwin's eyes than his father had been in King Stoneforge's.

####

The next few months brimmed with strife and tension as Haskell strove to gain control of the castle and the surrounding kingdom. Not everyone in the Velidred village was happy with the change in ownership and a feeling of betrayal and anger built up within the village.

Dissidents within the kingdom had taken matters in their own hands and staged minor uprisings in their attempts to sabotage the viscount's efforts to solidify his control. The Kallurian and Goodwin royals were vocal about their disapproval of Haskell.

Gadiel sat with Haskell one evening. "Realize that these men are familiar with power and political connections. They are using you to solidify their own power, both within their kingdoms and with hopes of defeating you some day."

"But I'm the seat of power in Velidred. The most powerful kingdom within the country." Haskell felt frustrated at the turmoil. He had assumed he'd walk into the throne room and everyone would bow to him. But he noticed the looks of distrust and hate within the staff that used to wait on King Stoneforge and now waited upon him. He had enlisted someone to become his chief food taster to ensure he wasn't poisoned.

"You will have to learn to grow into the role. I told you to be happy where you were, and now you've opened a big can of worms." Gadiel took a sip of tea. "Garrick is getting the Council of Nine under control and one of your first steps will be to make him a member of the council."

"Why can't you just crown me this minute?"

Gadiel shook his head.

Haskell sent soldiers into a few of the large villages in the kingdom to suppress riots.

Sims came into Haskell's inner chamber and bowed.

"What do you want, Sims?"

"My eyes and ears have heard rumors in the taverns. There is talk of a large uprising in two days' time, that will target you directly."

Haskell was tired, and frustration with the struggle to control the kingdom weighed heavy on his mind. "Have you told the guard's captain?"

"I have, Your Majesty. But I fear he is too relaxed about the dangers."

Haskell fingered the Imperium Wand he held at his side. "This has to stop. Who is in charge of the riots?"

They discussed the problem and the instigator for a few minutes. Then Haskell said, "I will handle it."

"Should I tell Gadiel?" Sims asked.

"No!" Haskell already knew that Sims had gone to Gadiel first, but he didn't care. It was time for him to put a stop to the naysayers and his enemies.

Two nights later, one quarter of the village burned. The fires started at the Green Dragon Inn and unexpected winds fanned the flames and picked up the sparks, sending them to neighboring buildings. Both dissenters and supporters died in the fires. But the person most vocal against the new regime had died early in the conflagration.

Support for Haskell grew from that point on, while fear and concern marked the faces of all those in the kingdom.

# # # #

Eight months later, on the day of his coronation, Haskell paraded into the grand hall, wearing a richly embroidered robe of royal blue outlined in white. The back of his robe displayed the new symbol of his kingdom, a hammer and anvil, to let the people know that he grew up as a working man. His pulse beat fast as the excitement of the day built with each step toward the throne.

Leading the procession to the throne were several young ladies of neighboring kingdoms, chosen for their ability to forge a relationship between Haskell and possible allies. They wore elaborate dresses of white and blue.

A group of thirty musicians played lutes, flutes, drums, and harps.

He had heard rumors of a possible revolt from friends of King Stoneforge and two of the insurrectionists who thought they should be king, so he carried the Imperium Wand in his hand to make sure he quelled any uprisings immediately. Two members of the Council of Nine had trained him on how to use the powerful weapon.

Haskell had never worn jewelry before, but today he wore a gold ring on his right hand third finger. After the ceremony, he would have a signet ring that would bear his symbol.

Hundreds of people had crowded into the grand hall, but Haskell still knew only a few of the many dignitaries. When he reached the throne, he stopped and turned toward the people in the coronation venue.

The young women that accompanied him to the dais removed his cloak and placed a ceremonial mantle, gold with red trim, over his shoulders which was secured with a chain and clasp made of pure gold.

Ambrose, the elder wizard from the insurrection, stood on the dais wearing a purple robe and holding his staff. When Haskell stopped in front of him, the musicians finished their song and the room went quiet.

Haskell turned toward the dais and Ambrose stood over him. Using magic to enhance his voice, Ambrose said, "By the authority vested in me and in accordance with the traditions of Velidred Kingdom, I proclaim and acknowledge Count Haskell as the rightful sovereign ruler and king of Velidred."

"In the name of the goddess of Velidred and with the blessings of the divine, I anoint you with this sacred oil," Ambrose stuck his thumb in the oil and outlined a circle on Haskell's forehead. Within the circle, he wrote the letter V, representing Velidred. Then he continued. "May this anointing represent the sanctification of your rule and the divine favor of Velidred upon your reign."

Ambrose nodded to a servant dressed in black trimmed in red who held a pillow with a crown on it in his hand. The servant walked to Ambrose and held out the pillow.

Haskell's mouth grew dry at the significance of the golden crown enhanced with jewels and diamonds about to be placed on his head.

Ambrose lifted the crown from its resting place. "May you bear the weight of the crown with wisdom, justice, and benevolence. As you ascend to the throne, you accept the sacred responsibility to govern and protect the people of this realm." He placed his right hand in a bowl of water and sprinkled water on the front of the crown.

Ambrose continued, "As a symbol of your royal authority and the trust placed in you by the people, I now place upon your head this crown, the emblem of kingship. May it rest there with dignity and grace, signifying your commitment to the welfare of the kingdom.

He gently placed the crown on Haskell's head.

Haskell adjusted it a little, so it didn't feel like it would fall off when he walked. The young former blacksmith's son's heart pounded in his chest. *This is it. I am KING!*

With a slight bend of his knees, Ambrose whispered, Turn and face the people.

Haskell turned.

Ambrose said, "Behold King Haskell, our anointed king! Long may you reign and may your rule be a beacon of hope and prosperity for the kingdom."

The people in attendance all bowed to one knee and in one voice chanted, "Long live King Haskell."

After that, Haskell sat on the throne as nobles, military leaders, members of the Council of Nine, and officials pledged allegiance to their new king and offered gifts of gold and silver. Haskell looked for Princess Noreen in the crowd, but did not find her. He didn't know if she had attended the ceremony or not.

The day ended with a royal banquet to celebrate the coronation, and Haskell watched the partygoers from his place on the dais. Many people came to him to have private conversations about striking a deal to move goods from their nation to Velidred. One of the last people to talk with Haskell was his co-conspirator, Garrick. They exchanged pleasantries, and he thanked the new king for adding him to the Council of Nine to replace one of the fallen council members.

Haskell went to bed that night, his wish to be king fulfilled, but with a heaviness in his chest. His thoughts were on Princess Noreen, whom he longed to see once more.

MORE FROM THIS SERIES

The Mountain King Series by Kenneth Brown

Haskell – Orphan to King – Prequel to the Mountain King Series

Eclipse of the Triple Moons

Zita's Revenge

Rescue of the Stone Warriors

Quest for the Crystal

Alpherge the Mighty Series by Kenneth Brown

The Ancient Tomes of Tolero

Go to https://kenbrownauthor.com for more details.

AUTHOR KENNETH BROWN

Kenneth Brown has been writing professionally since the release of his first book in 2018.

He loves to hike, spend time with his family and sings in the church choir. Even though he started writing late in life, he loves to create worlds, creatures and characters, and to have exciting adventures in those fantastical worlds.

Check out https://kenbrownauthor.com for novel release dates and details about the author.

ACKNOWLEDGEMENTS

I want to give special thanks to the people that helped make this book the best it can be.

Developmental Editor: Mary-Megan Kalvig

Copy Editor: Joan H Young, Author, Editor and famous Hiker

Thank you all for your willingness to educate me on word usage, story flow and grammar. Any mistakes you find are from the author himself.

BONUS MATERIAL

Thank you for purchasing this book. We hope you enjoyed Haskell Orphan to King. Please take the time to write a review of this book on your favorite book buying website.

To find out more about the author, Kenneth Brown, and get advance notification about future books, check out the website, kenbrownauthor.com, https://kenbrownauthor.com. Join the Readers Group to receive these great benefits.

- Get the latest information on New Releases
- Insider Looks at Outlines, Plots, Characters, Deleted Scenes and Exclusive behind the Scenes Glimpses at Kenneth Brown's Writing
- Sneak Peeks of Upcoming Chapters
- Ask the Author Questions
- Exclusive Offers
- And MORE

The cover artwork was created by Kenneth Brown using images from BookBrush and Shutterstock. His creative director, Mary Brown, was instrumental in getting the final image into a format worth presenting to the world. We hope you like it.

THANK YOU

I hope you enjoyed this copy of Haskell – Orphan to King. Please take time to visit https://kenbrownauthor.com and find more great books by Kenneth Brown.

Milton Keynes UK
Ingram Content Group UK Ltd.
UKHW022031230824
447344UK00012B/854